ZAPATA

The Border Series Book One

HARPER MCDAVID

SOUL MATE PUBLISHING

New York

ZAPATA

Copyright©2019

HARPER MCDAVID

Cover Design by Laura Bemis

Published in the United States of America by
Soul Mate Publishing
P.O. Box 24
Macedon, New York, 14502

ISBN: 978-1-68291-939-2

ebook ISBN: 978-1-68291-914-9

www.SoulMatePublishing.com

The publisher does not have any control over and does not assume any responsibility for author or third-party websites or their content.

For my father.

Always my hero.

Acknowledgments

This book would not have been possible without the love, support, and tolerance of my family. Martin, I appreciate your willingness to proof anything I throw at you, and always indulging my lack of enthusiasm for cooking after a long day of writing. Emily, I really hope you're not scarred for life, but your insight has been invaluable. To Lily and Addie, thank you for listening without laughing. Dave and Jason, thanks for not making me clean out the storage unit before this was done. And Mom—you taught me to love books and gave me the writing bug. What fun it is.

Charlotte, you're a gem. You've been a constant source of inspiration and wisdom. Someday soon I'll be holding *your* book in my hands.

Much appreciation to those friends who have selflessly and patiently listened to my book ideas, read drafts, and secretly wondered when I would master the use of commas. Pinky, your help has kept me grounded and made this a much better book. Danielle, thank you for being willing to read whatever I give you and trying to make me social media savvy. Liesje, your enthusiasm will keep me going for years, and yes, I'll fix the first one! Mary Lee, thank you for letting me bore you with my book woes and being my walking buddy. And finally, T, thanks for agreeing to do your tedious, and much appreciated, work as *The Comb* and always boosting my confidence.

Bunches of thanks to my clan. Hope you prefer that to tribe. Without you two there would be no book. Muchas gracias, Elizabeth and Melissa. You're the best!

Finally, a note of appreciation to my editor, Sharon Roe. Thanks for taking a chance on me. You've made this so easy.

Chapter 1

Avery stepped down on the tarmac. From what she could see, Zapata was just another uninhabitable and godforsaken border town. Rattlesnake country, dusty and desolate. A gust of hot wind blew an affirming layer of grit over her freshly applied lipstick.

"Ms. McAndrews." The copilot met her at the base of the stairs, holding her suitcase. He shot her a sympathetic smile. "We'll return for you whenever you're done."

A small rush of panic pulsed through Avery. She glanced up at the corporate jet, tempted to hike right back up those stairs. "You mean you guys aren't hanging around?"

He laughed. "Cancun, yes." He glanced about at the forbidding terrain. "This place, afraid not. We're based in San Antonio, though. When we get your call, it's thirty to forty minutes, tops. The captain says you have his number. Just let us know when you're ready to head back. We'll be here for you."

"Thanks." Avery grabbed the handle of her wheeled suitcase. A black SUV, with heavily tinted windows and the Rockforth logo emblazoned on its rear bumper, was parked just beyond the chain link fence. Next to it, an older man with a sizable paunch waited, his gaze focused on some point beyond her.

"Hi. I'm Avery."

"I'm looking for someone named Derrick. Was he on the plane with you?"

"No. I'm his replacement."

"Hmm."

"I'm sorry, you haven't told me your name," she said, trying to ignore his obvious skepticism.

A second man stepped down from the SUV, extending a hand. "I'm Manuel, and he's Bruce. We're the security team."

"Security team? My boss didn't say anything about that."

"He didn't mention security was an issue out here?" Bruce asked.

She gritted her teeth. She should have known. Eric had spent ten minutes dismissing her concerns about safety along the border, assuring her repeatedly that she had nothing to worry about. Typical. He only cared about one thing, and that was keeping Sam Rockforth happy. She didn't blame Eric for that, though. Working on Sam's projects came with a lot of perks. Today's private jet had been one of many.

"No. He didn't mention a security team. But I just found out last night that I'd have to take over for Derrick." She hefted her bag into the back of the SUV and climbed into the back seat with her field gear in hand. She tried to stifle any misgivings about her so-called security team. At five-six, Avery had seen the top of Manuel's head. And neither he nor Bruce appeared anything like the retired Navy SEALs or even night club bouncers she might imagine. But people weren't always what they seemed to be. Being a female engineer meant she'd been the target of that enough to know.

"Facility's about thirty miles out of town," Bruce said, as they accelerated along the road.

And this is town? Avery choked back a laugh. The sameness of the highway was broken up only by the occasional run-down restaurant or abandoned gas station. Tumbleweeds seemed to be the sole evidence of plant life, and only plastic bottles, cans, and other assorted garbage punctuated the fallow expanse of dusty terrain.

She retrieved the site map from the file folder. Derrick's projects were always such a mess. Nothing but a few random notes and receipts from bars with names that sounded suspiciously like strip clubs. With her index finger, she traced and retraced the production line. There was nothing unique about this particular tank battery. Based on the schematics, it looked just about like every other one she'd seen throughout the Gulf Coast and Rocky Mountains. The engineering was basic. Flow lines, separators, and pumps. It made no sense. Leaks and mechanical issues were hardly uncommon. Why go to the expense of sending an engineer at her pay grade when a local operations manager should be able to handle it? She chewed her lip. And why had Derrick let things spiral into a crisis mode?

Her thoughts were interrupted by the driver's voice. "Mr. Rockforth probably would have sent more guys with us if he'd known we'd be guarding a woman." Bruce's eyes met hers in the rearview mirror. "What made 'em change their minds and send a pretty thing like you? Surely you don't want to work in the oil field. Do you?"

It was a question Avery had had to answer many times before. Typically posed with a bit more tact. She remained focused on the plant diagrams.

Bruce persisted. "Where are you from?"

"Denver," she said with a sigh.

"Welcome to Texas."

"Thanks," she said. "It's good to be back." Time to shut the man down. "I got my master's at A&M. I've been working in the oil field for years."

"Well, here on the border, they play by different rules than what you're probably used to. You need to stay in the car unless we tell you otherwise." Bruce paused to turn up the radio, which was playing an unfamiliar country song. "Manuel and I are both armed." He drew out the syllables of the other man's name with an exaggerated twang. "Guess it don't matter that they sent a woman. When you're dealing with low-life drug lords, it's all the same. A bullet don't show preference."

Her head shot up. "Drug lords? Like cartel drug lords?"

"That's enough, Bruce," Manuel said. He shot a glance at Avery, shaking his head. "I grew up here. Zapata's not that bad. Nothing like Juarez."

She set the paperwork aside and leaned forward, her nails digging into the back of the driver's seat. "Are we really likely to encounter someone like that at a tank battery?"

Bruce continued: "Don't know what they was thinking when they sent you. Can't think of no one that could attract much more attention around here. And attention ain't what we need in this place."

"Shut up, Bruce," Manuel turned back to Avery. "No. We're not likely to encounter anyone out there in the middle of the day."

She let out a sigh of resignation. Manuel wasn't exactly reassuring. But she couldn't back out now. She'd assess the situation when they got there. For now, it was probably best to learn as much as she could about the site operations. She leaned toward Manuel with the map in hand. "Tell me about the facility. I've got production schematics, but not much more in the way of info."

"That makes two of us." Manuel gave her a weak smile. "I'm more of a translator than anything else. Sam thought I'd be useful since I grew up around here, but as you probably know, Bruce and I are out of the San Antonio office. I haven't been back here in years."

Great. What sort of mess had she walked into? An angry redneck and a translator. Neither were field technicians nor security experts. This was the last time she'd clean up one of Derrick's messes.

"The site superintendent is meeting us out there. His

name is Hector Rodriguez. I went to high school with him," Manuel said.

"I was hoping to get maintenance schedules and actual production data."

"Hector should have that stuff."

Her phone rang. Her mother. She was quick to silence it. No way would she answer it now. To do so would only be a confirmation of everything Bruce believed about her. Plus, she'd deliberately avoided telling her mother where she was today. It would only bring on another lecture about her unfortunate career choice, and how it left her with no personal life. Avery tossed the phone into her purse.

"How much farther?" As the words left her mouth, she spotted the iconic blue and gold stripes of Rockforth Petroleum. An assembly of petroleum storage tanks, production lines, and processing equipment stood inside a double enclosure of twenty-foot-high razor wire. She'd seen prisons with less security.

A pickup truck bearing the Rockforth logo was parked along the street. Manuel made a low throaty sound. "That's Hector. Fat as ever."

Bruce put the SUV in park and turned to Manuel. He bent over to retrieve a handgun from beneath his seat and tucked it into a holster attached to his belt.

"Pull your shirt down. Concealed. Remember, man?" Manuel gave the older man a chastising glance, then opened the door.

"Lousy job," Bruce said.

His negativity was increasingly irritating, but Avery elected to ignore it. She scrambled to gather her paperwork and slid to the opposite side of the car. For a moment, she fixed her attention on Manuel, who'd assumed a casual approach, smiling at Hector as if they were long-lost friends. From her angle, it looked like they were discussing nothing more important than the weather.

Avery fingered the door handle. Bruce shot up in his seat, releasing a string of obscenities as she opened the door. "You were s'posed to give me a heads up. Wait for me to tell you it's safe."

"My worst threat's probably a rattlesnake." If she waited on Bruce, this job would take all day. Hard hat in hand, she stepped down and slammed the door.

She approached Hector with her hand extended. "Hi. Avery McAndrews, mechanical engineer. You must be Hector." The man seemed to be oblivious to her outstretched hand. "You were probably expecting Derrick."

"Yes," he said.

She attempted to put his doubts to rest. "Let's take a look. You can give me a condensed version of the history here. I couldn't find much in Derrick's file." Hector didn't make eye contact, but instead stared at the ground, picking nervously at his thumbnails. Avery wasn't sure if he was embarrassed by his failure to resolve the problem or something more. "Don't worry. We'll get to the bottom of it. Sometimes the leaks aren't always so obvious. Especially if they're in the subsurface. But it shouldn't be that difficult." She stepped up to the chain link enclosure and pointed to the padlocked gate. "Do you have the keys?"

"Um, yeah," Hector said, as if her request to enter the facility was a surprise.

As Hector fumbled with the lock, she glanced up at a security camera positioned to capture activity at the gate. Cleanly cut wires dangled in mockery. With a sigh, she retrieved a notebook and made a note to have the security system repaired. It wasn't that uncommon, she reminded herself. Tank batteries were never in the best part of town. Storage tanks made the perfect canvas for graffiti artists, and she'd been to more than one site littered with drug paraphernalia and condoms. By comparison, this place was pristine.

Avery clipped Derrick's engineering schematics in her field notebook. Following the two men through the gate, she glanced over her shoulder to see Bruce still in the SUV. So much for her security detail.

Once inside the fenced area, she climbed over the berm designed to contain fluids in the event of spills or leaks. Hector and Manuel followed in silence. She studied the area. The soil showed no evidence of dark stains, which would be indicative of sizable crude oil spills or leaks.

She turned to Hector. "I understand production rates are down. Is that true with specific wells, or . . . ?" She hoped he might help her out, but he only nodded. "You do have the production numbers for the individual wells, don't you?"

Hector turned away. Maybe he did deserve to lose his job.

She sighed. "I'm going to walk the production line over to the tanks." The facility was relatively small, no more than a few acres. Between aerial photos and the site schematics, she had no difficulty following the line between the array of small and large storage tanks. The soil was clean. She checked the valves, circled each tank, and then retraced her steps.

"Hector?" He kept his distance, standing at the edge of the berm. "Can you tell me what this is for?" She pointed at a valve in the production line. So inconspicuous, she'd missed it on her first pass. Underneath it, a small patch of soil was stained with crude. "It's not on any of my drawings."

He approached slowly. "It's a security valve."

"A security valve?" She tilted her head. "Not sure I understand."

"A collection point for protection," he mumbled.

It still made no sense, but before she could try to force an explanation out of him, he had turned away. There was a slam of car doors, and Hector hustled over the berm. A voice rang out beyond the gate, calling his name.

Manuel crouched down next to her, inspecting the valve. "Is that where the problem is?"

"It's a problem for sure. You can see whoever installed it just basically cut into the line. They did a really sloppy job. But even if it's leaking, it's not enough to explain how they're ending up so short every month," she said.

"Well, well. What do we have here?" a voice said. Two men sauntered in their direction. Avery glanced at Manuel for an explanation, but he seemed as clueless as she.

Both men wore tailored dress shirts untucked and open at the collar, and mirrored aviators. *GQ* all the way. The taller of the two men paused at the top of the berm, peering down at them. Bruce lingered behind, barely inside the gate.

The smaller man continued over the berm in their direction. Even from this distance, he struck her as pampered. His lower lip jutted out defiantly as he approached. "Hector." His tone was a scolding taunt. "You didn't tell us you were entertaining." His gaze rested on Avery. "We would have been here earlier." He kicked at the ground with expensive Italian loafers. "Please join us down here, Hector." A sneer crossed his face as he took obvious pleasure in watching Hector struggle to scramble over the berm. The man clapped his hands and said, "Now who'd like to explain what the nature of our little gathering is all about?"

Her shoulders tightened. This guy was deranged. Who was he? And how was it that he felt entitled to walk on Rockforth property in such a manner? She glanced at her so-called security detail and site superintendent. Never before had she seen three people more interested in their own shoes. She sighed. Dealing with this guy would obviously fall to her.

She stepped forward. "I'm Avery McAndrews with Fenster Engineering." Her words came out a little faster than she'd intended, though her hand remained steady as she held out a business card. The man snorted dismissively and made no effort to take it. "I'm in the process of conducting a facility inspection. It was arranged by Mr. Rockforth's office. And, I'm sorry, but I don't know who you are."

Despite her declaration otherwise, she was afraid she knew exactly who these two were. Their tailored clothes and expensive haircuts made her think of Bruce's words: drug lords.

She shifted her attention to the tall man. Broad-shouldered and nothing like his fidgety partner. He stood with his arms crossed and a lizard boot resting on an overturned bucket.

Even through his sunglasses, she felt his gaze, calm and controlled. Irrationally, she felt a tinge of disappointment in his career choice. He was easily the best-looking man she'd ever seen.

Meanwhile, the smaller man made a series of pronouncements in Spanish. Hector stared at the ground, blinking, as if he were about to cry. The man repeated himself a second time, louder and sounding angry.

Hector turned to Avery and pointed to the crazy man. "His name is Javier Ramos, and he says to tell you he doesn't like redheads."

Her blood surged, and she felt her face growing hot. She turned to face the cocky little man. "And I don't like people who can't speak for themselves. Is the name Javier Ramos supposed to mean something?"

For a second, no one moved. She held her breath, wishing she could take it back. But she never could shut her mouth when she was angry.

Her eyes shifted to Javier's partner. Was it her imagination, or was he shaking his head? It was subtle, but now she was sure of it. And it wasn't a threat. It was a warning.

He was telling her to back off.

Manuel squinted. His attention was focused on something outside the fence.

An engine revved, and Javier jumped, waving a threatening fist. There was no missing the sizable gun at his hip. "Contreras! What the hell are they doing here, Hector?" He didn't wait for an answer but made a dash for the gate.

"What's going on?" she asked.

"Come on," Manuel said, heading for the gate. "We need to get the hell out of here. Stay behind me."

"Where's Bruce?" she asked.

"Probably back in the car," Manuel said, gazing through the chain link at a white Range Rover idling at the end of the gravel drive. The Rockforth SUV and a red Porsche were blocked in by the vehicle. Manuel swore under his breath. "We need to stay out of sight. I think it may be a rival gang."

Her heart pounded, and she couldn't catch her breath. Bruce was right about one thing. The rules were different here.

A shot rang out, and Avery froze. Javier stood in front of the Range Rover, his gun pointed toward the sky. It took her a moment to realize Manuel was no longer at her side. He called out for her to run, but she couldn't see him.

Frantically she searched the area, finding nowhere to hide. Running to the SUV was out of the question. The gate was not much cover, but it was the best she had. Javier's partner was crouched behind the SUV, a large gun in his left hand. His eyes met hers, and he gestured to her. She didn't understand. He repeated the hand gesture. He was telling her to get down, lower herself.

Javier fired another shot into the sky.

The sound was jarring. She was halfway in a squat when the shock of it landed her on her butt. Javier's partner sprinted across the barren expanse and through the gate to her side. His fingers locked on her wrist. She didn't resist. He yanked her to her feet and hustled her behind a water tank. They were well out of sight, but hardly safe if this became a gun fight. For several seconds, the two of them leaned against the tank side by side, panting. He shot her a sideways glance. In spite of her terror, she tried to force a grateful smile.

Javier was making a lot of noise. To her, the Spanish chatter made no sense, but from the sound of it, Javier was threatening. His partner let out a deep sigh and shook his head. Without so much as a signal to her, he took off toward the SUV.

She closed her eyes. Cartel member or not, she didn't want to see him hurt. She counted to three before daring a glimpse at the SUV. He was safe. She let out a sigh of relief.

There was a crunch of gravel nearby. Manuel crept up next to her. "Bruce is in the car. When I say the word, we need to run. While all eyes are on Javier. Okay?"

She nodded.

He put a hand on her shoulder and squeezed. "Go!"

She lunged forward. Ahead, the tall man's voice rumbled. "*Basta*, Javier!"

Javier seemed to ignore the man's words, continuing to sway with his gun in the air. Fortunately, it no longer mattered. The driver of the Range Rover floored it, spraying Javier in a fountain of gravel as he took off toward the main road.

Avery let out a small cry of relief as the car disappeared over a ridge. Of course, they still had crazy, gun-waving Javier to deal with. But a second ago, she was certain her life would end in the crossfire of a gang war.

There was a strange silence among them now. She and Manuel still hadn't made it all the way to the SUV. Hector emerged from the far side of the Porsche, and a few feet away Javier's partner rose to his feet.

The effect of the tall man's gaze on her was palpable. It was as if she could feel a comforting hand on her back and his voice low and smooth in her ear, asking if she was okay. Avery waited for him to speak, hoping he might somehow bring logic to this unreal situation. Amongst the other men, he seemed to be the single adult in a room full of children. It was ridiculous to have that sense about him, but it was a feeling she couldn't dismiss. He'd risked his life to protect her.

Something brought on a bout of hysterical laughter from Javier. He turned to the tall man and spoke in a stream of rapid Spanish. His gestures were dramatic. The man made a low *hmph* sound, then straightened, stroking the dark shadow of his few days' worth of beard. It occurred to her that she hadn't heard the man speak English. Nor had anyone addressed him in anything but Spanish. For some reason, she found it surprising.

A car door slammed, and heads turned as Bruce stepped down from the SUV. He was older than she had realized. He ambled painfully, one hip dipping lower than the other. "Ma'am, Man-u-el, Mr. Rockforth suggests we get checked in at the motel."

She halfway expected to be detained by Javier, but he only stood and watched. "*Hasta luego*, Red," he said. He spoke louder. "Maybe I wouldn't mind a piece of that. It looks pretty good from here." He whistled. "Alejandro knows, Red, I usually get what I want."

He turned to the other man. "*¿Qué piensas, Alejandro? Incluso alguien como tu tienes que apreciar eso.*"

Manuel spoke softly over her shoulder. "Just keep walking."

So, her hero's name was Alejandro. She glanced back over her shoulder, hoping to see his face once more, as if this final glimpse would allow her to detect a crack in his façade. Something that would tell her who he really was, and exactly why he risked his life for her. But he was already in the driver's seat of the Porsche. Only Javier remained, leering with satisfaction.

Chapter 2

"Why the hell do we have to stop in Laredo?" Javier asked.

"Because I make it a rule not to transport guns across the border," Alejandro said. "It's not worth the prison time. If you want to take the chance, then drive yourself next time. We're dropping everything off at the apartment."

"Oh yeah. I forgot." A moment later Javier's face lit up. "We could get some girls." He held up a small plastic bag, swinging the white powder from side to side. "Maybe we should stop there for the night. Have some fun."

"I can't. I have a meeting with your father tomorrow first thing in the morning." Not that he would ever waste his time partying with Javier and a bunch of hookers anyway.

Javier lifted a bottle of vodka to his mouth. "I'm going to kill every last one of those stupid Contreras."

"Not tonight, you're not," Alejandro said.

"You're no fun."

"It's not my job to be fun. It's my job to keep you out of trouble."

"Okay, lawyer man," Javier said. He was beginning to slur his words. "What about that red-headed bitch? Best ass I've seen in a long time. Man, you know what I'd like to do to her?"

"No. And I don't want you to tell me, either." Alejandro rubbed his forehead. The thought of it made him angry. He pictured her mouthing off to Javier. No one who knew Javier ever talked to him like that. Everyone just tolerated his cruelty and inappropriate behavior, tiptoeing around him as if he were a landmine awaiting the faintest trigger.

There was irony in how the situation with the redhead had turned out. Javier was so out of his mind this afternoon, tripping on who-knows-what. If time had allowed, Javier would have tried something, even though she wasn't the type he usually went for. Too brainy, to start with. But her defiance seemed to turn Javier on. Alejandro draped his wrist over the steering wheel. He always feared that one day he'd be forced to kill Javier. Silently, he thanked the Contreras that it wasn't today.

Javier turned to stare at him. "You don't like me, do you?"

Javier's perceptiveness caught Alejandro off guard. It was one of several traits that made Javier so dangerous. "I don't like what you're becoming." Alejandro had to be careful here. Javier wouldn't go after him the same way he would others, but he had other ways of doing damage. "You're losing control. And you're hurting your family." Alejandro pointed to the bottle. "You need to get rid of that." He grabbed Javier's free arm and flipped it over. At least the track marks weren't fresh. "And this has got to stop."

"You think you're perfect, don't you?" Javier said with a hiss. Alejandro ignored him. "Well, you know what? I'm going to get the Contreras without any help from you. And I don't even have to go back to Zapata to do it."

"Oh yeah?" Alejandro didn't hide his skepticism. "How do you propose to stop them?"

"She's going to do it for me."

"Who?"

"Who do you think? The redhead." Javier took another long drink. "Yep. You just wait and see. You'll be sorry you didn't think of it first."

"I doubt it."

"Turn left here," Javier said. He pointed at something excitedly. "I almost forgot."

"Forgot what?"

"My new project. This time Papa will see that I know best."

"What are you talking about?" Alejandro asked. Javier was always trying to prove himself to his father, but his schemes never seemed to work. The futility of it was probably what turned him into an addict.

"Turn!"

Despite his better judgement and the fact that he should be preparing for court, Alejandro turned off the main highway onto what was once a paved road. Infrequent travel had left the thoroughfare as nothing more than a pathway of asphalt blocks lined in vegetation.

"It's the back road to the quarry."

"Quarry?"

"You know, the one that backs up against the river."

The one Diego had collected from for decades. His protection money demands had nearly driven the small company into bankruptcy until the Contreras had managed to shove the Ramos family out. Alejandro glanced up at the rearview mirror. If the guys in the Land Rover had decided to follow them, they were as good as dead. "I don't think this is a good idea."

"If you're worried about those Contreras, don't be. I bought this place last month and kicked those assholes out."

"You did what?" Diego had said nothing about it, and it was up to Alejandro to authorize large expenditures.

"Papa doesn't know about it. It's a surprise," Javier said.

"What would your father possibly want a quarry for?" Alejandro glanced at the time on the dash. It was tempting to turn the car around and get back on the highway.

"See?" Javier pointed at the idle heavy equipment ahead. "It's not the quarry I bought it for. I mean, I will hire someone and get it started again. In fact, I think you should do that for me."

Alejandro sighed and shook his head. One more thing he didn't have time for. "So why did you buy it?"

"Look. He pointed to a small grove of trees across the river. "That's Mexico. And those dirt piles over there are where I'll put the opening of my tunnel."

Alejandro's senses spiraled into full alert. He straightened in his seat and removed his sunglasses. "Why are you building a tunnel when the river is no more than a hundred yards wide? Even a child can cross here."

"You have to ask?" Javier stared at him with a self-congratulatory smirk. "It's my supply tunnel." He waved the vodka bottle about. "I bring our shipments in through the tunnel and load them into the big quarry trucks on this side. You know, the ones they use for rocks and shit. Whatever they're getting out of those holes."

And another advantage would be the ability to move guns and cash undetected to the south. Alejandro shook his head. "You can't tunnel under the river. It's sand. You'll be drowning." It wasn't the craziest idea Javier had ever had. But the sheer feasibility of dewatering would send costs sky high. "When are you telling your father?"

"Not before it's finished. So keep your big trap shut." He lifted the bottle to his lips once more.

"Have you had an engineer or anyone knowledgeable draw up plans?"

Javier shook his head. "But that's an excellent idea." His words were becoming more slurred, and his eyelids were only half open. "She's an engineer, right?" The bottle began to slide from his hand.

Alejandro was quick to intercept the bottle before it hit the floorboard. He set it behind Javier's seat and out of reach. It took less than three seconds before Javier slumped against the door. Good. Now Alejandro could leave him in Laredo and let him sleep it off. And hopefully tomorrow would be like most others: Javier would have very little memory of the encounter with the Contreras or redheaded engineers.

Alejandro inched the car forward, wary of punctured tires. The last thing he wanted was to be stuck out here. Between piles of gravel, someone had started excavation efforts on the U.S. side. He rubbed his chin. The possibilities were huge. He'd keep Javier's secret. Shut up and authorize any expenditures. Even send a structural engineer to help him out. Yep, he'd help Javier build the best tunnel in this part of the country and let him transport drugs to his heart's content.

Until it benefited him.

Chapter 3

The Tumbleweed Inn was one of four motels in town, if one didn't count those that charged by the hour. Unfortunately, the other three were booked. One glance at the room and Avery knew she'd need at least a couple of drinks to actually sleep here.

Lucky for her, the Tumbleweed had its own restaurant: Catfish Cal's. It smelled every bit like its name. Bad fish cooked in old grease. Avery stepped down two grimy steps connecting the lobby to the restaurant.

The conversation between Manuel and Bruce came to an abrupt halt as she pulled out a chair. "What's the word from Sam?" she asked. "Do we have a plan?"

A waitress stepped into her line of view, producing a pencil from behind her ear. "What can I get you to drink, Miss?"

"A glass of your house red would be fine," Avery said.

The woman stared at her as if she were a complete idiot. Avery's eyes went to the men's drinks. Bruce was drinking a Bud. Manuel seemed to be abstaining.

"Scotch?" Avery said tentatively.

The waitress nodded. "Fusty Mule. It's distilled here in town. On the rocks?"

Avery massaged her brow bone. "Sure."

"Sam's not happy," Manuel said, as the waitress walked away. "He didn't know you were here. Said it wasn't part of the plan, and he wants you out of here."

Avery pursed her lips. "That makes two of us. What were his exact words?"

"He said this project was a waste of your talent and that he intended to 'have a word with that son of a bitch Eric,'" Manuel said. "Is that your boss?"

She nodded as a grin spread across her face. Another reason why she loved working for Sam Rockforth. The feisty old East Texas billionaire would put her boss in his place in a heartbeat. She'd pay money to watch Eric squirm and talk his way out of this one.

"The plane will be here for you tomorrow at nine. Man, Sam likes you a lot. He said he knew you'd get to bottom of the problem." Manuel laughed. "You know how he talks. He said something like, 'that Avery can find a whisper in a whirlwind.'"

"Good. Did he say how he plans to address the production problem?"

"He don't want to do nothing," Bruce said.

"That's not exactly true." Manuel said. "But it's complicated."

"You can't tell me he's going to overlook the fact that he's losing money. Someone is accessing that valve—"

Manuel held out a hand to stop her. "You have to understand how it works. These gangs or families operate a lot like the mafia. Javier's father is a very powerful man. Very rich. His name is Diego Ramos. He's been the worst of the worst for many years. Even when I was a kid, his name meant something. To operate in Zapata, the oil companies always had to pay off the Ramos family."

She frowned. "Really? Sam, too?" It was impossible to imagine a man as tough as Sam giving in to their demands.

Manuel nodded. "Yeah, even Sam. The consequences are bad if you don't."

"You mean to tell me you didn't know that?" Bruce asked.

"This isn't my project," she snapped at Bruce and turned

back to Manuel. "So, the valve in the production line? Hector called it a 'security valve for protection.'"

"I'll get to that part. But first you need to understand everything else." Manuel cupped his hands around his water glass. "Recently, another family, the Contreras, have been growing stronger. They live on this side of the border."

"The white Land Rover. Those were the Contreras?"

"Yes," Manuel said.

"Does Sam know about them?"

"He does now," Bruce said. "We gave him an ear full."

"They ought to be easier to stop," she said. "If they're here in the U.S., I mean."

"Law enforcement don't want no part of neither of 'em," Bruce said. "They prefer to see 'em kill each other off. Saves them the trouble."

"Bruce is right," Manuel said, with a nod. "And Sam has no intention of paying off two cartels. I think it's what brought Javier out there today. He's worried the Contreras are going to be Sam's choice for protection."

"Protection." She scoffed. The waitress set a glass of amber liquid in front of her. Avery sniffed it and then raised her eyebrows, her eyes watering. She took a small sip as the two men watched in apparent fascination. The liquid sent fire down her throat. With a small cough, she said, "Okay, so Sam paid off Javier's family in the past. But what about the valve?"

Manuel nodded. "I think that was the work of the Contreras. From watching Javier today, I don't think he's aware of the valve. He'd have no way to know how low the volumes have dipped in those tanks. It's part of Hector's job to make sure the Ramos family gets their share through the loading area. Normally, they would have no reason to set foot anywhere near that valve."

"Why not tell the Ramos family that the Contreras are

stealing? Let them fight among themselves for the protection rights," she said.

"Of course," Manuel said. "That's normally the way it works down here." He held up an index finger. "Except there's another issue."

She took another sip of the scotch, shuddered at the taste, and stifled a cough. At least it was alcohol. "What?"

"Tell her, Man-u-el. What you was telling me before she sat down."

Manuel glanced around the restaurant, then leaned forward, keeping his voice low. "Hector called me after we checked in here. He told me that he's only been site manager a few months. His cousin Rodrigo worked there for years. Sam trusted him to keep the crude oil stealing down to a minimum. And with only one gang to work with, Rodrigo did. Two months ago, Rodrigo was killed out in the driveway where we were standing today. Shot in the face. Middle of the afternoon. No witnesses."

Bruce gulped his beer, and Avery reached for her glass.

"Hector was working as a mechanic here in town then. Javier came driving up with Rodrigo's blood all over him. Told Hector he had to quit his job as a mechanic and work out there."

Avery leaned back in her chair. She might as well be a million miles from home. It was impossible to believe this was happening in the twenty-first century. She covered her mouth as she remembered how she'd acted out there. Taunting a cold-blooded killer. She took another slug of the Mule. Her voice cracked as she said, "Because Rodrigo had started allowing the Contreras to steal, too?"

"Yep," Bruce said. "Neither gang gave him much choice."

She considered calling Sam's pilot and asking him to meet her at the air strip tonight. If it didn't require driving through this town at night, she'd do it.

"That's not the worst part," Bruce said. "Tell her."

"Javier said he would kill Hector's family if he ever heard of the Contreras doing business with Sam. Hector's got a wife and two little girls. Javier called them each by name."

Avery swallowed back the lump in her throat. "So, Hector's been allowing the Contreras to steal by a different method and hoping no one would notice."

Manuel nodded. "And no one would have noticed, at least for a while. But the Contreras started getting greedy. Siphoning off just a little too much."

"No wonder Hector didn't want to speak to me today," she said.

"Can't really blame Hector," Manuel said. "He wasn't smart about things, but who would be when their kids and wife are being threatened?"

Avery toyed with her glass. "Javier's English is perfect. What's his background?"

"He's had every advantage possible," Manuel said. "He went to boarding school in the northeast, then college in Florida. I don't know why he's like he is."

"And Alejandro? Is he as bad as Javier?" She took an overly large swig of her drink.

"Alejandro De Leon." The Spanish pronunciation rolled off Manuel's tongue, sounding exotic. "He didn't grow up around here. Hector thinks Alejandro was hired to be a bodyguard for Javier's father, but Javier wanted him for himself. Like a playmate. That's how Javier is. Always wants something. He has a crazy life. Drugs, women, big houses— you can imagine. Hector says Alejandro doesn't talk much. Doesn't speak English. Just puts up with Javier. Reins him in a little, too." His eyes narrowed. "But to answer the question I think you're asking, no, he wasn't there that day."

Her interest in the man was, at a minimum, very unhealthy. The man was handsome, but he was still a gangster, for god's sake. She rested her forehead in her hand. She was already feeling the effects of all of it. The place, the drink, and the fact that none of it seemed real. "So, what's the plan?"

"I believe there's no choice for Sam but to put it back on Javier's family," Manuel said. "He needs to communicate directly with Diego Ramos. The man is bad, but not insane like his son. Sam needs to insist that they actually provide protection. And that includes taking care of the site superintendent and his family."

"But you don't sound convinced," she said.

Manuel shook his head. "As long as Javier's free to do as he pleases, I think the Ramos family is in trouble. And trouble for the Ramos family means trouble for us."

She took another swallow of Fusty Mule. It was beginning to grow on her.

Chapter 4

Avery struggled to sleep. The window unit air conditioner churned and hissed, then abruptly shut off, only to restart with an explosive bang thirty seconds later. The cycles were endless. Her head was throbbing from the rotgut whiskey, and she pretty much hated everyone that had anything to do with the fact that she was sleeping on sheets that didn't quite smell like detergent.

It was impossible to stop thinking of her boss's deception. Had he known how dangerous Zapata was? Her anger surged, and she imagined things she might say when she returned.

Maybe her mother was right. At twenty-eight, she should focus on her personal life. Giving too much to the company wasn't worth it. What kind of career was this, anyway? She couldn't even trust her own boss. Sure, there were monetary rewards. Especially working with Sam. She squeezed her eyes shut, trying to picture her custom-ordered metallic pearl Audi, scheduled to arrive the week after next. But was she selling out just for a material lifestyle?

Her thoughts jumped to Javier and Alejandro. Were they so different? They were sacrificing it all for fast cars, beautiful women, and—no doubt—serious money. She rolled her head against the pillow. This was absurd. Drunken rationale. Comparing herself to cartel members. She was nothing but a boring mechanical engineer who worked hard for a few luxuries. It wasn't like she'd sold her soul to the devil. She was simply doing what it took to get ahead.

The air conditioner imploded another time. She draped her forearm across her eyes, groaned, then turned on her side. The neon Cal's Catfish sign radiated a rainbow of light through the gap in the sagging curtains. She needed sleep. Tomorrow she would tell Sam he needed to sell that facility and take his business elsewhere. Why was he hanging on to it, anyway? The money made from it was nothing compared to what he had throughout East Texas and the Rockies.

God. Who cared. She didn't ever have to come back out here. She squeezed her eyes shut.

It seemed like only minutes before she was jolted awake once more. Damn that stupid air conditioner. If she had a gun, she'd have used the air conditioner for target practice. It was too late to ask for another room. And unlikely it would be any better.

Shadows danced intermittently, disrupting the neon glow. Fusty Mule was some kind of nasty stuff. Was she hallucinating?

But the biting grip on her wrists was no hallucination. She struggled, turning side to side. Someone's dirty hand covered her mouth. The smell of oil gagged her. She tried to bite the hand but couldn't.

With a bang, the air conditioner did its thing. The dirty hand moved, quickly replaced by a cloth covering both her nose and mouth. She knew better than to inhale.

Voices hissed in Spanish. She rolled from side to side kicking, attempting to make contact with something or someone. The figures darted about. Someone pinned her ankles.

She tried not to inhale, but it couldn't last forever. The figures gathered now, waiting.

Finally, she gave in. The smell was overpowering and sickeningly sweet. But it was only one breath.

She pretended to be unconscious. The grips on her arms loosened.

She counted to ten and then kicked with all her strength.

It wasn't enough. Firm hands pushed down on her again. There were more Spanish words she didn't understand. She took another desperate breath.

Her body slackened, and her limbs grew leaden. It was impossible not to breathe. Two more gasps for air, followed by a prick to her arm, and all she could feel was a slow burn.

Chapter 5

Small eyes peered at her from behind wire-rimmed glasses. A stethoscope hung about the person's neck. She shook her head and pushed against him.

"Shh. It's all right. You're going to be fine. I was just a little worried."

A ceiling fan wobbled noisily above her head. There was just enough light to see the dingy mint-green walls with their peeling paint. Her eyes panned the room.

"Water?" the man asked.

"Yes, please." The rusty iron bed frame screeched as she pulled up into a sitting position. The thin mattress was no buffer against the jagged metal springs. The man handed her a bottle from a case on the floor. In her uncoordinated effort, the water cascaded down her front as she attempted to drink. She blinked slowly. She was still wearing her pajamas. Really, just a t-shirt and boxers.

She rubbed her eyes. It was as if someone had switched her brain into slow motion. This wasn't the motel room in Zapata. This was far worse. Her thoughts were fragmented and repetitive. An attack. People holding her down. Making her breathe something. Trying so hard to hold her breath.

Kidnapped.

And this man? She regarded his face. Something told her no. He wasn't a kidnapper.

"You're a doctor?"

"Yes."

His reply sounded a little like *jes*. Maybe the slightest of Spanish accents. "Where am I?"

He only smiled and shook his head. Sympathy or maybe pity crossed his face. It made no sense. Why wouldn't he say where they were? Then she began to understand: someone had told him to keep quiet.

"What day is it?"

"Today is Friday."

"Friday," she said, repeating the word slowly. Friday? She blinked, as if it would clear some of the fogginess from her mind. Monday, staff meeting in Denver. Tuesday flew to Zapata. Went to the Rockforth facility. Cartel thugs were there. Wednesday? What had become of Thursday? Friday? She'd been unconscious for more than forty-eight hours.

The doctor crossed the room and opened a set of dark green wooden shutters. Rusting but ornate bars lined the windows. "I think a little sunshine might help. I have asked them to bring you some food. Please try to eat. Your body needs to recover." He bit his lip. "You still have a lot of drugs in your system."

"What kind of drugs?"

He said something under his breath and shook his head in disgust. "I cannot be sure. The important thing is that you're awake now. Your heart sounds good."

"They covered my face with a rag."

"Chloroform." He reached for her arm, pointing to the multiple injection marks. "This is what worries me." He lowered his voice. "They don't know what they're doing. Every time it's worse."

"Every time?" She swallowed with difficulty. "Who are these people?"

He looked away.

"What comes next?" Her voice shook.

"They don't tell me these things. I am only a physician." He handed her another bottle of water and perched on the edge of her bed. "But they don't call a doctor if they plan to kill you."

"Please." She grasped his sleeve. "Am I in Zapata?"

He frowned. She understood that to mean he'd never heard of the place.

"Mexico?"

He gave her the smallest of nods.

Mexico. The room seemed to whirl. A million miles from home. A place where the cartels ruled, and laws didn't matter.

"Who did this? What do they want?"

He shrugged. "I'm sorry. I don't know."

"Can you get a message to—"

He shook his head. "I am searched as I enter and as I leave." His expression was sympathetic. "You are in the hands of very powerful people. You must not take chances. Do as they say." He rose to his feet. "And whatever you do, eat. Sleep. Get strong before all else." He moved to the door and gave her a final smile before knocking. "Good luck to you."

In his absence, Avery felt the reality of her situation sinking in. Missing for three days. Eric and Sam surely knew of her disappearance by now. Had Eric notified her mother? Probably not. He would avoid such a dirty job. Pass it off to someone else, but only once they were certain she wouldn't be returning any time soon. Other than Eric and her mother, there was no one. She had given everything for her stupid job and sacrificed all personal relationships.

The truth of it was jarring—in some ways, more horrifying than the room she now occupied. Her chest felt heavy. There was no one in her life other than her mother that would truly be affected if she vanished.

Avery turned and swung her legs off the bed. Her thin pajamas clung to her. The air was stifling. Hot and humid. She wiped the sweat from her forehead and ran a hand through her hair. She wanted a shower. She gripped the bed, attempting to stand. She shook, her heart raced, and she collapsed back on the edge of the bed. Her legs were virtually worthless. Whatever they'd been doping her with was still in control. She leaned back and took another gulp of water. The bottle slid from her hand, spilling across the floor, and she didn't have the strength to retrieve it.

~ ~ ~

She must have slept through the remainder of the morning and into the afternoon. A tray rested on a small table next to the bed. Not much but rice, beans, and a tortilla. She was too tired and too nauseous to eat. By her calculations, she had not eaten since the flight. Dinner at Catfish Cal's had consisted of three glasses of scotch. She reached for the tortilla. Even her fingers barely moved in sync.

The tortilla steadied the shaking. She groped her way into standing. Across the room, a door hung unevenly on eroding hinges. She staggered toward it, then gripped the frame for support and peered inside. It was a bathroom. Dripping water left a dark orange pathway across the cracked sink. The toilet was even worse. Her heart sank. There was no shower.

She hobbled her way across the room to the open window and peered through the bars. Judging from the distance to the ground, her room was on the second floor. The fact itself had little meaning. There were no clues as to what this place was, or where she was. The terrain seemed similar to Zapata. Hardly a helpful indicator. Most of the interior of Mexico probably looked like this: dusty and dry. She squinted her eyes. On the horizon was the faintest outline of low mountains.

The room itself was quiet. Oddly quiet, actually. No sounds of traffic or other people. Only the fan. She scanned the room. No obvious cameras. Or anything else electronic.

She knocked on the wall. Solid. Plaster. Cracked and painted a mint green shade she'd always disliked. The whole room looked old. Its high ceiling and exposed pipes suggested it was maybe fifty years old? A hundred? Impossible to guess in Mexico.

She supported herself against the window frame, evaluating the doorway where the doctor had made his exit. Heavy double doors with a single antique brass knob. She inched toward the door like she was a hundred years old. She twisted the knob, but the door didn't budge. The doctor had knocked. She tried, but there was no response. The second time was no better. Anyone sitting on the other side would be able to hear. The effort only made her dizzy. She steadied herself before shuffling to the bed. Tomorrow she would be stronger.

~ ~ ~

It was impossible to stay awake for any length of time. Her brain seemed to be growing foggier, and each time she dozed off her dreams were stranger. It seemed like she was relapsing, getting weaker when she should be growing stronger. She rubbed her eyes, as if that would help.

The door clicked, and she struggled to hoist herself up into a sitting position. Someone flipped the light switch. Fluorescent bulbs flickered and buzzed, sending the room into a frenzy of haunting white light. She shaded her eyes. Something skittered across the floor. She covered her mouth in horror. It was a virtual army of cockroaches.

A large man moved toward her, holding a tray. Her heart pounded. She clawed the bed and dug her heels into the mattress.

He put out a hand and pointed to the tray of food he'd brought. "Hello." His pronunciation sounded forced. She blinked. It was the tall one from the tank battery. Alejandro. Minus the sunglasses and red sports car, she hardly recognized him.

"You." The word came out as a croak.

He cleared his throat. He nodded to her, his dark eyes skirting over her t-shirt and boxers. She glared at him and groped for the sheet, feeling it necessary to cover herself despite the oppressive heat. Tentatively, he set a fresh plate of rice and beans down next to her. His attention went to the virtually untouched lunch plate. His brows drew together, and he said something she couldn't understand before moving to the stash of water bottles.

Her hands shook as she accepted his offer of the water. "Thanks." She struggled to remove the cap, but there was no strength in her hands. She stared at her fingers, willing them to behave normally. Hopefully, this was just a temporary side effect of the drugs retreating from her system. She sighed and tried a second time. Gently, Alejandro lifted the bottle from her hands and unscrewed the cap.

Slowly, he backed away. Watchful. The man was like a sphinx, his brown eyes penetrating. It was completely unnerving.

He held up a finger. "*Un momento,*" he said, then knocked on the door.

His departure left her feeling abandoned. She glanced at the food. As hungry as she was, it was almost a certainty that she couldn't manage a spoon.

The door swung open, and Alejandro stepped inside once more. Despite his size, he was silent and graceful. He casually balanced another tray of food in one hand as he waved her to the side of the bed.

She slid over, though not fully realizing his intention was to sit next to her. His nearness left her slightly confused. When his arm grazed hers, she nearly jumped out of the bed. A small smile crossed his face.

He held a spoon to her mouth, and for several seconds she stared at him dumbly. "Eat," he said with a whisper, then followed the demand with a string of Spanish words.

Why was she so slow to comprehend? He intended to feed her. She opened her mouth, feeling somewhat like a stunned baby bird. Allowing the warm chicken soup to fill her mouth, she closed her eyes and swallowed. He repeated the action. His behavior was almost paternal. He paused to stir the soup. His eyes, downcast and focused on the action, were framed in dark, thick lashes. It added a slightly angelic dimension to his otherwise very masculine and in no way cherubic appearance. Even over the fragrant aroma of the soup, she could smell soap. She inhaled deeply. It made her consider her own hygiene. Someone besides the doctor must have been attending to her. The realization sent a wave of horror through her foggy brain. She prayed it wasn't Alejandro.

He nudged her, pressing the spoon to her lips. She offered him a slight smile before her lips parted, wishing her Spanish wasn't crap. There were so many questions.

Their eyes locked as she swallowed. He filled the spoon once more, but she grabbed his wrist before he could bring it to her mouth. She spoke softly. "Why am I here? What can possibly be gained from kidnapping me?" She didn't expect an answer, but it felt right to say the words.

She waited, but he said nothing. Somehow, his eyes told her what she already knew. The kidnapping wasn't his doing.

He passed her the water bottle and then retreated to the opposite side of the room, gathering trays and dishes. Disappointment lingered in her gut. She wanted to beg him to stay. Keep her company with his comforting silence and clean smell. He started to the door, then turned to face her. He gathered the fabric of his shirt and pointed at her.

Her t-shirt was damp from spilled water. She grasped it and made a face. "Yes. A clean shirt would be great." She covered her mouth and shook her head. "This is crazy, but I think I have Stockholm Syndrome already. It's only been three days. And I've only been awake for one. Isn't that what they call it when the prisoners start to see their captors as some kind of saviors?"

He stared at her kindly, listening as if he understood every word of her rambling speech. What she saw in his expression was neither cold nor vacant. There was something more.

~ ~ ~

It was at least thirty minutes before the door opened again. But this time it wasn't Alejandro. Bile rose in the back of her throat as Javier sauntered into the room, engulfing her small domain with cologne. On another man it might not be offensive, but on him the concoction of leather and herbs was nauseating. He must douse himself in the stuff. He crossed his arms and lorded over her, wearing a white starched shirt and coral-colored shorts. Not exactly a gangster look.

His eyes held nothing but cruelty and disdain for her. "What do you think of the place?" He made a sweeping gesture with his arms. "You got the Presidential Suite. Enjoying it?"

She stared back at him in silence. Something shot across the wall. She jerked back against the pillow.

He sneered. "You're afraid of a small lizard? If you're here long enough, you will learn to appreciate them. They eat insects." His eyes gleamed.

She said nothing.

"I see. You're going to be uncooperative. Just like Sam Rockforth."

"Sam?"

"He's not forthcoming with the money."

What? She blinked. He was hitting Sam up for ransom money? She couldn't even imagine the old man's response.

There was a slight curl to his lips. He sensed her fear. She'd have to do a better job of hiding it from him. The man was a predator. And, like most, the chase seemed to be his ultimate thrill.

Javier strutted across the room. "What do you think your price is?"

She fought to steady her voice. "I have no idea."

"Apparently neither does Señor Rockforth. He can't decide whether you're worth it or not."

Her stomach lurched. Sam liked her, but this was preposterous.

"I'm not one of Sam's employees."

"No, I know that. No one would pay what I'm asking for an employee."

What was he implying? She was Sam's girlfriend? His mistress? She coughed. That was beyond ludicrous. She started to deny it. Point out how he had the wrong idea. But she stopped herself. Just maybe, it was best that Javier believed she was important to Sam. Otherwise, wasn't she a liability? He'd have to get rid of her. Even kill her. A man as crazy as Javier wouldn't just set her free.

She gripped the edges of the bed as he drew closer. She was glad to be wearing dirty clothes and have unwashed hair. Someone that dressed and behaved like Javier would never stoop to touching someone in her present state.

As if reading her mind, he said, "I don't think Sam would pay much for the way you look right now."

"That man, Alejandro, said he would bring me some clothes."

Javier spun around, reacting strangely as she spoke. "Oh, he did, did he? How can that be if he doesn't speak English?"

"There are other ways to communicate, you know."

"Oh, trying to seduce your way out of here? Good luck with that." His laugh was tyrannical. "Alejandro doesn't like women."

His words stung. Javier's teeth gleamed as he watched her reaction.

"It wasn't like that," she started, then stopped. It was futile to attempt a rational conversation with this man.

"Well, too bad for you. Alejandro is spending the next few days with *mi papa*." His fingers danced over the foot rail. "Shopping for polo ponies. So you won't get any clothes from him." There was an undeniable edge of jealousy in his tone. "But if you want something to wear, I'll get you something."

"Could I have a toothbrush, too? Please."

He flipped his head in a non-committal manner, then turned to the door, knocking loudly. He shouted in Spanish.

When the door swung open, she took advantage of the three or four seconds she had to assess her situation. Directly outside, a man clad in military fatigues gripped the barrel of a rifle. She fought back the lump in her throat. Javier had his own army. Merely the hope of an accidently unlocked door wouldn't be enough. She'd have to find another means of escape.

Javier was back in less than two minutes. Dangling from one finger was a red negligee with black laces. He flung it in her direction. It landed on the sheet, covering her shoulders. Even without touching it, she could smell it. Cigarettes mingling with filthy unwashed bodies. She knocked it to the floor.

"Oh, you think you're too good?" He cocked his head. "Should I show you what you will become if Mr. Sam Rockforth doesn't pay? We don't have to go far. Any one of the girls down the hall will be more than happy to show how you'll spend your days."

Bile rose in her throat again. A brothel. It made sense. Javier's family would have a hand in prostitution. When the law was of no consequence, it was just another way to get rich.

He smiled with satisfaction, watching her face. "That's

right. We have a place for you here." He turned to the door. "I guess some men don't find redheads repulsive."

She bit her lip until the door closed behind him, then buried her face. Her wracking sobs were only slightly muffled by the pillow.

Chapter 6

"Alejandro." Diego Ramos's administrative assistant toyed with the ends of her hair and spun in her chair. "Señor Ramos is in a meeting." Every breathy syllable of her Spanish sounded like a purr.

"With whom, and how long has he been in there?"

"The mayor." Madia batted her eyes. "He hasn't been here that long."

The mayor. Alejandro stifled the urge to roll his eyes. The irony of it. He'd sat through many such meetings, watching Diego and the mayor posturing, both pretending to be upstanding citizens. Praising one another for their civic chivalry in front of anyone naïve enough to believe it. He rolled his head from side to side.

"Looks like you need a massage." She ran her tongue over her red lipstick.

Alejandro turned away. "Anyone else in there?"

"Someone from the American Embassy."

He let out a surprised cough. Fortunately, Madia didn't seem to notice. Since when did those two start meeting with the U.S. government? "You don't happen to know who it is?"

She shrugged. "Some guy."

"What did he look like?"

"Like maybe forty. I don't know."

Could be a hundred people that fit that description. "Blond hair, black hair, no hair?"

"Maybe balding. Light brown hair I think. Or maybe not," she said with a dismissive wave of a hand.

He'd never understood why Diego kept her around. It wasn't sex. The man had his share of mistresses, and none of them appeared to be as lazy or stupid as Madia.

Alejandro stared out the window in indecision. He couldn't barge in. He'd be risking his cover if the guy happened to recognize him. Plus, Diego would want to keep his son's latest antics quiet. But Alejandro needed to know who that American was. "I'll be in my office. Call me the minute they're out."

"Sure you don't want that back rub?"

"Positive."

She raised an eyebrow. "All right, then."

He shut the door to his office with a little more force than necessary. Who was this person from the embassy? The meeting was unlikely to be a result of the kidnapping. It was Alejandro's job to keep Diego in the dark with regard to Javier's antics. Ignorance made the pretense of being an upstanding Mexican easier.

Alejandro thought about the files he had locked away in a safe. Dozens of documents that had the potential to put Diego in prison for at least the next ten years. But it wasn't enough. His goal was much greater. And it would be achieved with the complete annihilation of the Ramos cartel.

His thoughts skipped to Avery. Red hair spilling across the sheets. Her face colorless. It was an image that he would never forget. God only knew what Javier's thugs had doped her up with. What had possessed Javier to do something so stupid? He was lucky she hadn't died. Alejandro banged his fist on the desk. It was his fault. He should have paid more attention to Javier's drunken rambling in the car that afternoon.

Thank God Dr. Martinez had given him a heads up. The doctor had sounded desperate when he called. *I know it's not my place to call. But I thought you should know . . . it's just that three days in this state is too long. Her vital signs are fair, but it would be my recommendation to have her in a hospital. I know that it's not likely, but someone must see to it that she is cared for.*

Would it have been different if she'd been intimidated by Javier? Kept her mouth shut? But it was that exact feistiness that made her fascinating, and he'd found it impossible to take his eyes off of her.

His phone rang, bringing him out of his trance. "Alejandro," Madia said in the breathy voice that turned his stomach. "Diego will see you now."

Alejandro took a deep breath. Dr. Martinez had risked his life by calling him. And now it was his turn to risk everything to stop Javier.

He made a detour by the elevators, hoping to spot the American without being seen. Unfortunately, it was too late. He caught only a glimpse of the mayor as the doors closed. Someone behind him cleared their throat.

"Looking for something?" Diego said.

"Oh, I was afraid I'd missed you."

"No," Diego said, drawing the word out. "If I remember correctly, you were to be shopping for ponies today."

"Something else has come up. Mind if we speak in your office?"

Diego's expression was impossible to read. "After you." He extended a hand in the direction of his office.

Diego shut the door quietly behind him. Before Alejandro could speak, Diego said, "If this is about Javier and the girl, I know all about it already."

"You do?" Alejandro's eyes narrowed. "How?"

"My question to you is, how did you let this happen?"

Alejandro sighed. It wasn't often he allowed himself to feel vulnerable. "Javier and I drove back from Zapata together. He passed out, and I left him at the house in Laredo with the car. The last I knew, he was planning on heading to Monterrey the next morning to check out the shipment coming from the south. And as you know, I caught a flight back to finalize the paperwork for yesterday's hearing."

Deep grooves formed in Diego's forehead where his eyebrows angled together in a V. "I had to learn from that American what my son had done."

Alejandro felt a surge of relief, though he attempted not to show it. If the U.S. government had intervened, then she was safe. "What do you need from me?"

"Nothing. It is to be kept quiet. As far as anyone knows, the Contreras were responsible."

Alejandro waited for more details, but Diego offered none. "Javier has released her already, right?"

"You've never let me down before. This can never happen again."

Alejandro met Diego's gaze with equal determination. To do anything else would be a confirmation of his culpability.

"He will continue to be a liability if we don't get him into rehab," Alejandro said. "Next time it will be worse." He'd said it before, but Diego never listened.

"No." Diego rose from his chair. "From now on, Javier will not be left alone. I want someone watching him at all times."

"Am I to serve as legal counsel or Javier's nanny?"

"He trusts you."

Alejandro wanted to laugh. Nothing could be further from the truth. Javier trusted no one. Paranoia flowed through the man's veins. But it wasn't the time to debate this with his father.

"Do whatever you must. Bring in people we can trust. It will be your job to oversee them. As always, discretion is key. Ultimately, Javier's your responsibility. And let me be clear. I do not intend to make a habit of negotiating with American officials."

Chapter 7

Her days were a feverish blur. During periods of intermittent awareness, her head swam with panicked and jumbled thoughts of escape, though she lacked the concentration to formulate any kind of logical plan.

This morning was better. For the first time in what seemed like months, she felt the heat of the room. She'd been so cold. Maybe the fever was finally breaking. Her head felt as if it might split in half, but it was still an improvement over yesterday.

She glanced about the room as if seeing it for the first time. If only there was a way to determine how long she'd been here. Though maybe it was better not to know. Forcing herself into a sitting position, she tried to recall the circumstances of her capture. Had she screamed loudly enough for anyone to hear? The walls were paper-thin at that motel, but the air conditioner was ridiculously loud. She pictured Manuel and Bruce, realizing she'd been abducted. Manuel would have been upset. Guilt-ridden and blaming himself. Bruce, on the other hand, would waste no time getting out of Zapata.

If either of them survived the night.

The possibility snapped her further out of the dreamy fog. Her heart thudded in a rapid and irregular rhythm. Javier might have killed them. She tried but failed to push back the thought. The law held no meaning for Javier.

She stiffened. Had the whole thing been her fault? If she'd been smarter in keeping her mouth shut would it have made a difference? "God, what have I done?" she said to the empty room. If she ever got out of this place, she'd learn to keep her mouth shut.

Her thoughts shifted to work. By now, Eric must have assigned some fledgling intern to inform her mother that her only child had been kidnapped. Within twenty-four hours of learning Avery was in the clutches of a Mexican drug cartel, her mother would hunt down Sam Rockforth. She'd learn his business, home, and cell numbers and recite them by heart. She'd stalk him, demanding answers. Follow him to the golf course, disrupt business luncheons, and keep in constant contact with his attorney. Avery laughed out loud. Margie McAndrews could be counted on to hound Sam Rockforth worse than Javier ever could.

Her thoughts were interrupted by the rattling of the door. The nasty scent of his cologne flooded the room before she saw him. "Miss me?" Javier strutted toward her.

"No," she said. Her hate for him flared, overpowering her resolution to keep her mouth shut. "I will never be that desperate."

"Next time it will be seven days of solitary, then." He coughed as he drew closer, then wrinkled his nose. "God, you look awful." He took several steps back, crossed his arms over his chest, and tilted his head. "I'm not sure if pitiful or beautiful will work better on Sam."

"What's that supposed to mean?"

"Time to take your picture. Remind Sam Rockforth of what he's missing. The old man is not very cooperative." He frowned, studying her face through lowered lids. "If I bother to have you cleaned up, do you think Sam will pay more?"

Saying yes could mean a shower and clean hair. She'd feel better. It was a temptation, but she didn't dare show any interest. Javier would only do the opposite. And the filth was beginning to bother her less. It ensured no one ever got too close. She turned her head toward the window, hoping to demonstrate her disinterest.

He shook a finger at her. "I need to get you a newspaper."

Like someone kidnapped by Al-Qaeda. Good luck with that strategy. If Sam had waited this long, then he probably had other plans. And her appearance would be inconsequential to anyone but her mother.

Javier left the room and returned minutes later with an older woman in tow. They spoke in Spanish, the woman looking at Avery critically. Periodically, the woman waved a hand under her nose. Avery grinned every time she did, not sure whether it was her unwashed state or Javier's cologne the woman found more offensive.

"Inez will take you to the shower," Javier said finally. He pointed a finger in Avery's face. "If you try anything, I won't kill you. That would be kinder than what I will do to you. Inez has some clients with very unique tastes. If you are smart, you will listen to my advice. You don't want to meet these people."

Avery fought back the image of what the patrons of this dump might prefer. Her stomach churned, and she gripped the rusty iron bedframe.

Javier jerked his head toward the door. "Out of bed now."

The woman pulled Avery to her feet. She moved unsteadily. Upon Inez's beckoning, two armed guards met them at the door. One stepped forward to cover her eyes with a dark piece of fabric while the other held her shoulders. There'd be no chance to explore her surroundings, though she did have a limited view of her feet. Each man held an arm and guided her along a tile walkway.

She smelled the rank and moldy bathroom long before they delivered her across the threshold. One of the guards removed the blindfold, though it was hardly a relief. The walls of the shower were coated in rings of filth, and every crevice was a thriving colony of black mold. Inez hastened the guards away, then bent to turn on the tap. Within seconds, yellow water began to collect in the slow drain. Before Inez managed to stop her, Avery stepped into the lukewarm shower without removing a single stitch of clothing. The action incited a string of angry shrieks from the woman, which Avery calmly ignored. The older woman threw up her hands in exasperation. Avery shed her clothes piece by piece. With careful deliberation, she wrung water from each, then stepped out of the shower to spread them across the counter.

"Laundry time," Avery chanted.

Inez embedded her lengthy red nails into Avery's shoulder and shoved her back under the shower head. The water level was mid-calf now. It wouldn't be long before the bathroom floor was flooded. Avery gritted her teeth and felt for the drain with her foot, shoving aside a mass of hair and other indeterminate solids, while Inez dumped a generous amount of shampoo across her scalp. The smell was foul. The viscous formula meandered down the sides of her head. She recognized the scent: flea shampoo. It would probably leave her bald. She leaned under the stream of water to wash it out as quickly as possible.

Inez swore.

"I don't care what you have to say about it," Avery shouted back. "I didn't need to be deloused. If I had fleas or lice or whatever, I'd be the first to know."

With a scowl, Inez shoved a sour gray towel at Avery and pointed toward a small dressing area. A red-and-black flowered polyester dress hung nearby. Garish and too low cut. Avery rolled her eyes. So, this was how it was going to be. Sam would get a glimpse of life in a brothel.

The woman handed her a bra. Overly padded, hot pink, and guaranteed not to fit. She'd barely stuffed herself in it when Inez tugged the dress over her wet head. The combination was every bit as hideous as she imagined. Exposed cleavage. Pink bra straps hanging out. Inez pulled down on the neckline.

"No." Avery swatted at her hand. "You're making it worse."

A stupid thing to do. Inez's patience was thin at best. Avery backed off as Javier's threats resonated. Arguing with this woman any further would only get her into trouble. "Sorry."

But it was too late for an apology. Inez delivered a hearty slap across Avery's cheek.

Avery staggered and let out a small gasp of surprise. Inez faced her, holding a comb like a weapon. The whorehouse madam had made herself perfectly clear.

Avery froze at the sight of herself in the mirror. The outrageous outfit. Days' or maybe weeks' worth of tangles. Dark circles ringed her eyes, and her face was devoid of color other than the red handprint. A photo of her in this state would lead them to believe she was already in the morgue.

Inez's brutality did not cease with the slap. She battled Avery's matted mess, seeming unconcerned that half of it ended up in the comb. Only periodically did Avery receive a reprieve from the pain, as Inez paused to marvel at the color of her hair. Inez uttered a satisfied grunt as she violently eliminated the final tangle. She bent over, reaching for a pallet of eye shadow. Before Avery could object, Inez slammed her head back. No one could accuse the woman of being ineffective in getting her point across.

Inez took her time. Eyebrows, lips, then finally cheeks. When Avery opened her eyes, she was hardly surprised to discover that her eyelids were painted a shade of blue not found in nature. It was difficult not to laugh. Her eyebrows were lined in heavy black pencil, and her lips painted fire-engine red.

She no longer looked dead.

No. She pursed her lips. This was far worse.

Inez let out a shrill whistle. A guard led Avery to a small room across the hall. Another followed, holding a newspaper and camera. It all felt absurd. Did they really believe a photo of her looking like the cheapest of hookers would somehow motivate Sam to pay? She had to believe that Javier, with his expensive tastes, wouldn't approve. But as far as she could tell, no one had bothered to consult him. Inez pushed her against the wall and pressed the newspaper to her chest. At least this might hide the worst of the hot pink bra. The guard eyed her, then said something to Inez. Chattering angrily, the woman yanked the newspaper down to waist level and grabbed the pink straps of the bra, hefting it upward.

Avery debated whether appearing desperately sad or scared would be more likely to convince Sam she needed his help. In the end, she decided it was neither. Didn't Sam always say he liked her for her determination? She straightened her shoulders and grinned like a maniac as the guard clicked away.

Chapter 8

A thud at the door jolted her upright. There was only one person who took pleasure scaring her like that: Javier. Her stomach knotted. Lately, he'd begun to stop by only long enough to fling insults. When he managed to sense her irritation, or even better — her anger, he'd leave.

"Get up." He glared at her through bloodshot eyes. He was twitchy this morning. Not a good sign.

"What time is it?"

"It's eight thirty. Why are you still in bed?" His voice was strained, rough.

"Because if you haven't noticed, there's not much else to do around here besides sleep."

"That's about to change." He managed to misstep and swayed into the side of her narrow mattress. She pretended not to notice. To acknowledge anything so trivial could send him into a rage. "I have a project for you."

Her eyes narrowed. She'd grown less afraid of him over time. It wasn't conscious; it had just happened. "What kind of project?"

"Engineering." He closed his eyes, and it looked as if he might fall over sideways. "I want you to design a tunnel."

"What for?"

"That's none of your business."

"I don't design tunnels. Civil engineers do that." Not that she was totally ignorant of the construction. What someone like Javier would want was probably simple enough. But he'd have to make it worth her while.

He peered down his nose at her. If it was meant to intimidate her, it wasn't working. Something about him was off. Maybe he was hungover. It was impossible to tell, but she got the feeling that if she shoved him hard enough, he might just collapse.

It was tempting.

"You will design this tunnel." Even his usual disdainful expression wasn't quite right.

"Or what?"

"Don't screw with me. I don't have the energy for you. You know I can make your life a living hell."

She kept her eyes on his, wondering if he expected her to rise from the bed. "All right. But you need to tell me what it's for."

"To move people from one side of the river to the other. Without getting wet."

"The Rio Grande?" No. Not even Javier would be that crazy.

"No." He spat the word at her. "A small river on one of my father's ranches."

Even a small river would require more expertise than she had. "What kind of information do you have for me?"

"What kind of information do you need?" He began to pace.

"The width, the depth, soil types. Average monthly flow rates. Flood stages. What kind of construction you want. Cement. Metal pipe. And those are just the basics. There's much more to consider." She tilted her head. A project like this would take months or more, depending on equipment and labor. But it would be something to do in this godforsaken place. A challenge. Like a puzzle that she never intended to finish. And it could buy her some time. Maybe he wouldn't kill her right away if Sam or someone didn't find a way to get her out of here soon. And best of all, she'd insist upon visiting the location.

"So you think you can do it?"

"Give me some answers, and I'll let you know. I'll need supplies. Paper, pencils, and a calculator to start with." She might as well have asked for an abacus. With no data, there was nothing to calculate.

"*Abres la puerta*," he shouted in the direction of the door. It was the biggest and meanest of the guards that finally opened the door. He looked only slightly less ragged than Javier. "He'll bring you pencils and paper," Javier said. "Make me a list. This job is top priority. I want you working on it right away."

She shrugged and turned away as the door closed. It was only after the final click that she allowed herself to smile.

~ ~ ~

It turned out that the big mean guard spoke English. He ran his finger under each word as he read through her list aloud. "You want Javier to find out the soil type?"

"Yes. It's really important. And he can't just tell me 'sand.' Some samples would be best. From different depths."

The man ran a hand over his gleaming scalp. "You want to know how wide the river is."

"Yes. And how far away from the river's edge the tunnel should begin and end. If there's flooding, I need to know that. What's the source of the water?" She sighed. "Oh God, there's water quality to consider. Sorry, I'll get to that later. I need to know, if the channel is narrow, then are the banks steep?"

"You are going too fast."

She rubbed her hands over her face. It was like playing the telephone game at a six-year-old's birthday party. This man could never really convey her messages to Javier effectively. And no one could even pretend to design a tunnel without having a clue about the scale.

"Tell him I need photographs. That will help me to get started. If he's around, tell him to come see me."

The man nodded and wasted no time making his exit. She toyed with the pencil and paper. Her single class in civil engineering was really not enough education for this. The course had been nothing more than an introduction to the design of tunnels, bridges, and dams. But at least it would give her the vocabulary to fake it.

The door opened. "You wanted to see me?" Javier said. He sounded almost civil.

"I need way more information. If you could start by telling me how you visualize this tunnel...?"

"I want it big. Big enough to stand inside."

"Okay. How wide is the river now?"

"Right now?" She nodded. Javier stared up at the ceiling. "Maybe a hundred yards or so. Maybe a little more."

"Wow. A hundred yards." He'd lied. Of course he'd lied. This was no small river. And in the event of a flood, it might become significantly wider. "I told the guard I need photos. I need to see what the topography is like. Does the river flow fast or slow?"

"Slow in this spot. Most of the time," he said.

"Okay. We'll start with photos. I need to know what the river bed is like. Big rocks, small rocks, or a mixture. Take lots of pictures."

"We already dug a little. There are all sizes of rocks there. And it's sandy." He might have told her this to begin with. Though from the way he said it, he sounded reluctant to admit they'd even attempted anything. He cleared his throat. "No one can know about this tunnel."

No surprise there. Otherwise he'd be building a bridge. "All right, I get it. The construction needs to be secret. Anyone that sees it might think you're repairing a road or something?"

"Exactly. You know, sometimes I think you're not as dumb as you look."

She returned the jab with a dazzling smile. "Thanks. I assume it needs to be completed quickly."

"Of course."

"And what's your budget?"

He thrust his chin in her direction. "You tell me."

"Take me out there."

"No."

"Yes."

"No."

"Then at least get me some pictures," she said.

He nodded, then turned to leave. "I'll have them this afternoon. And you will have some plans for me this afternoon."

"No, I—"

But he'd already left.

Chapter 9

Open-mouthed, Alejandro stared at the image on his phone. He reread the caption for the third time. *How much do you think Sam Rockforth will pay for this?*

What the hell? He tossed the phone aside, feeling sick. Avery was still in Mexico. Still at "Madam Inez's Playhouse," as Javier so graciously dubbed it. Like an idiot, he'd assumed Diego had released her to the American Embassy. Diego had said that was the plan. Or had he? Alejandro closed his eyes, trying to remember.

No. He hadn't. He'd dodged Alejandro's questions about Avery. Apparently, the only action he'd taken was to pay off that embassy official for silence.

Alejandro leaned back in his chair, staring at the ceiling in disbelief. Diego was allowing Javier to continue with this kidnapping scheme. As if it were just an expensive hobby. And as long as Javier continued to claim the Contreras were responsible, Diego would ignore it.

It went against everything Alejandro had been hired to do. His job was to ensure that Diego's reputation in Mexico City was clean. Rock-solid. If word got out that his son had kidnapped an American and dragged her across the border, Diego was done.

He pounded his fist on the desk. "Damn!" If only he'd known she was still locked up. He'd have had her out of there by now. And maybe he would have paused long enough to beat Javier within an inch of his life.

He reached for his phone and took another look at the photo. The date on the newspaper was nearly two weeks ago.

She looked terrible. He glanced at his watch. He could be there in forty-five minutes.

But first he needed an update on Javier's schedule. He reached across the desk for the most recent security report. Until now, he'd barely glanced at it. It was the aspect of this job he hated most. He ran a finger over the notes. The newly hired security team was having trouble keeping Javier sober. No big surprise there. By next week, Javier would have them shooting up with him, and Alejandro would be hiring replacements. He returned to his phone and texted the security chief in Cancun.

The man's response was exactly as he feared. Javier was already back at Inez's.

Alejandro stroked his chin. He had to get some guys inside the brothel. They could report back to him and keep her safe until he could get her out.

He touched the screen of his phone. "Oso. I need a cook. How're your institutional skills?" Alejandro held the phone away from his ear to avoid Oso's reaction, which he knew would be an onslaught of vulgarities. The man considered himself to be a master chef; even undercover he would balk at the idea of cooking for Javier's brothel. "I was just kidding. It's that cousin of yours I was thinking about. You know, the big one. No, the one that has the telenovela actresses tattooed across his ass. Yeah, Ivan. He's a cook, right? Good. Tell him to give me a call. The job will involve some general maintenance work as well. I'll double whatever he makes if he can start tomorrow."

Chapter 10

Alejandro stood in the doorway. *"Hola."*

She stared at him wide-eyed. His voice was like velvet, deep and rich. Her heart thudded as she fought to pull the sheets over her dirty clothes.

He studied her. She could imagine what he was thinking. Same nasty pajamas, now filthier than ever. Pasty white skin, matted hair. And she was losing weight. She'd seen it herself the day of the shower. Her face was growing gaunt. Nothing but sunken eyes and hollow cheeks. It could only be worse now. Nervously, she picked at her fingernails. Any signs she'd ever had a manicure were long gone. This place had made her a nail biter.

He set her dinner tray on her small bedside table. His nearness left her self-conscious, but at the same time desperate for more attention.

"You've been gone." Her tone sounded a bit too much like that of an abandoned child. She struggled to eliminate any whine from her voice. It felt weird getting no response, but she was convinced that speaking out loud helped to prolong whatever threads of sanity she had left. The guards really didn't know what to make of her.

His gaze hovered on the list she was holding. Her revised list for Javier. She waved it about. "You're wondering about this? When you came in, I was wondering if I'd really be designing a tunnel, or if by some miracle I might get out of here before Javier's demands got too specific." Alejandro's expression was sympathetic. But it was meaningless. There was no flicker of understanding. "I think either way, I need to appear vested. Don't you?"

Maybe his comprehension of English was better in written form. He seemed mesmerized by the list. In fact, he wanted to hold it himself. She relinquished her grasp on it. To her surprise, he set it down, pulled out his phone, and snapped a picture of it.

He pointed a finger toward her fresh tray of food. The plate was askew—there was something underneath it. Her first instinct was to clap her hands. Like a child. She was forgetting what it was like to be an independent adult. The effects of solitary confinement.

Alejandro patted her arm. She wanted to beg him to stay.

They exchanged a silent look of disgust at the cockroaches busily digesting the remains of her breakfast. As he bent to retrieve the tray, she whispered, "Please don't leave me here. Take me with you. I'm nothing to Sam. Javier's going to kill me when I finish the tunnel. Please."

Alejandro didn't react. He barely looked her way.

Her shoulders slumped.

The moment the door clicked shut, she kicked off the sheet. Beneath the plate was a virtual gold mine. A toothbrush, the smallest tube of toothpaste she'd ever seen, and a tiny wedge of soap. If she ever had the chance, she'd hug him for this. Her hands shook with excitement as she shoved the goods under her sheet.

It was several minutes before she realized that he'd also left her with a full set of silverware. A knife, fork, and spoon. The most she'd ever gotten before was a spoon. What was his intention?

Her heart sank as she inspected the knife. The blade was paper thin. Cheaply made, and in no way a weapon. She rubbed her forehead. He could have easily hidden something more threatening under that plate. A pocket knife would have been easy enough to conceal.

She sat back on her heels, her eyes focused on the distant mountains outside the window. Her eyes narrowed. There were possibilities. She sprang to her feet.

She'd known since the first day that this window offered the only possible means of escape, but she'd never come up with a plan. The ornate iron bars were covered in layers of paint. She ran a hand along the frame that attached to the sill. It took her two passes to detect a slight indentation where, long ago, someone had used a screw to attach bars. She slid her hand along the top and sides, locating seven more buried screws. Only eight screws, and she could be out of here. It sounded so easy as she spoke the words aloud.

She turned the knife over in her hand. Would it withstand the abuse of scraping layers of paint? And, more importantly, was it strong enough to turn the screws? She glanced at the barren ground below. Even if she managed to rid the window of the bars and rigged up a system using her sheets to lower herself, it was crazy. The expanse beyond was a virtual wasteland. She'd have no food, no real clothes, and no way to communicate. And if Javier caught her, he'd probably kill her.

She'd also have to contend with the added threat of his frequent visits to her room to confer on the tunnel. If she'd had the knife a week or two ago, she might already be gone.

It didn't matter. The fact was, she had it now. She'd work on the window at night and the tunnel during the day. Sleep would happen somewhere in between. God knows, she'd slept enough in the past weeks to make up for it all.

~ ~ ~

Moonlight was her only source of light. At the slightest sound, she jumped. Her stomach cramped at the constant threat of Javier's return. In her mind, it was made worse by the fact that he'd been gone for three long days. As if the length of his absence might somehow be correlated with the scale of his rage upon return.

Work on the tunnel was not exactly at a standstill. The guard had brought photos. She'd made thorough notes, sent more lists of requests, and was currently awaiting a response.

Exposing the first screw had taken three sleepless nights. By her calculations, the remaining seven would take three weeks to uncover. And that didn't even include loosening the screws. She rested her head in her hands and tried to ignore her rising disappointment. The knife would never survive the entire process.

Chapter 11

The sound of Oso's voice echoed across the marble entry of Alejandro's apartment. "Sorry I'm late. I was getting an update from my cousin."

Alejandro slid a beer in his direction. "Anything significant?"

"Nothing we didn't already know. Javier has the brothel guards on twelve hour shifts now. Midnight to noon. Apparently, he's short-staffed."

"Damn. Ten to six was better. Easier to catch someone asleep." Alejandro drew a line in the condensation along the neck of his beer bottle. "She's close to having the tunnel design done. Javier's planning on putting her to work if he doesn't hear from Rockforth in the next week."

"I'm assuming you don't mean putting her to work as an engineer," Oso said.

"No." Alejandro didn't bother to hide the anger in his voice. "Downstairs. Working for Inez. Making her one of his girls."

"So, we have what—a week to devise a plan?"

"Rockforth's definitely not going to pay. I won't let him. Javier would kill her once he got his hands on the money. The only way to save her is to get a jump on Javier. I want to be ready to go within forty-eight hours."

Oso's furry eyebrows shot up. "You expect a plan with no holes? We need a week."

Alejandro shook his head. "We've got two days."

Chapter 12

It was the morning after she'd uncovered the third screw that Javier made his appearance. The sun was streaming through the window, and though she was awake she hadn't yet made it out of bed.

He kicked at the side of the mattress. "This is what you do all day? Eat my food and sleep?"

"I've been sick." She coughed and pretended to struggle with breathing, sounding surprisingly raspy.

He backed away, apparently terrified of any contagious disease she might transmit. His upper lip curled in revulsion. She wanted to smile. It was impossible to determine what scared him more: the threat of contagion or her unwashed appearance.

In his hand were her notes. She and the guard had met two more times. "You saw the pictures," Javier said.

"Yes. Very helpful." Javier's tunnel location was no more a ranch than this brothel was a hotel, and the river looked suspiciously like the Rio Grande. But none of that mattered.

"I need to know what you think about construction," he said.

She'd thought about little else. It occupied her thoughts during the mind-numbing hours of working on the window. In fact, she'd become so interested in the prospect of the tunnel that she'd had some regret about not seeing it through construction.

"You obviously can't dam the river, and with your time frame, your options are limited. I think you should find a driller. A company with horizontal drilling capabilities. I've put together a rough drawing for you. Unfortunately, I don't have the reference materials to give you pipe specifications, but a good driller will know. It's how they install pipelines. Your pipe will just be a larger diameter than what they're used to, but for the right price they can probably make it happen." She reached for her notes. "Three hundred yards is a long way. You'll have to install supplied air, lights, and also pumps in the event of leaks or flooding. That means a source of electricity at one end or the other, and switches on both ends. I've marked a spot on the photos that should work. Based on what I could tell from the photos, the riverbed has minimal slope at the banks. It looks perfect for a pipeline."

"And there won't be too much activity during construction? Not too many trucks?" he asked.

"A lot less activity than there would be by any other method. There will be a drill rig. Couple of other service trucks. The biggest thing will be the size of your pipe. It might be a flag."

"But if I can pass it off as something else . . ."

"You can pass the pipeline work off as lots of things. Sewer or drainage. But three hundred yards' worth of very large diameter of pipe is a lot. You can't hide it behind a tree. You can't even hide it in a forest."

"So what can I do?"

She exhaled heavily, then remembered to cough. "You're next to a river. If anyone asks, tell them that during the last flood you had major problems. No access to the ranch, or whatever excuse seems plausible. Now you've decided to put in culverts. Lots of them. Big ones, because you're tired of messing around. Everywhere you see a low spot, you're putting in a culvert. So that you never, ever get trapped again."

Anyone who knew Javier would recognize this as his usual obsessiveness. But anyone who *really* knew Javier would know that the culvert story was a pile of crap.

But that was his problem, not hers. She was only the engineer.

"How long will it take?"

"You'll have to ask the driller. Generally, it's pretty fast if the terrain's not too tough and access is easy."

"Access is very easy." There was a light in his eyes she'd never seen before. It nearly eradicated the crazy look. Intelligence, excitement, and even hope were there. It was disturbing to think she might see the same thing in a mirror.

She remembered to cough. She placed a hand on her chest, dramatically hacking away, careful not to cover her mouth.

He buried his nose and mouth within the collar of his shirt. "I'll be back once I've found some drillers. I might have you on the phone with me."

And a gun to her head at the same time so that she didn't scream for help? No thanks.

"Hopefully I'll be better then. Not contagious."

He could fend for himself.

She was out of bed the moment she heard the final click of the door. Her heart raced. There was so little time. The key was not breaking the knife in her panic. If she could remove just one screw, the pointed end would be stronger and sharper than the knife, and she could use that to carve away at the excess paint around the others.

She inserted the knife into the closest screw. There was a moment of resistance before she felt it give. She smiled.

At this rate, she could have the bars off by dawn.

~ ~ ~

Her concentration was interrupted by a sound at her back. The door. A wave of cold flushed through her veins. It didn't seem like she'd been at it too long, but it was possible she'd lost track of time. She glanced at the light on the window sill—her method for telling time. Too early for the guards to deliver lunch.

She resisted the urge to jerk her head back. Instead, she reached between the bars and carefully set the knife on a small section of the window ledge that jutted out unevenly. A furtive maneuver. One she'd practiced repeatedly for the eventuality of this moment.

The knife wasn't completely concealed, but it also wasn't in plain view. At her feet lay scattered chips of paint. Casually, she did her best to kick the scrapings against the wall, then set her feet over the heap. Her heart thudded heavily in her chest. She kept her back to the door, pretending not to hear, gazing dreamily at the hellish landscape. A place even birds avoided.

She could feel the person edging closer. Any closer and her work would be evident. She turned and leaned against the window, trying to appear calm, though one look at her grasp on the window sill would say otherwise.

Alejandro. He pinched his shirt. "*Lo siento.*"

She frowned. Her Spanish was bad, but even she could tell he was apologizing for something. It took her a moment to understand that it was a reference to the clothes he'd never brought. She shook her head. "I don't need more clothes just to spend my time rotting away in this place."

He nodded as if he understood, then turned his attention to the bed. More specifically, to her notes.

"You can look at them. Take a picture. I wish I could give you the specifics. But I don't know where he's planning on putting it. I can tell you there's a quarry nearby. But he refused to let me see the site. No surprise there, I guess."

Alejandro had already finished photographing her notes before she ceased her rambling. She wanted to make him stay. The room always felt brighter when he was there.

"Thank you for the toothbrush and everything else." She mimicked brushing her teeth. "You can't imagine . . ."

This one small acknowledgment seemed to cause something inside her to snap. She bit her lower lip, trying to keep it together. But from somewhere within, she couldn't stop herself. Her voice was barely audible. "You know, you're the only person that's even spoken to me in I don't even know how long. Not counting Javier and that brute of a guard." She didn't look at him, but instead focused on the ceiling. "In all those studies of prisoners in solitary confinement, at what point do they start to lose it? Because I'm fighting it every day. And do you know what it's like when the only people that speak your language are the devil and his spawn? I know you don't understand a damn thing I'm saying. But thank you for standing there and pretending, even if you are a drug-dealing scumbag. God only knows what your motivation to help me might be."

A hysterical laugh escaped her, immediately followed by an uncontrolled sob. "Why does Javier think Sam Rockforth gives a crap about me? I mean, I barely even know the man. Not on a personal level, anyway. He's never going to give Javier a red cent for me. I'm nothing but a contract engineer. The only one stupid enough to take that crappy Zapata assignment. All because I wanted a promotion I was never going to get." She wiped her eyes, then blinked a few times. Oddly, it was the best she'd felt in weeks.

He glanced at her feet. It was obvious from his expression that he'd seen the paint.

"You won't say anything, will you?"

Suddenly, the door was flung open, banging against the wall. Both of them jumped. Avery's heart skipped a beat.

"What the hell are you doing? My orders are no speaking to her," Javier shouted. He switched to Spanish as he drew closer, jabbing a finger at Alejandro's broad chest.

Calmly, Alejandro swatted his hand away. He fired back, his voice so much deeper than Javier's.

But something in their conversation changed. Without another glance in her direction, Alejandro stormed toward the door, then turned. He uttered a few final words to Javier.

Avery understood only one word: Guadalajara. Her heart sank. He was probably leaving. The only person who had demonstrated compassion in this hellish captivity, and Javier had chased him away once again. She wanted to scream.

Javier paced the room. She moved toward the bed, hoping to draw his attention away from the window.

"What did he say to you?" Javier was back to looking as crazy as ever.

"Nothing."

"What was he doing in here?"

"He probably heard me banging on the door. He was just decent enough to respond."

"I heard you talking to him."

"Yeah. I called him a scumbag drug dealer, which, by the way, I enjoyed saying, since he doesn't understand a single word I say."

Javier's jittery pacing slowed slightly. "Well, you won't have that luxury anymore. He's leaving for Guadalajara in an hour. I sent him away for two weeks. By the time he comes back . . . well, you'll either be back wherever you came from or you'll be working down the hall. Either way, I'll be making some money off of you."

All because of one stupid mismatched conversation in two different languages? And now she would pay. Why was he so jealous of Alejandro? Javier had the money and the powerful father. He didn't have to work for a living. Women who somehow didn't know he was crazy probably found him attractive. There might even be women out there who didn't mind a little craziness, but his insecurities were so blatantly obvious.

"If I'm going to be your employee, why don't you give me a Spanish dictionary?"

He lurched forward. "As if that would be useful. You'll learn everything you need on the job, and the new vocabulary you'll be acquiring . . ." He shook his head. "You won't find in a dictionary."

It took everything she had not to spit in his face, but she was almost certain he would hit her if she did. Or worse.

"Why don't you let me talk to Sam on the phone? I might be able to convince him to pay."

"Do you know how many times I've called him?" Javier's eyes narrowed. "He's never asked to speak to you once. Not a single time. Tell me why that is."

She was tempted to mention that sending Sam pictures of her dressed like a hooker might not have been the best strategy.

"Tell me why he doesn't ask to speak to you." Javier's tone was growing more demanding.

She could think of absolutely zero reasons why a person in Sam's position wouldn't ask to speak to his wife or girlfriend. Most desperate husbands or boyfriends would be beside themselves demanding to speak to the victim. Unless that victim wasn't really a loved one. From the look on Javier's face, he'd reached a similar conclusion.

The truth probably wouldn't hurt at this point. "Sam doesn't ask to talk to me because Sam Rockforth barely knows me. Like I told you the first day, I'm an engineer for a consulting firm, not his girlfriend or wife or even his employee. I don't know where you ever got the crazy idea that Sam cares about me."

Javier's eyes flashed. "You've lied to me."

"No. You had the wrong idea from the beginning."

"Then why didn't you speak the truth sooner?"

"Because I thought Sam might be willing to get me out of here. I thought he might pay you."

"Stupid bitch. You've wasted my time."

"No I haven't. What about the tunnel?"

Javier breathed heavily through his nose. He seemed not to have heard her. "You are going to pay."

He began to pace. Avery closed her eyes and began to cough. He didn't seem to notice. With each lap, he grew closer to the window. She knew what would happen next.

He kicked at the paint chips lining the wall. It took a moment for him to process what he'd just seen. His eyes moved over the wrought iron, and he leaned forward, inspecting the window sill. He shook the loosened frame. Then his eyes paused on a single location. There was a tremor in his grasp as he lifted the knife from the ledge. "How did you get this?" he asked with a hiss.

She remained still. Coughing and staring at the floor.

"Stop it with that fake hack." Javier flew across the room. "Where?" He screamed the word. Blood vessels surfaced at his temples, and there were beads of sweat on his forehead. "I should break your neck."

"It was on my tray."

"I don't believe you. My guards don't make those kinds of mistakes."

Her knees felt weak. She braced herself against the bed frame, not ready for what she feared would come next.

His hand stung the side of her face. She made a low noise in the back of her throat. Outrage. Until her kidnapping, no one had ever hit her before. Not deliberately. Now, both he and Inez had done it.

She took a step in his direction, clenching her fist. His face was only inches away. She swung. But he anticipated it, effortlessly catching her wrist in mid-air. He gripped it so tightly she screamed, convinced she could hear the small bones cracking.

"Tell me." His words seethed.

"I told you the truth."

She stood still, fighting the urge to touch the place on her face where he'd hit her. It throbbed. Her eyes met his. She realized the look of confidence she was trying to create only enraged him more.

He struck her a second time. This time harder. She turned away, covering the sting with her hand.

"Bitch. You will pay." Still gripping the knife, he moved to the door and kicked maniacally. As it opened, Javier shouted at the person on the other side. The man's voice called out to others. Javier stormed out of the room, the door slamming in his wake.

She fought back tears. This wouldn't end well.

Five minutes later, the guard and a second man appeared, armed with a toolbox. To her relief, Javier was not with them. They crossed the room to the window, and her heart sank.

The guard was someone who routinely delivered her lunch. The other man she didn't recognize. She would have remembered. He was obese. Maybe three hundred pounds, and incapable of focusing on the job of boarding up the window. Repeatedly, the guard chastised him for his clumsiness and apparent lack of skill.

The man bent over to retrieve a screwdriver, revealing much more of his backside than she cared to see, but it was impossible to keep her eyes away. Tattooed across his lower back and butt were the faces of women.

He turned, grinned, then winked at her. She moved to the opposite side of the room, as far away as possible.

Nail by nail, they eliminated the natural light from the room. There would be no more fresh air. No view of the outside world. No more hopes of spotting a random bird and gazing at the distant mountains. And, worst of all, no hope of escape. All of it taken away. It was now truly a prison.

It took less than ten minutes before the shutters were nailed shut, and the men collected their tools. While the guard banged on the door, the larger man shot her a fleeting grin and allowed a screwdriver to slide from his hand. The sound of contact with the floor was muffled by the pummeling of the guard's fist against the door. The guard was out the door by the time the man paused to kick it in her direction.

The darkness weighed upon her. She retrieved the screwdriver and tucked it into her waistband, then returned to the darkest corner of the room and gathered herself into a ball. Tears poured down the sides of her face.

Javier reentered the room. He flipped on the fluorescent lights, sending a troop of cockroaches scurrying in all directions. Their spasmodic movement no longer bothered her. She withdrew further into the corner. He paused to inspect the men's work. She'd never seen him so calm, no longer fidgeting and taunting. But something told her this controlled version of Javier was far more dangerous.

"Tomorrow you will start work. It's time you earn your keep." His gaze rested on her lazily. "Your nights will no longer be for sleeping. I suggest you use your next few hours wisely."

She made no effort to hide her tears. Crying seemed to have absolutely no effect on him, anyway. But her foolish words did. "I hope the Contreras cartel gives you what you deserve."

In a flash, he was across the room. This time it was no slap. Nearly wrenching her arm from its socket, he yanked her to her feet. His fists came as a surprise. First to her jaw, then to her abdomen, knocking the breath out of her. Slowly she straightened, completely ignorant of defense mechanisms that might have spared her further pain.

She slid the screwdriver from her waistband. Holding it low, she jabbed him in the side.

"Bitch!" The screwdriver clattered to the floor. It hadn't even been enough to break the skin, but it fueled his rage.

He slammed her head against the wall. The jarring force left her ears ringing and the room spinning.

She swayed as he followed up with alternating punches to her gut and face. Her entire body was engulfed by pain.

One blow followed another, and she could never anticipate where he'd strike next. He was much too fast, and her ability to react seemed to take place in slow motion. Her knees buckled, and she slid against the wall, landing on her back. Next came a series of kicks, to her sides, arms, legs, and once or twice to her head.

By the time he paused to collect the screwdriver, she was broken, certain she'd die.

He peered down at her, clicked his tongue with a sound of disgust, and headed for the door.

Chapter 13

More than once she attempted to hoist herself from the floor to the bed, but the pain was too intense. She settled for the corner. If Javier chose to take out his anger further, she would at least have the protection of the two walls at her back.

She curled into a ball. Every movement sent more shivers of agony raging throughout her body. It brought back memories of her bicycle wreck from when she was seven. The worst pain, a fiery stab at her waist, was exactly as she remembered it. She'd had two cracked ribs then. Probably more now.

She tried to imagine how she might have defended herself better. He'd anticipated her every move. She knew nothing about fighting, and now she was facing... she forced thoughts of the brothel away.

There was a bang at the door. The horrible lights flickered on once more, and three men moved toward her. She groaned. "No, please." Her words were barely audible.

One of the three waited at the side of the bed holding a metal toolbox, while the other two pulled her up by the arms. She cried out, but it changed nothing. Resistance only meant more pain, and she didn't have anything left. The two men slung her onto the bed. The landing left her shuddering in agony. The third man opened the toolbox and began to withdraw a series of small instruments as the others pinned her against the mattress.

She closed her eyes. A small motor hummed, sounding like a dentist's drill. What could they possibly do next?

Disturbing images of the ways Javier might silence her floated through her mind. Removing her teeth. Cutting out her tongue. "No." She clamped her jaw shut.

But no one touched her face. Instead someone twisted her left arm, pressing it firmly against the mattress. She couldn't catch her breath. Part of her wanted to know what they were doing, but it was easier to just close her eyes and shut it out.

Needles pricked the inside of her arm. A sting coupled with small vibrations. What the hell had that psycho Javier thought up this time?

Realization struck her. This was a tattoo.

Tears leaked from her eyes. The violation was far worse than any pain.

~ ~ ~

Sometime later the door opened again. She couldn't find the strength to lift her head. What would be the point, anyway? "If you're here to kill me, just get it over with, would you?"

Whoever it was made a serious effort to be quiet. Probably not Javier. She waited, dreading the lights. But no one turned anything on. She squinted in the darkness. Two figures moved silently toward her.

"No more." She let out a pleading half-cry half-moan.

"Shhh," someone said. Definitely not Javier. She would have smelled him by now.

She held her breath. A figure leaned toward her, and she let out a cry of recognition. "Alejandro." As he leaned forward, she grabbed desperately at his collar. He stroked her hair and whispered to her in Spanish.

"Señorita," another voice said. She raised her head to see the outline of a large man, shorter than Alejandro but broad-chested. The man kept his voice low. "We need to get you out of here quickly."

Alejandro reached for her hands and gently pulled her to her feet. She tried to stifle a moan but wasn't successful.

The second man whispered, "Are you hurt?"

"Yes."

"Can you walk?"

"I think so."

"We have something to cover your clothes," the man said.

Alejandro produced something from around his neck. In the minimal light, it appeared to be a dress. Alejandro gathered the length of it and carefully placed it over her head. This was going to hurt. Feeling childlike, she raised her arms. The process was excruciating, but his touch was warm as he guided her arms through the short sleeves.

A lump formed in her throat. Stockholm Syndrome. It was real now. He was her captor and her hero. A fantasy realized.

In near-silence, the threesome crept toward the door. Alejandro held her hand in his. The security guard was crumpled in an awkward slump. She moved on, refusing to let herself think about it.

They wasted no time. The other man led the way, and Alejandro followed closely behind her. The full-length dress dragged, and she gathered the excess fabric in one hand, cautiously stepping down in measured increments. Walking didn't bother her, but the stairwell they came to was nearly pitch black, and her steps were tentative. Either Alejandro sensed her apprehension, or he was becoming impatient. He moved next to her and grasped her free arm. With easy assurance he guided her into the descending darkness.

His hand never left her arm even as they reached the hallway below. The corridor was almost as poorly lit as the stairwell. The air was stifling and the accompanying odors oppressive: rotting meat and stale cigarettes. Probably body odors too, but her own standards had become so low that her sensitivity to personal hygiene was virtually eliminated.

The hallway was lined by a series of doors on either side. She shuddered. One of these might still be her room, if they didn't make it out quickly.

The silence of their exit was broken by a crash. Steps away, a door flew open. With a backhanded sweep of his arm, Alejandro pressed her into the shadows, his large body hiding hers. Something glass shattered against a wall. A high-pitched shriek was followed by a groan. The other man glanced at Alejandro, who shook his head. An angry male voice, speaking in Spanish, muffled the echo of small sobs.

Avery's heart pounded against Alejandro's broad back. She wasn't out the door yet. Tomorrow night these could be her cries.

A silhouetted figure emerged from the room. He paused only to utter a few words in Spanish before his footsteps thudded in the opposite direction.

Avery let out a small sigh of relief. He'd never even sensed their presence.

Alejandro made a low sound. His partner stood in the doorway, inspecting the scene.

The crying had stopped. Either the person was seriously hurt, or worse. It was wrong to assume the cries came from a woman, Avery realized. It had sounded more like a child.

Alejandro signaled for her to stay put as he joined the other man. Their movement took on a hurried sound. Panic washed over her. She didn't want to be left alone in the corner.

She inched her way just inside the doorway. A series of candles provided the only light. She covered her mouth, choking back her feeling of horror. The girl was small. Maybe not even a teenager. Alejandro snapped his fingers, pointed to the bed, and bent to lift the naked girl from the floor. Avery yanked a rumpled sheet from the bed and covered the unconscious girl, who was now in Alejandro's arms. Her head left a trail of blood as it rolled across his shoulder. The other man stripped the remaining bedding, trying to fight a losing battle against the sizable pool of blood on the floor. Alejandro shook his head. The man kicked the saturated sheets to the corner.

Alejandro's partner took the lead as they resumed their escape along the shadowy corridor. The addition of the girl slowed their progress. Avery hovered behind Alejandro. They stopped at an intersection of hallways. The other man disappeared around a corner, while Alejandro signaled that they would wait. The girl dangled like a rag doll in his arms.

Time crawled as they waited for the man to reappear, though Alejandro seemed unfazed by the weight of the girl. The idleness gave rise to Avery's nerves, which sent barbs up the back of her legs. She fidgeted; Alejandro shook his head in warning. She stilled herself.

Unexpectedly, the girl moaned. Alejandro closed his eyes. Avery drew closer. She'd cover the girl's mouth if necessary. Her eyes met Alejandro's, where his own impatience was beginning to reveal itself.

A distant rattle sent them into the darkest section of the hallway. Seconds later, Alejandro's partner turned the corner breathless. In a loud whisper he said, "*Vamonos!*"

She exhaled.

The night air was welcomingly cool and damp as they made their exit. With every step, a small amount of tension began to ebb from her body. An idling car waited only steps away. Alejandro assumed the lead.

"Señorita, do you mind sitting in the back with the girl?"

It was the first time in weeks someone had offered her a choice of any kind. "No. Of course not."

Alejandro climbed into the passenger seat. He glanced over his shoulder, watching Avery and the girl. Avery caught his eye under the dome light and said, "*Gracias.*"

She closed her eyes as they accelerated through the night. No need to bother asking where they were going. It didn't matter. For now, the simple feeling of the night's air whipping through the open car window was enough. And if she never laid eyes on that horrible place again, she had no complaints. She glanced at the girl. Hopefully, the same would be true for her.

The driver cleared his throat. Peering at her in the rearview mirror, he said, "Your face. It's kind of a mess. Are you hurt? Alejandro would like to know what happened."

Avery took a deep breath and immediately regretted it. The pain was excruciating. She uttered a single word. "Javier."

Alejandro demanded something else from the man. "Is it bad?" the man translated.

"The girl's the one you need to worry about," Avery said, sounding tougher than she felt. In truth, she wondered what kind of internal damage she had from Javier's kicks.

"When it's light outside, you'll need to hide yourself and the girl. Are you well enough to do that? We didn't plan to have two of you back there."

"We can make it work." Though exactly how, she wasn't sure. "Are we taking her to a hospital?"

The driver shook his head. "Too dangerous. For all of us."

The harsh reality. They still weren't safe from Javier.

Chapter 14

The morning sun drew Avery out of a light sleep. The girl's eyes were open now, and focused on her. She'd been right in thinking the girl was young. Nothing but a child. Avery smiled at her, but the girl drew back. Avery should have known better. Her face must be such a mess, it was scaring the girl.

They were in a city now, or at least the outskirts of one. The air was heavy with diesel fumes. Avery tried but failed to find a painless way to hunch down in the seat. Horns blared, and the car slowed. Stop and go. Each lurch was a reminder of Javier's beating.

She studied the girl's wound. In the light of day, it seemed less dramatic than last night's amount of blood had suggested. She leaned toward the girl and tentatively swept the hair from her forehead, carefully avoiding the wound itself. She half expected the girl to react, but she remained still. Avery touched the area next to the wound as gently as possible. She'd always heard head injuries bled a lot. Hopefully, that was the case here. A bigger concern was probably a concussion. Of course, the way Javier had smacked her own head against the wall, she might have a concussion, too.

The girl shifted, and Avery gasped as she caught sight of the girl's wrist. *J-33*. Nearly an inch in size. It sent a jolt of rage through her. She'd almost forgotten. The pain was so insignificant compared to the rest of her injuries, and she hadn't allowed herself to watch its application. She turned her own arm over.

J-41.

Branded like livestock. Javier's forty-first prostitute. At least that's what she assumed it meant. At the sight of it, the girl's expression changed from fear to something that resembled trust.

Avery's own anger waned. As much as she hated the man and the fact that he'd dared to leave his mark on her, it was meaningless. Unlike the girl, Avery hadn't suffered the consequences of the label.

The driver peered over his shoulder. "How's the girl?"

"It looks like she's going to be okay," Avery said. "I can't say that for sure, but it's not as bad as I thought it was last night. If I had something to clean it off with, I could tell you more."

"We'll be stopping soon," he said. "But you need to close your window. We're getting very near the heart of the city."

"What city?"

He didn't answer.

"What time is it?" she tried instead.

"Just a little after six in the morning."

They hadn't been in the car too long. It seemed odd. The brothel felt like it was a thousand miles from anything, but obviously that wasn't the case. All along she'd been on the outskirts of a city. Maybe if she'd gotten the bars off the windows she would have survived, after all.

Alejandro peered over the back of his seat. He said something in Spanish to the driver.

"Señorita, you need to move down in the seat. Mexico is not exactly full of redheads. You have to hide yourself."

Avery helped the girl into a reclining position, allowing her to occupy the entire back seat. Trying her best not to cry out, Avery lowered herself to the floorboard and propped her legs against the opposite door. The position was excruciating. She held her breath and inched her upper body back, just the tiniest amount. She closed her eyes, praying the ride would be a short one.

From this uncomfortable and awkward position, the only thing in her line of sight was Alejandro's profile. She was glad, at least, for the opportunity to observe him without feeling his unnerving gaze on her. A welcome distraction. He was wearing a gray t-shirt and jeans. Last night's blood had dried, leaving random spots dotting his sleeve. The tendons of his bronze arms were lined with the veins of an athlete, and the short sleeves of his t-shirt allowed her a glimpse of his well-defined triceps and biceps. Anyone that perfect had to be a gym rat. Or maybe not. If Bruce was right, and Alejandro had been some sort of bodyguard for Javier's father, then it made sense that he'd be in great shape. He leaned forward to retrieve his phone from the far corner of the dash. The t-shirt clung to every muscle spanning his back and shoulders.

He held the phone to his ear, though he didn't speak. He clicked it off, tossed it on the dash, and then ran a hand through his hair. Perfect hair. Dark brown in enviable loose waves. She felt an overwhelming urge to touch it, allow a strand to wrap itself around her finger. Why did the gay ones always have to be so good looking?

She jerked and winced, caught by surprise at her own thoughts. Too long in captivity was making her lose perspective. Alejandro was a member of a cartel. Sure, he was saving her from Javier, but who was to say he didn't have other plans for her? He might even be selling her off to someone else. Anything was possible, and she couldn't afford to let her guard down. One glance at the girl, and she could see in her wary expression that her thoughts ran along the same lines.

Alejandro spoke to the driver. He pointed out the window, his low voice rumbling in what sounded like anger. The phone message must have done it.

She rocked painfully against the edge of the seat as the car took a sharp turn. The sky disappeared, and there was a shrieking of car tires as they spiraled upward.

The car idled before coming to a complete stop. She rose up on her elbows but then grimaced, regretting the decision. Alejandro opened his car door, stepped out, and then turned to peer into the back seat. His eyes caught hers, and he said something to the driver.

"Where's he going?" she asked.

"He'll be right back. You can sit in the seat now. It's dark enough in this garage, I think." He turned to the girl, apparently instructing her to make room for Avery. Avery sucked in air as she hefted herself from the floorboard and into the seat. The man glanced at her in the rearview mirror and removed his cowboy hat. "He wants you to wear this."

The hat was black, bedazzled with rhinestones, and slightly damp with sweat. She hesitated, gripping the brim. But this was no time for vanity. This hat could mean the difference between life and death for all of them. She shoved her knotted hair into the hat and did her best to tuck in the stray strands.

"I'm Avery, by the way. I need to thank you for last night."

"I'm Oso, and you don't need to thank me. Thank Alejandro. He made all the plans." He hopped out of the car and opened her car door with a grin. "Feels good to be out of that terrible place, I know." A gold molar gleamed in the light of the parking garage. "Alejandro's ready for you. Do you need help getting up?"

"Maybe a little," she said. She swung her bare feet around.

"You need shoes." He held up a finger. "Stay there." The trunk popped open, and she could hear the shuffling of paper. He returned with a pair of pink flip-flops in hand. "They're small. But better than nothing." The much-too-small shoes were decorated with sparkly dragons.

"It's okay, I'm fine without them," she said. "I haven't had any in weeks now."

"You have to. You'll need something." He squatted before her, slipping the shoes onto her feet. Another inch's worth of sole would have been ideal.

She watched his hands. Each of his fingers was clad in gold. Only one thumb was without jewelry. He stood and held out a hand to help her. His oversized belt buckle dazzled with an array of gemstones, and a pearl-handled pistol was tucked into the waist of his jeans. About his hairy neck was a massive gold chain.

And yet he was father or grandfather to some little girl who wore sparkly dragon flip-flops. It was all so surreal.

"Thank you."

He led her to a navy Jeep and opened the door. "Can you get up there yourself, or do you need help?"

She began to back her way into the seat, biting her lip to stifle a groan. "I can do it. Thank you for everything." She rotated in the seat, catching a glimpse of Alejandro behind the wheel. Eyes hidden behind aviators, two days' worth of beard, and a baseball cap on backwards. He nodded at Oso and put the Jeep in gear.

"Wait." She called out to Oso through the open window. "Where's he taking me?"

He shook his head and gave Alejandro a knowing look. "Somewhere you'll be safe. Until things are better." He slapped the windshield and backed away from the idling vehicle.

Until things are better? But she had no chance for further questions. Alejandro hit the gas, and they were off.

The traffic was heavy, though Alejandro seemed to find ways to dodge the congestion. She leaned back and pulled the cowboy hat low over face. Cobbled one-way streets and hurried commuters dressed in business attire. There was no doubt this was Mexico City.

With no common language, there was little conversation. Alejandro spent much of his time on the phone. It was on speaker, so she heard all of the conversations but could understand none of them. The only thing she knew for sure was that none of the callers were Javier. She'd recognize his voice in an instant. Twice a woman called. Her deep, rich voice could only be described as sultry. Alejandro's replies were calming, as if for some reason he needed to pacify her. There was something about it that Avery didn't like. Whatever their relationship might be, she was sure of one thing: the woman was manipulating Alejandro. She smiled to herself. Amazing how some things just didn't require translation.

After a solid hour of stop-and-go traffic, the cars began to thin. The terrain was turning hilly, and distant mountains were becoming visible through the haze. Somewhere in the back of her mind, Avery had expected to be delivered to the American Embassy or something along those lines. But wherever they were headed was obviously not to the embassy. She thought about Oso's words. *Until things are better.* She wished she'd had a chance to ask what that meant. Now she was in a car with a man she barely knew and no means to communicate.

She forced herself to pay attention to the landscape, trying to establish landmarks. It was important to have some idea of direction. They were driving parallel to a highway, but Alejandro seemed to be deliberately avoiding it. Instead, their route was a series of stops and starts, turns and twists. It wasn't until they veered back in the direction of the elevated highway and she spotted the tollbooth that it made sense. He was avoiding cameras. Whether it was for his benefit or hers, she couldn't begin to guess.

Out of range from the effects of the city, the sky was now a clear blue, and she was beginning to catch glimpses of what seemed like a mirage. A snow-capped mountain, it was a perfect peak. Even after spending nearly all her life in Colorado, she'd never seen anything like it. It dwarfed all other mountains, both in height and with its spectacular beauty.

Alejandro, following her gaze, pointed. "Volcán."

"Volcano?"

"Si."

"Wow!" Her amazement seemed to please him. "It's beautiful."

"Popocatépetl."

"I wish you spoke English. This would be so much easier. I have no idea what you just said."

It was impossible to keep her eyes off of the breadth of his hands. There was reassuring strength there. And somehow it seemed more than just physical.

He rested his left wrist on the steering wheel and leaned his head toward hers. He pointed to the volcano, repeating the word very slowly. "Popocatépetl."

"Couldn't you teach me something easy? I'll never be able to pronounce that word."

He watched her with an intensity that made her squirm. She'd prefer he keep his eyes on the road. He repeated the word a third time. "Popocatépetl."

She laughed. Then said, in her very American accent, "Po-po-cat-tip-etty."

It was his turn to laugh. A deep laugh. The first she'd ever heard from him. His face lit up, almost childlike.

Something about it brought on an unfamiliar feeling. Stockholm Syndrome? No. She felt indebted to him, but it was more than that. Until now, the past few hours had been about escape. The panic of flight. But leaving the city had brought on a sense of calm. She saw it in the way he leaned against the door as he drove. He was no longer tense. It made her want to know him better. Understand him, and why he was willing to risk his life for her.

The sun was high in the sky when they pulled into a small village. She was starving. He parked at the edge of an outdoor market, far from any other cars. The bustling marketplace seemed like a fantasy. It was so different from anything she'd seen in weeks.

She had no intention of being left to wait in the car. As she moved to open the door, he placed a hand on her arm and then handed her a pair of sunglasses. She understood. No drawing attention to her eyes or the bruises.

She put the glasses on and turned to him for approval. He leaned toward her and carefully lifted the hat a fraction of an inch. With his other hand, he brushed the stray hair from her face. His touch was light, and his nearness radiated warmth. It was impossible to believe that this man, who'd risked so much, had any ulterior intentions.

He helped her out of the Jeep. Though it wasn't terribly painful, she hunched her back just in case, protecting her injured ribs. His reaction was a mixture of irritation and something else. He didn't understand and probably misunderstood her reaction to his help, she realized. She reached for his arm and led him behind the Jeep, glancing about to be certain that no one was watching. Slowly and painfully, she raised the long dress. She was still wearing her dirty pajamas underneath, and he helped her as she lowered the waistband of her shorts. The flesh around her lower ribs was now a full-scale exhibition of Javier's violence in varying shades of purple, blue, and black.

He grimaced and turned away.

"Javier," she said. "Broken." Not that he understood the word. But he didn't need to. The bruises said it all.

He straightened her dress and took her hand. His grip was firm and surprisingly calloused. Not the hand of someone who spent their days simply racing sports cars with Javier and shopping for polo ponies.

Chapter 15

It was crazy to bring her here. It might be a couple hundred miles from Inez's, but Javier had informants everywhere. And her clothes didn't quite make sense. To the locals, the long dress meant *turista*. But the shoes and rhinestone cowboy hat were . . . ridiculous. He tried not to drag her, but he didn't want to give anyone the chance to stare at her for too long.

He wrapped an arm around her waist, trying to encourage a little haste. She flinched. Damn. She must have at least three broken ribs.

She slowed at every stall. He tried to be patient, chewing his lower lip and surveying the crowd. It was mainly women, a few older men, and kids. He urged her along. Better to keep the dawdling to the covered area of the market, where the aisles were narrower and darker.

Dark enough that the bruises on her face weren't visible at first glance. The thought of it made him draw her closer. She smiled, the contours of her face radiating adulation despite the remnants of Javier's beating. He couldn't take it to heart. It was simply Stockholm Syndrome. She'd said it herself.

As they rounded a darkened corner, he spotted Eduardo and smiled. The old guy was amazing. At least seventy, and yet he was perched like a wiry monkey on the counter behind his stacks of books. He launched himself at Alejandro, enclosing him in a hearty embrace, then ran a hand along his face. A paternal gesture, treating him as if he was still eight years old.

Alejandro turned to Avery and presented her to the old man. "Avery." For some reason he couldn't explain, he pronounced it with an American accent. With this, he gained her admiration. She grinned at him and then at Eduardo.

In Spanish he said to Eduardo, "I need a copy of *the* book. Also, she's going to need a Spanish-English dictionary."

Eduardo raised his eyebrows. "*The book?*"

Alejandro nodded. It had been years since he'd resorted to this method for communication. But he couldn't afford to contact Sam Rockforth himself. Nor could he ask anyone else on his task force to do so, either. Avery McAndrews wasn't part of their assignment. Her situation was incidental, for the most part unrelated, and he could not allow it to jeopardize two years' worth of hard work.

Eduardo drew a deep breath and disappeared between two towering stacks. Avery's attention was drawn to the inventory, and he took the opportunity to reach for a paper and pen behind the counter. He copied the number from the contact in the burner phone, occasionally glancing at Avery, though she didn't seem to notice. At the top of the page he wrote Sam's name.

The book was a hollowed out copy of *Cien Años de Soledad*. Eduardo's bookshop had served as a contact point for dozens of American agents over the years. Alejandro suspected that the bookshop, which was nothing but a few tall stacks of used bestsellers, was supported almost entirely by Eduardo's covert activities.

Eduardo hung his head over Alejandro's shoulder. The old man held the book open, deliberately looking away while Alejandro dropped the slip of paper inside.

"Tell Roger I need his help." Alejandro lowered his voice. "He needs to let this guy know that the girl is safe. She'll be home soon. No ransom required. Little trouble with the embassy, though, so it won't happen right away. Roger knows the logistics. And most importantly, Roger needs to remind this guy that under no circumstances is he to alert anyone. No press, no family, no friends. For the contact's eyes and ears only." Alejandro grinned at Eduardo. "It's a lot to remember. You're not getting forgetful yet, are you?"

The old man laughed. "Forgetful." He ruffled Alejandro's hair. "Not me. My parents are still alive and running their restaurant. Senility doesn't run in our family."

"Tell them I said hello."

Avery peered over the counter. Eduardo slammed the book shut. "*A Hundred Years of Solitude*," she said. "I love Gabriel García Márquez!"

Alejandro groaned inwardly. He would have to be more careful around her. He turned to Eduardo. "Bring me another copy in English. You do have one, don't you?"

"This girl's going to cost you some money," Eduardo said with a grin.

"It's not what you think," Alejandro said.

The old man shot him a doubtful glance. "Are you sure about that?"

Avery's eyes filled with tears as Alejandro handed her both an English copy of Márquez's book and a dog-eared dictionary. Her sudden display of emotion seemed a little out of character. But she wasn't the same person he'd seen in Zapata. Her face was a constant reminder of the hell she'd endured with a great deal of dignity. Recovery, both mental and physical, would be slow.

As they made their way back to the car, he forced her to move a little more quickly. One stop to buy lunch for the road was all he'd allow. He tapped her shoulder, pointing to a food stall. To his surprise, she threaded her fingers through his. He glanced at her small hand in his own. His reaction was one he couldn't identify. He'd never felt so responsible, and yet there was something else. A possessiveness he didn't understand.

She swung her arm forward. Something caught his attention. It was several seconds before he realized what it was. Rage washed over him, causing a physical burn through his gut. He twisted her arm gently to get a closer look. The black ink was haloed in red. Fresh.

He took a deep breath. This was no time to let her see how angry he was. This was his fault. He should have removed her from Inez's weeks ago. Stormed in and told Javier that Diego wanted her gone.

She shrugged. "Last night. After he beat me up."

He forced himself to meet her gaze. Sometimes he wondered if she had a sense of his comprehension.

She needed medical attention. Feeding her would be a start. He directed her to a food stall, ordering enough food for six people. She could use it.

They waited as a woman wrapped their lunch. Two men lingered two stalls away. It was the third time he'd spotted them. They were empty-handed and directionless. This was never a good sign. Paranoia rose within him. He leaned over the counter, impatiently reaching for their food.

Yanking on Avery's arm with a little more force than he intended, he put an apologetic arm around her shoulders. He leaned toward her, speaking Spanish. "I'm sorry, it's just we're going to be late if we don't get on the road."

"*Si*," she said, picking up on his game.

He spoke louder, and his remarks grew more flirtatious. Not quite inappropriate, but close. She'd resent it if she knew what he was saying, but it was his best hope at misleading those guys. He paused at a fruit stand. The two were nowhere in sight, but he wasn't confident that they'd lost them. He led her between two stalls. Even mostly hidden by the cowboy hat, the red hair was eye-catching. And it was starting to make its way out of the hat. Something would have to be done about it.

The proprietor of one of the stalls shooed them away from his food prep area. Alejandro ignored the man's angry chastisement and continued to lead her on a march toward the Jeep. He glanced over his shoulder, then bisected a small gathering of people.

The Jeep was in sight. One final glance over his shoulder left him hopeful that they'd lost the men. He unlocked her door and hurried her in. Nonchalantly, he tossed the burner cell under the wheel. Even if someone reported having seen a redhead fitting her description, he knew the backroads in this part of the country, and within ten minutes the two of them would be impossible to find.

Chapter 16

It had been at least thirty minutes since they left the market, though the unpronounceable volcano continued to loom ahead. Abruptly, Alejandro took a sharp turn toward it. The decision seemed to be last-minute, surprising even him. Other than the towering volcano, the mountains seemed almost familiar—so like the foothills just west of Denver. Alejandro steered the vehicle off the road. He reached behind Avery's seat and lifted out two water bottles and a plastic bag. With a nod, he indicated that she should get out. From the back of the Jeep, he retrieved a tarp.

She fell behind. His stride was long and deliberate. He spread the tarp in a sandy patch, then sat down facing the great snow-covered volcano. Stretching out his long legs, he turned his face up to the sun. God-like. If she weren't starving, she might stand back here and just watch him.

He tilted his head in confusion. At least she wasn't too obvious. He patted the tarp.

She sighed. Lowering herself to the ground was the last thing she wanted to do.

"Tacos al pastor," he said.

The sight of it was enough to make her forget her pain. She lowered herself to the ground and snatched the taco from his outstretched hand. She peeled back the corn tortilla. The filling was thin strips of pork with onions, cilantro, and pineapple. She took a bite and closed her eyes. Never before had anything tasted so good.

Alejandro laughed. Again, that deep, musical, surprising sound. He continued, and she opened her eyes to find him watching her. So, she was the source of his amusement. Her face grew hot. She'd been so absorbed in her food that she'd paid no attention to how quickly she'd been stuffing it in her mouth. She turned away in embarrassment.

He stretched out, rested his head on one arm, and lowered his baseball cap over his face.

A nap? He must be kidding. She needed to get home. Her projects would be piling up.

Or not, come to think of it. By now, Eric probably assumed he'd never see her face again.

She wouldn't let herself go there. Dark thoughts were no longer allowed. But her mother missed her. And hadn't given up on her. She knew that for sure, and the thought made her chest ache.

She gazed at Alejandro's long, lean form. What were they doing? Mexico had highways. Today's drive had been nothing but backroads. Sort of fun, but not exactly a beeline for the consulate or border. She'd let it happen. Just happy to be well-fed and, as much as she didn't want to admit it— watching him.

She struggled to her feet.

He slapped the tarp. "*Siéntate.*"

"Do you really intend to get me home or not? If so, you have a strange way of showing it. Is a siesta really a requirement here?"

He moved the cap no more than an inch, peering at her with one eye. "*Diez minutos.*"

An estimate of time. Her dictionary was in the Jeep. Might as well entertain herself while he took his nap. Maybe she could string together enough words to ask him where they were going.

She flung open the passenger door. As she reached for the dictionary, she noticed the keys dangling from the ignition. It was crazy and careless. Anyone could have shown up and driven off. She glanced across the meadow. He was still sprawled on the tarp.

It was tempting. She could navigate by the sun. Stop and ask for directions to the nearest big city. Someone would speak English. She could find a consulate and be home tomorrow.

She moved to the driver's side, all the while watching him. She hefted herself gracelessly into the seat.

As tempting as it might be, she couldn't leave him here in the middle of nowhere. Not after he'd saved her. But she should at least take the keys out. Not that there'd been too many cars coming this way, but still. Her fingertips grazed the spot where the key should be. She peered through the steering wheel. Nothing.

Alejandro stood next to the open window of the driver's door. His face was devoid of expression. Not even smug.

She closed her eyes and sighed heavily. The man was definitely part cat. Big and silent. He opened the door for her and helped her down as if nothing had happened.

"I wasn't going anywhere. I just wanted to get the keys out of the ignition before someone took off with the Jeep and left us stranded."

His eyes were black, his mouth a straight line. He didn't believe her.

Chapter 17

They drove in silence. He didn't even talk on his phone. She wished he would. A distraction would be welcome. They were in the middle of nowhere. Finally, she reached for the radio knob. Anything to break the silence.

He shook his head. "*Sin musica.*"

She wasn't sure if he was telling her there was no reception or if he just preferred silence. She turned her back to him. The volcano was behind them now. They'd been on a dirt road for the last twenty minutes. Dusty and ridden with potholes.

"I know you don't believe that I didn't intend to steal the Jeep. But I seriously doubt I could drive it with my ribs like they are. The clutch would be a killer." It made her feel better to say the words, even if he didn't understand.

They drove through a small town, and he surveyed a row of shops. He brought the Jeep to a halt and held up an index finger. Making a hand gesture someone might use to make a dog sit, he stepped down from the Jeep. She watched as he disappeared behind a small grocery store, and then she reached for the dictionary. This game of charades was growing old. She flipped through the book, wondering how long he intended to keep her in Mexico. Her heart sank in realization: you don't buy a dictionary for someone who's about to leave the country.

He was back two minutes later holding a paper sack, and they resumed their jostling drive along the backroads. She was beginning to question whether they were still in Mexico. Finally, after passing through what seemed like the hundredth small village, he turned down a small dirt lane. They stopped outside a garish blue gate. Beyond the gate stood a stucco two-story building strangled in overgrown vegetation. Chickens were everywhere.

He hopped out and reached between the wrought iron scrolls, drawing forward a combination padlock on a long chain. She wrinkled her nose. Was this his house? Chickens? Somehow, she couldn't imagine it. The way he fumbled with the lock told her no. It took no fewer than seven tries before he finally succeeded in unlocking it.

Concrete walls topped with broken glass enclosed the property. He inched the Jeep along the gravel drive, causing waves of chickens to flee to the sides.

This wasn't an airport, bus station, police station, or border crossing. And she despised chickens. Why were they here?

A middle-aged woman peered down from the balcony as he brought the vehicle to halt. He waved to her. She responded with a threatening fist. Avery laughed. Good. The woman didn't want them here. Served him right.

Alejandro circled the vehicle to open Avery's door. She shook her head. "No."

His face tightened. He pointed to the ground.

"I hate chickens. I don't need to get out. I'll just wait here until you're done."

His face was a picture of calm as he reached across her and unbuckled her seatbelt. He grasped her upper arm firmly. She shook her head. This time she received a warning look. He'd force her if necessary. She felt her lower lip jutting out. He placed his hands under her arms in the way one would lift a child, then hefted her from the seat. She shrieked in pain as he set her on the ground. Looping the ring of car keys around his index finger, he held them up—a taunting gesture—then moved toward the house, abandoning her in a circle of at least eight chickens.

Avery drew in her arms. Did chickens sense when someone was afraid? What kind of person kept poultry in their front yard? Weren't they supposed to be in a coop? She tried fruitlessly to stifle her sense of panic. "Ugh," she said with a shudder. She couldn't move. They'd peck at her. Follow her. Maybe even chase her.

The woman was no longer on the balcony. Alejandro's voice rose, coming from somewhere inside the building. The woman was mad. Arguing. Saying no. Over and over again.

Good. It meant they wouldn't be here too long. A black-and-white chicken strutted dangerously close to her. She desperately needed them to end their conversation soon. The chicken moved even closer, trying to peck at her foot. She screamed and jerked back. An awkward little dance.

This was absurd. She'd survived weeks living in a brothel under the command of the craziest drug lord in Mexico, but she was going to die here. Out here in the middle of nowhere. Pecked to death by a herd of chickens. Pack of chickens. Flock? Whatever.

A door slammed, and Alejandro stormed across the yard, parting chickens as he went. He seemed too angry to notice her plight. He moved to the back of the Jeep and dropped a black plastic trash bag to the ground. Hopefully it was trash, because this place was probably crawling with chicken poop. He slammed the rear door and retrieved the trash bag and the brown paper sack.

Unsmiling, he regarded her. "*¡Ándale!*" His voice was harsh.

"No."

He spun on his heel, took two steps, grabbed her arm, and led her toward the house. The chickens darted away as they moved. She groaned in pain. He ignored it.

The house was dark and smelled of day-old onions. Stale and muggy. He pulled her along into the kitchen. Unwashed dishes were stacked around the sink.

Alejandro slid the paper sack across the kitchen counter toward the woman. She shook her head, then peered at Avery over reading glasses. "I don't know why he thinks he should leave you here."

Avery gasped. She was American. At least her accent was. And she was almost as pale as Avery. "Leave me here?" Avery shook her head. "No. No. He can't leave me." She glanced at Alejandro for an answer, but he averted his gaze. "I have no intention of staying."

The woman raised a heavy salt-and-pepper eyebrow. "He thinks you are."

"Well, I'm not. Take me to a bus station. Call a cab. I don't care. I'll walk, damn it. Just point me in the right direction, and I won't waste your time or mine."

The woman snorted and said something in Spanish to Alejandro. He rubbed his forehead.

She chewed her lip and pushed a stray clump of gray hair off her forehead. "You'll stay. Until I say you can go." The woman's voice was gravelly. "You've got *entitled bitch* written all over you, and I'll be damned if I let you get him in trouble." She swore under her breath and shook a finger at Alejandro. "I'm retired, damn it. This is the last time." As if he somehow understood. She barked at Avery. "Take your stuff upstairs. Room's on the left."

"Where's he going?" Avery said.

"Ask him yourself."

"He doesn't speak any English."

"Then that's your problem, girly. When in Rome . . ."

Alejandro grabbed the trash bag and started up the stairs. Reluctantly, she followed. The place was hardly cozy. The bedroom was barely a step up from the brothel. A single bed buried in old newspapers occupied one corner. Canned goods flanked the opposite wall, and Venetian blinds hung unevenly from the one small window. Worst of all, the air was still, the room was stifling, and there was no fan.

"You're really going to leave me here?"

Alejandro sighed and let the plastic bag slide to the floor.

"What's with the trash bag?" She nudged it with her foot. He pulled it open. She made a small noise in the back of her throat. "My clothes!" She glanced up at him. "How did you get this?" Of course, he didn't answer. "You dropped it in the chicken poop."

For a moment, it seemed like he was stifling a laugh.

"When are you coming back?" she asked. He turned his back to her. She stomped with all her might. Waves of pain shot up her back. She opened the dictionary and flipped through it as quickly as she could. "*¿Cuando?*"

He turned to her. In the fading day's light, his eyes were golden. Not brown. How had she not noticed before? His dark, thick eyelashes accentuated the striking contrast further. It only made her resent him more for ditching her.

He shrugged and shook his head miserably.

What was this? Regret for dumping her here? Some kind of apology? Never before had she had such difficulty understanding another human being. Of course, language wasn't typically a barrier. She thumbed through the book. "Why? *¿Por qué?*"

He spoke quickly. She couldn't distinguish a single word. Syllables, inflections, everything melted together. There were no clues. Finally, he spoke the words slowly: "*Una semana.*"

"*Semana, semana, semana,*" she repeated, furiously searching for the meaning. "Week?" She gritted her teeth. "Like hell you are. I am not staying here for a week! No *semanas*. Do you understand?" She poked him in the chest with the spine of the book. "You have two days." She held up a pair of fingers. "Not a second more."

He drew closer. Their faces were only inches apart. He held up a hand. "*Cinco dias.*"

"No! It's too long." She pointed at the stairs. "You heard her. That woman doesn't want me here. And I'm not living with chickens!" The final sentence came out as a shriek.

A smile spread across his face. He *was* actually stifling a laugh. As if he understood. How dare he?

She took a swing at him, now certain he understood the bit about the chickens. He dodged it. The smile on his face continued to grow. He touched her arm, then reached for her wrist, rubbing his thumb lightly across it. "Avery."

She tried to ignore the gesture. Ignore what it was doing to her heartbeat. His attitude was infuriating. "Three days." She pulled away from him. "After that, I'm out of here. And it's not a threat. It's a promise."

Chapter 18

Leaving her with Harvey left him digging his fingers into the steering wheel. Harvey would lighten up eventually. He hoped. As for Avery . . . it would take time. One look at her ribcage and Harvey would appreciate how tough she was. But it wasn't the physical aspect that worried him. Solitary confinement could be more damaging that any beating.

The sound of the phone interrupted his thoughts. Spider's voice came in over the speakers. "Checked in last night, just like you told me to. Used your credit card."

"Good. And you parked the Audi out front like I asked you to?"

"Yeah."

"Who was working the desk?"

"Some old guy. Half asleep. Didn't bother to even look at me. Wore exactly what you told me to. Black cap, sunglasses, black hoodie zipped up, jeans, and boots. And don't worry, no one could see the tattoo."

Alejandro let out a sigh. "Good." Spider wasn't quite as tall as he was, but in general appearance he was close enough to pass the test with a low-grade hotel security camera. "I'll meet you at that dive on the west side of town about nine. We can switch cars there."

"How long are you planning on staying here?" Spider asked.

Alejandro floored the Jeep. He'd never intended to let Javier coerce him into going to Guadalajara, but it would give him an alibi for last night. "Two days, three max. Just long enough to eliminate thoughts that I might have had something to do with the girl's escape."

"What does Javier want you to do here?"

"He wants me to do the impossible. Negotiate some work with *La Anguila*," Alejandro said with a yawn.

"The Eel? Slippery Dude? No one negotiates with him. Javier must want you dead."

"He does. But lucky for me, I happen to know that the Eel is busy doing a little jail time. So, I'll waste two or three days hanging around, make sure I'm seen by anyone who matters, then head back to the city."

"And the girl?"

It was a rhetorical question. There were few people in this world he trusted more than Spider. But too much knowledge was a liability in their world. It was always best to remain vague. "I'll work on that next."

He set the phone aside in indecision. Removing Avery from the brothel was a risk from a thousand angles. But he'd had no choice. He couldn't leave her there, with Javier planning to put her to work. Just the thought of it was enough to send him off the road.

The guys in D.C. would be pissed. They were already on his case to wind things up. The San Antonio office was different. They understood the precarious balance of infiltrating a cartel. Carelessness only got you killed. But that didn't mean they were thrilled by it, either.

He scrolled through his contacts and found Arturo. "Need some documentation," Alejandro said. Arturo had been his contact in the San Antonio field office for nearly two years.

Arturo cleared his throat. "Would this be for the girl that Javier's looking for?"

"Might be."

"You know he's offering a reward. Rumor is it's a million dollars."

A million? The thought of it made Alejandro's blood boil. Javier would never pay it. But a number like that would attract a multitude of idiots stupid enough to believe they could collect. "All the more reason to get her out of here quickly."

"What are you thinking?"

"Cancun. A week or ten days from now. Get a copy of whatever identification you can. Javier's guys got her driver's license, so maybe use a passport photo if she has one. You'll want to alter the hair color to black."

"Will do. Boss wants to know what progress you've made this week."

"Another shipment due in at the end of the week. Tell him I plan on being there to document everything."

"All right." Arturo let out a heavy sigh. "Watch your back, man. You don't need to be side-tracked by this girl."

"Not planning on it."

Chapter 19

Avery and the woman evaluated one another. Circling the kitchen like prize fighters. The woman was grizzly. Long gray braids flanked her barrel-shaped body. Her arms and legs were stick-like. She wore denim overalls and an ill-fitting t-shirt that might have been green in 1973.

The woman sighed as if in resignation and made a smacking noise. "Name's Harvey. You'll be responsible for doing the cooking around here. He says you got some broken ribs. I'll take a look at them later. And I won't make you do anything to make them worse. But no screwing around." She arched an eyebrow. "I mean it. You do anything stupid, and I'll make your life a living hell. I don't know what made you worth risking his ass for, but . . ." She didn't finish. Just shook her head, turned, and left.

Avery frowned. Who was this woman?

She wrinkled her nose at the dirty dishes and moved to the living room. More random piles of junk. Harvey was a half-step away from being a serious hoarder. At least there were books. Scattered everywhere. These piles could keep her entertained for months.

The first title made no sense. German, maybe? The second book was the same. She shifted to another area of the room. One book after another, all in Spanish. She glanced about, trying to identify book covers. The woman was American. There had to be something in English.

Instead, her attention was diverted to a series of photographs displayed on the far wall. Most were black-and-white photos with horses in them. In fact, horses were the dominant theme. She drew closer to one. It was an old photo of a young girl grasping the reins of a horse with a trophy clutched in the opposite hand. Avery leaned in, studying the girl's facial features. A long thin nose and prominent eyebrows much darker than her hair. It was Harvey. Avery stepped back, assessing the collection as a whole. Harvey through the years. Pretty as a young girl. Blonde, still tough looking, outdoorsy but undeniably attractive. Difficult to equate this long-limbed equestrian with the abrasive person she'd just met wearing overalls. Interestingly, the landscape was always the same. Tree-covered rolling hills. Not Mexico. At least not what Avery had seen of it.

She moved on to a cluster of faded color photos. Older Harvey. Late twenties, maybe. Still outdoorsy, but glamorous, too, and standing arm in arm with someone vaguely familiar. Avery moved on to a second photo. The two of them together. Heads bent in admiring gazes. The man's striking physical presence practically jumped out of the frame. Not traditionally handsome, but someone who exuded strength. Avery removed the photo from the wall to get a closer look.

"General Rodrigo Salazar. In case you're wondering who that it is."

The raspy voice made her jump. Her hands shook, and she nearly dropped the photo. Pain streaked across her side. She turned awkwardly, embarrassed to be caught snooping.

Avery recognized the name. One of Mexico's heroes. She racked her brain to remember why. It was a long time ago. She had fuzzy memories of this man's face in the news.

The woman seemed to sense her questions before she asked. "You would have been pretty young then. One of the cartels got to him. Never did know exactly who."

Avery blinked, at a loss for words. Carefully, she returned the photo to its place.

"He was your . . . husband?"

"No." Her voice was steady. Emotionless. Whatever this man was to her was in her past, and she wanted it left there. "Let me take a look at your mid-section."

Avery made a face. "I should probably take a shower first."

The woman made a dismissive sound. "I've been around a lot filthier than you. Come on."

Avery didn't bother to argue with her. She pulled the long dress over her head.

Harvey whistled as Avery lifted her shirt and lowered her waistband. "Got you good, huh? Alejandro said it was Javier."

"You know Javier?"

The woman laid her hand flat against the bruised area, then slowly moved it upward, palpating. "Can you take a deep breath for me?"

"No. It hurts too much."

"As big as you can, then." Harvey continued palpating as she obeyed, then tugged Avery's shirt back down. "No way to tell if they're broken without an x-ray. Treatment's the same either way. Ribs generally heal themselves. Six weeks or so. But you need to work on your breathing. I know it hurts like hell. It's happened to me a few times. One of the hazards of being a horse owner. Take the deepest breath you can stand, then let it out slowly. Several times a day. Goal is to prevent pneumonia."

Pneumonia? Really? It was way down on her list of concerns. Avery smiled anyway. "Thanks. I'll work on it." She brushed a strand of hair from her face.

"Whoa. And what's this?" Harvey reached for her arm. "The little shit branded you?"

Avery kept her voice low. "Yeah." The indignity of his mark seemed worse now.

"Need to get some antibiotic ointment on it."

At least the woman didn't go into the myriad infections and diseases that could be brought on by dirty needles. It was one thing Avery refused to let herself think about.

The woman gestured to the paper sack on the kitchen counter. "We'll do your hair in the morning. I don't have the energy for it right now. And you do need a shower."

"My hair?"

"He thinks you'll blend in." Harvey made a face. "Take a lot more than hair dye."

"Hair dye?" Avery thrust her chin out. "No way."

"I'd say it's not your decision to make. If you want a chance at staying alive, black hair it is."

"Black?" The word came out as a croak. It was almost laughable. She'd never pull it off. Not with her coloring. Her college roommate used to call her Casper. And though she'd often wished otherwise, red hair was part of her identity. It was who she was. She twisted the end of her knotted mass of auburn hair.

Mexico was taking her apart. Layer by layer.

"Now, I need you to go get a chicken. Not the black one. Any other one is fine."

Avery froze, then blinked.

"They're out back now."

This woman expected her to kill a chicken? Make dinner from one of them? She despised them, but no way would she do this. She shook her head. "I'll cook anything else, but no. I can't."

Harvey's gaze blackened. She shrugged, then moved to the door. "Suit yourself, then. I expect dinner at six."

Avery rubbed her temples. She felt like a wimp. But one could survive on rice and beans. That was one thing she knew for sure.

~ ~ ~

If Harvey was dissatisfied with her cooking skills, she didn't show it. The two sat across from one another, each staring at empty spots on opposite walls.

"You must speak several languages," Avery said.

Harvey grunted. "I do."

"I saw German and Spanish books."

Harvey ran her tongue along the front of her teeth, regarding Avery but saying nothing.

"Do you speak more than English, German, and Spanish?" For all she cared, the woman's native tongue was Swahili. She was just trying to keep the awkwardness at bay.

"Yep." The word was delivered with a loud smack.

Clearly, Harvey wasn't bothered by social conventions. Like doing her part to keep the conversation going. Avery dangled her fork over her food.

"What'd you do to get yourself in trouble with Javier?"

Avery shrugged. "Opened my mouth when I should have kept it shut."

Harvey's watery blue eyes glowed. "Is that right? I think that's a story I'd like to hear."

"There's not much to it. Javier was trying to collect his extortion money from a client of mine. I was just trying to get my work done. Instead of waiting it out, I walked straight into his trap. He insulted me, and I gave it back to him. Totally stupid of me. Next thing I knew, it was two days later, and I was in Mexico."

"He brought you across the border?" Harvey's eyebrows arched dramatically.

"Someone did."

"And from there?"

"Alejandro rescued me. I'm not sure why." The woman gave her a long, hard stare. Avery tried not to appear fazed by its intensity. "I didn't ask him to," she said defensively. "Javier had some idiotic idea that my client would pay the ransom. He didn't, and Javier was going to put me to work in his brothel."

"And Alejandro took it upon himself to save your ass," Harvey said. "Foolish. Like messing with a rabid dog." She shook her head and uttered a string of curse-like words in a strange language.

Hopefully, it was Javier that she was calling a rabid dog. "You don't have horses anymore?" Avery asked, hoping to change the subject.

"Nope. I've got the land—in fact, there are stables on the south end of the property. But they're too much work for one person. You a horse person?"

"No." Avery shook her head.

"What kind of work do you do?" Harvey asked.

"I'm a mechanical engineer." Something changed in Harvey's expression. It might have been a hint of approval.

"Good. Maybe you can get my tractor started in the morning."

"I'm not really a mechanic." Irritation crossed Harvey's face. Avery toyed with her food. Messing around with a tractor was definitely better than killing a chicken. "But I'll see what I can do."

~ ~ ~

It was sheer luck when she got the tractor running the next day. From that point on, Harvey saddled her with a variety of dysfunctional power tools. Most were hopeless. Those that weren't required parts that probably weren't available within a hundred-mile radius.

In the afternoons, blue skies morphed to gray and torrential rains turned the property into a swamp. It was during the daily downpours that Avery took advantage of Harvey's absence to declutter. Harvey made a habit of materializing only at mealtime. Not that she ever left—

Avery could always hear her. The floors creaked and doors slammed, but she always kept her distance.

It didn't take long to discover that Harvey was diabetic. Empty insulin vials were everywhere. Tossed aside, as if Harvey injected herself and then dropped the small bottles wherever she stood at that given moment. Never any needles. How someone managed to dispose of syringes but not bottles was a mystery. One of a dozen weird things in this house.

Though Avery searched, she found no telephones or computers. No TVs or radios, either. Harvey said she didn't own a car, and groceries were delivered every few days by someone Avery never saw. Otherwise, Harvey's existence was one of complete isolation.

On the third day, Harvey found Avery in the garage attempting to repair the burned-out motor from a cheap hand mixer.

"You don't give up, do you?"

Avery straightened her back and stretched. "This one may be a lost cause."

"Even I could have told you that. But don't worry about it. I'm not baking too many cakes these days." One side of Harvey's mouth curled in irony. "You work this hard on everything you do?"

Avery wiped the grease off of her hands but didn't answer.

"We've got to do something about that red mop of yours."

"Why? Is he coming tonight?" Avery rose to her feet a little too quickly, then grabbed her side.

"Not as far as I know. I think he's planning to be here over the weekend," Harvey said, as she started toward the house.

Avery ground her teeth and followed Harvey out of the garage and into the house. She'd known he would be longer than three days. "Have you ever dyed hair before?"

Harvey gave her a sideways glance. "Do I look like a person who routinely colors their hair—or anyone else's, for that matter? Pretty sure it doesn't require a PhD."

"Let me see the box," Avery said.

Harvey slid the box across the kitchen counter. The outside of the box boasted a radical change in lifestyle, depicting a stooped, graying man magically morphing into someone twenty years younger with his newly blackened hair. Avery made a dismissive sound. "It's for men. And it's all in Spanish." She spun the box around. "Why did he have to go for jet black? Dark brown would have been better. Does this stuff contain bleach?"

Harvey adjusted her reading glasses. "No. And you'll be happy to know it says semi-permanent. I bet it starts to fade fast. Probably six weeks or less."

"In six weeks I plan on being back to my natural color," Avery said with confidence she did not feel.

Harvey's mouth twitched, but she said nothing.

~ ~ ~

Harvey was right. Dyeing one's hair from red to black did not require years of education. But just because it worked didn't mean it looked good. Avery stared at herself in horror. The bruises left by Javier's fist did nothing to improve things. "I look like a freak."

Harvey peered over her shoulder into the mirror. Her silence was a confirmation of Avery's declaration.

"Give me that stuff. I need to make my eyebrows match."

Harvey stripped off the provided gloves. "Be my guest."

Avery leaned closer to the mirror, smearing the concoction across her eyebrows. "Maybe my eyelashes, too."

"Be careful—" but before Harvey could finish, Avery had produced a small brush from her toiletries bag. "I was going to say watch out, you might blind yourself. Who knows what chemicals might be in that stuff."

Avery wrinkled her nose. She hardly cared at this point. This whole scheme was a bad idea. Alejandro should have found her a wig. In her current state, she'd garner more attention than ever. She leaned over the sink, rinsing away the excess dye.

Harvey handed her a towel. "Better," she said with a nod.

Avery dried her face, then chanced a look for herself. It was better. If one could ignore the black and blue marks lining the sides of her face, the contrast of her newly darkened brows and lashes with the sage green of her eyes was surprising. Less freakish, but she'd still never get used to it.

Chapter 20

Eventually, Harvey ran out of repair projects for her. Avery evaluated the chaos of the living room from the hallway. Dust-covered books everywhere, and not a single bookshelf. Who did that? Books were the absolute easiest things to deal with. She scratched her head. Possibly, there'd be some boards and cinder blocks in the junky garage. It was dorm room decorating, but at least it might minimize the chaos.

She made her exit through the door behind the kitchen. The garage was a thousand times worse than the house. Overflowing trash cans. Chicken mess. She stepped over the pieces of an old washer and dodged random tools in various stages of decay. Amidst all of it, there were no cinder blocks, though a dilapidated book case stood in one corner. She ran a hand along its ruptured veneer. Not likely to withstand the move inside, even if she could have managed it.

The situation was exasperating. Was Harvey's health so bad that she couldn't take care of anything? Or did she just not care?

As Avery turned to leave, she spotted a padlock hanging from an unlatched door. She stepped gingerly over an old tarp, afraid of what might scurry out of the folds. The handle of an unseen rake sprung up in her face. She caught it within a centimeter of her face. "Damn it!" Its steel teeth bit into the sole of her shoe. It was amazing Harvey was still in one piece. She propped the rake against a wall, then turned her attention to what appeared to be a small closet. The ramshackle door hung slightly ajar. She glanced over her shoulder, paranoid that Harvey would materialize. So far, she hadn't objected to Avery's reorganization of the kitchen or bathroom. But that was organizing, and this was snooping. The hinges creaked as she opened the door a few more inches.

Her heart stopped, and she gasped a little too loudly. If Harvey had been anywhere nearby, she would have heard her.

An electric light switched on automatically as Avery opened the door. She gawked at the state-of-the-art gun locker. No one would imagine such a place on this ramshackle property. Beyond the dusty outer exterior, a double-doored steel enclosure stood wide open. It was a virtual arsenal the size of a small bedroom. Dozens of rifles, handguns, and boxes of ammunition occupied felt-lined cubbies. Enough to arm a police force. She moved inside, drawing her arms across her chest as the room's lethal potential made it difficult to breathe.

The upper shelves were lined with scopes, silencers, and an assortment of things she didn't recognize. Her knowledge of this stuff was from cop shows on TV. What made it stranger was the level of organization. It was nothing like the rest of the house. She backed out, steadying herself against the garage wall as she tried to catch her breath and fight back a wave of nausea that threatened to send her to the floor.

It was time to get out of here.

The way Harvey lurked around, she'd make an appearance any second now. Avery shut the flimsy garage door and made her way back into the house on unsteady legs.

She leaned against the door frame separating the kitchen from the living room. Who was this woman? The room full of scattered books offered no answers. The titles at her feet were French, Spanish, and even Russian. What kind of person possessed enough guns to eliminate a small village? The photos on the wall were no help.

She rubbed her forehead. To look at Harvey, one wouldn't expect a linguist. An organic farmer, maybe. Perhaps a horse person. Old hippie, definitely. But sharpshooter? Terrorist? No. Too old and too grounded. Her gaze shifted to another small stack of books. The Arabic print stood out.

There was always spy. Harvey was secretive enough. And there were the guns. But shouldn't she be younger? Healthier? Of course, she claimed to be retired.

~ ~ ~

Avery was making a bigger mess as she dug through the piles for the magazine. It was frustrating—she was certain she'd seen it earlier. Finally, she spotted the dog-eared copy of *Newsweek*. A special edition with General Rodrigo Salazar on the cover.

The surroundings were so stark, the photo could have been taken in the wasteland behind the brothel. Dressed in fatigues and a bandana about his neck, he leaned against a stone wall for support. His body sagged, and his eyes reflected defeat. The photo was probably not selected to illustrate the winning side in the battle against the cartels. The text was in Spanish. She flipped through the pages, searching for more photos. Most were Salazar with other military leaders. The last page was a photo of the General looking at least ten years younger. Next to him stood a woman and three young children.

The stairs creaked, and she shoved the stack of magazines under the table. The photos left her wanting to know more. But it was time for dinner, and she'd have to be creative. Not that it seemed to matter much to Harvey, but tomorrow they'd have only eggs for every meal if one of them didn't get groceries.

~ ~ ~

She managed to throw enough leftovers together to make soup, though the broth had simmered away. What was once soup was now stew. She'd banged on Harvey's door nearly two hours ago and was told to disappear. If she refused to eat, Avery couldn't make her. But the woman was diabetic, and she couldn't totally ignore that fact. Avery stomped up the stairs. "Harvey. Soup is ready. Beyond ready." She banged on the door loudly. A second attempt still didn't produce results. She turned the knob.

Harvey lay sprawled across an unmade bed. Avery whispered her name. There was no movement. Drawing closer, she could see the rise and fall of Harvey's chest.

"Harvey."

A spent syringe balanced on the edge of a bedside table. She shook Harvey by the shoulder. The woman mumbled. Thank God. She was alive and semi-conscious. "Harvey!" Avery took her hand. Diabetic coma or diabetic shock? Impossible to guess which. One required insulin and the other sugar. Her grandmother's final years had been like this. A roller coaster of blood sugar levels.

Avery glanced about the room. It was the first time she'd been in here. No telephone—cell or otherwise. She could run to one of the two neighbors. That is, if she could even get out of the gate. Or chance it and give the woman a glass of juice. It was what her mother had always instructed her to do with her grandmother.

She squeezed Harvey's hand. Clammy. Most likely shock. "Harvey, I'm going to get you some juice. Hang on. I'll be right back."

It was a crapshoot. Did they even have 911 in Mexico? She ran for the stairs, trying to ignore the excruciating pain of her heavy breathing. Juice. If that didn't work, insulin— on the off chance that she could find an unused vial and clean syringe in this dump.

She returned, breathless, raised Harvey's head with one hand, and slowly introduced the mango juice with the other. It ran down the sides of her mouth, streaking the bib of her overalls. Avery tilted her head back just a fraction more. Harvey coughed, spraying juice everywhere, but Avery continued. Eventually, Harvey's eyes opened as she attempted to push Avery away.

Avery shook her head. "You have to finish it." Harvey made a face. "What did you do, take your insulin and then forget to eat?"

Harvey pushed her back. "Enough. I'm okay."

"Finish it," Avery said firmly. "I'll bring you up some soup."

Harvey was sitting up and holding an empty glass when Avery returned with the soup. She set the tray at the end of the bed before clearing the nightstand of trash and empty vials.

"How'd you know? What to do, I mean."

Avery moved the tray to the nightstand, then handed Harvey a napkin and spoon. "I didn't for sure. It was a guess." She held Harvey's gaze. "But my grandmother was type two." She stood over Harvey, watching her face. "I suspected that you wanted to avoid me. And then you waited too long to eat."

Harvey dipped the edge of a tortilla in the soup. "I don't need you snooping around here. Messing up my stuff."

Avery ignored her. "How many languages do you speak?"

Harvey turned away.

"And how many guns does one person need?" Avery crossed her arms. "Look, I'm not trying to snoop. I'm just trying to figure out why Alejandro parked me here."

"To keep you alive."

"He could have dropped me off at the embassy and been done with it. I don't get it."

Harvey glanced down at her soup and pushed it away. "No, you don't get it."

"Then explain it to me." Avery didn't bother to hide her growing frustration. "I didn't grow up in this godforsaken country."

"What do you want to know?"

"I want to know why Alejandro didn't just drop me off at the embassy."

Harvey rubbed her forehead with a pained expression. "Because the corruption runs so deep. Because these organizations are like bacteria that's resisted every antibiotic. To outsmart them, you need to be one of them."

"So, you're saying that even the American Embassy is full of corruption?"

"I didn't say *full* of corruption. But there is a problem there."

"And what's Alejandro's role in all this?"

"It's complicated. Starting with that shit Javier. And the fact that he works for Javier's father. He's playing with fire. I can't imagine what possessed him to take you out of that place."

"Is Javier's father as crazy as he is?"

"No. He's not. Nothing like him." She closed her eyes. "Javier's mother is from one of Mexico City's wealthiest families. Almost like royalty. Diego Ramos, Javier's father, came from nowhere. He rose up through the ranks of the cartels by being tough and smart and lucky. Now they live like the Kennedys. Rubbing shoulders with celebrities and flying to Milan for an afternoon of shoe shopping."

"And Alejandro?"

"He's been with the family a couple of years. Diego Ramos has his favorites, and Alejandro is one of them. Probably the reason he had the balls to take you out of that whorehouse. He assumed Diego might forgive him for it if he found out." She let out a sigh. "I don't see much of Alejandro these days, but I know he spends a lot of time cleaning up after Javier. Diego has begun to distance himself from certain activities. Or at least try to give that impression to his neighbors. Javier is a liability for his papa."

Avery removed the bowl. "What about Alejandro? Did he grow up in Mexico City with Javier?"

"No."

"Where, then?"

"Is there more of that soup?"

Evasion. Harvey wasn't going to tell her anything meaningful.

"By the way, Alejandro said to tell you he wouldn't be here till Friday night."

Avery's eyes narrowed. She'd communicated with him. But how? This old witch must have a cell phone squirreled away somewhere. Harvey's eyes were on her now. Analyzing. Avery shifted uncomfortably, feeling two steps behind. "Friday means nothing to me. What day is it today?"

"Monday."

"What's the date?" Avery asked.

"May fourth. Why?"

"Just wondering how long I've actually been in Mexico." Avery licked her lips, steeling herself and trying to make her face a blank. She'd been here over a month. And now he was delaying things another four days. Her blood began to boil. Neither of them gave a damn that she needed to get home. Or that she had a mother who was probably going through hell just now.

It was becoming clear that she needed to take control of the situation. Waiting for Alejandro could mean she'd be here next May. She took a deep breath. "We're out of food. Vegetables and bread. Meat, too."

"That could be taken care of if you weren't such a wuss about the chickens. For everything else, a boy will be by tomorrow to get my order." Harvey's sagging jowls and a blasé expression made her look like a Bulldog. "Make him a list."

"I'll make him a list." Avery lifted the tray and moved toward the door. "But I'm not touching your damn chickens."

Chapter 21

Avery had been practicing her pronunciation all morning. The sentence structure wouldn't be correct, but if the grocery boy could understand her at all, she could get her message across. All of it would depend on Harvey. Primarily, where she was when he showed up. Avery only needed a minute alone with him.

It was mid-afternoon when the boy arrived by bicycle. She ogled the bike enviously, considering the possibilities. But there was no way. Stealing it wouldn't work. He and Harvey stood no more than twenty yards away. Plus, riding it could be a killer on her ribs. Her mind raced. This kid was the first person she'd seen in the days she'd been here. No phones. No computers. No other obvious means of communication. He'd be back on that bike and out of here in minutes. Quickly, she scribbled down the few phrases she'd memorized and tore out the back door.

The boy climbed on his bike just as she dodged the vile chickens moving up alongside him. "*Hola.*" She grinned.

He gawked at her. She'd completely forgotten about the lingering bruises and black eye. A stupid mistake. She should have worn the sunglasses.

Harvey, who'd just started to return to the garage, turned. Suspicion was etched across her face.

"I just had a few more items for him. Wrote them down in Spanish. Thought I might as well practice," Avery said, hoping the woman would continue into the garage.

But Harvey's feet were firmly planted.

There was no choice. With Harvey watching, she couldn't exactly whisper to him. She sighed and handed the boy the paper.

He frowned, then glanced at Harvey.

Avery's heart raced, and her hands shook. She stuffed them into her pockets.

The boy said something in Spanish.

Avery's heart sank. Busted.

Harvey's hands went to her hips. "He can't read your scrawl. Why don't you go ahead and tell me what it is you'd like to convey to him? Or should I just guess?" She marched across the yard and snatched the note from his hands. "Let's see here." Her voice was cutting. Avery wanted to run. "Best I can tell from this butchered attempt at Spanish is that you'd like either a phone, a ride to town, or," she raised an eyebrow, "a hearing aid." Harvey crumbled the paper and sent the boy on his way. She crossed her arms and with a disparaging glance said, "That the best you can do?"

Avery's face burned. She turned her back on Harvey, bracing herself for the return through the chickens. She kicked at a clump of dead grass. Maddening. Ridiculous. Infuriating. All of it. This was barely an improvement over the brothel. She was still a captive. She stomped her foot, hoping to scare away the chickens. "Why am I here?" She yelled the words, assuming Harvey was already back inside. "I have a job. People counting on me. And my mother is all alone. I didn't do anything to bring this on—"

Harvey surprised her by grabbing her by the collar of her shirt. "Get your ass inside."

Avery didn't fight back. For a sixty-something diabetic, Harvey was incredibly strong.

Harvey pointed to a kitchen chair. "Sit your butt down." She planted her hands on her hips, feet spread a mile apart. "Even if you could manage to get yourself into town, Javier has a big price tag on your head. Rumor has it he's offering a million bucks. Every little low-life around is hunting for you."

"But—"

Harvey held up a hand. "You let me finish." She wiped the sweat off her forehead with the back of her hand. "I have exactly two neighbors on this street. They're rarely around, and it's the reason I live where I do. That boy you just saw rode that bike seventeen miles to get out here. That fact is important for exactly two reasons. You know what they are?"

Avery shook her head. She wasn't about to open her mouth.

"Number one is obvious. He's not used to seeing anyone out here. That someone else is out here is automatically news in the village." Her eyes narrowed. "Number two is you. Look at you. You and your battered face. You think he's not going back to the village to tell everyone who will listen about the green-eyed monster that's out here with me?"

Avery chewed her lip. She understood that Harvey wanted to fly under the radar, but the poor excuse for a town that they'd passed on the way here probably had no more than twenty residents. It wasn't like he was going to post it on social media.

Harvey stared at her. "You've got one of the most dangerous cartels in the country searching for you. That bastard Javier is as mean as they come, and he hates to lose. If anyone believes you're the person that Javier might be searching for, then I'm as good as dead. And you'll have a lot more than just a few cracked ribs." She reached inside the pantry, shoving aside boxes and cans, then extracted a bottle of tequila. Avery's eyes widened. She'd searched the pantry thoroughly yesterday. "More than a hundred million people living in this country, and yet when someone like Javier is looking for someone, it gets small real fast." She set out two shot glasses. "You do anything like that again, and I'll lock you outside that gate. Leave you there for the vultures to fight over."

"And what am I to do if you go into a diabetic coma?" She shouldn't have said it, but more than anything she really wanted to know if the woman had a phone.

Harvey threw back her head and swallowed the contents of her glass. "You mean if I drink too much of this stuff worrying about who's going to show up at my door looking for you?"

Avery gave a small laugh. "Basically, yeah."

"The green house at the end of the street. The man who lives there was a medic in the army."

"That's not exactly the same as a hospital."

Harvey poured herself a second while Avery toyed with hers.

"I'm missing three toes. Can barely see out of my right eye, and my kidneys aren't looking too good. I'm not going to last forever. But that doesn't mean I'm going to let Javier dictate when my final day will be."

Avery shrank down in her chair and downed her shot. Amazingly smooth, with a slightly smoky taste. "Whoa."

Harvey's eyebrows flitted upward. "Good stuff, isn't it?" She brought the bottle to the table. "Now, what are we going to eat for supper?"

"When does the boy get back?"

Harvey shrugged. "Sometime tomorrow if we're lucky." She poured Avery another shot.

Avery held the glass up to the light. "Then it's tortillas and beans." She closed her eyes as the rich tequila warmed her throat. "And don't you dare mention those chickens again."

Chapter 22

Alejandro read Harvey's email for the third time. One paragraph in particular bothered him.

The girl barely sleeps. She thinks I don't know it, but she cannot tolerate being closed up alone inside a room. Every time a door shuts, she practically hyperventilates. She jumps at every sound and seeks out the corners whenever possible. Seems to be okay during the day as long as I keep her busy. In the long term, I think she'll be fine. It will just take time. But for now, I've figured out that a little tequila at night calms her down.

Harvey was using Avery as an excuse to ignore her diabetes. He'd thought maybe the two would be good for one another, but both of them would be better off without the tequila.

Avery's psychological state gnawed at him. He rubbed his forehead. Even in his line of work, he'd never encountered a woman quite like her before. She went to extreme lengths to hide any vulnerability. Why this need to prove that she could handle anything? She'd been beaten far worse than the young girl, yet didn't let him know how bad it was until that moment at the market.

He lifted the envelope from his desk. It was all there. He flipped open her new passport. The photo was passable. After weeks of mild starvation in the brothel, Avery's face was far more angular than the picture they'd used. He returned it into the envelope and read through the itinerary. Mr. and Mrs. Lopez would be flying from Cancun to Phoenix in four days. The role of Mr. Lopez was to be played by Spider. The thought of it hit Alejandro with an unexpected stab of envy. But traveling with her himself was out of the question. He couldn't risk sacrificing his cover just to take her home. It was a job anyone could do.

Maybe Oso was right. Too long without a woman messed with your head. His head was certainly messed up where Avery was concerned. Oso always claimed that getting laid was a cure for distraction, but he'd never known the man to actually put it into practice. And in this instance, Alejandro was sure that casual sex with some random woman wouldn't put anything back in perspective.

Chapter 23

On good days, Harvey declared happy hour at five o'clock. The battle over the wisdom of drinking tequila as a diabetic was continual, though typically Avery was able to keep her fed and cut her off at two shots. And she couldn't deny that it made her own nights a little easier.

As Harvey relaxed, Avery plied her with questions. Both knew it was a game. Avery tapped her fingers, waiting until Harvey threw back her first shot. The answers were always consistent. Tight-lipped. Rarely did she get more than a single yes or no.

"Why'd you get involved with a married man?" Avery asked.

This time she actually got a laugh out of Harvey. "Someday, someone might ask you how you fell for a cartel member."

It took a minute for her to comprehend Harvey's implication. Avery's face grew hot. She straightened and snorted. "Like that's going to happen."

Reaching for the tequila, she hoped Harvey didn't notice her shaking hands. If circumstances were different... but they weren't. It was impossible. They didn't share a common language, and he was a cartel member. If that wasn't enough, Javier had said that Alejandro didn't like women. Sometimes she questioned it, remembering the look on his face the night he fed her soup. Or the way he'd fixed her hair in the car.

She glanced up to find Harvey watching her smugly. Avery took another sip. "On to the next subject. Why so many guns?"

"I think I've told you enough about life in this country that you don't need to ask that question."

"But that's where you're wrong. You only have two hands, and you have dozens of guns out there."

"Fair enough. The guns don't belong to me." Harvey set down her glass. "At least not all of them."

"I suppose you won't tell me whose guns they are."

Harvey leaned toward Avery's glass with the tequila bottle in hand. "I suppose you're learning a thing or two."

"What languages do you speak?"

"Alejandro is delayed again. Probably will be several more days, maybe even a week, before he can get here."

Avery nearly dropped her glass. How was she communicating with him?

"Before you work yourself into some kind of state, let's put dinner on the table."

Avery banged the dishes a little too loudly. If nothing else, she needed to reassure her mother that she was alive. There was no guarantee she'd ever make it home, but to her mother it would mean hope. Phone or computer had to be Harvey's method of communication. She'd searched every inch of this house, except for Harvey's bedroom. There must be something in there. But so far, she hadn't managed to find a way in without Harvey finding out.

~ ~ ~

It was late one afternoon when Avery finally got her break.

There was a clanging noise she recognized as the sound the grocery boy made to get Harvey's attention. But it hadn't been a full week since his last delivery. It had to be someone else. As far as she knew, Harvey kept the padlock on the gate at all times. Since the day of the grocery boy incident, Harvey had insisted that Avery remain inside. And even if she'd been allowed outside, she couldn't have let someone in. Harvey wasn't about to tell her the combination to that stupid lock.

"Harvey," she yelled down the hallway. "You know, since you've got me locked up like Rapunzel it's up to you to attend to the guests at the gate."

She laughed to herself. Goth Rapunzel. Jet-black hair, a ghostly complexion, and a battered face. No tower was necessary to keep the prince away.

Harvey made a sleepy exit from her bedroom, carefully closing the door firmly behind her. "Any idea who?"

"That would require that I go outside."

Harvey shot her a go-to-hell look and started down the stairs. Avery supposed that her sarcasm might have been a little excessive. She traipsed behind Harvey, feeling more like her canine companion than the princess in the tower.

It occurred to her that the visitor at the gate might be unwelcome. "Harvey?"

"Yeah?" Harvey halted mid-stride and glanced over her shoulder, waiting.

"Should I be prepared to do something?"

Harvey snorted. "You a sharpshooter?"

"No."

"Then just go back upstairs and stay in your room."

Her hands shook. She didn't want to be alone upstairs. She took a deep breath, hoping to calm herself. Instead, what she felt was an unexpected and overwhelming rush of guilt. If something happened to Harvey, she'd never forgive herself. The thought caught her a little by surprise. But it confirmed that she couldn't just sit back and do nothing. Slowly, she made her way up the stairs, wondering if she could manage to sneak out behind Harvey. Unlikely. And there were the chickens. She stuck out her tongue at the thought. But there was the veranda off Harvey's room. And she was fairly certain she knew how to reach it.

Tentatively, she opened the bedroom door. Things were a great deal neater than the day she'd found Harvey passed out. No syringes or vials lying about. No clothes tossed aside. She tiptoed across the room.

The veranda's wooden deck was damp and mossy and enveloped in foliage. The greenery seemed to swallow her. A perfect hiding place. She positioned herself within a nook that presented an optimal vantage point.

A smallish man waited for Harvey as she plodded through the chickens. There was no car. That was a good sign. Javier's thugs would probably show up in something conspicuous—bright red and expensive. The man raised a basket, and Harvey grinned. There was friendly chatter between the two as Harvey reached for the padlock.

Avery took a step back. She wasn't aware until then that she'd been halfway holding her breath. For the first time in weeks, it was fear for someone else. She had been terrified that someone might try to harm Harvey.

She returned to the bedroom and paused to shut the veranda door. Something blinked red under the bed. She froze. The red light blinked a second time.

She made a rib-killing dive for the charging computer.

Surprisingly, the laptop wasn't even old. She closed her eyes and ran a hand over the cool metallic surface, then cracked it open. No password necessary.

The front door slammed, and she shoved the laptop back under the bed. She made it out of Harvey's bedroom and back into her own only seconds before Harvey yelled up the stairs, "Come on down, Rapunzel. We got a basketful of mangos."

Harvey had already sliced one open by the time Avery had pulled herself together enough to make her way down the stairs.

Avery bit into a chunk of the ripe mango, savoring the sweet tanginess with raised eyebrows.

"Damn good, huh?" Harvey said with her mouth full.

She nodded. "Would you teach me to shoot?"

Harvey blinked. "That came out of nowhere. What would possess me to do something that foolish?"

"Well, you said yourself that we could be in danger, since I revealed myself to the grocery boy."

Harvey scratched her head. "We'd have already known about it if he talked. My neighbor didn't know I had a guest." She chewed her lower lip. "If I could trust you to not turn it on Alejandro . . ."

"Turn it on Alejandro? Why would I do that?"

"He told me you tried to steal the Jeep."

Avery threw up her hands. "I knew he thought that. He left the keys in the ignition. I moved over to the driver's seat to get them out. That's all."

"You sure about that?"

She set aside the mango slice she was about to eat. "I'd be lying if I told you it didn't cross my mind. But no one bothered to explain to me why I couldn't be handed over to the embassy. Or that Javier had such a high price on my head. The fact is: I didn't leave him. I couldn't. Not after all he's done for me."

"Still don't know why he did any of it," Harvey muttered under her breath. "That boy never has been able look the other way when he sees something he thinks he can fix." She rubbed her forehead, then rested her chin in her hand. "And that includes me."

"What do you mean?" Avery asked.

Harvey turned away.

"Come on, does everything have to be such a secret? You won't even answer the simplest of questions. How many languages do you speak?"

Harvey rubbed her forehead. "Promise me something. Don't allow revenge to consume him."

"Revenge? What are you talking about?" Avery glared at her, but Harvey seemed unfazed. "You might as well convey your thoughts in Mandarin, as I'm sure you could." Avery slid her chair away from the table. "Forget I even asked."

"We start tomorrow," Harvey said. "Seven a.m., and I better not regret it. Truth is, he's still got to get you out of this country. And it isn't going to be easy. You might as well know what you're doing with a gun. Be some use to him."

Chapter 24

"Which one's your dominant eye?" Harvey led the way past the garage into a small wooded area.

"My dominant eye?" Avery frowned. Her ex-boyfriend had never bothered with details. Just handed her safety glasses and earplugs and told her to aim at the target.

"Stand here." Harvey held her shoulders firmly. "I know it's early, but too much coffee will give you the shakes. Aim the gun at the target. Both eyes open first. Then close your right eye, then your left. Whichever is closest to your view with both eyes open is your dominant eye," Harvey said.

"Oh, wow. That makes a difference." Avery aimed with her left eye closed. "Why is this gun so long?"

"Silencer. So we don't wake up the neighbors. The pistol you're holding is a twenty-two. Bullets are smaller. Nine-millimeter is a bigger bullet, and the gun will kick more. This is easier to learn on."

"But you can't kill someone with a twenty-two, can you?"

Harvey raised an eyebrow. "Bobby Kennedy was killed with a twenty-two. Now tell me, is the safety on or off?"

Avery fumbled with the pistol. This was less intuitive than she remembered.

"Give you a hint. This gun is easy. The saying goes, 'red you're dead.' Meaning the safety is off."

"Safety's on, then. But I guess you knew that. Otherwise you probably would have stopped me before now."

"That's exactly right. Now line yourself up. Let's see

what that ex-boyfriend taught you. Tin can on the left is your target."

Avery fingered the trigger nervously. Harvey's eyes were burning holes in her back. What was she thinking when she asked for this? She took a deep breath, pulled the trigger, and squeezed her eyes shut as the gun jerked upward.

"That's a technique I've never seen before."

Avery flipped the safety on and turned to her. "I can't do this."

"Yes, you can. And you will. Turn back around and nail that can." She crossed her arms. "We've got all day, if that's what it takes."

Avery swatted a bug out of her face. The humidity was oppressive. She couldn't stay out here all day. She lined herself up, steadied the gun with her left hand, and fired.

"Better. The cartridge holds twenty bullets. Keep going."

Her shooting was slow to improve. Her arms ached. The gun was heavy, and the feeling of Harvey's eyes on her never went away. In the process, she reloaded the cartridge a couple of times. Finally, she grazed the can enough to knock it off the wall.

As she started to flip the safety, Harvey said, "Now go for the can on the right."

Avery stifled a sigh and fought to still her shaking arms. She closed her left eye, straightened her shoulders, and pulled the trigger. The resounding pop came as a surprise. This time she'd hit it squarely. She glanced over her shoulder at Harvey, then turned and eliminated the middle can as if it was nothing at all. From the corner of her eye, she caught the briefest glimpse of Harvey's approving grin.

~ ~ ~

Weeks had passed since Alejandro had left her here. Harvey continued to deliver the bad news then evade the question of why he was so slow in returning, but it had begun to matter less to Avery. Shooting lessons became part of their daily routine, and Avery loved it. She was now familiar with nearly every gun in the locker.

She finished cleaning the Ruger they'd been working with today. Harvey hung over her shoulder, inspecting her work as she reassembled it. Ironic, since the rest of her life was such a mess.

"Someone's banging on the gate." Harvey held up a hand to silence Avery's activity. "It's the delivery boy."

"Good. We're down to nothing but eggs," Avery said.

Harvey headed to the front yard while Avery launched herself toward the back door. Since Harvey continued to insist that she remain inside, she brought the groceries in without Avery's help. Typically, it required several trips. Avery had been waiting for this day. She took the stairs in twos. It would be just enough time to get her hands on that computer and send her mother an email.

To her relief, the computer was still under the bed. Time for only one email. Let her mother know she was alive and safe. She'd keep it simple. No details about her location or her captors. No putting anyone at risk.

She choked back her excitement. Her heart swelled at the relief her mother would feel. She'd never typed so quickly in her entire life.

Carefully, she shut the laptop, wiped off her fingerprints with a corner of the sheet, and then slid the laptop back under the bed. Surprisingly, what she now felt was guilt. And worry. Could Javier track her email? No. That was a ludicrous thought.

Harvey was shelving groceries when she returned to the kitchen. The woman paused at the sight of her face. Avery turned away, busying herself with making coffee.

"Something happen while I was paying the grocery boy?"

"Hmm?"

"You're looking a little flushed."

"No. I just took the stairs too fast. My ribs still hurt." Though as she said the words, she heard her own lack of conviction.

"Feel well enough to tackle the henhouse? The door isn't quite hanging right."

Avery wanted to gag at the thought. It was as if Harvey knew she'd done something on the sly and would make her pay. "You're serious?"

"Someone's got to."

~ ~ ~

It was later than usual when Avery made her way to the kitchen to cook dinner. Harvey was already parked at the table. Her face was pink, and her behavior was suspiciously jovial. It would take more than just a repaired chicken coop door to make her look like that.

"What's with the good mood?" But before Harvey could answer, Avery spotted the bottle. "Tequila? That bottle was three-quarters full last night." Dinner was more than an hour from being ready. Avery ran a hand through her hair. Harvey needed food now, and most likely insulin, too.

This was crazy. Harvey wasn't usually this cavalier. Though she acted like death was around the corner, usually she sipped no more than a couple of ounces. Avery slapped some cheese between two tortillas. "When was your last injection?"

Harvey smiled. Her eyes were glazed. "This afternoon."

"I'm going to test your blood sugar, then."

"You chust go right ahead."

Avery frowned at drunk Harvey. How long had she been at this? She slid the quesadilla toward Harvey. "Where's your meter?"

Harvey waved a hand aimlessly. "Upstairs."

Harvey had consumed more than half the quesadilla when she returned. Avery grasped the first finger she could grab on the woman's left hand. She pricked it with a lancet, then squeezed a drop of blood on a test strip. Harvey barely seemed to notice.

Avery stared at the results in confusion. "Your blood sugar is *low*." As drunk as Harvey seemed, she'd expect it to be sky high. She turned the meter off, then on again. Harvey's head started to droop. Avery handed her another wedge of quesadilla. "Keep eating." Harvey stared at the food in her hand. Casually, Avery removed the tequila bottle and filled Harvey's glass with water. "Let me check once more."

"It's right," Harvey said with a slur. "It's what happens with booze. Liver can't keep up. Make me another one."

"Another quesadilla?" Avery peeled apart the tortillas, not waiting for an answer. She'd like to kill her for this. How could she be so careless? "Don't suppose you'll tell me what brought this on?"

Harvey raised an index finger. "Twenty years."

"Twenty years?"

"He's been gone."

"Who? The General?"

Harvey nodded, then rested her head in her hands. "And he thinks revenge is the answer."

"Who thinks?" Avery frowned. Was the woman hallucinating? Then it occurred to her. "Alejandro? Alejandro is seeking revenge for the General's death?" She blinked. It was the second time Harvey had mentioned revenge. Why would Alejandro be seeking revenge? And revenge from whom? The General was purportedly killed by a cartel. A rival cartel?

Harvey raised her head. "Need to go to bed. Help me upstairs."

After half-carrying and half-dragging Harvey up the stairs, Avery helped her into a ratty pair of pajamas she'd found draped over a chair. She pulled the bedsheet up around the woman, though the room was warm. "I've brought you a Coke. Let's get some down before you pass out on me, okay?" Harvey's response was slurred laughter. Avery shook her head. "I'm going to leave the door open. You can yell if you need anything."

She leaned forward to adjust a pillow, and Harvey patted her face. Avery rolled her eyes.

"Thank you for the maternal reassurance." The woman could make a pretty funny drunk, if not for the riskiness.

As Avery started out of the room, Harvey added, "Seven."

"Seven?"

"Yep." Harvey closed her eyes.

Avery paused for a second in confusion before smiling. Seven languages.

Chapter 25

For the hundredth time, Avery glanced at her wrist, checking for the watch that she no longer possessed. She'd checked Harvey's blood sugar two more times before going to sleep. It was fine then. But it wasn't like Harvey to blow off their morning shooting practice. She seemed to thrive on teaching.

Avery frowned. When she'd checked on her in the middle of the night, Harvey was her usual sober self. Mean. Barking at Avery to get out of her face and get the hell out of her bedroom. But one never knew with a diabetic. She closed the door to the gun closet and started toward the kitchen.

"Harvey!" Her voice echoed up the stairwell. "Harvey!" She took the stairs slowly, expecting Harvey to emerge from her bedroom, but there was only silence. She banged on the door and twisted the knob. The door was locked.

"Feed yourself," Harvey said. "I'm fine."

She'd make her breakfast anyway. Harvey would eat it eventually.

Avery contemplated their very odd friendship. If one could call it that. It was all on Harvey's terms. Which meant that other than the fact that she spoke seven languages, Avery still knew very little about her. On the flip side, Harvey seemed to read her like a book. On most things, anyway. She certainly knew how to get under her skin.

The offhand comments about her falling for Alejandro were a little misguided. It was surprising. Harvey claimed to know him well, but for some reason, she wasn't aware of his sexual preference. Maybe he wasn't that open about it. Or maybe Javier was lying. She stopped herself. It didn't matter.

She was sick of eggs, so she fished in the pantry for oatmeal. Maybe Harvey was hung over. Toast might be better. On second thought, it was silly to put so much thought into it. Harvey was Harvey. She'd probably be downstairs bossing Avery around again in another fifteen minutes and eating whatever she dished up.

With resignation, Avery pulled out a chair and seated herself facing the wall. She'd taken way too big of a bite when she heard the car engine. She froze, trying not to choke in the process. It sounded like it was coming from directly outside the kitchen window. Whoever it was had made it past the gate.

Her breath caught in her throat. Had Harvey heard it? She slid the half-full bowl across the counter and moved toward the stairs.

"Harvey!"

There was no answer. She could hear her, though. Harvey's voice rang out from upstairs, yelling in Spanish. She must be on the veranda.

Avery's mind was a whirlwind. Would someone seeking Javier's reward go so far as to hurt Harvey? Of course they would. It was a lot of money in a land with no laws.

She didn't care what Harvey said. It was too cowardly to lock herself in the bedroom. And she wouldn't wait for someone to break down the door. She needed to stand by Harvey no matter the circumstance.

Avery made a beeline for the gun closet.

When she returned, the hallway was silent and Harvey's bedroom door stood open. The weight of the gun tucked into her waistband made her movements awkward. She tried to peer through to the veranda but didn't see Harvey. Her heart raced, and her ribs ached. If she could slip out the back door she could—then she heard it. The deep rumble.

Alejandro.

Her heart pounded, and she found herself smiling in anticipation. She took the stairs down two at a time, as if her feet were operating on their own volition. Until she heard his anger. Fury. She backed up, but he must have already seen her. He moved to the bottom of the stairs, glaring up at her, his perfect face contorted into a shadowy cloud of rage.

Harvey moved to his side. Irritated but not furious. "Get yourself packed up," Harvey said. "You're out of here."

Avery nodded and returned to her bedroom. Obediently, she stuffed her belongings into the trash bag, feeling like a child. The sight of Alejandro in this state was disturbing, but worse was Harvey. There was no sarcasm in her tone. No smartass remarks.

When she returned to the kitchen, Alejandro was nowhere in sight. Harvey stared out the kitchen window at the side of the garage. She kept her back to Avery. There was a heavy silence between them. Avery cleared her throat, but before she could speak, Harvey said, "Alejandro's waiting. But hang on a minute," she said as she started toward the back door.

"Wait." Avery pulled the gun from her waistband. "When I heard the car…"

Harvey gave her a look of approval. It was a first. "Wait here, and I'll get the case."

The seconds seemed like hours. The hammering in Avery's chest continued. If only she understood what had happened. She knew better than to hope for answers from Harvey.

Harvey returned with a canvas satchel in one hand. "Put the gun in here and keep it somewhere out of sight. I hope you won't need it, but you'll know what to do if the time is right."

A lump rose in Avery's throat. "Thank you. Thank you for—"

"Go now." Harvey wouldn't meet her gaze. "Don't you dare put him in danger."

"I would never intentionally . . ." The words came with difficulty. "But you still haven't explained revenge."

"You'll know it when you see it."

Chapter 26

He drove like a crazy man. Avery thought she was going to be sick. If only Harvey had explained. Alejandro never looked at her. Never met her eyes. His phone rang continuously. Periodically, he'd pick it up, look to see who the caller was, then fling it on the dash in disgust. The only thing she knew for sure was that her situation had somehow worsened. The cause was a mystery. She gripped the door, praying he didn't roll the Jeep.

Even in his frustration with her when he thought she'd tried to steal the Jeep, he'd been so calm. A little angry, maybe. But not full of rage. This was a different man. Alejandro the cartel member. The bodyguard for one of the most dangerous men in Mexico, and friend of the craziest. Why had she imagined him to be incapable of this behavior?

The wheels on the passenger side lifted from the ground as he took a sharp left. She shrieked. He really was going to kill them.

"I know you don't understand me, but you're being an ass. No one is behind us. I've been watching ever since we left Harvey's." She turned in her seat now, facing him. The muscles in his jaw were hard. She could almost imagine the sound of his teeth grinding. He took a jarring right, slamming her back against the car door. They'd left the main road. "What is your problem?"

Harvey seemed to believe he walked on water. Apparently, she'd never seen this side.

He swerved a few more times before slamming on the

brakes and throwing them both forward. The nails of her right hand carved out grooves in the door handle.

For several minutes she rested against the seat back, eyes closed. Neither spoke. There were no clues as to what had put him in this state, though something told her she was at fault.

She opened her eyes to a pathetic roadside park. Long abandoned and overgrown with weeds. In the distance stood a decrepit shelter housing a graffiti-covered picnic table.

With apprehension, she turned to him. His left elbow rested next to the window, his hand covering his mouth. His right arm was slung over the steering wheel. He stared straight ahead, not even blinking.

It wasn't good. He could be planning to kill her. What was he doing here? Trying to decide where he'd bury her body? No. Not necessary when one was a drug lord in Mexico. He could just toss her in a ditch.

He flexed a hand against the steering wheel, exhaling deeply. The minutes seemed suspended, leaving her nerves a ragged mess. He flung open his door. With a sweep of his hand, he indicated that she should follow.

He leaned against the cement picnic table, staring at the ground. His posture was rigid, and each breath seemed measured. When his eyes finally met hers, she sensed a lot more than simple anger.

He cleared his throat. "Sit down."

Her breath caught in her throat. English? For a second, she thought she was imagining it.

Until he spoke again.

"You refuse to listen to those who risk their life on your behalf. I cannot seem to convey to you the seriousness of your situation and the lives of those you endangered. What were you thinking? Emailing your mother."

English. American English with zero Spanish accent. Whatever he was trying to say was lost on her.

"Are you listening?" he asked.

She blinked, struggling to recall his words. Emailing her mother. He knew about it. Her mouth went dry, and she felt like a child who had just been caught setting the drapes on fire.

"She needed to know I was okay." The words sounded choked. Why had he refused to speak English to her until now? If he'd just told her how dangerous it was in the first place, she'd never have contacted her mother.

He spoke through his teeth. "She would have seen you day after tomorrow. Nearly a month's worth of planning, all undone. Do you have any idea what you've done?"

Her chin was quivering, and she couldn't speak for fear of crying. She shook her head.

"Let me tell you, then. Your mother went straight to the press, announcing that she'd heard from you and that you were safe but still in Mexico. In that moment, you and your mother reminded the Ramos family, and the Contreras family, and every other cartel from here to Argentina who has a beef with Javier Ramos, that Avery McAndrews is still out there. Up for grabs. And, for the right price, one of them still might just be able to get their hands on you. Until yesterday, they'd pretty much forgotten about you. Javier had moved on to his latest obsession. But today, the new game begins. He's doubled the reward for finding you."

"That's ridiculous. Can he really afford it?"

He threw up his hands in exasperation. "You're missing the point."

"Of course I'm not." She wasn't an idiot. She knew they were in serious trouble. But two million dollars? Sam didn't even want to pay a hundred thousand. "It's just that that's an absurd amount of money."

"Yeah." He rubbed his chin, and the corner of his mouth curved up for a split second. She wondered if he was tempted to collect it himself. He sighed and met her gaze again, and she knew that was not the case. All his earlier frustration and fury seemed to be replaced with something new. Anguish? Defeat? Or maybe just exhaustion.

"The worst is . . ." His voice was barely audible. "I don't have a plan for getting you out of this country alive anymore."

Silence hung between them. He sank to the bench.

"So where are we going now? I mean—are you going to ditch me out here?"

"Don't tempt me." He closed his eyes. "I don't know, Ms. Avery McAndrews. Exactly where do *you* think we should go?"

Her anger began to surface. She hated his mocking tone. "I was right to call you an ass."

His eyes widened in surprise.

"You drive me around the country playing your little game of charades in Spanish. Dump me out in the middle of nowhere with a gun-fanatic crazy chicken woman, all without explaining anything to me. Oh, and really nice touch with the whole Spanish dictionary thing. What the hell was that?"

She took a step toward him, raising her face in challenge, as she continued the rant. "Look at things from my perspective. I know virtually nothing about you except that you're a member of the Ramos cartel." She held out a hand to stop any interruption. "In spite of that, I've trusted you. But that's all the more reason I would have been respectful of the need for discretion. If you'd only bothered to take the time to explain it to me." She gasped for breath, causing a sharp pain in her lower ribs. "Tell me what *you'd* have done when you saw that laptop. Sat back and ignored it? I don't think so. You don't really strike me as the passive type. Well, I'm not either."

He stared at her in disbelief. "God, you're incredible. I've never seen anyone turn a situation around and blame the person trying to help faster than you. You should have gone to law school." There was no amusement in his expression. "You finished?" His voice was low but controlled now. "And by the way, I thought you might at least make an effort to learn some Spanish."

That was low. She seethed.

"While we're on the topic of discretion." He rose to his feet, stepping closer to her. "There are very few people in Mexico aware of my command of the English language. I have no intention of increasing that number. And if you do, then you can say goodbye to your ticket home. Is that understood?"

She didn't respond.

"This isn't a game, Avery."

"Fine." She started to turn away, but he grabbed her arm. She attempted to shake it off, but he only tightened his grip.

"You will do as I say from here on, or I deliver you to Javier. Understood?"

This was a threat he'd never carry out. It was the one thing she knew for sure. But her desire to continue with the argument was waning. She nodded. "Okay, I'll do whatever you say."

His grip on her arm loosened, and his hand slid down the length her arm. Inadvertently, her fingers curled over his.

Confusion crossed his face, and she felt heat rise to her cheeks. He withdrew his hand with an awkward smile and started toward the Jeep.

She tried to ignore the sting. "Are we leaving?"

"Nope." He opened the back of the Jeep and withdrew a blanket.

"What are you doing?"

He spread the blanket in a shady spot under a small tree, never bothering to glance in her direction. "I'm going to take a nap before we get back on the road."

"Is taking a daily siesta a necessity for you?"

"No. But thanks to you, I spent the night driving." He stretched out across the blanket. "The Jeep is locked, and the keys are in my pocket. So is my cell phone." He cut his eyes at her. "I suggest you keep your hands to yourself."

Chapter 27

Arrogant, presumptuous man. His words stung. *Keep your hands to yourself.* She made a face at him. Fortunately, he couldn't see it.

She'd only held his hand for a second. And she knew he was gay. His reaction was so . . . something. Did he actually believe she meant it as more than an apologetic gesture?

She cringed. His temper was surprising. He'd succeeded in making her feel flighty and irresponsible. Things she'd never been accused of in her entire life.

She'd been gone from home a long time, with very few answers and endless rules. She maintained that what she did was not wrong. *He* was wrong to be such a jerk about it. She merely did what anyone would have done, given the opportunity. A lot of people would have done more. Given up their location. Or Harvey's name. Told the story of the rescue. She was careful to avoid all of that. Okay, maybe if she'd thought about it more she might have guessed that her mother would speak to the press. It was her style. She was relentless. And a retired publicist who still craved the attention.

Avery stretched her legs across the concrete pad, resting her back against a support post. Not the most comfortable position, but she wanted to keep her distance from him. In spite of herself, she watched him sleep. His face was anything but peaceful. She'd never seen anyone frown like that when they were asleep before. She looked away, refusing to take responsibility for his miserable nap.

Had she sensed somehow that he spoke English? Since his first visit to her room at the brothel, she'd spoken to him as if he understood. She'd never in her life displayed any psychic or even particularly intuitive instincts, so what was it about him? And why was his ability to speak English such a highly guarded secret?

She tossed a pebble at a crack in the cement, then reached for another while considering the advantages this gave him. People would drop their guard around him. Resort to speaking a language they presumed he didn't understand. It allowed him to understand conversations not meant for his ears. Probably a big advantage in the world of illegal drugs and prostitution. Brilliant, actually. Unprompted, she'd confessed to him that Sam Rockforth would never pay her ransom. She'd also called him a drug-dealing scumbag, or something of that nature. Regret colored her face. What other things had she said to him that she could barely remember? All that hero worship nonsense about Stockholm Syndrome, for one thing. Ugh. She made a frustrated swipe at her hair. God only knew what he thought.

She couldn't focus on it anymore. Cartel member or not, he was trying to help her. He'd risked his life. It was just so difficult. He didn't fit into any boxes. Good, bad, dangerous, kind. None of it seemed completely true or false. Only unpredictable.

~ ~ ~

Eventually, her pile of pebbles had multiplied to form a small hill. More than once she'd dozed off herself. It had to be mid-afternoon by now.

She knelt at the edge of the blanket. He'd turned onto his side, looking younger and less stressed. She leaned in closer, peering at his face.

"Avery." His eyes didn't open. "What are you doing?"

"Nothing." She wasn't about to admit that she'd been thinking about brushing a strand of hair from his face. "It seems like it's getting kind of late."

He yawned and glanced at his watch. "You're right, it's after two." His eyes widened as he studied her, as if seeing her for the first time. "Your hair looks good."

She shot him a dirty look. "If you're into witches."

"You pull it off well." He bit his lip. "But your eyes... you need to keep your sunglasses on."

"Harvey called me a green-eyed monster."

He snorted. "You've got thick enough skin to not be bothered by anything she says." He rose to his feet and extended a hand to her. "We should get on the road."

"Where are we going?"

"I'm not sure. Harvey's was the safest place I could think to park you until I got things arranged."

"Is she going to be safe?"

"Yeah." He stretched his neck from side to side, then shot her a sideways glance. "She said there'd been talk in the village about you."

She threw up her hands. "I didn't know being seen by the grocery boy would be such a big deal. But she said if he suspected anything we would have already known about it."

"True. But we can't afford to take any more chances. Your picture is posted throughout Mexico now."

"Have you seen the photo he's posting?"

He started the car. "Yeah."

"Was I holding a newspaper?" He nodded. "And do I look anything like that now?"

His grin was one of concession. "No."

~ ~ ~

He stuck to the backroads once again. The only thing she knew for sure was that they were headed northwest, based on the position of the sun. Neither spoke much, each of them seeming to be lost in their own thoughts. The Jeep was loud and rough. This time, it was a comfortable silence. Much better than the drive to Harvey's, when there had been no choice but to coexist in silence. Or so she'd been led to believe.

So far there had been no stops for gas or food. Alejandro searched the radio for anything but static.

"Who is she?" she asked.

He made a face. "Who exactly are we talking about?"

"Harvey—who'd you think?"

"There was no context," he said. "Do you expect me to read your mind?"

He had before. So maybe she did. "You didn't answer my question."

"She didn't tell you?"

"She's the most tight-lipped woman I've ever met."

He laughed. "That's an accurate description."

She rotated in her seat to see his expression. "What's wrong?"

"Nothing. I'm just thinking how much easier this is. Being able to talk to one another."

He was so different, and at the same time so familiar. His sense of humor was just as she imagined it would be. The easy banter between them came naturally. "You know, you're just like her. You answer my questions with another question. Is she an arms dealer?"

This brought another round of deep laughter from him. Even though his eyes were hidden behind sunglasses, there was a sparkle in his expression. "Hardly. She was a journalist."

"That doesn't explain how you know her. And I really don't buy it. She's no journalist," she said.

"She is a journalist, but her secrets are not mine to divulge." He shook his head. "I've known her for a very long time. Perhaps it's best that we just leave it at that."

"Why does she have all those chickens?"

"I noticed you have a problem with chickens." A slight dimple appeared along the side of his mouth.

"It's not funny. I don't like them. And she kept wanting me to kill one for dinner."

His eyebrows shot up. "Really?" He leaned back against the seat, laughing heartily.

"Yes, really. Why are you so surprised at that?" she asked.

He continued to laugh. "Because the reason she has so many is that she can't do it herself."

Unbelievable. Avery ground her teeth. Harvey had made her feel so incapable, so . . . pampered.

She stared out the dusty windshield and tried to find a comfortable position. The constant jostling was a challenge to her healing ribcage. Was Mexico really so lacking in paved roads? Or was it just his method of avoiding crowds? It seemed that he migrated to the most desolate places around, never drawing too close to the mountains. But they were always there looming in the distance, setting the boundaries for their path. He avoided water, too. The few times she'd spotted a lake or river, he'd veered way out of the way as if to steer clear. He tapped the steering wheel, though there was no music. His face had lost the tension she'd seen when he was sleeping. Maybe the backroads were just less stressful. A time to forget who he really was.

"Tell me why you're bothering to risk your life to save mine."

"Oh, now that's the real question, isn't it?" He grinned, his teeth brilliantly white and straight. It was a feral look. "That much I can tell you. It's simple. I work for Diego Ramos. Javier's father. Part of my job is to clean up after Javier."

She rubbed her forehead. "Javier's father doesn't approve of kidnapping?"

He shifted in his seat. "Not a good idea when the victim is a U.S. citizen. It makes things messy," he said.

"So then why all the effort to hide me? Why doesn't Javier's father tell him to call off the hunt? Let me go? Leave me at the American Embassy."

"It probably won't surprise you to learn that Javier is hated by just about everyone. The fact that he's labeled you as his property makes the whole situation complicated. His father prefers to turn his head and pretend none of it's real. Hide all of Javier's mess from his crowd in Mexico City. My job is to keep the news of Javier's activities at bay. As long as none of Diego's legitimate business partners or anyone else of any social standing finds out, then he's happy." He ran a hand through his hair. "Plus, there's a problem with the embassy. Javier did something similar about a year ago. The person involved went to the embassy for help. His body was found the next day. In pieces."

She tried to suppress the shudder his words sent through her. "So, Javier has connections at the embassy?"

He shrugged. "Money buys power."

"And that's why you do what you do?"

"Buy myself power, you mean?" He let out a small laugh. "Does it look like it?"

He'd done it again. Evaded the question by answering with a question.

"If we're playing twenty questions," he said, "then it's my turn."

"Go ahead. I have nothing to hide," she said.

"We'll see about that."

They'd reached the outskirts of a moderately sized city. Embedded in rolling hills, houses of multi-colored stucco glistened in the late afternoon's golden glow. Who knew Mexico could look like this? "Don't suppose you'll tell me what town we're in."

"Nope."

"Are we staying here?"

"Afraid not," he said, smiling apologetically. He must have detected the hope in her voice.

"You know we've circled this roundabout twice now."

"I'm aware of that. Just deciding what to do with you." He exited the traffic circle, heading east. "Back to twenty questions. My first one for you, Avery McAndrews, is I'd like to know why you work for Sam Rockforth. Greedy old bastard."

She had to laugh at the irony of his question. As if her own code of ethics was somehow not quite what it should be. "Isn't that the pot calling the kettle black? I like working for Sam. Oil and gas are my area. He's pretty much my favorite client. He has a lot of work. Normally, it's not quite like Zapata. Kidnapping usually doesn't come into play."

"But money does."

"How do you know that? How do you know anything about Sam?" she asked.

"I know he's not that different from my boss."

She frowned. "What are you saying?"

"Oh, I'm not suggesting that Sam dabbles in the same things that Diego does. It's just the way he does business. He's got a reputation."

Her anger began to escalate. "A reputation? You have the audacity to speak of someone's reputation when you don't even care about your own? Plus, on the other side of the border, Sam's reputation is fine."

"You realize you're defending someone who refused to pay your ransom," he said.

"I told you already. He doesn't even know me on a personal level."

"What about the little bonuses you get on the jobs you do for Sam?"

"Where are you getting your information?"

"Diego makes it my job to know our clients."

"You're calling Sam a client?" she asked.

"The Ramos family provides protection." He shrugged. "So, yes."

She crossed her arms across her chest. "Protection?" He was delusional. "Kidnapping your client's engineer is *protection*?"

He ignored her. "Have you ever questioned why your take-home pay was significantly above the average for someone with your education and years of experience?"

How could he know about Sam's bonuses? It was obvious he was trying to justify his own corruption. She turned away from him.

"You don't want to jump out. Hospitals aren't that great around here. Plus, it would probably just prolong your stay."

"I wasn't going to jump. I'm not an idiot. How do you know about Sam and how he pays?"

From the crinkles in the corner of his eyes, she detected smugness in his expression. "I didn't. Just a guess. Sam would have to pay well to get someone like you to work in Zapata."

"Someone like me? Exactly what does that mean?" She glared at him, but the effort was wasted since he was obviously amused by her reaction. "You're delusional."

He tilted his head in mock consideration. "If it's a contagious disease, then you're probably right. I certainly have enough exposure to others that are affected."

"God, you're—"

"Incorrigible?" he said with a grin. "And you're impetuous. You act without regarding the consequences. Like just now. Thinking about jumping out of the car. If you don't get yourself under control, it's going to kill both of us."

"For the last time, I was not going to jump." Her eyes narrowed. "Where did you learn English?"

"Same place you did, I guess. At home."

"Did you grow up in Mexico?"

"Define grow up," he said.

She sighed. He was the most exasperating person she'd ever met.

He turned to her, the levity in his expression gone. "Look, I'm not in a position to provide you with my life history. Not that you would find it that fascinating anyway. So, our little game has its limits."

"How did you end up working for Diego Ramos, then? Were you already in the business?"

"That's two questions." He rubbed the back of his neck. "I ended up with the Ramos family by word of mouth." He seemed to consider the second question. It should have been a simple yes or no, but he was taking his time. "And yes, I was in the business."

"And which arm of the business would that be? Drugs, arms, sex trafficking?"

"Wow," he said.

"Well, it's what the Ramos family is known for, right?"

"If so, I'm failing at my job."

"Are you telling me the truth?" she asked.

"You do realize that's another question."

"I still have plenty left. So, answer it."

"The answer is yes," he said.

"Why do I constantly get the feeling you're not who you pretend to be?"

He tossed his head back with a laugh. "Exactly who do you imagine that I might be? Making me out to be some kind of good guy? A hero? I already told you I'm employed to clean up the image of one of the most corrupt families in Mexico."

There was more that he wasn't telling her. He'd done his best to watch out for her in the whorehouse and then risked his life to get her out. There were probably other ways he could have handled Javier without putting himself at risk.

"Have you ever killed anyone?"

His voice was low. "What do you think, Avery?"

"Lots of people?"

Silence followed. The game was over.

~ ~ ~

Once again, he'd managed to find the most desolate dusty road on the North American continent. Her head rolled against the headrest as her eyes grew heavy.

"No!" Alejandro said, slapping his palm against the steering wheel. He shouted out a few lines in Spanish that were unmistakably obscenities.

"What?"

"Jeep is starting to overheat." He reached for his phone, glanced briefly at the screen, then flung it onto the dashboard. "No service."

She could have told him that just from their desolate surroundings. The landscape was divided into plots, though as far as she could see, there were no crops. "How far are we from this undisclosed location where you're taking me?"

He shot her a look. "We might as well be on a different planet." He pulled the vehicle to the edge of the road and shut it off.

"I guess it's not a good time to tell you I'm hungry."

"Afraid not," he said.

"Any idea what's wrong?"

"No. Apparently my mechanic doesn't know, either. It was in the shop all week."

Her hand went to the door latch. "I'll take a look."

She knew better than to ask what kind of traffic to expect around here. She hadn't seen as much as a farm truck for at least an hour, and there was nothing but a handful of decrepit buildings in the expanse of rolling acreage ahead.

They stood shoulder to shoulder as he unlatched the hood. Nothing was smoking, and there was no steam. "Are you an automotive genius?" he asked.

"No." She rolled her eyes at the false idea that being a mechanical engineer somehow implied expert knowledge of engine repair. She knelt to inspect underneath the car for leaks. He squatted next to her, their faces less than an inch apart and their arms touching, as they surveyed the dirt road for evidence. "I don't see any coolant."

He didn't seem to be focused on coolant. In fact, he never looked at the ground, but only at her. His breath warmed her shoulder. She waited, uncertain of what this was. If Javier was telling the truth and Alejandro was gay, then . . . his intent was all in her head.

He cleared his throat. "I've already replaced the water pump."

She felt so awkward. Her heart was racing, and for what? Her stupid fantasy. She gripped the bumper and pulled herself up. She pointed inside the hood.

"Yeah," he said before she could form the words. "The thermostat. I was thinking the same thing."

"Given the age of the car," she said, hating the nervous edge to her voice.

"I'll be rebuilding the engine before too long."

"No new Jeep?"

"No. I've got other cars, but this one is different," he said.

"Cars plural?"

"Diego. His way of rewarding his employees."

She raised her eyebrows but said nothing, continuing to peer under the hood. "Alejandro?"

"Hmm?"

"You should probably replace the hose clamps on the radiator with spring clips. Plastic radiators tend to crack and . . ." Avery couldn't finish. Alejandro cleared his throat as if stifling a laugh.

There was an element of humor in his tone as he spoke, "Thought you didn't know anything about cars."

"You asked me if I was an automotive *genius*. And I'm not." She turned to meet his gaze.

One side of his mouth inched upward, but he said nothing. He let the hood drop and, rubbing his hands together, moved to the side of the Jeep. He leaned against the vehicle, staring off into the distance. Removing his sunglasses, he gave her a long, hard look. In the light of the early evening, he was a visionary object. Golden. Otherworldly. She was already struggling to breathe after that thing a minute ago. She forced herself to turn away.

"It's probably ten or twelve miles to the main road. After dark, there won't be any traffic out here. Not even much on the main road. Not that we could make it before dark. The nearest town is fifteen miles," he said.

Streaks of orange and pink lit the horizon. Alejandro moved to the back of the Jeep, muttering in Spanish. She turned to find their belongings strewn across the dirt road as he heaved the rear seat from the back of the Jeep.

"Do you need help?" she asked.

"We're setting up a sort of campsite here. It's too late in the day to do anything else. Help me find whatever wood we can before it gets dark."

"Out here?" Glancing about, she spotted nothing but a single distant tree and an occasional scrubby bush. Was he serious? She'd be lucky to find sticks longer than three inches.

"Whatever you can find. It doesn't have to burn all night. It's not as if we're going to freeze. Just thought it might be nice to have some firelight for dinner." In one hand he held a bunch of small red bananas, and in the other he clutched a bottle of wine.

She was starving, but it was impossible to be irritated with him for not stopping to get food. He was making the best of a bad situation. "Sorry, I had bananas and wine last night," she said with a twisted smile. She could easily put away the whole bunch of bananas. "And I guess since you're the hunter, it's up to me to be the gatherer."

"Yep."

She marched toward the fleeting sunlight, crossing her fingers that this wasn't an active time of day for rattlesnakes. Small gusts of wind left the air almost cold. She crossed her arms and searched along the rows of barren dirt.

She hadn't managed to get very far before she heard him calling. He waved her back across the road. At his feet was a heap of old boards.

"Someone's old outhouse."

"Great," she said with a raised eyebrow. "I'm going to see if I have long pants in the *clean* trash bag Harvey gave me." She spun on her heels. "Any particular reason why someone took my suitcase?"

He shook his head. "Hopefully you realize by now that I wasn't a participant in Javier's kidnapping operation. As soon as I learned what happened, I sent someone back later to search the motel. They found the remains of your belongings in the dumpster."

That was probably something she could have lived without knowing. It wasn't difficult to imagine the contents of the Tumbleweed Inn's dumpster. Catfish carcasses and half-eaten corn cobs.

He waited by the burgeoning fire with a corkscrew in his hand. "No glasses or cups."

"You know, after learning where my clothes have been, drinking straight from the bottle seems fitting."

"Banana appetizer?"

"Of course. Do the peels burn?" she asked, catching the banana he'd tossed in her direction.

"No. Trust me. I had a cousin who was a pyro as a kid. Banana peels require an accelerant to burn." He pointed to the Jeep seat and said with an undeniable hint of sarcasm, "Make yourself at home."

Removed from the Jeep, the back seat was less than a foot above ground level and not very wide. Seated shoulder to shoulder, they stared at the fire in awkward proximity.

He handed her the bottle. "Not to worry. When this one's done we do have several more. Or I could just give you your own."

She took a sip. "God!" She coughed. "What is this stuff? It's incredible."

His teeth flashed brilliantly in the firelight. "Diego's. Left over from one of his parties. Told me to take home the whole case." He gazed at the label. "French Burgundy. Last time I checked this stuff ran eighteen-hundred dollars a bottle."

"Thank you, Diego," she said in a mock toast. "Life is good."

"That's gracious of you. I'm not sure if I'd been kidnapped by his son and dragged around the Mexican countryside I'd be ready to thank him just yet."

The flush of the wine warmed her cheeks and infused her bloodstream with a sense of relaxation. Leaning back against the headrest, she closed her eyes. "I'm glad you weren't part of the kidnapping."

He said nothing, but leaned forward and rested his elbows on his knees. His head hung down. Avery passed him the bottle, sensing he needed it.

"How did you ever get mixed up . . ." She didn't finish. One glance at his face told her it would take a lot more wine. He was a closed book. He'd said it himself. Only a few people in Mexico knew he spoke English. This made it almost a certainty that he'd grown up in the U.S. And that made it that much more confusing. Why come to Mexico? Of course, there was the lure of money. She shook her head at her own ridiculous persistence. Why did she keep wanting him to be something more? It was naïve.

She watched him from the corner of her eye and followed his gaze. "Wow, the stars are just popping out one by one, and they're incredible."

"They say you've never seen the stars until you spend the night on the ocean or in the desert." He pointed. "Leo." She tried to follow his outstretched finger. He leaned closer to her, the warmth of his skin welcome. "It looks kind of like a coat hanger."

"Yeah, I see." He dropped his arm and resumed his previous position, farther away. She crossed her arms at the invading cool air.

"No lights," he said. "No clouds. You know, the elevation is higher than Denver. That's why it's so cool."

"You know where I'm from." Her words had taken on a slight slur.

"I do. Part of my job."

"What else do you know?" She gave him a sideways glance.

"I know that as camping spots go, this place isn't bad," he said.

Not bad at all, she thought as she took another swig of Diego's wine. In fact, this was the best night she'd had since landing in Mexico.

No. She set the bottle at his feet. Sadly, it was one of the best nights she'd had in months. Maybe even this year. Long before she'd ever heard of Zapata.

Her life was nothing but weeks of being alone in motels. Weekends spent recovering from the work week. A vicious cycle leading to an empty life. So empty, in fact, that she was enjoying being stranded in the Mexican desert with a gangster. Inadvertently, she made a small noise in the back of her throat.

"You cold? I have a jacket in the Jeep. Let me get it." He didn't wait for a reply.

He returned holding a heavy windbreaker. She threaded her arms through the too-long sleeves. His musky scent was infused in the cloth. Something about it made her sad to think that tomorrow it would smell only of campfire.

"Another banana?" His question brought her out of her semi-dream state.

"I guess so. But it does seem to dampen my ability to detect the aromatics of the wine."

His eyes were wide. A small line creased his brow.

"Oh, come on. I'm just kidding." She rolled her eyes. If only he'd seen her putting back the Fusty Mule or Harvey's tequila. "The way we're drinking this wine, you'll understand me really well before too long." She covered her mouth with her hand. "Oops, I didn't mean it to sound like that." She carved out random lines in the dirt with the heel of her tennis shoe. Her mind was succumbing to the wine haze maybe a little more quickly than it should.

He set aside the empty bottle and withdrew the corkscrew from his shirt pocket. "Is your mother the only person you contacted yesterday?"

That had come out of the blue. And sitting here in front of the blazing outhouse remnants, it was impossible to believe that it was only yesterday.

"Yeah, why?"

"Just wondered if there was someone else."

"Like a boyfriend?" Her laugh was high-pitched. As if she were in middle school. "God, no." She raised her eyes to the sky.

"I didn't mean to embarrass you."

"I'm not embarrassed." A lie. "It's just relationships. They're complicated." She stumbled over her words. "I mean, I'm not very good . . . at that. I've got something missing. Not missing, just . . ." She buried her face in her hands. God only knew what he thought. She was definitely getting drunk. It was time to shut up.

"Missing, huh?" His voice rumbled, and not only did she detect a note of humor in voice, but she could see that dimple surfacing again. "Like what?" He coughed as he struggled to swallow his wine. "I think I'll use a couple more of my questions on this subject."

"Please don't. It came out wrong." She was still sober enough to deflect his focus. "What about you? Do you have a partner? I guess I don't know what Mexico law is—I mean, being a Catholic country. Do you have a husband?"

"Do I have a husband?" He ran a hand along his jawline, as if this was something that needed to be calculated. He hitched an ankle over the opposite knee, a slightly awkward position in the Jeep seat. "No one has ever asked me that question before." He rested a forearm across his lizard boot. "What have I done to give you the impression that I'm gay?"

"Oh." She squirmed. Thank God it was dark out. "Javier . . ." Her face must be beet red. "He told me you didn't like women."

"Interesting. And you believed him?"

She shrugged weakly. "I never had any reason to doubt him. I mean . . ." She had no idea how to stop this hole she was digging for herself.

He stretched out his long legs and rested his woven fingers on his head. He seemed to enjoy watching her squirm. "Yeah. Go on."

"Stop it. Now you're just being mean. How could I know anything about you? You only spoke Spanish around me."

"You're right. I guess I've had the advantage there." He shot her a look. "Since you tended to tell me what you thought even when you believed I didn't understand."

She pushed him half-heartedly. "I think somewhere inside I knew differently."

"Is that right? So, the drug-dealing scumbag comment was intentional?" He turned. His closeness left her increasingly aware of her own heartbeat.

"Why does Javier think you're gay?"

He made a dismissive sound. "Javier always wanted me to patronize Inez's place." He tossed a twig into the fire. "And the kind of women that he surrounds himself with in Mexico City—well." He raised an eyebrow. "I guess I gave him reason to believe it. Never occurred to me."

She stared at the fire. He'd just become someone else. Once again. She reached for the wine bottle. Straight Alejandro was a concept she'd need to process.

"Do you have a girlfriend or a wife?"

"No." He launched a larger branch into the blaze. "Doesn't work too well with my career."

Career? It seemed to her that working for Diego Ramos was not exactly a career. But she kept her mouth shut on the issue. Instead she said, "I know the feeling."

"I thought you had something missing." He let out a low laugh.

"Funny." She snatched the wine bottle from his hand. "What I tried to say earlier is that my relationships usually don't last very long." The alcohol was giving her the strength to be candid. Or stupid. Something told her she might regret this tomorrow. "I've been accused, more than once, of being emotionally unavailable." She threw her head back and spoke as if addressing the luminous night sky. "I'm an idiot. I've sacrificed everything for my stupid job."

He said nothing, and his silence left her feeling a little foolish. She turned to find him watching her. Lightly, he traced the side of her face with his index finger and whispered something in Spanish. A warm sensation flooded her body. She moved closer, tilting her face into his. His lips were soft, and his mouth tasted of wine.

It was a brief kiss. But it left her on fire. She threaded her hand through his hair and leaned back for more, her lips parting.

He stiffened, clasping her wrist as he pulled away. "Avery." His voice was rough. "This can't happen. I'm sorry. It was my fault."

He touched her arm, and she flinched. Humiliation flushed through her, and she wanted to run. Rejection was unfamiliar. She rose to her feet, swaying just a little. She shrugged her way out of his jacket, deposited it in his lap, and turned to the Jeep.

"We have eleven water bottles left. You need to drink some before you go to sleep. We have a long walk in the morning, and you don't want to be hung over." He paused. "Avery."

"Leave me alone." She wove her way back to the Jeep and climbed inside.

Chapter 28

It was impossible to find a tolerable position in the Jeep seat. This morning her ribs ached more than they had in the past week. She shielded her eyes. The glare off the hood was blinding. She reached for her water bottle. Glancing around, she caught sight of Alejandro hitching his backpack over one shoulder. Her eyes narrowed. He hadn't even bothered to wake her up, and now it looked like he was leaving.

She flung open the door and shouted, "Where are you going?" He'd wasted no time—he was nearly at the top of the first small rise.

As she took a few steps in his direction, she had to admit he'd been right: a couple more bottles of water last night would have made all the difference. Her mouth was dry, and her head pounded. It didn't help that the sun was relentless.

"You're leaving me here?"

He turned but made no effort to come back. "I left you a note. Thought it might be better if I just went myself, since you didn't seem like you were in any shape to walk it. I shouldn't be gone much more than a few hours. I can run most of the way. I've set up a little campsite for you. It's on the other side of what remains of the outhouse. You'll be out of sight. Barricaded and out of the sun."

She rocked back on her heels. It seemed like the stupidest idea she'd ever heard. She hadn't told him about Harvey's gun. As far as he knew, she was defenseless. "You really think the chances that I'll be okay out here alone are better than if I just go with you?"

"No one's been down this road in days. Not since the last rain, which was more than two weeks ago. So yes. If we end up in some little town, I'm afraid someone might recognize you."

Ass. He might have mentioned this last night. The truth was, he just didn't want her around. The realization made her angrier than ever and furious with herself for kissing him. She clenched her teeth. "Fine. Go." The intensity of the sun was making her queasy, and she spotted a small boulder only a few feet away. She could wait. And if he never returned... it wasn't like she would get lost without him. One single dirt road. In frustration, she kicked at a small rock, pretending it was him. It didn't help.

She wiped the sweat from her forehead with her sleeve. Every minute seemed like a new kind of hell. It seemed like years ago that her life had been her own. Hard to believe that she ate, worked, and slept guided by a universe of order based on logic and principles. Now, there was no order. Work was a distant memory. Sleep and food weren't always an option. Trapped in a place where she couldn't speak the language. And, worst of all, she'd allowed herself to become vulnerable and been rejected. All because of one man's misconception. That idiot Javier.

She heard the rattle just as she unscrewed the cap from her water bottle. At first, she didn't see it. Its earthy brown markings were a perfect camouflage, blending with the soil and scrubby vegetation. It was the gaping red mouth that held her attention. A massive rattlesnake. No more than two feet away. Fangs protruding as its tongue flitted. It was coiled and ready to strike.

She didn't move. Hopefully, it would go away if she was still enough. The thing must sense her heartbeat, it was thudding so loudly.

She called for Alejandro. Not so loudly, at first. She

needed to be certain the snake wouldn't react. It didn't. The second time, she belted out his name.

He peered down at her from the crest of the hill. Dropping the backpack, he sprinted toward her.

"Rattlesnake," she said as he drew closer. Her heart was thundering now.

"Be still." In his hand was a pistol. His every silent move was calculated. "Turn your head away from the snake. Slowly! Now, don't look at me either." There was a small click. "That was just the safety." She drew in a tiny, shaky breath and closed her eyes. "Good. Now keep still."

The explosive force sent dust over her shoes and up the legs of her jeans. She jumped, but by then the bullet had already done its work.

Alejandro moved toward her with his free hand extended. "Best not to look down." Squeezing her hand, he tilted his head toward hers. "Are you okay?"

"Yeah, I'm fine." It was hardly the truth. Her legs were wobbly as she stood up.

"I'm sorry. I guess I didn't factor in snakes."

The adrenaline had eradicated any remnants of her hangover. "You can't leave me alone." She hadn't meant to say it. The words just slipped out.

He pulled her close, encircling her with an arm. "I'm so sorry, Avery." For a moment, neither of them moved. She let herself relax against him. "We'll come back for the big stuff. Whatever you can't live without can go in the backpack." He set Oso's cowboy hat on her head and touched her chin with his thumb. "You okay now?"

It only took about ten minutes before she was second-guessing her decision to walk. The sun was brutal. By her estimate, they had at least eleven more miles. They weren't exactly making great time, thanks to her pace. It was hillier than it looked, and breathing was painful. At this rate, it would take them nearly three hours to reach the main road and then another one to reach the town.

Gradually, the bare soil turned to grass, and eventually that gave way to scrubby trees and tall cactus. Along with the nearly verdant vegetation came rocky, rolling hills. It was beautiful, but with each increasingly steeper uphill step, Avery's already-slow pace grew slower. Every breath was a struggle. They walked in single file, keeping to the side of the road as if somehow it mattered. It didn't. Not a single car had passed.

"Interest you in a banana?" He asked over his shoulder.

"Ugh. No thanks."

He peeled one for himself, humming a tune she couldn't identify. "Kidnapped, beaten, and now cornered by a rattlesnake. You're tough, Avery McAndrews."

Whether it was heartfelt or just a means of calling some kind of a truce, she didn't care. She only wanted a soft bed and eight hours of uninterrupted sleep out of the sun.

The main road was a great disappointment. She'd spent hours building it up in her mind. But the only noticeable difference was the intermittent black top and the volume of garbage delineating the shoulders.

She began to lag behind. Sweat ran in lines over her face. Her sleeves were soaked from wiping her face.

Something roared in the distance. She glanced over her shoulder, hopeful someone might stop for them. A beater, dusty purple with a flapping bumper, made a raucous approach. In spite of the fact that it was obviously missing a muffler, she could still hear the rumbling of the bass.

As the car drew closer, she could make out two men seated low in the front seat. Alejandro's head jerked back, suddenly aware of the car's proximity and her diminishing pace.

"Avery, no. Don't pay any attention."

But it was too late. The man in the passenger seat was now hanging out of the open car window. His bald head was a collage of tattoos bouncing in time to the music, and he was readily demonstrating his interest in her. "*Hola, chica.*" This was followed by a whistle.

Alejandro wasted no time inserting himself between Avery and the car. His tone was cool as he spoke to the two. He apparently attempted humor, his laugh sounding forced.

But whatever he said wasn't working. The driver stepped out. Clad in a stained undershirt, he flexed his fleshy biceps as he spoke. No need to understand Spanish. He was taunting Alejandro.

Avery took a step back. Must everything in this country turn into a display of machismo?

"Shit," Alejandro said under his breath, then added in a loud voice, "No." His right hand hovered over the holster barely concealed beneath his cotton shirt.

Had they recognized her? She stepped closer to Alejandro, hiding behind the breadth of his back. It seemed like a chicken maneuver, but like an idiot she'd left her gun in the Jeep and was at a loss for any other ideas. The men continued to exchange words. Still facing the tattooed man, Alejandro reached for her behind his back. Her palm was sweaty as she gripped his hand, taking refuge in its strength. He pulled her closer until their clasped hands rested against the small of his back. Slowly, he guided her hand up his back a couple of inches.

Her breath caught in her throat as she felt another gun beneath his shirt. How many guns did one person really need? And what was she supposed to do? She couldn't exactly move her hand up his shirt without those two noticing. Or maybe she could. She hovered closer, peering over his shoulder, then rested the weight of her body against him.

Though both men looked like they might have seen the inside of a jail cell, neither was a physical match for

Alejandro. He was probably a head taller than the driver. The tattooed man was wiry. But this wasn't about physical strength. If the threatening taunts didn't stop, it would be about who took the first shot.

She released Alejandro's hand and ran her fingers under his shirt tail. His muscles were taut as she removed the small gun from its holster. She continued to peer over his shoulder, and he leaned his head toward hers. Hopefully, the two men took it as an intimate gesture. Alejandro's lips never seemed to move as he said, "Not yet."

Neither man noticed anything. The driver was too busy talking. Strutting as he spoke and playing the tough guy. The more worrisome thing was what the bald guy was doing. He kept his hands low and out of sight. It couldn't be good. But shouldn't Alejandro anticipate it? This was his world.

In the distance, an engine backfired. Moments later, a truck crested the hill, barreling toward them. Its slatted wooden sides swayed noisily with every bump, catching the attention of the two men.

"Now," Alejandro whispered. "Just hang on to it. Only use it if I tell you."

It was a small thirty-eight. A few weeks ago, this would have been a disaster, but thanks to Harvey she possessed some degree of confidence. He hadn't mentioned the safety, but she could see that it was on. She tucked the gun in her front pocket and kept a hand on it.

The bald man's head whipped around at the sound of the truck. His eyes narrowed, and he turned back to Alejandro, mouthing off angrily.

All the gun knowledge in the world didn't make up for her inability to understand what was being said.

Alejandro's voice was calm as he responded to the bald man. He tilted his head back toward hers. Another fake demonstration of affection for their benefit. She played along, resting against him with an arm about his waist.

The car, with its doors open, was blocking the oncoming lane. The truck horn bellowed.

"Juan," Alejandro shouted, then waved. He started toward the middle of the road, dragging her along. It took her a moment to understand that he planned to stop the truck. He released his grip on her hand. Waving both arms back and forth, he planted himself in front of the approaching truck. He rattled off something in Spanish, and she nodded, pretending to understand. Together they waved frantically. The driver would have no choice but to stop. Alejandro called out again. "Juan!" Eventually, the lumbering truck came to a noisy halt. Alejandro pulled her toward the passenger side.

The elderly truck driver frowned at the two in confusion. He shook his head. "No."

"Point the gun at him," Alejandro said. She glanced at him in disbelief. "Now! And don't let those two see you." Alejandro slid a hundred-dollar bill toward the man.

She did as she was told, though the way the gun wavered in her hand, it didn't seem like much of a threat. Alejandro growled at the old guy in low tones, though for the benefit of the other two men, he maintained an expression of someone finding a long-lost friend.

The old man gripped the steering wheel with arthritic hands. His eyes were partially obscured by a straw cowboy hat worn low, but his mouth was a perfect line. No need to know Spanish to understand. *Too old for this.*

It was a crazy idea. But it might just work. Her eyes darted nervously from the old man to the other two men. The driver of the car began to swagger toward the truck. A bottle of beer dangled from his hand. She prayed he was too drunk or high to stop them.

But Alejandro didn't wait to find out. He began to push her up into the cab of the truck. "Get in." The old man banged his fist on the steering wheel, but with the gun still pointed at his chest, he had no choice but to let them in. With the stick shift on the floor, there was hardly enough room for the three of them. "*Vamonos*," Alejandro said. But she was in the way. The old man could hardly put the truck in gear. Alejandro pulled her into his lap in a not-so-gentle manner. She let out a small pained gasp.

There was no apology. His attention was focused on the situation ahead. The driver of the car now stood in the truck's path, and the old man was at a loss for what to do. Alejandro reached across and slammed on the horn.

"Can I take the gun off the old man now?" she whispered.

"Not yet. I need him to keep the truck moving."

The truck edged forward, gears grinding. Alejandro kept a hand planted firmly on the horn. The driver of the car stared at them, swaggering in defiance. Avery's fingers curled around the handle above the door. This couldn't really be happening. Alejandro yelled out the window. The man didn't budge, but merely held up his bottle in a mock toast.

"Stand up," Alejandro said to her, then raised himself through the open window. He perched on the door, attempting to wave the man away. Her eyes went to the tattooed man, who was now exiting the car.

"Alejandro!" She gestured frantically. The tattooed man was holding a gun, and it wasn't small.

Like a flash, Alejandro's hand was at his hip. In the next moment, he and the tattooed man leveled their guns at one another.

Avery whimpered. "No."

His gaze and gun fixed on the tattooed man, Alejandro sent a warning to the old man. The driver hunkered down, flattened himself against the seat, and murmured to himself.

"Floor. Now!" Alejandro said to Avery. "Take the gun off of him. But don't put it away just yet."

The tattooed man fired first. The bullet struck the driver's door with an explosive bang followed by a whizzing sound.

The old man yelled, and Avery shrieked. She clawed at the filthy floorboard. She covered her ears and tried to stifle her whimpering.

Alejandro fired back. From the floor of the truck, it was impossible to tell what was happening. He shot off more rounds. Each one sent racking pain through her body as she jerked in response. A shell casing bounced off of the seat, landing next to her. She attempted to make herself smaller, but it was impossible.

The truck backfired. The sound launched her off of the floor, sending her body into some kind of spasmodic tremor. If the bullets didn't kill her, this constant state of near heart attack would.

Her back was to the old man. Hopefully he was okay. The fact that they were moving was a good sign.

Finally, there was silence.

Alejandro remained outside the window for what seemed an eternity, then holstered his gun. He lowered himself into the seat and reached for her. "You okay?" he whispered, pulling her into his lap.

She buried her wet face in his shirt as he wrapped his arms about her.

"Maybe you should give me the gun back now."

She'd forgotten about it, though it was still in hand. Luckily, it was pointed at the floorboard. "You're speaking English," she whispered.

Alejandro glanced at the old man, who seemed oblivious. "It will be the least-memorable aspect of our encounter."

The truck began to gather speed. Alejandro stroked her back. She moved her head to his shoulder while he continued to hold her. The old man removed his hat and wiped the sweat from his forehead with the back of his hand, muttering to himself. Alejandro passed him another hundred.

"What just happened?" she finally asked.

Alejandro peered down at her as he spoke. "I winged the bald guy so he'd drop his gun. Then took care of their tires. That's it." He rested his cheek against the top of her head.

"No one's dead?"

"Nope. Those two gangbangers will live to see tomorrow."

She rubbed her forehead. How did anyone live like this? "They won't come after us?"

"No."

He turned and spoke to the old man.

"I hope you're apologizing."

"That's what the cash is for."

"There's a hole in your door," she said.

Alejandro fingered the bullet hole. His eyes followed the likely trajectory. "It went through the driver's door and must have passed right by you and into my door. Another inch or two and it probably would have hit me in the leg."

She closed her eyes. "I heard it." She shivered. A sound she hoped never to hear again.

He brushed a stray strand of hair from her face. "We'll be in town soon. Get some lunch, and you'll feel better."

It would take a hell of a lot more than food.

Chapter 29

He held her back from entering the small café. "You go to the bathroom. I'll order our food. If anyone talks to you, act like a bitch. Flip your hair. Look bored. Look away. Act mad at me. Keep your sunglasses on, and please don't attempt any Spanish."

She nodded and began to step away, and he grabbed her wrist. "And try to keep that tattoo covered."

Act like a bitch? She was drenched, thanks to a torrential downpour that had started the minute they were out of the truck. Difficult to pull off much of a superior attitude when one resembled a wet dog. She struggled to wring the water from her hair into the sink.

At least the old man had brought them to the edge of town. They wouldn't have arrived until dark, otherwise. An image of the other man's tattooed head flashed through her mind. If they'd arrived at all.

When she came back out, Alejandro had found a table in a breezy canopy-covered courtyard some distance from the few other patrons. To look at him, no one would believe he'd run through pouring rain to get here. He lifted his beer bottle. "I wasn't sure what you wanted to drink, so I ordered you a margarita. Thought you might need it."

She polished off two bottles of water before the waiter brought her margarita. The sight of the salted rim made her mouth water. If she stayed in this country much longer, she'd be an alcoholic.

She waited until the waiter walked away to speak. "This

is the town we could see in the distance yesterday, isn't it? The colorful one."

"Yes. It's Valerone. And don't say we should have stopped then."

"I wasn't going to. But what's after this?"

He reached for his phone. "Call the garage. See if they'll tow the Jeep before it's stolen. Then find a hotel."

She started to speak, but he held up a finger and began to talk on the phone. He clicked it off and set it aside. "I've got someone willing to go out there, but we'll have to go along." He toyed with his silverware. "Unless I leave you here in a hotel."

It surprised her that he'd even consider it. His tension seemed to be fading. But the real question was, could she handle a hotel room alone for a couple of hours? "And if I go with you?"

"We better hope the tow truck doesn't break down." He shook his head. "We still have a four-hour drive tomorrow when the Jeep's fixed. You might want to avoid a few hours of driving." He switched to Spanish as the waiter set their food on the table, pretending to argue with her.

Once the waiter was out of hearing range again, she said, "Just out of curiosity, what did you say to me in Spanish?"

The edge of his lip curled devilishly. He shook his head. "You don't want to know."

"Oh, but I think I do. I saw the way that waiter looked at you."

"Yeah, and what way was that?"

"Like he felt sorry for you."

He grinned. "A nap might be a good thing after the day you've had."

"Evasion. Just change the subject and think I'm too stupid to notice." She licked the salt from her upper lip. "But you're right. After this morning, I have a pretty good idea of what's out there."

"Today was nothing. Those guys were just locals looking to cause trouble. If anyone going for Javier's reward money happens to find you, you'll learn how bad it can be."

~ ~ ~

In a town where vibrant buildings lined curved cobblestone streets, Alejandro managed to find a hotel that was easily the worst-looking place in town. No arched doorways leading to spiral staircases or wrought iron gates draped in bougainvillea. It was the only brown flat-roofed building for miles. The windows were orange-mirrored glass, as if someone had swiped a few panes from a 1970s office building, and the odor of stale cigarette smoke spilled out onto the street. Anyone who could afford to pass out hundred-dollar bills like they were nothing didn't need to stay in a place like this.

"You're kidding, right?" She'd said it under her breath, though maybe a part of her wanted him to hear.

"Keep your sunglasses on," he said with a hiss. "Remember to act mad at me."

It shouldn't be difficult. This was a dump of a hotel. Dirty and dark. Would a decent hotel room honestly pose a danger?

The lobby, if one could call it that, was empty. The only sign of activity came from a black-and-white TV emitting little but static. A heavy-set woman lumbered out from a back room. Alejandro spoke in Spanish, asking for someone named Victor. The request irritated the woman. She stuck her head through the open door and called out.

Victor seemed shocked to find Alejandro in his lobby. He bounced excitedly as he spoke, in no apparent hurry to show them to a room. Avery was feeling the weight of the margarita and the day's hike bearing down on her. She made an impatient huff. He'd said to act like a bitch, hadn't he?

Alejandro rolled his eyes, and the man nodded, grabbing a key from a row of hooks. "*El mejor.*"

It was her turn to roll her eyes. She knew the man was suggesting it was his best room. Alejandro nudged her and discreetly shook his head.

Victor led them up a narrow set of stairs to a room bearing the number two. Fortunately, her sunglasses allowed her to avoid making eye contact with Victor as he proudly extended an arm into the bedroom.

Gaudy was the second thing that came to mind. First was *no way*. No way was she spending a night in this room. Her skin itched just looking at it.

She shot Alejandro a dirty look in the mirror headboard designed to resemble a Mayan temple. The base of the temple was a collection of greasy imprints from the heads of previous guests. The mattress slumped woefully in the middle. Any more sag and the thing could be mistaken for a canoe. Even all the small-town motels that she'd stayed in for work couldn't hold a candle to this place.

Alejandro and Victor talked loudly and laughed as she stewed. Finally, Alejandro slapped Victor on the back and shut the door behind him.

Defensively, he held up two hands as he turned to her. "Look, before you say anything, I need to explain." He sank to the bed, and she hoped the whole thing would curl up and swallow him. "People know me in this town. If I parade someone like you into a nice hotel, word will eventually get around."

"Someone like me?" She spit the words as if they were shards of glass.

"Come on, Avery. You know what I mean. Men notice you. Not just men. *People* notice you."

"Because I'm an American?"

"Yes. Because you're a *gabacha.*" His voice was low,

his tone patronizing. "And don't be coy. It's not just that. You're beautiful, and I'm surely not the first to tell you that."

"I look like a witch!"

He shook his head, then glanced at his watch. "I've known Victor nearly my whole life. He's trustworthy. And you'll be safe here. Safer than anywhere else. Okay?" He tilted his head, waiting for her response.

"How long will you be gone?"

"Two to three hours."

She didn't address the fact that there was only one bed. That discussion could wait.

"I have a friend who owns the garage. He promises me he'll look at the Jeep as soon as we get it there. There's a chance we could even get out of here tonight."

"Maybe I should go with you." She sank onto the foot of the bed, not looking at him. "What happens if . . ." She couldn't verbalize it.

He slid closer to her. "Nothing's going to happen." He turned her face toward his, holding her chin. "That is what you were going to say, isn't it?"

"Yes." But it was more than that, and she didn't know how to tell him. What would she say? *I'm afraid of being alone?*

"I'm coming back." He studied her face. "And think about it. It's your choice to lock the door from the inside. No one's locking you in."

She crossed her arms, feeling suddenly exposed. How did he know?

Alejandro continued in a pacifying tone. "Worst case is like I said: the tow truck breaks down. If you start to get worried, go find Victor. He'll know what's going on. He's a good guy. Here's some cash if you get hungry." He handed her a hundred-dollar bill and rose to his feet. "Sorry, it's all I have. You know, on second thought, you'll definitely want to keep the door locked." His smile was sardonic. "It will keep Victor's mother out."

As he started to leave, her voice took on a more panicked tone. "When will you be back?"

"Before dinner."

She clawed the mattress as the door shut. There was no reason to be paranoid. It was completely illogical. She'd existed in the brothel for weeks without as much trepidation as she felt at this moment.

Against her better judgment, she pulled back the bedspread and climbed under the covers. A shower could wait. Clenching the money in her fist, she closed her eyes, wishing the next few hours would fly by.

~ ~ ~

She ran a comb through her wet hair. The nap and shower had left her feeling a thousand times better. The damp towel smelled faintly sour, but she wasn't quite ready to step back into her dirty clothes.

The room had grown dark, and the sounds of raised voices mixed with traffic floated in through the open window. A chorus of barking erupted in the distance. Still wrapped in the towel, she moved to the window and edged back the panel of dusty fabric serving as a curtain. She gazed down at the restaurant across the street. Chairs clustered around small tables dotted the sidewalk. Her stomach growled at the thought of dinner.

Her thoughts of dinner came to an abrupt halt at the sound of that rare but familiar laugh. Alejandro. She shoved the makeshift curtain aside further. An awning partially obstructed her view of the restaurant, and there were no street lamps. It was impossible to single him out. She watched for several minutes, hoping to hear his voice once more.

She felt a small pang of envy. Relaxed, laughing and drinking. Surrounded by people. But even in the best of times, that was rarely her life.

The soft knock at the door brought her out of her self-pity. The knob turned before she could reply.

"Avery?" It was a whisper. She pulled the towel tight and moved to the darkest corner. Just as she began to speak, he flipped the light switch, illuminating the room with a single low-wattage bulb hanging from the ceiling.

"Over here."

"Oh, sorry." He turned away, but not before taking in the sight of her in the unusually small towel. "Um," he started, then cleared his throat. "I've got your clothes. I'll set them down here by the door. There's dinner for you, too. I'll be in the hall. Just yell when you're dressed."

She moved toward him. "It's all right." She put a hand on his arm, then took the trash bag from his hand. She paused and smiled up at his face, lingering just a moment longer than necessary. "I'll just be a second."

She banked herself against the bathroom door and took a deep breath. What the hell had she just done? He'd made his feelings clear last night. She couldn't explain what made her act like she did around him. Loneliness, maybe. Whatever it was needed to stop. When she got home, she'd make an effort to meet someone. Make her mother happy. Maybe even succeed in making herself happy. In the meantime, she needed to stop with him.

She opened the door and took a deep breath. His back was to her. Casually leaning against the wall, watching the street below. He'd switched on a bedside lamp and turned off the awful overhead light. Only his silhouette was visible.

"I saw you at the window earlier. From the street," he said.

"You should have stayed. With your friends, I mean." The knot in her belly hardened at this pretense.

He waved a hand dismissively. "My friend, the mechanic, wanted me to have a drink with some of our old friends. But that kind of thing usually leads to too many questions."

"What do you mean?" She glanced at the plate he'd placed on the bedside table. Her appetite had vanished.

"Not about you." He avoided her gaze. "They want to know why I'd be crazy enough to work for Diego Ramos."

"Did you live here? When you were a kid, I mean," she said.

"No." He continued to stare at the street below. "I grew up in Austin. That's not common knowledge, by the way. Just my close friends around here know. Kind of like my command of the English language."

"What about your family?"

He shrugged. "I was raised by my aunt and uncle. Pretty much from day one. I have two younger cousins that are like sisters to me. My uncle is an attorney, and my aunt hates what I do for a living. She worries. I don't see them very often. But if you're wondering about my connection to Valerone, my grandmother lived here. I spent every summer here till college."

"I see. You were a good kid. Not someone who would work for a cartel. And your friends can't figure it out."

"It's worse than that." He ran a hand through his hair. "You know about the General?"

"Yes." She sank slowly onto the foot of the bed. "He might have won the Nobel Peace Prize if he'd lived long enough. At least that's what the press thought," she mumbled.

Something darkened in Alejandro's expression. "Did you know that Diego Ramos killed him?"

"Harvey said no one knew who killed him."

"She knows perfectly well who killed him."

This had to be what Harvey was taking about: Alejandro's obsession with revenge. She held her head in her hands. But Harvey might have mentioned that his mission was to avenge a national hero.

"Everyone knows Diego killed the General and got away with it. And yet I work for him. It's amazing any of my old friends can even stand to be around me. It's why I didn't want to come here. Even driving through . . ." His voice trailed off.

"Harvey warned me about revenge."

"Yeah, Harvey." He leaned against the wall, closing his eyes. "We have a long and very complicated relationship. Harvey was his mistress, not his wife. In a Catholic family, that's not such a great thing. A lot of demons to contend with between Harvey and me." He rubbed his eyes with a groan. "Enough of this." He glanced at her untouched plate. "Not hungry?"

As tragic as it had been at the time, General Salazar had been dead for twenty years. Why was Alejandro risking his life to avenge the death of someone long dead? And who cared if Harvey was his mistress? Alejandro had immersed himself within a cartel. That alone meant he should see his share of needless murders. Women and children caught in the crossfire. Why make the death of the General his crusade?

"Avery?" His voice brought her back. "Are you okay?"

She paused. "No, I'm not. I don't understand. Why this single event in a long string of violence and corruption? Why are you letting the death of one single man govern your life?"

His face lost its color, his amber eyes large like that of a child. His answer was slow to arrive. "I was there that day. The General was about to give a speech. The crowd was large, noisy, chaotic. Diego Ramos was his security advisor." He turned away, back toward the window. "It was the perfect setup. The few witnesses that actually saw what happened eventually disappeared or changed their stories."

"How old were you?"

"Ten."

"And someone protected you. Kept you safe from the Ramos family."

"Yes. Harvey." He stood and moved to the window. There was tension in his stance. "I'm not sure why I told you any of this. But I prefer to drop the subject. Do you mind if we get some fresh air?"

"Of course not. But I thought you were afraid I might be recognized."

"I think you're safe enough at night. Plus, my friends know I'm traveling with someone."

Alejandro led her along the curving streets of downtown Valerone, saying something about the history of the town. She couldn't listen. Her mind raced, while her body felt numb. There was something about the General's death he wasn't telling her.

"Tell me about your family," he finally said. She could feel his eyes on her. Searching for something to bring her back into the conversation.

She shrugged. "There's not much to tell. I'm an only child. I lost my dad to cancer four years ago. It's the reason I worry about my mom. Without me, she's all alone."

"Hopefully she won't have to wait too much longer." He sighed heavily. "What made you become an engineer?"

"My dad. Sometimes he took me out to rigs by helicopter. I thought it was great. But he wasn't thrilled when I decided to follow in his footsteps."

"Really? Why not?"

She struggled with the words. "He didn't think I'd be accepted in the business because I was female." Her gut tightened at the memory of father's reaction to her career choice. "That's not exactly accurate. *He* didn't believe women were capable."

"But you've proved him wrong."

"No." She sighed. "I'm here talking to you right now because I'm a woman. I've spent the last four years trying to prove him wrong. Sacrificed everything. I agreed to go to Zapata because I thought it would mean a promotion. I was working twice as hard as anyone else at my level, and it didn't matter. I wasn't ever going to get that promotion."

The parallels between them brought her to a halt. Their obsessions were different, but so clearly alike. Unattainable goals.

"You don't know that you weren't going to get a promotion," he said.

She gazed up at him. "I've had nothing but time in these last few weeks to think about it. And I do know it. It's amazing what you find when you step away and take a look at your decisions. People always say life is short. But I never appreciated it until I thought I might die in that brothel."

He shrugged. "So, you had a bad boss. And maybe you were slow to realize it. We've all been there. It doesn't mean you should give up if engineering is something you love." The rain had started again. In a matter of seconds, it went from a random raindrop to a blinding downpour. He tugged at her arm. "Can you run?"

The pain in her side was diminishing every day. But running was still a struggle. "Not fast."

They were both drenched when they reached the room. "Mind if I grab a shower?" he asked. She was already running the damp towel through her hair.

"It's your room, too." It sounded strange, and it made the room seem even smaller. It left her unsure of how to occupy herself while he showered.

She combed out her hair and waited. For what, she didn't really understand. When he emerged from the bathroom, she was pacing nervously next to the bed.

A smile crept across his face. "Avery, don't worry. I'm planning on sleeping on the floor."

Her heart sank, while at the same time she breathed out an audible sigh of relief. "It's not necessary. I know you're not going to—"

"You don't know anything. In fact, you have no idea."

She wrung her hands. It was a gesture she associated with nervous old ladies, and yet she couldn't stop herself.

"It's okay." He patted the end of the bed. "Just sit down. You should eat."

She was slow to sit, and when she did, she carefully distanced herself. His phone buzzed, and a name she didn't recognize appeared across the screen. He practically launched himself across the bed to silence it.

"You can take that," she said.

"Later." He held the untouched plate out to her. "Eat."

She still wasn't hungry but didn't refuse. Maybe he'd explain a few things if he was a little less preoccupied. She took a small bite. "What happened to the girl?"

"The girl?" He frowned.

"The girl from the brothel. The one that went with Oso."

"He took her to his cousin's."

"And what will happen to her?" she asked. "Does Javier have a reward out for her, too?"

Alejandro shook his head. "I doubt it. The girl will probably end up doing the same thing somewhere else. Unless they can somehow keep her off the streets." He cocked his head in her direction. "Why are you asking about her now?"

"Because it's been on my mind a lot. Why do you think it will be difficult to keep her from returning to prostitution?"

"Because it's all she knows." He sighed. "Javier gets those girls when they're ten or twelve years old."

"*Gets those girls?* You make it sound like they're stray cats. You think kidnapping ten-year-olds is acceptable?"

"Of course not, but I'm not part of it. I work for his father. Not Javier."

She'd expected this to be his excuse, and it was the reason she'd raised the subject now. "And yet you're all about the PR. Does Diego have any daughters of his own?"

"Yes."

"And he knows about these places Javier has?"

"Avery, it's not that simple."

"It is. Why can't you people just be satisfied making your damn money off guns or drugs? Whatever it takes to make you ultra-wealthy." She flung her arms out. "But leave the children out of it." She angled away from him. "And don't say you're not part of it. By doing nothing, you're condoning it."

The muscles in his jaw flexed. He seemed to be considering how to defend himself. It was exactly what she wanted. Back him into a corner and force him to talk. To hear, out of his mouth, what his goal was in working for Diego Ramos.

He spoke slowly. "I have to choose my battles with the Ramos family carefully. You're right. Allowing Javier to kidnap children to staff his brothel shouldn't be tolerated. Is it enough for me to assure you that it won't always be that way?"

"How?"

"It just won't." His gaze was intense, unwavering. "You have to understand. There are things I just can't tell you." He drew closer. "But what I can tell you is that life is cheap in Mexico. It's what the General was trying to change. Children here leave school and enter the drug trade before they can read. Those guys we saw today . . ." He shook his head. "There's no legitimate work for them that pays. In a few weeks, they'll be running drugs for someone, if they're not already. And in a year or two, they'll be dead. Killed by a rival gang. Leaving behind widows, girlfriends, and fatherless kids. The cycle is short."

"So, Harvey's warning about your obsession with revenge . . ."

"She's wrong. It's not about revenge. It's about doing my part to change things in a country that I love."

She didn't doubt his passion. His face said it all. But she wasn't convinced that revenge didn't play a part. "And you believe that, working from within the Ramos cartel, you can do all that?"

"It's an oversimplification. But yes."

"Are you working alone?"

He responded with an unwavering gaze. She understood it. It was a warning to back off.

"I see." She leaned against the headboard. He couldn't undertake it alone. There had to be others. And what did that mean? That he was DEA or FBI? She drew the sheets up around her. She was shivering, though not cold.

He moved next to her. "Don't let your career become all you've got. Ditch that boss of yours and get a new job. Meet new people. Just take time to enjoy all that life has to offer."

She wanted to scream. Ask him if he could actually hear himself. What a hypocrite. She rubbed her face. "And while you're saving Mexico, I'll be out having cocktails with my new friends and feeling fulfilled?" She twisted the sheet in her hands. "Do I really appear to be that shallow? Do you think I can leave here, find new friends, get a new job, and remain unchanged by all of this?"

Lightly, he traced the outline of the *J-41*. She wanted him to stop, and at the same time, she hoped he never would.

His voice was quiet when he finally spoke. "I think you understand why I pushed you away last night. It can't work for us. I chose a path that puts those close to me in danger." He removed his hand from her arm. "In a few weeks you'll be home, and . . ." He tilted his head. "I'll be thinking about a night I spent with a girl under the desert stars. Wishing it could have ended differently."

Chapter 30

True to his word, he'd slept on the floor. She'd heard him get up, go into the bathroom to shower, and eventually leave the room. Sometime later, he'd returned with breakfast. All the while, she'd feigned sleep. Now he perched on the edge of the bed, cup of coffee in hand, and she couldn't pretend any longer.

"The thermostat for the Jeep is on back order. No word on when it will be here. But it doesn't matter anyway, because it seems my help is needed today," he said with a sigh. "Javier has information on a redhead he wants me to check out." The corner of his mouth curved up in irony. "A friend of mine is loaning me his motorcycle. Apparently, you've been spotted in a town about two hours from here."

She sat up and reached for her coffee. "Well then, you'd better track me down."

"Will you be okay?"

She nodded. "Is this town somewhere we've been?"

"No. It's on the coast. Barely more than a fishing village. It's a nice place. Under different circumstances, I'd be happy to take you."

"Does he know you've been here in Valerone?"

"No. He thinks I'm about two hours south of here. None of the Ramos family knows anything about my history with this town. And Valerone is hardly a destination. You should be perfectly safe here. Victor will bring you lunch and anything else you need. He's dug up a couple of books in English for you."

"Who does Victor think I am?"

"My American cousin. He believes you have some crazy ex-boyfriend that's got some gang connections. Your ex is supposedly pulling out all the stops to find you." He patted her leg, which was covered by the thin sheet. "You understand I have to go, don't you?"

"Sure," she said, trying her best to sound convincing, though the thought of spending the day alone in the room left her feeling tense. "I'll park myself in here and behave. When will you be back?"

"After dark sometime." He rose to his feet, glancing down at her with the same paternal-like fondness she'd experienced in the brothel. Now it made her want to run. "Victor has my number if you need me."

"One question on the cousin thing. He obviously knows we're sharing a room. Isn't that a little weird?"

"Yeah." He scratched his head. "I'll make it clear I'm sleeping on the floor. Maybe you could ask him to bring me a blanket, if you don't mind. It got cold down there last night."

And with that, he was gone. Her chest swelled, and she wrapped her arms about her waist. Not only would she spend the day alone in the room, but she'd been rejected. She hated it. Rejection was agonizing hell. It made legends out of poets and filled psychology textbooks. All she'd wanted was . . . but when she thought about it, she didn't know what she wanted. None of it made sense. There were so many reasons she shouldn't be attracted to him. Starting with the obvious fact that in a couple of weeks, she'd never see him again. But maybe that was a good thing.

Chapter 31

Alejandro hadn't hesitated when Javier called. The hotel room seemed to be growing smaller by the minute. This trip offered a way to kill a few hours by hanging out near the beach and looking for redheads. Plus, he could plant a few false leads of his own on the way down there. Send Javier's thugs scurrying to the border until he came up with another plan to get her home.

The sooner he could get her out of Mexico, the better. Last night had been hell. He'd sounded like a sanctimonious ass. Harvey's version of revenge was closer to the truth. His work was not altruistic, nor had he intended to clean up Javier's messes once he eliminated the Ramos cartel.

Until last night.

But now she'd left him with no choice. The Bureau wouldn't love it. He could only imagine what they'd say when he asked for help with Inez's girls. Didn't matter. He had to see it through. In so many words, he'd promised her. If he didn't take care of it, another gang would be running the whorehouse within weeks. God, how his father would have loved her.

He could manage her idealism. What he couldn't seem to control was what she did to him in other ways. The line he'd dumped on her about the night in the desert was as much for his own benefit as hers. Sleeping with her would be a mistake. But when he was in that room, he thought of little else. It was an issue he hadn't expected. Something he hadn't felt since adolescence. And even at fifteen, he'd had more control over his mind. Something was going to have to change.

~ ~ ~

The hotel bar wasn't much, but neither was the town. The bartender slid a Modelo Negra in his direction. Alejandro could feel the eyes on his back. This was Los Zetas territory. They tolerated the Ramos cartel the way a panther would put up with a house cat. In other words, he needed to find the redhead, or at least pretend to, and get the hell out of here.

A barstool scraped the concrete to his left. He kept his gaze fixed on the muddy beach beyond the bar. The air smelled of salt and the decay of last night's high tide. There was movement to his left. He knew without looking that there were now Zetas parked on either side of him. Probably no fewer than six firearms between the two.

He took a long swallow of beer. The bartender swiped at a glass with a towel. He'd been messing with the same glass ever since the two men had seated themselves at the bar. Alejandro considered his options. Option number one was chug his beer, leave, and hope they didn't follow him out. Option number two was chug his beer, order a second, and ask them about a redhead seen in the area.

"Give me another," he said to the bartender.

At least one of them probably knew of Javier's search and reward money. Amazing how word got around the cartels. If they ever got their hands on Avery, they'd try to extort more money from Javier, he'd refuse to pay, and the next day she'd be dead. Simple as that. Except the Zetas never just killed someone. Their murders were tortuous events ending with a display of their results made public for all to see.

He turned to the one at his right. A trail of tattooed teardrops ran from the corner of the man's left eye to his cheekbone. Prison tattoos. Each teardrop represented an intended kill or one he'd already carried out. Alejandro gripped his beer bottle with a little more force. At moments like this, he wondered why the hell he wasn't practicing corporate law in the U.S.

He pulled the photo from his pocket. It was the photo taken in the brothel, except it had been altered by one of the Bureau technicians. Her nose was slightly larger and her hairline different. Her eyebrows were heavier and severely arched, but the most significant alteration was to her cleavage, now enhanced to the point of distraction. It was hideous. She looked like a crazy porn star. The sight of it made him sick, but most of the gangbangers he knew would search far and wide for a woman like that.

He slid the photo toward the man. "You know what I'm looking for, don't you?"

The man remained impassive, his eyelids lowered. "Is that little prick Javier really going to pay for her?"

"Do you really think he's stupid enough to screw you over?" Alejandro asked.

The man to his left cleared his throat. "You got another one of those pictures?" His tongue was practically hanging out of his mouth.

Alejandro nodded and produced a stack. "Here's several. Pass them out to your friends." He took another swig of beer. "I heard she was here. But so far, I haven't seen her." He nodded at the warped image of Avery and laughed. "Be hard not to recognize her." The guy to his left guffawed, but the man with the teardrop tattoos maintained his silence. Alejandro slid his nearly full bottle toward the bartender, along with a stack of bills. "You know how to reach us if you find her."

He debated whether to head straight for the motorcycle. Hanging around would bring on more trouble. And the two at the bar could rally their men. But his search needed to be somewhat convincing.

He scanned the beach for redheads. No obvious tourists anywhere. From what he could tell, it was mainly locals. Kids digging in the sand, and a few teenagers clustered about.

And Zetas. Standing out like sore thumbs in their black t-shirts.

He sauntered back to the bike, acting as if he weren't feeling the Zetas' presence pulsing throughout every blood vessel in his body. He reached for the helmet just as a voice said, "Tell your little piece of shit friend he's—"

But Alejandro never heard the rest. Someone clipped him in the jaw with a right hook, immediately followed by a second to the right cheekbone, which sent him reeling. Somehow he managed to stay on his feet, though he was jumped from behind by another guy. He spun, forcing the attacker to release his hold, though it was meaningless. Six men now stood in a small semicircle around him, each of them holding a gun pointed in his direction.

The guy with the teardrop tattoos spoke. "You're not welcome here. I never want to see your pretty boy face again. I don't think it would make a very good football." There was laughter among the men. Alejandro's stomach lurched. His wouldn't be the first face removed by a Zeta's switchblade simply for the purpose of reconditioning a soccer ball. "Do you understand me?"

"Perfectly."

"If we find the girl, we decide whether we want his shit money or not. If any of you Ramos scum show up here again, it's war. And I think you're a little shorthanded." He laughed maniacally. "Now get the hell out before my boys decide to use you for target practice."

Alejandro didn't bother with the helmet. The rush of air cooled the physical sting of his beating. He gritted his teeth, trying to recall the last time he was sucker punched. It would be some time before his dignity was restored.

It was at least sixty miles beyond Zeta territory when he pulled over. He switched on the burner cell.

"Arturo here," the voice said.

"Any progress on the girl's travel plans?"

"Boss wants you to hold on."

"Why?" Alejandro asked.

"Politics. If anything happens to this girl and it gets out that we're involved . . . I don't need to tell you. Her mother's making lots of noise already. We need that twisted little maniac to give up his search."

"He's easily bored, but it still means at least a couple of weeks." *At best*, he thought with a sigh. "But you'll have her docs ready?"

"Already done, *amigo*."

"Any way you can get them to me?" There was hesitation in Arturo's silence. "I take that as a no."

"Sorry. The boss."

"Doesn't trust me, I guess. He really didn't want me involved in Javier's kidnapping mess to begin with." There was no comment from Arturo. "Any progress on the embassy rat?"

"Zero."

"Damn." If only he'd been able to catch a glimpse of the guy that day in Diego's office. But blowing his own cover would have undone more than two years' worth of work. "I went through the security footage from the meeting, but the guy knew what he was doing. Kept his head down at every camera location."

"Same with the audio. Dude didn't say much more than yes or no," Arturo said.

Alejandro glanced at his watch, then at the sun low on the horizon. "Better go."

"Yeah, man, stay in touch."

He dropped the burner in the dirt and dragged the bike over it a couple of times. He'd toss the bigger pieces along the highway to Valerone.

He switched to the company cell. Javier answered on the first ring. "Find her?"

"No. Just some Zetas who would prefer to kill us."

Javier made a dismissive sound. Easy for someone who never ventured into enemy territory to do. "Hope you told those assholes they better stay away from her. I don't pay reward money to scum."

"Yeah." Alejandro rubbed his forehead. "Who was your source?"

"My source?" Javier hesitated.

And for the second time that day, Alejandro realized he was becoming sloppy. There'd never been a redhead sighting. Javier had sent him down there deliberately.

"I think it was one of my guys," Javier said.

Liar. Alejandro banged his fist down on the bike. Not only had there been no redhead, but the Zetas had been expecting him. It was a setup meant to scare him.

Alejandro kept his tone even. "I'd like his name." Javier had played this game before. Whenever he believed Alejandro was attaining too much power within the organization, he backstabbed him with some juvenile stunt.

"I'll think of it. Got to go, man."

A thought struck him, sending a mixture of anger and terror coursing through his mind and body. What if Javier somehow knew he had Avery? Knew where they were? Got him out of the way, banking on the fact that he wouldn't bring Avery into Zeta territory?

It was irrational. There was no way. Javier couldn't track this phone. He'd bought it himself, deliberately refusing one from Diego that was certain to have a tracker installed to monitor his every move.

His heart raced. He couldn't take any chances. He gripped the bike handles. If only the Bureau would give him the go-ahead to kill that little bastard.

Chapter 32

Alejandro crashed through the door, launching Victor off of the end of the bed and causing Avery to have a near heart attack.

"What the hell, dude?" Victor demanded.

Alejandro's eyes swept over the room, finally resting on the bottle of tequila she and Victor were sharing.

She frowned. "What's wrong?"

He shook his head and stepped out in the hallway. Victor took it as signal to follow. "He no look happy."

Alejandro's voice bellowed out from the hallway. "And bring the bottle with you."

~ ~ ~

It was more than an hour before Alejandro returned. When he finally made his entrance, the bottle in his hand was nearly empty, and he paced nonstop, keeping his face turned away at an odd angle.

"Is something wrong?"

"What'd you do all day?"

Something in his voice was off. She tried to catch his eye, but he seemed to be somewhere else. "Laundry. Hung out with Victor and learned some Spanish, too."

"Let me hear it," he said, finishing off the tequila.

"*Lo siento Fernando, pero el bebé no es tuyo. Gloria tiene un tumor cerebral y sólo siete días de vida.*"

He snorted. "First of all, I see your cheat sheet. If you want to be convincing, you need to memorize it. And how exactly did you learn that the baby is not Fernando's, and

Gloria's brain tumor will leave her dead in seven days?" He held out a hand to stop her. "No, let me guess. Telenovelas?"

"Yeah. If Harvey had a TV, I'd be fluent by now. Victor says it's how he learned English. Watching the American soaps. And by the way, you neglected to tell me that my name is Constanza. I didn't know what he was talking about when he first came in here."

"Sorry. It was the first name that came to mind."

"Constanza? Really? It doesn't exactly roll off the tongue. It's awful. And it sounds like someone's great aunt." She rose from the end of the bed. "Is that what I seem like to you?"

Alejandro's laugh was followed by a wince. "You're anything but." He stopped his pacing to stand directly in front of her. His eyes held a devilish gleam she'd never seen before.

"What have you done?" She reached out to touch his face.

"It's nothing. Just a small collision with a fist."

"Your cheek is swollen." Her fingertips danced lightly over the spot. "It needs ice." His eyes lingered on hers, and neither of them seemed compelled to move. She struggled to breathe. "I'll be right back."

"No." He put a hand on her wrist. "I'll get it."

"It's okay. Victor showed me where the back stairs are. They lead directly into the kitchen. If you're hungry, I can get something to eat as well."

He hesitated before releasing her. "You'll come straight back?"

"Well, I'm not hanging out with Victor's mother, if that's what you're asking. The old lady doesn't like me."

"Yeah," he said, running a hand through his hair. "You're not alone."

~ ~ ~

He'd had a shower by the time she returned. Moisture hung in the air, and the room smelled of soap. She barely touched the ice pack to his face, though it might as well have been a torch, the way he reacted.

His voice was gruff. "Give it to me. I'll do it myself."

She retreated. "This room is so small, you have to either eat at the bathroom counter or in bed." It was nervous chatter, but she couldn't stop herself. "A chair would be great."

Lost in his own world and edgy, he said nothing. The empty tequila bottle stood next to an open wine bottle. She stared open-mouthed. Anyone else would have passed out by now.

"What happened today?" she asked.

"Javier made sure I was acquainted with some rival cartel members."

"He set you up?" She covered her mouth. "Why?"

He shrugged. "Because it's what he does." He reached for the wine bottle.

Evasiveness. It ran through his veins. To learn anything, she'd need to be a lot less direct. He turned his attention to the wine, filling his glass to the rim. She put a hand on his arm. "Eat. Then we can go for a walk."

He stared at her. Something was amiss. It was as if pessimism had displaced his usual self-assurance.

He shoved aside the untouched plate. "Not hungry."

"Then we have to get out of here. Let's go for a walk."

~ ~ ~

The sidewalks were busier than the previous night. Music played in the distance.

"Do you know what's going on? Where's the music's coming from?"

"Live music on the square." His words ran together in a slight slur. "I forgot about it."

The streets grew more crowded as they drew closer to the town square. He reached for her hand. Sounds of brass and guitars echoed off the surrounding buildings.

"Maybe we should get back to the hotel. This probably isn't a very good idea," she said, though the thought of being cooped up in there and watching him drink himself into oblivion held no appeal.

He seemed not to hear her. His attention was elsewhere. "No," he said with a groan.

"What?" But by the time she understood his reaction, it was too late. They were engulfed by a small group of people.

"Alejandro," someone said.

He was quick to drop her hand. He answered in Spanish. She let out a small sigh of relief. Obviously, these were his childhood friends.

They were friendly, smiling at her occasionally, though no one really attempted to speak to her. Alejandro was the center of their attention. He'd say something, and they'd laugh. His melancholy was gone, and she'd been forgotten.

There were only two women. The shorter of the two hung on the arm of one of the men, periodically grinning at Avery. The other woman had eyes for one thing only.

Alejandro.

There was no denying she was beautiful. Long black hair framed her doll-like face. Her short red dress flared at her hips like a skater's outfit, emphasizing every curve as her long brown legs moved to the beat. She was impossible to ignore, and Avery felt herself oddly drawn in. The music stopped, and the woman reached for Alejandro's arm, swung herself around, and effectively shoved Avery aside. Alejandro did nothing to stop it.

Avery crossed her arms, trying to control her irritation. He was drunk, she reminded herself.

As the music resumed, the subtle movement of the

woman's hips expanded the distance between Avery and Alejandro. Her moves became more exaggerated, and it was tempting to nudge her away. A little shove would be more satisfying. The woman's gyrating body blocked her view of Alejandro, and Avery needed to see his face.

As the crowds grew, their little group morphed into a tighter cluster. Now completely displaced, Avery could finally see him. His eyes were downcast, making it impossible to read his reaction. The woman ran a hand along the length of his arm, eventually entwining her fingers with his while her hips continued to move. He shook his head. One of his friends shoved him in the direction of her gyrations. The others clapped and chided. Avery stomped. It was probably a good thing no one noticed. Alejandro continued to shake his head in refusal. But his friends didn't give up. Their game continued until, finally, his eyes went to Avery.

Was he seeking her permission to dance? Exactly what did he expect her to do? Insert herself and tell this girl no? Avery clenched her fists. Any move she made could shift the focus on her. Minus the tequila, this would occur to him. Part of her wanted to go stomp on his foot. Leave him too crippled to dance. They needed to get out of here, and the last thing she wanted to do was stand here and watch. But as his cousin, Constanza, she had no choice.

The woman tugged on his hand and tilted her face upward. She reached for his other hand and backed her way toward the dancing crowd. All of this while wearing six-inch stilettos. Avery felt herself hissing at the sight of it.

One of Alejandro's friends shouted in her ear. "Watch them. They're beautiful together. Your cousin's an excellent dancer."

"Yeah," she said. "But he's pretty drunk." Maybe drunk enough to wipe out. She laughed silently.

She crossed her arms. Every fiber in her body itched to

leave. But he'd left her no choice. She had to stand here like some bimbo and act like she was having the time of her life.

It was a salsa. The woman's feet moved quickly, and her timing was perfect. Despite having consumed half a bottle of wine and even more tequila, Alejandro danced with easy grace. Surprising in someone so tall, but Avery could see this was not their first time together. Every move was polished, and seemingly second nature. Their bodies moved in rhythmic unison. The perfection of it only made her angrier.

"He doesn't look drunk," the man said.

"No." It would be a lot easier if he did. The woman heaved against him. Avery resisted the urge to turn away.

Their circle of onlookers grew. Alejandro's friend leaned toward her again. "It's always this way with these two." The crowd began to chant.

"What are they saying?" She practically had to scream to be heard.

"The people. They love them. They're asking the musicians for a tango."

Dancing had never been Avery's thing, but she knew the tango was considered the most sensual dance out there. As if anything could go beyond what she'd already seen. Gradually, the music drifted into something different.

Eyes closed, the woman threw her arms into the air and, with a dramatic turn of her head, ran her hands sensually along the length of her body while circling Alejandro. She stomped, assumed a domineering stance, and beckoned him with her index finger. He stalked her, and the two began to circle one another. Their expressions were fiery, as if there existed an invisible current passing between them. She rested a hand on Alejandro's chest.

The move seemed to initiate the actual dance. Their arms linked, and the woman's leg somehow wrapped itself around his waist. She ran a hand along the back of Alejandro's neck and pressed herself against him. The move sent her sliding down Alejandro's hips in a fashion so graphic, it left little to the imagination.

Blood pounded in Avery's temples. Enough was enough. She scanned the square for a restaurant or bar. Anything would do.

The man tapped her. "Would you like a drink?"

She turned to him. "Yes."

He nodded. "One minute. I'll let them know where we're going."

It was tempting to tell him not to bother. Alejandro could damn well hunt her down on his own.

~ ~ ~

The place was a short walk across the plaza. It was dark and virtually empty; the only clientele were a few older men slumped at the bar. She waited as Alejandro's friend ordered beers. Probably a good thing. If left up to her, they'd be doing tequila shots.

He led the way to a dark corner with a nearly hidden table for two. She hesitated. There were other empty tables where others could join them, but whatever.

She climbed onto the barstool and held up her beer. "¡Salud!" A toast Harvey sometimes recited before drinking tequila. It was the first moment she'd really taken the time to see the man before her, and what she saw surprised her. At first glance, it was his perfectly tousled shoulder-length hair that caught her attention. Definitely sexy. But it was his gaze that held her. Soulful, and yet edged with just that tinge of devil that was like a magnet for women who knew better.

"¡Salud!" he said with a grin. "You are Constanza?"

She nodded, nearly choking on her beer. Thank God she hadn't tried to introduce herself—she'd have never remembered that stupid name.

"I am José."

"Nice to meet you, José. I appreciate the beer. I was really thirsty."

"Alejandro never brought any of his cousins here before. You are from where?"

"Texas." A lie. She surprised herself with the ease of it.

"And you are staying in Valerone how long?" he asked.

"Just long enough to get the car repaired. I'm headed home after that."

"Back to Mexico City, then to take the plane?"

She nodded, though who knew what Alejandro's intentions were. He'd probably find some other place where he could abandon her for weeks on end.

José's eyes rested on her mouth. Something flickered in his gaze. It took her a second before she realized that it was not her mouth he was watching, but the exposed tattoo. Crap. Casually, she moved her hands out of sight and yanked on her sleeve. Damn Javier. She'd been so careful up till now. Hopefully, tattooing prostitutes wasn't common practice around here. She'd just assumed it was Javier's thing. But if this assumption was wrong . . . she had a problem. Anyway, there was nothing she could do about it for the moment.

"Angelica and Alejandro. They are beautiful dancers, yes?"

Angelica. If the name implied angel, it didn't apply to dancing. Forcing a smile, she spoke through gritted teeth, "Yes. Beautiful." The words burned as they passed her lips.

"You don't like her."

Avery shrugged. "I have no reason to dislike her. I don't know her. Have they been dancing together for a long time?"

He gave a low laugh, and she didn't like the sound of it. "Yes." He shook his head. "As much as he tries to stay away, it never really works. She always wants him back."

What exactly did that mean? Did she always get him back?

He stroked his chin. "But I'm surprised you don't know this. Since you are his cousin."

"Alejandro has never mentioned her." She came off sounding jealous, and from the look on his face José had picked up on it. She waved a hand dismissively. "How often do you discuss women with your cousins?"

His eyes gleamed. "Never."

"Are the rest of your friends coming over here?"

He shrugged. "I told them where we are. But Angelica can dance for hours. Especially with him. And everyone loves to watch."

She was done talking about Alejandro and dancing. "So tell me about yourself. What do you do? I assume you live in Valerone."

"Yes. I'm an artist," he said.

She might have guessed it. "Painter, sculptor?"

"Muralist." He toyed with his empty bottle, his eyes lingering on her a moment longer than necessary. All part of his game.

"I'd offer to buy the next round of beers, but I'm afraid I didn't plan on coming to a bar and didn't bring any money. I guess my dearest, sweet cousin should have told me what his intentions were." Alejandro's money was stuffed in her pocket, but a large bill could bring on unwanted attention in a place like this.

"Not to worry. I refuse to let you pay." He held up two fingers for the bartender.

"Are there places I might see your work? In the daylight," she was quick to add.

"Yes. Just off the square. Two blocks from here." He tapped his chin, studying her. "Have you ever been a model for an artist?"

"No," she said. At home such a question probably would have sent her scrambling for another table or another bar.

But tonight, it made her want to laugh. With his well-honed, ardent gaze, he was almost convincing. How often did women fall for this?

"The bones in your face are perfect. Your eyes are lovely, too. Though I think, if you don't mind me asking—is your hair . . . ?"

"It's a little darker than normal."

"Would you consider letting me paint you?"

The absurdity of it made her want to roll her eyes. "I'm afraid I won't be here long enough for that."

"Even a quick sketch of your face would help me remember."

"I don't know if Alejandro told you or not, but I have an ex-boyfriend trying to find me. He has some violent tendencies. I mean I'm flattered, but it's probably not a good idea."

But José wasn't listening. He'd already started a rough sketch on a bar napkin.

She reached for her second beer just as a large hand enclosed hers. Alejandro smiled down at her. "You don't mind sharing, do you?"

She withdrew her hand. The weight of his body resting against her back felt a little too familiar for a cousin.

"José, how you doing, man?" Alejandro asked.

José responded in Spanish, barely bothering to glance up from his drawing. If Alejandro realized what the man was doing, he didn't react.

Alejandro placed possessive hands on her shoulders. "We should get back to the hotel." The vibration of his voice against her ear sent a tingle down her spine. She arched in response. His satisfied grin was diabolic.

José's focus shifted to Alejandro's hands and then to his face. Neither man seemed happy at the sight of the other. In fact, José looked ready to choke the life out of Alejandro.

She climbed off the barstool and bent toward José. "Thank you, José. It was nice talking to you. My cousin owes you some beer. Make sure he pays his debt."

~ ~ ~

Alejandro slung a heavy arm over her shoulder, obviously still drunk. "Are you not speaking to me?"

"It's Constanza. Remember? And maybe you should turn the volume down a little when you speak English." She swung to the left, freeing herself.

"You're mad at me, aren't you? It's because I left you alone, isn't it?"

How did someone so intelligent become so stupid when drunk? As she started forward, Alejandro grabbed her arm and said, "Stop." The alcohol didn't leave him weak.

Fortunately, the music still playing in the plaza drowned out their words. "What do you want?" She yanked her arm away.

"I want to know why you're so angry."

"You lock me up in a hotel room all day, then return acting all weird with a messed up face and won't tell me what's going on. Now you're drunk, and you ditched me out on that square to dance with that—" She straightened her shoulders, regretting opening her mouth. Once again, sober Alejandro wouldn't have had to ask.

"You're jealous?" he asked. He smiled like a child at Christmas.

"Please just stop. Leave me alone." She pulled away from him. "I just want to go back to the hotel." But before she could move, he wrapped his arms around her.

He kissed her with a forcefulness she hadn't anticipated. There was nothing sloppy about it. In the desert he'd been so gentle. But she recognized tonight's desperation. It was there when they were together in that tiny little hotel room.

Everywhere. The intensity of it escalating by the second. Given enough to drink, she might have done the same thing.

She gave into him, allowing the worst of the night to be forgotten. For the moment, anyway. He squeezed her tight, and she clung to him.

"God," he murmured. His hands meandered up the back of her shirt. "You don't know what you do to me."

She drew back. How different would things be if he were sober? His eyelids were heavy.

"Avery."

She didn't correct him. Constanza was hardly the name she wished to hear him call out in the throes of passion, but his repeated carelessness was a problem.

"Let's go back to the hotel," she said.

He held her face in his hands, beaming. "Really?"

Part of her wanted to laugh. He was so eager. She hadn't even considered the insinuation of her request, she just wanted him to stop talking. She kissed him lightly.

A female voice shrieked in Spanish. From somewhere in the shadows came a flash of red. Angelica. Sobbing and hurling herself against Alejandro. Avery backed away.

His voice was soothing. He took Angelica's hands in his. Avery understood nothing but the word *no*, which Alejandro seemed compelled to repeat a thousand times. Angelica's sobs were punctuated by more angry Spanish. Nothing seemed to stop it.

Avery rolled her eyes. "Really?" More than enough drama here for a telenovela. Her own role seemed to have become undefined once more, and the hotel was within sight. It was beyond stupid to stand here, since neither of them seemed to remember she was only feet away.

She paused to watch the two for a moment. The ridiculousness of the situation eradicated much of her anger. She wanted sober Alejandro. Not the man who allowed himself to become embroiled in this drama.

Angelica continued to batter him with words and fists. Claw marks lined his cheek. The woman made a hissing sound in Avery's direction.

"Alejandro, I'm out of here." She was tempted to add that she hoped Angelica had had all her shots.

"Avery."

He needed to stop calling out her name. It was just another reason to leave. "Constanza," she said, and took off in the direction of the hotel.

~ ~ ~

She stared at herself in the mirror as she brushed her teeth. The more she thought about it, the more she realized that Angelica had just done her a big favor. She spat into the sink and reached for a bottle of water. If there was one thing she was missing, it was that fiery Latino passion. Not a single strand of her DNA, contributed by a long lineage of stiff British ancestors, possessed any of it. Maybe a little more of it might have helped her past relationships or made her a better dancer. But what she'd witnessed tonight was . . . too much.

She drew back the covers and glanced at the door. It was fine with her if he found somewhere else to sleep. The fact that she was alone wouldn't even bother her tonight.

~ ~ ~

It was just after two a.m. when she glanced at the clock. Light from the street filled the room. No one had bothered to close the shades last night. She frowned at the heavy lump at the foot of the bed. Alejandro. Probably too drunk to remember he was supposed to be sleeping on the floor.

The room was cold, and he was wearing nothing but a t-shirt and boxers. Part of her was tempted to let him freeze or shove him off the bed with her foot. But she'd never seen a grown man curled up that way. Like an infant. If their roles were reversed, he'd never do that to her.

She nudged his shoulder. "Alejandro. Wake up." Under normal circumstances, that would have probably launched him out of bed and reaching for his gun. But he just groaned. "Move up here. Under the covers." It felt as though she were speaking to a six-year-old. "You don't need to freeze."

His movement was sluggish. He cocooned himself in the sheets with only muffled thanks. She turned her back to him, facing the wall and drawing the covers over her bare shoulder. Just knowing he was inches away left her incapable of moving. Barely breathing. She couldn't risk waking him.

The tension left her rigid and made sleep a struggle. Glowing green, the ancient clock radio became impossible to ignore. Time passed in fifteen-minute intervals. Two-thirty. Two-forty-five.

More than an hour passed, and it was after the slightest move of her hand that he spoke. "Avery, I'm sorry." His words were so faint, she wondered if she'd really heard him. His warm breath against her shoulder told her it wasn't her imagination.

She rolled over onto her back. His eyes were closed.

"The wine was a mistake," he said.

"And the tequila wasn't?"

"No. I needed that to calm down." Though his eyes remained closed, the corner of his mouth turned up.

"That girlfriend of yours isn't going to come slit my throat in the middle of the night, is she?"

"No. She'll slit my throat long before yours. And for the record, she's not my girlfriend."

"Have you told *her* that?"

He propped up on his elbow, peering down at her. "What do you want to know about Angelica?"

She stared at him one long moment, wishing she could really get a read on the look in his eyes. It wasn't quite light enough. She had to assume his willingness to talk meant there wasn't much to tell.

"The truth is, Angelica is about the last thing I want to hear about." She started to turn away.

"Stop." He put a hand on her shoulder. "Then what do you want to hear about?"

He had her attention now. "I want to hear about the things you don't tell me. Or just won't tell me."

"The things I don't tell you are for your own good."

"See. The perfect example of saying nothing."

"What do you want from me, Avery?"

There were a million ways to answer that question. She wanted him. Even in spite of the Angelica drama. But the pain of rejection was still fresh. She couldn't rely on his earlier drunken behavior to represent anything valid. She put a hand on his arm. "I want to know what caused you to drink so much."

"Because I worry. Compulsively. I worry every second I'm away from you."

The way he said it was earnest and heartfelt. It was a declaration without motivation or expectations, and it left an unfamiliar ache in her chest.

"When I figured out Javier had set me up, I drove myself crazy imagining the worst. By the time I got back here, I was sure he had you again."

His face loomed over hers. She brushed back the hair from his forehead. The lights from the streets radiated off his sharp profile. The effect was something next to hypnotic.

"So, to answer your question. You're the reason I got drunk," he said. "Being with you breaks every rule." He ran a finger along the curve of her shoulder. "And I can't seem to stop myself."

His touch left a trail of fire. It would be so easy to succumb. But she had to keep her head. "Whose rules? Your own, or something larger?"

He withdrew his hand, and her heart took a small dive. "Maybe both."

"For God's sake, Alejandro. Are you DEA or something? Are you afraid if I'm captured and tortured, I'll give you up?"

Silence hung heavily between them. He rolled over on his back and stared at the ceiling.

"I'm sorry," she said.

"No. It's not your fault." He draped an arm across his eyes. "If it makes a difference, I'll tell you what you want to know."

She held her breath at the significance of his words. But she couldn't ask it of him. Not like this. "No." She peered over at him. "I just want you to trust me."

"This is not about trust. This is about getting hurt. Vulnerability. Anything that happens between us has no future."

Lightly, she touched his arm, forcing him to meet her gaze. "I'm twenty-eight years old. I think I'll survive."

It was a lie. Everything she'd felt in the last few minutes was from her heart. Age, and wisdom, and rational thinking had nothing to do with any of it.

He stroked her cheek. "Maybe it's not you I'm worried about."

Chapter 33

She wasn't sure who kissed who first. It was brief. The second time, he took her mouth with an urgency that resonated through her core.

She pushed back. "I do need to know one thing."

"What?"

"Did you touch her? Anything beyond dancing, I mean?"

His laugh was deep. A rumble. She started to push him away. "I thought you didn't want to talk about Angelica," he said.

"I didn't, I don't, but I can't help it. Don't laugh."

"Of course I didn't touch her. And I'm not laughing. It's just you. Jealousy doesn't seem to suit you. It's a little out of character. But maybe I should ask you the same thing."

"What do you mean?" she asked.

"Did you touch him?"

"Who? José?"

"Did he tell you that he was her husband?"

She froze. José had baited her. "No. He didn't say a word about it." But it explained so much.

"He typically avoids telling other women. But she's no better. They should have been divorced years ago, but the games are what keeps them going."

She raked a hand through his loose curls. It was her fault they were even talking about the two of them. Any further mention of their names had the potential to ruin what lay ahead. She inhaled deeply. His hair still held the faint scent of shampoo. It made her want to bury her face in the pillow next to him and never leave. "I want to forget about both of them."

Two days' worth of stubble grazed her cheek as he searched for her lips. Her movement was tentative as she was careful to avoid pain, while she allowed her body to mold itself against his. He slid a hand under her t-shirt, his fingers caressing her back.

She shifted, and he said, "I think you need to lose this shirt." She rose up and raised her arms, allowing him to tug it over her head. He kissed her, cradling her head, as he lowered her to the pillow, then leaned over her and left a trail of kisses between her breasts.

Her hands rested on his shoulders. "Your shirt needs to come off, too." She wanted to feel the warmth of him against her, flesh to flesh. His teeth flashed white as he smiled down at her, rising up to discard his shirt. There was nothing rushed about his movement. He seemed to want to savor every moment. Her hand glanced over his chest. His smooth muscles flexed in response. "Constanza and Alejandro. This might make us a little more than kissing cousins."

His laugh was sardonic. "Too much family intimacy for you, Constanza? You going to walk now?"

"Not likely." It was impossible to imagine anyone refusing him.

His hands caressed her back as she kissed his neck. Pressing against her, his chest was a series of taut, muscular ridges and valleys. The regular thrum of his heart was a statement of his confidence in every move. He flipped her on top with the same easy manipulation he'd displayed when he danced. Not even a twinge from her ribcage.

One hand moved slowly, tracing the outline of her breasts, while the other hand reached beyond the elastic of her shorts. A noise escaped from the back of her throat as his fingers continued downward, removing the remainder of her clothes.

Her hands moved to his hips. "We need to keep this fair." She rose to her knees, sliding his boxers below his hips and reaching for the length of him. He groaned and muttered a string of Spanish words. "Speak English. I want to be included."

"I hardly think you're excluded." Gently, he manipulated her onto her side, forcing her to relinquish her grasp on him. "Not yet," he said with a whisper. "Patience."

Their combined weight was centered in the middle of the bed. She stretched out an arm to combat the curling mattress. Never before had she kissed a mouth so sensuous. She leaned in to nip at his lower lip.

"Diagonal," he said, preventing them from being swallowed by the mattress. Angling under him, she pulled him closer. "What about your ribs?" he asked.

"You'll know if you hurt me."

Her hands went to his hips, his butt, and the back of his thighs. Smooth and solid. It made her wish for daylight. She would take in every square inch of him. Force him to stand there as she inspected him. But it felt as though she knew his body already. His agility revealed so much. And she'd made a practice of watching him for so long. Stifling the urge to imagine a night just like this . . .

"Hey, Gabacha, you're distracted."

"Hardly," she said, kissing his shoulder as he loomed over her. "I knew exactly what you were doing." She grazed her teeth lightly against his bicep. His skin was salty, with an underlying edge of something sweet. "I was concentrating. Just maybe not in the way you imagine."

"Tell me about it." His voice had grown rough.

Her hands moved up the rippling muscles of his upper back and shoulders. "I intend to." He kissed his way down past her belly. "But not now," she said with a gasp.

It was impossible to remember that just seventy-two

hours ago she'd believed him to be gay. She let out a small laugh.

"Something funny?"

As if somehow perceiving her thoughts, his tongue circled a spot that launched her back into the moment. She clawed the sheet and dug her heels into the mattress. "No. Nothing funny."

He moved up the length of her body, pausing to kiss the flesh of her inner thigh. "You're more beautiful than I even imagined."

So are you.

He hovered above her, bearing the weight of his body on his forearms. She studied his face. "You're worried," she said, smoothing his hair back. Indecision etched lines across his face. She stifled an impatient sigh. Inadvertently, her body arched upward. In every tendon, she could feel the desire of his body to match hers, but his mind was planted somewhere else.

Finally, she understood. She'd managed to find the only gangster south of the border with a conscience. "I'm not going to break."

He leaned in to kiss her. She could see it in his face that he didn't believe her. Seizing the opportunity, she used both hands and gravity against his doubt. And this time, she forgave him for resorting to Spanish.

~ ~ ~

The room was no longer cold. She rested her head on his chest as he stroked her hair. Amidst the tangled sheets, her thoughts sifted through the haze of the night.

He kissed her cheek. "What are you thinking about?"

"Oh, you know—valve repair out at the Zapata facility. Production rates. You?"

He caught her off guard, rolling on top of her and pinning

her wrists above her head. "Expense reports." His lips blazed a trail across her neck.

"I can tell," she said with a husky laugh that sounded nothing like her own.

So, this was how a real man made love. Love making. It was a phrase that never made sense until tonight. He was neither selfish nor selfless, generous but never hesitant to take his share. Everything was a balance. Her past was a trail of boyfriends that treated sex like a mountain to climb or a race to win. And they were boys by comparison.

There was only one aspect of Alejandro that was like an adolescent. He ran a hand between her thighs. His rebound.

Chapter 34

In the remaining minutes before sunrise, the square was empty. His footsteps echoed across the cobblestones.

It had taken everything he had to drag himself from the hotel room. Being with Avery was like dangling heroin in the face of an addict. But he had to get her out of Valerone. For one thing, Angelica and José posed a problem. He ran a hand along last night's claw marks. Angelica knew they weren't cousins. By noon, everyone else would know it, too. If they remained here, Avery would become an object of interest for all his friends. And a target for more of the game playing between those two.

His objectivity was questionable. He wasn't sure exactly what was governing his decisions: his brain or his libido? Parking Avery right in the heart of Mexico City was a crazy plan. But it seemed the only choice. He had to get back to work. His prolonged absence was already irritating Diego. And before long, it would raise questions. It meant she'd be right under the nose of the Ramos family. But it was this or send her back to Harvey. And with no car of his own at the moment, getting her back to Harvey's was not a realistic option. Or so he told himself.

He perched on a low stone wall and tapped his phone. "Oso."

The voice on the other end of the phone growled, "It's four in the morning. Don't you have anything better to do than call me? You need to get a life."

"Yeah, you're not the first to tell me that."

"Well, what is it?"

"Time for a little shift in lifestyle. I need you to pick me up. Bring the BMW."

"Where?" Even with Oso's expertise, there was always a chance someone would track his car. Valerone had to stay off the Ramos family's radar. It would mean taking a bus to somewhere else, preferably not too far away. He bit his lip. She might not forgive him for this.

"Xalapa. Don't use the navigation system. I had everything checked out two weeks ago, but you never know."

"I don't need a damn navigation system for Xalapa," Oso said groggily. "I'll double check everything else. Diego's boys are getting sloppier every day." He yawned. "What's the rush?"

"Diego wants me back in the city. Jeep's broken down, and it could be weeks before they get a part out here."

"Where do I pick you up?"

"Juarez Park. There's a coffee shop on the southwest corner. And I've got baggage."

"What kind of baggage?"

"Female."

"You're telling me you haven't gotten her home yet."

"Shut up," Alejandro said.

"What the hell are you doing in Xalapa?"

"We're not there yet," Alejandro said. "We'll be there by nine. Does that work?"

"Yeah."

"And my role this time?"

Alejandro laughed. Oso always liked this part. "Houseboy, cook, bodyguard, it's your choice," Alejandro said. "You'll be hanging out in my apartment when I'm not there."

"Babysitting?"

"Hmmm. Better not call it that. Also, do me another favor and find Roger. Have him reach out to my Texan friend again. He needs to know the Mexico vacation has been extended. At least until the weather improves. The forecast suggests we're about three weeks out."

Oso made a noise in the back of his throat. "Anything else?"

"No."

He slipped the phone back into his pocket and rubbed his forehead. Three weeks. He could probably get her out in two if he worked at it. He'd prefer three weeks. But it wasn't a choice. He sighed. This thing with her had no future. It was what nearly stopped him last night. Until she—

"Baggage?" Her voice sent a ripple of shock through his system. Though low, the sound of it seemed to fill the air. "That's how you see me?"

She leaped down from the top of the wall. His mind raced to recall what else she might have heard. Hands on hips, she stood before him, disheveled and sexier than ever. He pulled her into his lap.

"Three weeks?" she said. "Till I go home?"

He nodded, burying his face in her hair. "What else did you hear?"

"Obviously something about someone named Roger." He attempted to make his face a blank, but she continued. "Who does Roger talk to?"

He said nothing.

"Sam?"

What had happened to him? He was losing it. He'd made one stupid mistake after another. The setup by Javier, dancing with Angelica, and now this. Any more screwups on his part and they'd be in trouble. Why hadn't he insisted on speaking Spanish to Oso?

"Are you asking Sam for ransom money?"

His head shot up. "Of course not. Just the opposite."

Her fingers stroked his face. "I had to at least ask." She kissed him. "Your secretive side."

"Clearly, not secretive enough." He stared at the ground. He ran a hand along her bare legs, trying to smooth the goosebumps. "It's cold out here for shorts. Come on. Let's go get another couple hours of sleep."

"Sleep?" she asked. "That's what you intend?"

He made a low groan in the back of his throat. "No."

~ ~ ~

Alejandro wanted to laugh. His grizzly friend showed up minus the cap but was otherwise dressed as a chauffeur. Oso held the door for her and nudged Alejandro to join her in the back seat. Alejandro rolled his eyes and climbed in.

"Avery, you remember Oso."

"Oso," she repeated, sounding out the strange name.

"It means bear in Spanish," Alejandro said.

"The apartment, I presume?" Oso said with a fake British accent. Again, Alejandro fought the urge to tell him to knock it off. No one would seriously consider hiring Oso for any job that required sophistication. Unless that sophistication involved a gun.

"Yes."

This time Oso spoke in Spanish. "Preferred language for this trip?"

"Spanish is fine. Unless you need to practice your Arabic."

Oso laughed. "Hell no. I'll retire without a pension before they ever get me back to Beirut." His eyes met Alejandro's in the rearview mirror. "Nice claw marks. Someone did a dance on your face."

"I have some Zetas to thank for most of it."

"Those are the claw marks of a female." Oso laughed. "Is it her work?"

"No."

"I guess I don't have to tell you that half of Mexico is losing their minds over her."

"Over the reward money."

"Not just the money. Javier's guys have been distributing photos. You delay this much longer and she's going to be gracing billboards."

He kept his face a blank, trying to downplay his possessive reaction to Oso's words. And it might have worked until Avery leaned into him. The man's eyebrows shot up.

"Tell me you're not."

Alejandro ignored him.

Oso continued. "In all the years we've worked together. Damn. Knock me over with a feather." He switched to English. "I took the liberty of bringing your attaché case, sir." He slung the briefcase over the seat.

The fact that Oso brought it meant something. And whatever was in the case required his immediate attention. He winked at Avery, pretending to be unconcerned.

"Is she sick?"

Oso had picked up on something Alejandro had missed. Alejandro glanced at Avery. She was subdued. "She wasn't exactly a fan of the bus. The decent line didn't have a bus until late afternoon, so we took the local. Just about a thousand stops. No air conditioning, filthy, over-crowded, you know."

"You'll be alone again in no time if that's how you treat her. I wouldn't put Aunt Maria del Rosario on that bus. And let me tell you about my Aunt Maria del Rosario."

"You've already told me you spent your childhood dreaming of how to torture her. The bus wasn't a disaster. It got us there. And we weren't even stranded once. Plus, it's the safest thing I could have done. No one with two cents to their name would choose the local. No cartel members. Hell, not even a self-respecting gangbanger would be caught dead on the local line. I think it was probably the woman across the aisle with her chickens that got to her."

"She'll ditch you before tomorrow. Unless that fancy apartment of yours makes up for it."

"I'm sure it will be my butler that makes all the difference," Alejandro said.

"Oh, so now it's up to me to fix your love life as well. You'd better get a new butler."

"No way." Alejandro fingered the briefcase. "Before I open this case in front of her, what language are the documents in?"

"English," Oso said.

"Then you'll need to summarize what's in here. I'm not going to read anything in front of her."

"You're not going to like it. The orders came from the top."

"Bureaucratic crap, then."

"They want you to stop playing the hero. Proceed with the bigger task at hand. Someone thinks you're getting a little distracted."

"My local orders were to hold off, hide her for a few weeks. Let things die down. I spoke with Arturo yesterday." He clenched his fists. "And how does D.C. propose I get rid of her?"

"They recommend you take your chances with the embassy," Oso said.

His face grew hot. He couldn't even look at Avery. "Bullshit. They want to use her as bait. A way to catch their mole."

"I'm just repeating what's in there. But realistically, the odds are in her favor. She's big news everywhere. Anyone would be an idiot to mess with her at the embassy."

"Not if the money from Javier is enough." Her body flinched at the mention of Javier's name. He put an arm around her.

"Then pretend you never saw those docs."

Oso was right. He could ignore it. The two of them did it all the time. Especially when the orders came directly from D.C. Most of those guys hadn't spent ten minutes in the field. Somehow, a degree in political science and a mediocre command of an obscure foreign language entitled them to give orders. "Think I can buy two or three weeks before they notice she hasn't shown up at the embassy?"

"Easily. Take a month or two if you need to." Oso hated the bureaucrats even more than Alejandro did. "We've done a lot worse." Oso grinned. "Tell me why we're not going after the embassy mole."

"Not our jurisdiction. State Department wants us to stay out of it."

"Bunch of inbred ticks, that lot. We'd have the matter over and done with by now."

Alejandro glanced down at Avery falling asleep against his shoulder. "Yep." And last night would never have happened.

~ ~ ~

The elevator door opened, and Alejandro held out a hand to her as she lingered near the car. "Don't worry about your things. Hanging around the garage is not a great idea. Oso will bring everything up." She was quiet, and though it was impossible she'd understood the discussion he'd had with Oso, her mood nagged at him. She was good at picking up on cues. He pressed eighteen. The highest number on the panel. The penthouse apartment. She raised an eyebrow.

"It's Diego's apartment, not mine. It used to belong to one of his mistresses. He insists I live here."

"Why would he do that?" Realization crossed her face. "Oh. Because he can keep tabs on you. Is it bugged?"

"Absolutely." He smiled down at her. "And the staff here is on his payroll."

"Then why am I here?"

"Because Oso and I know how to work around it. It's amazing what you can do with a little misdirection. I'll show you. But just so you know, never enter or exit the garage on any floor except the fourth. And only use this elevator. Never the one on the left. He pointed to the ceiling. These cameras are mine. The feed is fake." Her forehead wrinkled, and he reached for her hand. "It's life in a cartel. You learn to be careful who you trust."

"Who is Oso?" she asked.

"My Chief of Security. Anyone high enough in the organization has to have a security team."

"And you're high enough?" He nodded dismissively. "How many security people do you have?" She stumbled over the words.

"Three of them handpicked by me. Two more provided by Diego. They keep him informed of my comings and goings. Of course, I'm not supposed to know about it. But it works well if Oso and I stay on top of it. Again, it's sort of the fake-feed principle. I'm very selective in what jobs they do for me. But I do have to throw them a bone periodically." He grinned. "Do something unexpected. Just to give Diego something to think about."

"So how are you able to travel around alone?"

"Depends. Sometimes I take them with me. It's rarely necessary for me to have a team of five in tow." His hand went to the bruised side of his face. It might have been nice to have had his guys at the beach, but showing up with a team often meant a fight. Something much more serious than a wound to the ego and a slight bruise. "I give them other tasks. Right now, a couple of them are looking for Javier."

"How do you ever accomplish anything? When you're busy managing that?"

"Oso. He's irreplaceable."

"But he's staying with me. Right? Until I leave?"

"Yes."

He kept his gaze focused on the floor. In a mere thirty seconds, she'd discovered the greatest weakness of his plan. Oso's assignment left holes in a hundred other places, but he trusted no one else with Avery.

The doors opened, and he guided her through the sizable foyer. The look on her face said it all. The massive rooms, the floor-to-ceiling windows. She was eating it up. To him, it felt sterile and impersonal. Colorless couches and chairs strategically located in clusters circling area rugs that offered zero warmth. But Diego's decorator had insisted it was him. *It screams sexy bachelor attorney* the woman had reminded him with irritating frequency. He should have fired her.

He thumbed through a small stack of mail. "Can I get you something to drink? Water? Wine?"

"It's a little early in the day for that, isn't it?" she asked. "Aren't you going into work?"

Even Avery seemed slightly foreign in this place. As if the façade of the apartment had eliminated a part of her that was genuine. "I am, but I'll show you around first."

She followed him into his study, where he held a finger to his lips and pointed to the small black spot on the ceiling. In silence, she glanced around the room. Her eyes went from the books to his not-so-neat desk. Something about it made her smile.

They returned to the long hall, refraining from speaking until the door to the study was soundly shut. "It's a device designed to pick up phone calls. We leave it alone deliberately. I make any important calls somewhere else. But sometimes, I go in there and give them something mundane and lengthy. You know, the tax attorney, my great aunt who can't hear and requires that I repeat everything seven times." He put a hand on her back. "I'll show you the kitchen."

"Wow," she said a moment later.

He couldn't disagree. State of the art. A world of sterile stainless steel and arctic white. Even a professional chef would find it impressive. And again, there was nothing personal about it.

"I don't cook much. When I'm in town, Diego usually requires that I attend dinners and fundraisers. So, you'll find it's seriously lacking in much but breakfast food. I'll have groceries delivered. And Oso's your cook. He's not bad. You won't starve."

She was barely talking. He didn't have time to deal with it now. He glanced at his watch and moved on.

"Get ready for the humidity," he said as he opened the heavy door. The view was one of a kind. Half of Mexico City. It was the only reason he'd agreed to live here. That, and the lap pool that ran the entire length of the glass wall. He'd miss it when the job came to an end.

Avery gasped. "I can't believe this."

"Yeah," he said, cocking his head. "I try to swim in the mornings." He pointed to a door. "Weights and machines. Maybe stick to the treadmill and bike if you can tolerate it. Until your ribs are a hundred percent, it's best to avoid the heavy weights. The pool might be a better choice."

"Except a swimsuit wasn't on my packing list for Zapata."

"We'll see what we can do about it. Maybe if I don't have to work late, we can go shopping." He reached for her hand and pointed. "Master bedroom. Only bedroom in the apartment."

"In this huge apartment—only one bedroom?" She stared at the king-sized bed.

"Diego didn't intend for his mistress to entertain. There are maid's quarters. On the back of the kitchen. Two very small bedrooms back there, if you can even call them that. Oso will probably stay there."

He led her back to the great room and held up a remote. "Red button opens the cabinet doors. Green button turns on the TV. You'll find some English channels. Hope you don't mind, but I need to have a shower and get to work."

In the silence, Alejandro felt her gaze with every step of his retreat. She was scared. And she had good reason to be. Leaving her felt a little like desertion. But she was safe with Oso, and Alejandro couldn't afford to waste time. He needed to get his head back in the game. No more mistakes.

Chapter 35

The person who lived in this apartment was someone she didn't know. This version of Alejandro was hiding more than he was telling. He was courteous but different. Whatever had made him angry in the car had changed things.

She raked her hair with her fingers. Maybe it was time to learn some Spanish.

She sank into the white leather couch and clicked the red button, then the green button. Flipping through the channels, she wondered when she'd last watched real television. The telenovela with Victor hardly counted. She landed on an American talk show. Four women seated around a glass table speculating about the insipid details of some celebrity wedding. She stared, transfixed. She'd never been one to waste time on these kinds of shows before, but now they seemed more ridiculous than ever. At least the telenovelas offered up some humor. She clicked off the TV.

Alejandro's footsteps echoed across the marble. His hair, still damp, was combed back in a way she'd never seen it before. He wore a blue suit. A suit no one could purchase off the rack. Perfectly cut to exhibit the breadth of his shoulders and the narrowness of his waist and hips. He and Diego probably jetted off to Hong Kong or London to visit their tailors.

His eyebrows knitted together at the sight of her. He adjusted the knot of his tie as he approached. Keys dangled from one of his fingers. Her breath caught in her throat.

He lifted her chin with one finger. "Avery, what's wrong?"

She tried her best to smile. "Nothing. Do you always dress like that?"

"Something wrong with it?"

"No, it's just so . . ." She steadied her voice. "You look great. I guess I didn't know PR guys dressed like that." She stumbled over her words. "But I don't really know any, either."

"PR was a loose term. I thought you knew. I'm Diego's attorney."

Something inside her twisted. He was in deep. Deeper than she ever imagined. PR was one thing. But being Diego's attorney meant he had access to a lot more. And this closeness put him in a much more precarious position.

He bent to kiss her. The absence of his days' worth of beard felt strange. As if Valerone wasn't real. It didn't help that while he smelled of aftershave and tasted of toothpaste, she sat in clothes bathed in the sweat and filth of the bus. Despite this, she refused to let him go. Instead, she pulled him closer, wrapping her arms around his neck. Somewhere in there was the Alejandro of last night.

There was a bang and a whistle. "Don't mind me," Oso said, with unnecessary volume. It wasn't difficult to see why his nickname was Spanish for bear. He resembled one in every possible way. Huge, lumbering, and fur covered.

Alejandro squeezed her shoulder. It might have been her imagination, but he seemed to be relieved by Oso's appearance.

"I'll try to be back by six or seven. Tell Oso what you'd like for dinner."

At the sound of the door shutting, she covered her face. His preoccupation with returning to work was so obvious.

~ ~ ~

Oso had left her alone to sleep the afternoon away. Following a ridiculously long shower, she stepped into

Alejandro's vast closet dressed only in a towel. She glanced about. It felt a little creepy to spy on him. But his level of organization was fascinating. It put hers to shame. Dress shirts separated by color. Sweatshirts and sweaters meticulously folded and stacked like a retail store. Despite the abundance, she couldn't even bring herself to borrow something warm. This closet belonged to someone she barely knew. Diego's version of Alejandro. Not the guy happy to drive backroads in his old Jeep.

Her gaze shifted to his duffel bag. Oddly, digging through it seemed less invasive than peering in his closet. She brought the jacket to her face. It still bore the lingering smell of campfire, with a slight hint of the Alejandro she knew. She threaded her arms through the sleeves.

Oso was watering plants when she tracked him down. It seemed a little out of character for a man of his appearance, but that was true of the entire apartment. He didn't fit here either. And for that, she liked him.

"What canna do for you, miss?"

"Where are you from?" She smiled. "You're not a native, are you?"

"What, of Mexico?" He grinned. "I'd like to think I'm a citizen of everywhere. Or nowhere, depending on how you look at it. But to answer your question, I was born here." He glanced at the paper in her hand. "It seems you have a list there. Is there something I can get for you?"

"I was wondering if we could go shopping. I don't really have any warm clothes."

His eyes rested on Alejandro's jacket. "I see that. I think Mr. DeLeon intends to take you himself."

"Mr. DeLeon," she repeated. It sounded so strange. She'd heard it spoken only once before.

She searched the room for a clock. Oso seemed to understand. He sighed. "It's nearly eight o'clock."

"Eight PM?" She'd recognized the workaholic side of Alejandro early on. It was a weakness they shared. "He'll never get home early enough to take me shopping, will he?"

Oso's expression was sympathetic. "Not really for me to say. Diego Ramos is not the kind of boss you say *no* to very often. But if you'd like, I can remind Alejandro." He set the watering can down. "I'm failing at my job if I don't feed you." She followed behind his massive waddling form. "Since you weren't awake, I took it upon myself to choose tonight's supper." He pointed to the stools at the bar. "Seat yourself there." He slid a water bottle in her direction. "It'll take me just a minute." He frowned, his caterpillar-like eyebrows nearly covering his eyes. "How do you feel about fish?"

"Without a tortilla?"

He winked. "My feelings exactly. Don't get me wrong. I don't have anything against rice and beans. But there's more to life than that."

~ ~ ~

A door slammed, forcing her abruptly into a state of panicked wakefulness. Alejandro bent over the back of the sofa, smelling of wine and cigarettes.

"You should be in bed," he said. She blinked. He draped his suit jacket over the back of the couch. "It's past your bedtime, Gabacha." He wound his way around the furniture and with little effort scooped her into his arms. "Sorry, but you were moving a little too slowly for me." He removed the nearly full wine glass from her hand. "Did I just hurt you?"

"No. It was just a twinge." She circled his neck with her arms and snuggled against him. It was the first time in hours that the weight from her chest had lifted.

He deposited her in the middle of the bed and then headed toward the closet. "Sorry to be so late. Diego needed to make up for lost time."

His excuses didn't matter. She'd used them all herself. She only cared that he was here. Warm and alive. She searched through her belongings for her toothbrush.

"You're quiet." He paused to watch her spread toothpaste and placed a brief kiss on the top of her head.

She shrugged. Her mouth now full of toothpaste, it was best if she didn't talk. Every thought she'd had for the last eight hours had circled around her obsession with his wellbeing. To verbalize any of it would make her sound silly. Or like his mother.

He was still in his closet when she climbed into his bed. It was impossible to ignore the significant improvement in bedding against her bare skin. She shifted in the crisp and yet silky smoothness of his sheets. He stepped into view, wearing only boxers and watching her writhe. Her gaze went to the finely sculpted muscles of his chest and abs.

"You're beautiful without your shirt on," she mumbled. Her eyes grew wide as they slid down to the visual sign of his readiness. The corner of his mouth turned up. He'd caught her reaction, and he liked it.

~ ~ ~

They lay side by side, equally breathless. The previous night seemed amateurish by comparison. He propped himself up on one elbow. "I thought I was tired. But I guess not." He twisted a strand of her hair around his finger and kissed her forehead. "You're making me crazy. You know that? I could barely concentrate at work."

She lifted a single eyebrow. It was the only muscle left in her body that hadn't been turned to liquid. "Good." Her voice was husky.

"Are you just a little drunk tonight, Gabacha?"

"No. You saw my wine glass. It was nearly full."

He reached for the lamp. Even in that momentary

absence, she wanted to pull him back. Feel his body snaking around hers.

"I don't know how I'm going to get through three weeks of waiting for you to come home from work. I feel like a fifties housewife. Except I have no casseroles to make, or whatever it was that they did back then."

"You are just the tiniest bit drunk, aren't you?" He pulled her close. "Don't worry. During the weekends we won't get out of bed."

She laughed. "Will we text Oso for food?"

"No. We'll give him the weekends off. Eat cereal if we need to even eat at all."

She kissed his neck and ran her teeth along his earlobe. His breathing shifted, growing more rapid. "God, Avery, you really are going to kill me."

Chapter 36

He hadn't anticipated the guilt that came with keeping her in the city. Five o'clock meant nothing to Diego. Neither did six or seven. For days, he'd intended to take her shopping. But even the weekend hadn't been his.

She was always cold. This morning he'd left her a sweatshirt and a pullover. For some reason, though, she insisted upon wearing his old navy jacket. The image brought a smile to his face.

Someone cleared their throat. Diego. Dread filled the pit of his stomach. The man wanted something. He knew by the look on his face.

"Tonight is the earthquake fundraiser. Marta and I had plans to go but can't. I'd like you to represent the family. Take Luisa."

"What about Javier?"

The old man shot him a sideways glance. "I don't know where he is. Any word from your guys?"

"No." Alejandro didn't allow his gaze to falter—a technique successful with everyone but Avery. The truth was, he'd almost forgotten about the guys he'd sent to tail Javier. And apparently, it was mutual. They hadn't reported to him in several days.

"Let me know when you do."

"If he does show up, would you prefer that he go in my place?" It would serve the old man right. Let Javier show up drunk or high and make an ass out of himself. Maybe then Diego could be convinced that rehab was the only place for Javier.

"No. Luisa wants you to escort her," Diego said. "It's black tie, of course."

"Of course," he said, barely able to disguise his lack of enthusiasm. Alejandro wanted to slam his fist against the desk. Luisa. Maybe twenty years old. A virtual baby. And Diego had set his sights on him as her future husband. He'd suspected it for some time now. It wasn't that uncommon in cartels. Sometimes it was a way of creating alliances with rival cartels. But more commonly, a way of strengthening the internal bonds and setting up the future successors.

Embedded was one thing. But marrying into the cartel was another.

Diego cleared his throat. It was a sound that always sent Alejandro on high alert. "Am I wrong in thinking that your attention is a little divided these days? Diego held up a folder. "It's the Martinez contract. I was under the impression that this had been handled several weeks ago."

Alejandro tried to remain calm. Neglecting the contract was costing Diego money. A stupid oversight on his part. "Forgive me. You're right, I should have been paying closer attention. I'll see to it that it's filed within the hour."

Wordlessly, Diego crossed his arms and studied Alejandro's face. Alejandro had seen him do this to others at least a dozen times. But he'd always been careful to avoid Diego's scrutiny. The man's cold stare left him wanting to check his holster.

"What's on your schedule for tomorrow?" Diego asked.

The question left Alejandro completely unnerved. Diego rarely asked and never micromanaged. A reality that always made Alejandro's other job easier. So how would he explain tomorrow's trip to San Antonio?

The corner of Alejandro's mouth curved up, and he let out a small laugh. "You won't believe it if I tell you. I'm meeting with the Solano brothers."

"Really?"

Alejandro nodded. It was the first thing that came to mind, but it was an alibi that would never be questioned either. The Solano brothers, American arms dealers, trusted few, but over the years, Alejandro had gained their trust in ways that would surprise and displease Diego. In addition, Diego would never send his security guys to tail Alejandro for this meeting. If detected, the move would be interpreted as a sign of distrust between allied organizations. No one could afford to be at odds with the Solanos.

"I'm surprised. It seems like a job for Oso."

Alejandro toyed with a pen desperately trying to maintain the charade. "Freddy has challenged me to a race on that swamp of a lake he lives on. He has a new speedboat, and he's letting me use his brother's. I've been putting him off for months." Alejandro shook his head. "But I suspect he wants me to see his new merchandise as well."

Diego's expression remained fixed. "I'll tell Luisa to expect you at six."

Alejandro let out a sigh as Diego shut the door behind him. It was impossible to tell what the man thought.

Alejandro picked up his phone and touched the contact information for his own personal attorney. "Max, do you have half an hour for me tomorrow morning?" Alejandro asked in Spanish. "We can make it quick. Just a couple of adjustments to my will and an issue with a safety deposit box."

~ ~ ~

The thrill in Avery's eyes at his early return from work only made things worse. She and Oso stood shoulder to shoulder in their matching aprons. The image launched an irrational flare of jealousy in him. They'd grown close. But why wouldn't they? Twelve hours a day, nothing but the two of them.

He paused to kiss her. "Tomorrow night we go shopping. Tonight, I have to fill in for Diego at an event."

She and Oso glanced at one another conspiratorially. Disappointment flashed across her face for no more than a split second. Always so quick to hide her feelings. An exterior of steel. It was probably why she said her ex called her emotionally unavailable. You always had to look below the surface.

"I need to change," he said.

The plodding of Oso's footsteps behind him was impossible to ignore. Alejandro didn't stop until they were directly outside of the bedroom and out of Avery's hearing range.

Oso began with a nasty curse in Spanish. "What the hell are you trying to do? Do you not know how to say no to that bastard?" Oso grabbed his collar. "Quit promising her things." The man's breath was in his face, and he still had a large knife in his hand.

"You're not planning on stabbing me with that, are you?"

Oso released the grip on his collar. "Don't tempt me."

"You know, you could help me out here. I saw that look between the two of you. *She* may not understand, but you know how it is with Diego. Our guys have lost Javier. They have no clue where the little shit went."

"I don't care about that." Oso's voice was a low rumble. "You're taking Luisa?"

"What do you think?"

"You want to know what I think?" Oso's eyes were narrow slits. In all the years Alejandro had known Oso, Alejandro had never been at the receiving end of this much emotional rage. With Oso, it was usually a quick verbal chastisement or a fist. "I think you've become a selfish son of a bitch. It's a single issue with you now. We both know you've got enough to bring down the Ramos family. The drug trafficking . . ." he raised a fist. "How many shipments of illegal arms do you have on record now? Ten? Twenty? Could be a hundred by now. And hell, now you can add kidnapping." Oso shoved him against the wall. "This is all about revenge. All about the General. And I hate to tell you this, but no matter what you do to Diego, it's not going to bring him back."

Oso backed away. His breathing was heavy. "I never thought I'd call you a fool. But you are. You're wasting your own life avenging the death of someone who's been gone for twenty years. And even though she doesn't know why, she recognizes it." He pointed the knife in the direction of the kitchen. "That's the best thing that could ever happen to you. You want revenge? Go after Javier for kidnapping her. Ironic, isn't it? You have Javier to thank for the ten minutes of sunshine you've allowed into your life."

Alejandro's own breath had become ragged. He pinched the bridge of his nose but didn't respond.

Oso started back toward the kitchen. "Don't include me on the guest list when you let Diego coerce you into marrying that child."

~ ~ ~

Alejandro fumbled with the buttons on his tuxedo shirt. Oso had exaggerated. There were only two major arms shipments he could absolutely pin on Diego. He probably should be going to see the Solano brothers. At least that way they'd have a third shipment on record. He tilted his head in the mirror. The documentation would most likely hold up in court, but *most likely* wasn't enough. He needed certainty. The drugs were easy. Just across the border in a sizable safety deposit box, he'd stashed two years' worth of tapes, photos, and documents all leading back to the Ramos cartel. He'd resisted telling anyone about it. Not even Oso. If the bosses knew, they'd pull the plug on the project and call it good, even if it meant that Diego's jail time was only a fraction of what it should be. The arms and the money laundering were different. Diego had been hands-on since the beginning, refusing to delegate. This is what would put Diego behind bars forever.

Oso was right. His obsession with revenge had left him unbalanced. But Oso was wrong about one thing. He'd never marry Luisa Ramos.

He tucked his shirt in and glanced up to see Avery's reflection in the mirror. Standing a few feet behind, she struggled to appear nonchalant, but her beautiful face masked nothing tonight. She was suffering. And he didn't have a clue what to do about it.

He flipped up his collar and reached for the bow tie. She lifted it from his hand. Their eyes locked for only a second. She centered the length of silk around his neck. Moving with silent confidence, she crossed the ends and fed the longer one through the neck loop.

He closed his eyes, taking in the scent of her. It was the tea she drank in the afternoons. Something Oso had concocted especially for her.

Even that felt like another affront. Was he really jealous of Oso? The slow burn in his gut told him so. He resented their camaraderie. Every time he walked through the kitchen, they were there together. Heads bent over some recipe or laughing at something on TV. It was as if Oso had reached a part of her that he couldn't. Or hadn't. And after tonight's lecture, he hated the man, almost as much as he hated himself. It left him incapable of saying anything halfway intelligent to her.

And how the hell did she know how to tie a bow tie?

She smoothed the front of his shirt. Her touch left him wanting to blow off the dinner more than ever. He opened his eyes as she straightened the tie. It was perfect. A much better job than he could ever manage. He wanted so much to kiss her. But Oso's words had left him feeling undeserving and unsure of how to even go about it.

At least she spared him his dignity. She raised up on tiptoe and kissed him lightly before turning away.

"Avery, don't . . . don't go." He grabbed her wrist. Even the J-41 tattoo seemed to glare back at him. Another testament to his failure to act quickly. There was so much he wanted to say. So much he needed to say.

"Alejandro, not now. I don't know what you and Oso are fighting about, but I know he feels the need to defend me. And I think . . ." her voice faltered. "I think it's best that I trust Oso's objectivity."

Anger welled up within him. He tightened his grip on her wrist. "Screw Oso's objectivity. What do you want?" It was too harsh. He wanted to take back the words. He released his hold on her. "Sorry. I didn't mean that as it sounded."

"No. You're right. I don't need to bring Oso into this." She looked away, and for the first time, he noticed the shadows under her eyes. "I just need to be something more than someone who keeps your bed warm at night."

~ ~ ~

The apartment was pitch black when he returned. No one bothered to leave a light on for him anywhere. He tiptoed through the bedroom and into the bathroom. Carelessly, he tossed the tux aside. He'd be just as happy to never see it again. There was one good thing to come from the night. Luisa Ramos had zero interest in him, and even Diego would never convince that girl to marry someone she didn't want.

But in every other way, it was one of the most miserable nights of his life. It was bad enough to have to leave Avery. But after she'd said the bit about only being there to keep his bed warm, he'd barely been able to drive. He'd never been so conflicted in his entire life.

He climbed into bed as silently as possible. The sound of her breathing was like a melody.

She smelled of cinnamon. It brought back old memories. The times when his *abuela* made his father's favorite dessert: *buñuelos*. It always filled her tiny house with that smell.

He draped an arm over his forehead. Maybe Oso was right. Maybe it was time to wrap things up. He turned onto his side, wishing he could see her face in the darkness.

Chapter 37

"Never pronounce the h's," Oso said. "You say ola, not hola."

"I don't think languages are my thing. I took two semesters of German in college so I could study abroad."

"And?" He handed her a lump of dough. "Knead that, please."

"It didn't go so well." She shot him a smile. With a single hoop earring and his bald spot covered by a bandana, only the flour-encrusted apron saved him from looking like a pirate.

"You want to learn it for him, don't ya?"

Oso's sentimental side amazed her. He was so gruff and still such a softy. It wasn't the first time he'd spoken to her in this way about Alejandro.

"I want to learn it for myself." She pounded on the dough with more vigor than necessary. Oso said nothing, though there was evidence of skepticism in his expression.

The silence stretched between them. "How long have you known Alejandro?" she asked.

"We've worked together for six years."

"That wasn't really what I asked, was it?"

He glanced up at her and shook his head. "No."

"So you've known him a long time. Do you know Harvey?"

Oso's face crumbled into a myriad of deep lines. "That old crow. Yep. Known her a good part of my life."

Harvey and Oso. She tried to imagine them in a room together. The two of them weren't so different. Except

Harvey was a lot less sentimental and a lot grouchier. In contrast, Oso treated Avery like some kind of princess, offering to bring her breakfast in bed. Even making her bed if she didn't beat him to it. He tried his best to never let her feel like a captive.

"This recipe was handed down to me from my great-grandmother. She lived on the Greek island of Santorini," he said, steering her away from any further talk of Alejandro's history.

Avery didn't question the fact that Oso must have had ten great-grandmothers. Every day was a new recipe from a different part of the world. Wherever he acquired his cooking skills made little difference to her.

"Now that you've mutilated this poor dough," he said, retrieving it with his paw-like hands. "He's a good man. Just a little misguided sometimes."

"Who are you talking about?" She wrinkled her nose. "Your great-grandfather?"

"Alejandro. He doesn't always know what's best for him. He works like a dog." He passed her the bowl of spinach. "Give that a stir, will you? Then you'll want to mix in the feta."

"In what way does he not know what's best for him?" she asked. She knew what she wanted to hear. And Oso had deliberately baited her with the comment.

"He's got tunnel vision. Anything for work. I keep telling him life's not that simple."

"Like last night?"

"You have nothing to worry about there. It was just Luisa Ramos. The boss's daughter. Like I said, he'll do anything for work."

It felt like a kick to the gut. She'd suspected there'd been another woman in there somewhere.

Oso eyed her work. "She's nothing but a teenager. Diego made him do it, and he agreed. All part of Alejandro's vendetta. I keep telling him he's wasting his youth. But he doesn't listen to me."

Vendetta. For some reason the word struck her, sending a nagging message to linger in her thoughts.

"Completely unhealthy," he said.

"Has he wrecked any other women's lives along the way?" It came out wrong, making her sound jealous when she was trying her best to sound unfazed.

"No. He never lets it go that far. Not that other women haven't tried. Even ones in our line of work." He tossed the towel aside. "I just think," he paused and rubbed his beard. "I think he's let his guard down with you. I've never seen him do that before. It would be nice if you could talk some sense into him."

"You want to use me?" She tilted her head. "In case you haven't noticed, I don't seem to be doing a very good job of influencing him. He comes home later every night." She bit her tongue before adding something about last night.

Something flickered in Oso's gaze. "Don't let him get away with it. Be direct."

Vendetta. The word rose to the surface of her thoughts as if to light a hidden pathway. The wooden spoon in her hand clattered to the floor.

"Something wrong?" Oso asked.

She shook her head slowly. "There's something I need to understand first." She pointed to the laptop Oso had been using earlier. "Can I borrow that for a minute?" From the way he cleared his throat, she knew he was about to deny her request. "You can look over my shoulder."

With a grunt, he slid it across the island. "No email. No social media."

"I learned my lesson." Her hands shook as she typed in the words. *General Rodrigo Salazar, death, images.* Hopefully no one had posted one of those horrible morgue shots. All she needed was to catch a glimpse of the crowd in the minutes leading up to his assassination.

"Internet's slow sometimes," Oso said. He wasn't kidding. She could barely stand still.

Gradually, small images filled the screen. She selected one where the crowd was obviously calm, a before shot. The thud of her heart was heavy as she zoomed in. The General stood to the side of the stage. To his left side were his bodyguards. Easily identifiable: black jackets, earpieces, and tough looking. But it was the right side that drew her in. Her stomach twisted. She let out a gasp and covered her mouth. The image left no room for doubt.

Standing next to the General was ten-year-old Alejandro. Already nearly as tall as his father.

Oso reached across the island, snatching the computer from her. His eyes met her tear-filled ones. It was the fastest she'd ever seen him move. He circled the island and took her in his arms. "So now you know what your competition is. It's not another woman."

"No one can expect him to overcome that." Her voice was muffled against Oso's shirt.

"His mother and I have tried. But he won't let go. He's too hard-headed. He got that from her."

She lifted her head. "Harvey is his mother?"

"She didn't raise him, but yes. She and the General felt strongly about keeping him out of the limelight. And it was a good thing they did."

Harvey. His mother? She'd never even considered it. But it made sense. All the secrecy, their bickering. Neither of them would even tell her how they knew one another. "What was she like then?"

"Not so different than she is now. Brilliant. Always said and did whatever the hell she pleased. She was a reporter, and a good one. Had a knack for interviewing people. Getting them to talk. She was beautiful then, too. Met the General on an interview and spent weeks traveling with him. One thing led to another."

"He was a lot older, wasn't he?"

"By the time Alejandro was born, they'd been together for ten years. She was probably in her late thirties and he was mid-fifties."

She sank to one of the barstools. "Why did it take me so long to figure it out?"

Oso didn't offer anything. "I don't want to put any pressure on you. But he's running out of time. Diego wants more from him all the time. He's got his hooks into Alejandro."

"He's going to do what he wants to do. Nothing I can do or say will change anything."

Oso shoved the spanakopita aside. "That's where you're wrong."

Chapter 38

Oso's eyes were on him. Playing the part of overprotective father. Self-righteous old blowhard. Alejandro could do without the scrutiny. He'd never intended to neglect her. And no one knew better than Oso that he'd spent two grueling years making himself irreplaceable to Diego. Strolling out of the office at five o'clock had never been part of the routine.

"It's four forty-five, and I'm here," he said. "Stop beating me up. And stop acting like her father."

He glanced at the bedroom door for the third time. She only had four changes of clothes to her name. How long could it possibly take to choose between them?

The door creaked open. His eyebrows lifted in surprise, and Oso whistled. Alejandro shot him a go to hell look. No playing both father and admirer.

Even after the guys had recovered her clothes from the dumpster, he'd never bothered to look in the bag. He'd just assumed that he'd seen everything in their time together. But obviously not. She was wearing high heels and a black dress that hugged every curve.

She smoothed down the front of her dress and looked from one man to the other. "What?" She grinned. "Don't make fun of me. I used to always keep this dress in my suitcase when I traveled. And since I haven't dressed up in months, now it feels strange."

Oso cleared his throat. "You two ought to get going. Stores aren't open all night." He winked at Avery, and Alejandro longed to punch him.

For some reason, their first few minutes alone bore all the awkwardness of a first date. He couldn't find the words. And she wasn't exactly talkative either. Maybe it was the clothes. Or maybe it was the fact that they'd seen so little of one another recently. Had they lost something? The ability to understand one another?

It seemed like years since Valerone, when all this began. He couldn't remember how they got here. Or life before her.

They were in the car before she spoke. "I think I've been unfair to you in the past few days. Last night I saw the tux and assumed . . . the worst."

And Oso had let her believe it?

"Oso explained to me that he was mad at you for working too much. I guess he knew I was getting really antsy in the apartment. Not that hanging out there is a hardship in any way . . ."

He cut her off. "He's mad at me for a lot of things. Being a workaholic is only part of it. But he's right, I've left you alone far too much."

"I know what it's like to immerse yourself in a job."

She was actually making excuses for him. He smiled weakly, wishing it were that simple. Her fingers curled around his hand. Amazing how her simple touch could send his thoughts elsewhere. But something was up with her tonight. She was jittery and couldn't quite sit still. She withdrew her hand.

He pulled up to the hotel. The black Audi convertible might have stood out in other neighborhoods. But not here.

He sensed her confusion. "It's a good location for shopping and avoiding the Ramos family. They hate this hotel." He laughed. "It was fully booked on the day they planned to celebrate the youngest daughter's *quinceañera*. Management refused Diego's bribe money to kick everyone out. That doesn't happen very often in this town."

A young valet offered a hand to Avery. Alejandro tensed as the boy's eyes drank in the sight of her.

She pulled on the blue jacket. He kept his mouth shut on the subject, but he intended to buy her something warm in her own size.

"You're sure we're not going to run into Javier?"

The answer was no. Not a hundred percent sure. Yesterday he'd surfaced in Guadalajara, but today he was nowhere to be found. It meant he was on a bender. Eventually he'd OD, nearly die, and someone would drag him home. "If he's in the city, I would know. Javier's party life usually leaves a trail. And his arrival back here is never understated."

Avery's attention was diverted by the streets lined with expensive shops. "This isn't necessary. Mexico's version of Target would have been fine. In fact, I really don't think I need a swimsuit."

He placed a hand on the small of her back and guided her toward a ridiculously ostentatious boutique with swimsuits in the window. "Let's check this place out."

One step inside the place and he knew it was a mistake. A saleswoman already had Avery by the arm. He launched himself into the role of domineering male. Under normal circumstances, Avery probably wouldn't have tolerated it, but in a place where money flowed like water, it was the norm. And this shop was the worst of its kind—a place where wealthy old men shopped for their twenty-something girlfriends. Leather chairs were situated around a raised platform. Racks of lingerie, with price tags greater than the average citizen's annual rent, lined one wall. He should have known better.

"We're here for a swimsuit," he said in Spanish. "For exercise. Swimming laps." With a nod, an older woman, sophisticated with her shock of gray hair amidst an otherwise black bob, evaluated Avery. The saleswoman's face was a blank. Neither approving nor critical.

Avery was instructed to stand aside as the clerk collected swimsuits. Periodically, the woman would hold one up to check it against Avery's coloring. From what he could see, the clerk had ignored his request. No one could possibly swim laps in that.

Avery's eyes were jade, a sign that, he was learning, meant anxiety. Her cheeks were growing increasingly more flushed. He stroked her arm. "Don't fight it. They have their ways of doing things here. If you don't love it, we're not buying it."

The clerk held a hand in the direction of the fitting rooms. Avery shot him a doubtful look. She'd hardly been allowed to see what the woman had selected.

"Señor, is it your preference to be in the room with her or to have her show you?" the older woman asked.

Either way, Avery would probably want to strangle him. "I'll stay out here."

He parked himself in a chair positioned directly in front of the stage encircled by mirrors. He nodded affirmatively at the complementary glass of wine offered by another clerk but shook his head at the open box of cigars. Finding him out here lounging with a cigar would send her over the edge.

It wasn't long before he heard Avery. "No," she said. Her voice rang out a second time, followed by sounds of a scuffle.

"Alejandro!"

He was already on his way. The saleswoman was in the process of shoving a pair of spike-heeled shoes at Avery as he opened the door.

"I'd better do this," he told the woman in Spanish. "My girlfriend is not used to our customs." He added quickly, "They do things differently in Ireland."

"Who swims laps in this?" Avery's words came out as a hiss. "What is this place? It's like Halloween for either

Brazilian supermodels or hookers. I'm not sure which." She pointed to a pair of six-inch heels. "She expects me to parade around the store in those nasty shoes."

It took everything he had not to touch her. She was right. She was no Brazilian supermodel. Standing before him, draped in narrow black bands of fabric, she was a thousand times sexier.

"Take a deep breath." He might as well have been saying it to himself. With both hands, he smoothed back the hair from her face. "There's no reason it needs to be like this." He stroked her bare shoulders. "Let's just get out of here." As he said it, his eyes were drawn to the reflection of her backside in the mirror.

"No." She grabbed him by the chin and forced him to meet her gaze.

So what? She'd caught him. She couldn't fault him for that one quick look. But there was something else in her gaze.

He'd imagined a slap. A retort. Maybe even a little lecture on objectifying women that would cause him to squirm. But what he hadn't expected was for her to launch herself at him. Together they slammed against the wall, sending hangers crashing to the floor. She wrapped her legs around his waist.

He let out a muffled groan.

"Lock the door," she said.

Somewhere in the fog of his mind, it occurred to him that this might be better handled elsewhere. She giggled as he attempted to quiet her with a kiss. There was still time to attempt a graceful exit before things progressed further.

But it was like stopping a runaway train.

~ ~ ~

Sometime later a voice said, *"Discúlpeme."* The saleswoman. She tapped on the door. At least she'd managed to ignore them for a respectable period of time. She cleared her throat.

Avery completely ignored her. Her defiant laugh was low and throaty as she retrieved the swimsuit pieces from the floor.

Alejandro buckled his belt and ran a hand through his hair.

The saleswoman repeated herself.

"*Un momento, por favor*," he said.

The dressing area was suddenly peppered with loud voices. "Anyone here speak English?" a man asked. "My wife has some bathing suits she wants to try on."

Avery rolled her eyes. "American."

He pulled her into his arms, taking advantage of the diversion to steal one more kiss. She ran her hands under the tails of his shirt. He was quick to grab her hands. "No," he whispered. "Not now."

The American spoke again. "Babe, I'll be out here. Do you know that they give you cigars and a drink while you wait? But the deal is, for me to get all that you got to model."

Avery opened the door and stepped out, head held high. Her utter confidence made him smile. The saleswoman was waiting, hands clasped and eyes on the floor as they made their exit. The epitome of discretion and professionalism.

Just beyond the entrance to the dressing area, the loud American babbled on his phone. Something about the man's drawl was more familiar than Alejandro had realized. It hit him like a brick, and there was no time to do anything about it.

"Alex?" The man exhaled a cloud of cigar smoke. "Damn, I can't believe it."

Neither could he.

"What the hell are you doing in Mexico City?"

He stiffened. Wariness crossed Avery's face, and he reached for her hand. "Scott," he finally said. It was all he could say. The man had grown pink and fleshy with time. Probably too much alcohol combined with excess hours behind a desk. They were the same age, though Scott looked somewhere closer to fifty than thirty.

"I thought I was seeing things. Someone was just talking about you today. Wondering where in the hell you'd gone to."

"Um, yeah, well, we're here," Alejandro said.

Scott cast an appraising glance over the length of Avery's body, not bothering to disguise his approval. "You always did have the most beautiful women hanging off you, buddy."

Avery's nails dug into his palm.

Scott licked his lips. "Don't tell me you're practicing law in Mexico."

"No," he said. "I'm sorry, Scott, but my wife and I are running a little late. We've got a dinner reservation with her parents across town."

"Your wife?" He leered at Avery. "Well, why don't you come on over afterwards. We're at the Hyatt. Not too far. There's a bunch of us there. Bar Association thing. You probably know half of them. All the Tulane gang. Everyone will be shocked to see you. There was even some speculation as to whether you were still alive or not."

Her nails dug deeper.

"We'll try. Thanks."

"Okay. You better. I'll be looking forward to catching up. Remember, we'll be in the bar. Bring your lady."

~ ~ ~

He was driving too fast. "Twenty-one million people in this city, and I run into him. I could have been walking down the street with Diego." He was thinking aloud. "Man. Do you know how bad that could have been?"

"No, I don't." Her words were delivered like shards of glass. "Because I don't know who you are. Tulane Law School?"

He rubbed his forehead. Slowly, her words began to register. "Why does it matter to you? Who cares where a drug-dealing scumbag goes to school?"

"That was low," she said.

It was. But he couldn't help it. He slammed his palm against the steering wheel. Scott Simpson. Of all the people. The man was the biggest gossip he'd ever known.

"What's your real name?"

They were stuck in traffic. It wasn't doing much for his mood. He could barely listen to her.

"I see. We're back to this again," she said.

"What? No. I'm just getting over the shock of it." He shook his head. "My name is Alejandro DeLeon Harrington. Alex for short."

"And why isn't there a Salazar in there anywhere?"

"What do you want? My life history? A few random facts won't change anything. My parents went to great lengths to make sure I wasn't linked with the General. They always said it was for my sake, but it was probably to keep his wife in the dark, too." It was impossible to curb the anger in his voice. "You think that knowing some random facts will somehow make things different?"

"Random facts? I asked you about your family—your *family*," she said.

The look on her face took him down about two notches.

"You're right, that sounded bad. I'm sorry. But nothing I can tell you will erase what I am." Avery turned away, leaning against the car door. He threw up his hands. "What is up with you tonight?"

"Nothing's up with me. And you're right. Everything I've learned about you has come in pieces. First, you can speak English, then the gay thing, and you couldn't even tell me you were a lawyer. Nothing you can say will make a difference. Everything is a lie." She bowed her head, and her voice grew quiet. "And because I already know who you are." She sighed heavily. "And you've proved to me over and over again that I can't win against a dead man."

It was as if his body had been infused with ice water. "I think I'd better take you home."

"No!" It was practically a scream. "I don't want to walk in and have Oso look at me that way one more time." Her breathing was ragged.

He swung the car into an empty spot along the curb. He rested his forehead against the steering wheel and then shot her a sideways glance. "Oso told you who I am."

"No. I figured it out for myself." She turned to him. "I'm sorry. It must have been terrible." Her words were genuine, though her guard was up.

"And now you know why I'm crazy. Good. Let's go home."

"Stop it. Stop acting like such a jerk. So what, you ran into some blowhard in a store. Statistically, it was going to happen to you some day."

She was right. It would have. But that wasn't why she was upset, and he knew it. It was the fact that he'd failed to tell her who his parents were. A lie of omission. She'd probably hoped that one day he'd spill his guts to her. Tell her about the General. But he wouldn't have. He couldn't. He'd never once said the words out loud. *Someone killed my father. Shot him in the back of the head while I was leaning against him.*

A familiar heaviness returned to his chest. It had been a daily part of his childhood and adolescence. In his early twenties, he'd almost been able to bury it, but it always resurfaced in the least-convenient moments. Until he took on the Ramos cartel. Then it became fuel for his days. His own brand of screwed-up therapy.

He stole another glance at her. She didn't deserve this. "I'm sorry, Avery. I'm trying to figure out how to apologize for acting like such an ass. I owed you more than my lame description of my home life." He started to say more, but for the first time in two years, he was at a loss for how to defend his mission. He was about to destroy another relationship. But the few times it had happened before, he didn't really care. This time was different. This time he'd be scarred.

He reached behind the seat. "I've been meaning to give you this. I'd like to pretend it's entirely out of the goodness of my heart."

Her eyebrows drew together in confusion. The hinged jewelry box had caught her off guard. He'd known that would be the case. As she opened it, her fingers grazed the edge of the silver cuff bracelet. Though he sensed her eyes upon his face, it was impossible to do anything more than focus on some obscure point in the distance. She lifted it from the box and slipped it on.

"It's beautiful. Is it handmade?"

He shrugged. "I guess. The truth is, I can't look at that tattoo. Every time you flip your wrist, I see one more way that I've failed you." The words just made him sound like that much more of an ass.

But she surprised him. She ran a hand under his collar. The fine hairs along the nape of his neck stood on end. And so did his guilt.

"After we left the Zapata facility that day, Javier was pretty messed up. Snorting coke, drinking vodka, and ranting about the Contreras," he said. "I could have prevented everything."

She shook her head. "Stop." She spoke through clenched teeth. "This is not your fault. You are not going to feel guilty about Javier. I'm the one who mouthed off to him. If I'd kept my mouth shut, I'd be at home right now."

"I want to tell you the story." He pulled away. "I need to tell you. Because you're right. I'm paid to be a liar. Lies of omission are part of it. But what I've kept from you is fundamental to . . ." He didn't know how to finish. Fundamental to what? Absolving himself of guilt? Being with her? Having a relationship? He couldn't say any of it. The harsh truth was that this relationship still had no future, and he didn't deserve absolution.

She intervened. "Tell me about Javier." Her voice held the slightest edge of defeat.

Alejandro kept his gaze down. "He kept saying he was going to use you to get revenge. I ignored him. Assumed he'd forget about it."

She chewed her thumbnail. "You want to know what I think?"

From the odd sound in her voice, he couldn't begin to guess. But it didn't seem like it would be a repeat of the dressing room.

She unbuckled her seatbelt and twisted to face him. He had no choice but to meet her gaze. "I think if Javier hadn't taken me across the border, I'd still be slaving away for a boss who's a liar and hoping for a promotion that wasn't going to happen. Do you want to know where I was before Zapata?" She didn't wait for a response. "Wamsutter, Wyoming. Twelve straight nights in a crappy motel all alone." Her eyes were huge, and he couldn't help but imagine what she must have looked like as a child. "Before that, it was six days in New Iberia, Louisiana, watching crews dig up pipelines. And I can keep on going."

He wasn't quite sure where this was leading, but probably best to let her keep talking.

"I think that's the reason that, out of our time together, my favorite night, even though you rejected me," she said, with a dip in her voice attempting to make him laugh, "was the night we spent in the desert. I barely knew you. And even though I thought you were gay for half the night," she shot him a look, "I still didn't feel alone. You were such a hero to me, I guess. And there was no one and nothing taking you away."

How she could manage in some strange way to forgive both him and Javier, he had no idea. He leaned across the console, reaching for her face with both hands. He kissed her long and hard.

"I want that night back," she said breathlessly.

"You'd do it over again? Really, in the desert?"

"Well, maybe I would choose to sleep somewhere besides upright in the front seat of a Jeep."

He stroked her face, memorizing every angle. If any woman could help him find his way, it was Avery.

Chapter 39

Oso deposited the box of hair color next to her dinner. At least this time, the person on the box was female. Avery glanced up at him. It was tempting to ask for his help, but he was all business tonight. Buried in paperwork and phone calls. Plus, she didn't see him dealing with hair color.

She grabbed the box and her dictionary. She couldn't screw this up. And as much as she still hated her dark hair, she didn't want to make it worse. Only Alejandro's bathroom had space to spread out, and he wouldn't be home for hours.

She documented each step with a sticky note. Maybe it would reduce the possibility of serious error. She made a face in the mirror. Her translations were questionable at best. Every time she reread the instructions, her interpretation was different.

She drummed her nails on the counter and inspected her roots for the thousandth time.

Maybe in different light they wouldn't look so obvious. How much could hair grow in another week? Her natural auburn outgrowth wasn't *that* different from the rest, was it?

The mirror shrieked otherwise.

She swatted at the box and sank to the floor. For no apparent reason, she started to cry. Tears spilled down the sides of her face, and her chest began to heave. Even after being battered by Javier, she hadn't cried this much. She buried her face between her knees. Racking sobs echoed through the bathroom. She didn't care. There was nothing she could do to stop it. And no one was around to hear her, anyway. Oso was at the other end of the apartment.

But as much as she wanted to blame it on her hair, that wasn't the cause. Nor was it eating dinner alone or missing her mother. It was the simple realization that she couldn't stop Alejandro's crazy mission of vengeance. He'd as much as told her that last night.

She stood, reaching for a tissue, and there he was in the mirror. It sent a shock wave bristling through her. She seemed to have a similar effect on him. He stared at her as if he'd never seen her before.

"Avery?"

She shook her head, still unable to speak. Alejandro was the absolute last person she wanted to see. He moved toward her, and she held out a hand to stop him. Her nose was running. She made another lunge for the tissue box.

"Can I get you some water?"

She nodded. A couple of seconds to clean up her mess and get out of here.

But he was faster than she. His fingers lingered on hers as he passed off the water bottle. "Can you tell me what's wrong?"

She'd managed to regain some composure. How much, she wasn't sure.

He didn't force her to answer, but instead reached for the hair dye box and scanned the directions. His gaze shifted to her hair. He seemed surprised at the outgrowth.

She hated him for it. He hadn't been around enough to even notice.

He set the box of hair color aside and moved closer. She took a step back. "Avery. Please don't run away from me. I'm sorry."

Why did he even bother? She looked awful. Her eyes were puffy, and her face was red.

He inched toward her. She was up against the wall. She

could have pushed him away. But she didn't. Instead, she allowed herself to be drawn into his arms. So much for inner strength.

He kissed the top of her head. This simple gesture set off a whole new round of tears. The more she failed to control her sobs, the tighter he held her.

His shirt was wet when she finally pulled away. He seemed to know better than to ask again for an explanation. Instead, he smoothed the paper instructions on the counter. "I need to give you an old shirt. This stuff can stain." He began to unbutton his own shirt.

She blew her nose. "What are you doing?"

"Getting ready to dye your hair." He tossed a t-shirt at her. "Sit on the counter. It's easier to see what I'm doing this way." He leaned over her, gathering up her hair and smoothing a towel over her shoulders. It seemed as if he'd done it a thousand times before. And tonight, he didn't smell of alcohol or someone else's smoke. It was all him: that mysterious spice mixed with the evening's misty rain. It made her want to crawl under the covers and curl up next to him, for no other purpose than to be held.

He was far more thorough than Harvey had been. Her neck grew stiff and her shoulders tired. Each section of hair was carefully divided, and he held the applicator bottle like he was Rembrandt. "You have a lot of hair."

"It's not a job for the impatient," she said.

"That's why you're lucky to have me." He smiled smugly.

Her stomach lurched. His words meant nothing. "I didn't expect you home so early."

"Diego and his wife are leaving for South Africa tomorrow night. Gone for two weeks."

The impact of this news must have shown in her face. He was quick to add, "I still have a court case to prepare for.

Can you turn your head a little? But it won't be anything like it's been these last two weeks." He frowned. "Wow. It really has been nearly two weeks since Valerone. Hasn't it?"

"Yes." Her voice broke.

He set the bottle aside. His words were a whisper. "I'm sorry for last night—and everything else. More than anything, I really do want to tell you everything. But I can't." She averted her gaze, turning her attention to the floor tiles. "You deserve better."

She ran a hand along his face, pausing over the barely detectable stubble. "That's not what I want."

His gaze shifted away, and she knew in that moment that she'd never really have him.

"I can rinse my own hair."

"Avery . . ."

She put a hand on his chest. "You don't need to say it."

~ ~ ~

She was halfway down the hallway to the kitchen when Alejandro called out from the darkened family room. The sound of a chair scraping across the tile sent her heart into its familiar traitorous flutter. She glanced over her shoulder to see him standing at the end of the kitchen island. "I need to buy you something warm to wear. Something other than my navy jacket."

"I like your navy jacket."

He moved up behind her. He was so close that his breath warmed her damp hair. "Why?"

She kept her back to him. One glance at his face, and all her resolve would vaporize. "Because it still smells like the campfire." She took a deep breath and closed her eyes. "And you."

He didn't move. The seconds seemed like hours. His hesitation was palpable.

Finally, his hands went to her shoulders. Slowly, he spun her around.

"This wasn't supposed to happen," he said.

"What?"

"I wasn't supposed to ever let go."

Chapter 40

The door rattled. Oso. This was at least the third time this week he'd gone to the rooftop to tend to his plants and forgotten his key. Avery set the Spanish book aside and moved to let him in.

She barely opened the door before dashing back to her Spanish book. The quiz she was taking was supposed to be timed. Lost in translating some conversation about a couple arguing over where to eat dinner, it was several seconds before she noticed something was off. Oso shuffled. These footsteps were lighter, sharper.

Her head jerked up.

She didn't need an introduction. She knew exactly who he was. Trench coat, expensive clothes, and graying temples: Diego Ramos. His mere presence seemed to come with a gust of frigid air.

The fact that he wasn't welcome didn't stop the man from moving toward her. Oso kept a small pistol in a drawer only six inches from her hand. She kept her eyes on him as she searched the open drawer. Finally, her hand made contact with the cold metal grip. She pointed the gun at him.

He seemed unfazed. It didn't help that the gun was bobbing in her shaking grasp.

"Put the gun down." His English was heavily accented.

"No. Why would I?"

"Because my men are in the hall. Even if you manage to kill me, which I suspect you won't, they will do worse to you."

He continued to move toward her. Where was Oso? If he was on the roof and this man was telling the truth, he could be ambushed.

There was no choice but to do as he asked. She set the gun in the drawer and leaned her hip against it. At least this way he couldn't grab it from her.

He moved like a young man, crossing his arms over his chest, casually leaning against the kitchen table. Her voice shook. "Are you Mr. DeLeon? My uncle Oso said it was okay to hang out here. I hope you don't mind."

Diego sighed, massaging his chin. "I know who you are. You're no niece of Oso's." He pulled out a kitchen chair. "Have a seat."

It was either the stupidest thing to do or the only thing to do. Her mind was such a blur, she wasn't sure which. All she knew was that it would be better for this man to leave before Oso's sudden arrival brought on a gun fight.

He patted the chair. "Please."

She did as he requested, her heart thundering and her palms sweating.

His eyes were Javier's, minus the lunatic element. Instead, Diego's held the appearance of icy indifference. "I assume by now you know who I am." She nodded. "Good, then introductions are not necessary."

"What do you want?" It sounded almost brave—hardly what she felt.

"I want you out of Mexico."

"Then we both want the same thing."

He pulled out a chair for himself. "It's not that simple, is it?"

"No. Your son is offering a ridiculous amount of money for my capture."

Diego leaned back in his chair. "I don't want your death linked with my family." He rubbed the back of his neck. "I'm getting too old for this."

"Then help me. You have resources."

He shook his head. "No."

His outright refusal made no sense. She got the feeling that whatever came next wouldn't be good. "How did you know I was here?"

"Because I know my attorney the way I know the back of my own hand. And ever since your arrival in Mexico, he's been losing his edge. I thought I had things taken care of, but it seems he was one step ahead of me. Rescuing you was a mistake on his part. He's too soft-hearted." He raised his chin and peered down at her. "Now it seems that it's more than that, and it is beginning to disrupt my plans for him."

"Which are?"

"None of your concern." He steepled his fingers. "You can find your way across that border yourself. And if you die doing it," he said with a shrug, "it's no fault of mine."

"But you just said you don't want my death linked with your family. Can't you at least guarantee me that your son won't kill me? Or someone trying to collect his reward money?"

"I think you know by now that Javier has a mind of his own. My wife and I are to leave for Johannesburg in four hours. If you are still here when we return from this trip, my men will kill you."

She didn't doubt him. His tone wasn't even threatening, he seemed to be merely stating a fact. She massaged her temples. "Let me get this straight. You are telling me I need to leave to spare your upstanding reputation, while you allow your son to continue with this crazy manhunt? Don't you think I'd be out of here by now if I could be?" Something in Diego's expression shifted, and she understood. He honestly believed that it was her choice to remain in Mexico.

"I can see now, you've misunderstood things." She leaned toward him, feeling a sudden advantage. "I have a career to return to, a fiancée, and a mother who is dying a slow death, wondering where I am. Contrary to whatever you're imagining, I am not free to roam this city. Alejandro has me captive here. If you've mistaken our relationship for something else, then you're wrong. We don't even speak the same language." She waved her hands about. "Nice as it is, this place is still a prison."

"Then why haven't you used that gun on him?"

"I've thought about it. At least a hundred times. But then where would I go? It wouldn't change the fact that I have a price on my head. And you're right: Alejandro's soft-hearted. More so than your son, anyway. So unlike Javier, Alejandro intends to maintain the fine reputation of the Ramos cartel while *also* sparing my life."

She sounded dangerously cocky and overly confident. The exact attitude that had caught Javier's attention that fateful afternoon in Zapata. She took a steadying breath and tried to play it with a bit more humility. "As I understand it, Oso will be taking me home in the next day or so."

"She's right." The sound of Oso's voice nearly launched her from the chair. Judging from the lack of color in Diego's face, he was also taken by surprise. Oso continued, "We leave in the morning. I'm working on some documentation at this very moment."

Diego crossed his arms and switched to Spanish. Oso's retorts were no more than one or two words. Meanwhile, she buried her hands under her thighs to stifle the convulsive tremors.

Their conversation had lasted no more than two minutes before Diego slid out of his chair. His eyes narrowed as he spoke to her. "I hope for your mother's sake you make it home."

~ ~ ~

After the door shut, she and Oso didn't even look at one another. She threw herself against the back of the chair and stared at the ceiling. She wasn't sure about Oso, but she didn't trust Diego not to burst through that door a second time.

"You couldn't have played it any better. Brilliant job," Oso said.

"But we need to leave by tomorrow."

"We don't have that long. Once the old man is out of town, Diego's guys will be looking for a way to occupy their time. Hunting us down would be exactly their kind of fun. We'll leave tonight."

"Do we go without Alejandro?"

Oso stroked his beard. "I'm afraid of how he'll react if we just take off."

"I know you have these sort of romantic notions about the two of us. But he has told me in no uncertain terms that this thing between us can't last. Maybe it would be best if we did just go."

Oso's face looked suddenly haggard. "I don't care what he's told you. If he comes home to an empty house, he'll do something foolish and end up getting himself killed. By leaving tonight, we have the whole weekend to get you across the border safely. And Alejandro can be back at work on Monday. Diego's guys won't dare touch Alejandro, as long as he returns. Diego did promise to have his guys offer a little misdirection to Javier. That will keep that little shit off our tails for a little while, but he's got plenty of snitches between here and the border itching to get that reward money."

She dug her fingers into her temples. None of it sounded good. "What kind of plans was Diego referring to?"

Oso snorted. "He wants his daughter, Luisa, married off to Alejandro. I think he sees Alejandro heading up the cartel someday."

Avery shook her head. "Javier would kill him."

"If I didn't beat him to it," Oso said. He slapped the table. "Let's get you started packing the coolers. I'll round up the team and load the other necessities."

"I assume you don't really have documents for me."

He squeezed her shoulder. "I'd give up my pension to get you a passport. But I'm afraid not."

A sound at the front door launched the two of them from their seats. Before either could react, Alejandro called out their names. They exchanged a quick glance before responding. "We're in the kitchen."

He was pale and breathless as he tossed his keys on the counter. "Javier knows where we are."

Chapter 41

Alejandro pulled her into his arms. His hold on her was tight, and his heartbeat was strong. Faster than usual, but it was not the same rhythm of fear that thundered through her body. He was all adrenaline.

"How?"

"José painted a mural of you. Someone saw it… and you can take it from there."

"I told him not to. I told him—"

He stroked her hair. "It doesn't matter. It was just a matter of time before something happened. And it wasn't actually José, it was Angelica."

Her hand balled up into a fist. "Shouldn't she realize this could a death sentence for you, too?"

"I think that was the motivation. But at least this way we got some warning. Javier is more than four hours away, so we need to be out of here in two."

Oso was already sorting through a staggering amount of ammunition. Alejandro started to speak to him in Spanish.

"Don't," she said. "Everything needs to be said in English."

The scowl on Alejandro's face told her this was exactly what he preferred not to do. Always better to keep her in the dark. Filter everything, as if she were a child.

Oso gave Alejandro a small, reluctant nod. "She's right. The more she knows, the better prepared we are."

"All right," Alejandro said. The look he gave Oso suggested that he wasn't thrilled. "Make sure to pack the vests. I'll contact the rest of the team. Get the word out that we're headed to Guadalajara."

"Why Guadalajara?" she asked.

"Diego keeps a house there," Alejandro said. "We all use it a lot. Javier might not believe it, but he'll be forced to send a couple of guys there to check it out. This will keep his security team divided, and that's what we want."

"Meanwhile, we head elsewhere," Oso said to her. He shoved a gun into the holster on his hip.

"What if he sends someone here?" she asked. "Doesn't he have guys here in town that aren't traveling with him?"

"Yes, and you can bet they're already scouting out this building," Oso held a small bullet up to the light and squinted at the markings on the bottom. "Probably a small team. Two or three guys."

"According to one of our guys who's traveling with Javier, the men sent to watch this apartment won't be here for another couple of hours. Javier's so screwed up that he wants to get us himself. In fact, he's bragging about it. So, he'll have a couple of guys watching this place, but they've been ordered to leave us alone until he arrives."

Like a big game hunter shooting a caged lion. It was easy to imagine. Brave Javier makes his grand entrance surrounded by an army of men.

Alejandro pointed toward the bedroom. "Let's get packed. I need to make a trip to the office before we leave."

"I thought you just came from the office," Avery said.

He shook his head. "I was in a meeting across town when Victor called and told me about the mural."

Gathering her few outfits and toiletries took no more than two minutes. She stuffed the black dress into the trash bag. Meanwhile, Alejandro swore to himself from inside the closet. Drawers slammed, and there was the occasional sound of something thudding against the wall.

"Do you still have those steel-toed boots of yours?"

"Yes." She was preoccupied, rummaging through the trash bag in search of Harvey's gun.

"They might have some value. Depending on where we end up," he said from the closet. "And that cowboy hat of Oso's."

"Okay." Not like she was planning on leaving anything behind anyway. Sitting cross-legged at the end of the bed, she unzipped Harvey's small satchel. She withdrew four boxes of twenty-two bullets. The pistol was buried somewhere at the bottom.

The sight of it sent a jolt down her spine. She'd never really imagined putting it to use. It had been her favorite during their morning practices. Harvey could have given her any one of a dozen less-impressive guns. Avery stroked the pearl handle. The unexpected gift left her feeling unusually sentimental.

Alejandro grumbled about the need to pack for all kinds of weather. "Don't worry, I'll bring the blue jacket."

"Thanks." She slid open the chamber, double checking to see that it was empty. Not that Harvey would ever make such a stupid mistake.

"What the . . ." Alejandro stared at her. "Where did you get that?"

She slid the chamber closed and returned the gun to the bag. "Harvey."

"Harvey gave you a gun?"

At any other time, she would have laughed hysterically at the strange look on his face. "Yeah."

"Harvey? Gave you a gun?" He seemed to be talking to himself. "She must be losing it. She had to know you might be tempted to kill me."

"Obviously, she trusted that I wouldn't shoot you."

He raised a skeptical eyebrow. "Surprised you didn't use it on me when you found out I spoke English."

"It crossed my mind."

"And you know how to use it?"

"Of course. She taught me how to shoot all her guns. But this was my favorite."

"Your favorite?" He scratched his head and mumbled something in Spanish. "Are you ready otherwise, Annie Oakley?"

Oso called out from down the hall. "Loading the cars."

"Two minutes," Alejandro shouted back in reply. "I really need to get going. But first I want to give you something. There's so much that we need to talk about. But I guess we'll have plenty of time on the road for that." He lifted a sizable painting from the wall. The painting itself was so bland that it hardly seemed like a surprise to find a wall safe behind it. He continued to speak as he tapped out a code. "It's very important. And it's one of many things I intended to talk to you about this weekend, but we only have time for the short version right now."

Following the electronic hum of gears, the safe door swung open. She shifted to get a glimpse of the contents. Stacks of paper, cash, and what appeared to be passports. Everything she imagined a spy would possess.

He tossed several bundles of American dollars toward his duffel bag. "Not sure whether I'll need to be an American or a Mexican this week." He grinned at her, though she could see it was forced. "And this is it." Whatever it was, it was too small to see from her vantage point. He shut the door and returned the painting to its hanger.

He knelt beside her and held out a small key. "Do you have a safe place to put this?"

A look of horror crossed her face. She pushed his hand away.

"Listen to me Avery. We can talk about this more later. But what you need to know is it goes to a box at Zapata County State Bank. Box number is nine twenty-eight. Can you remember that?"

She refused to meet his eye. He squeezed her shoulder. "Please tell me you'll remember."

She nodded.

"Good. My attorney has made sure that you're authorized to access it. Like I said, we'll have time to talk about it in the car. Is your bag ready to go?"

"Yeah."

"I'll take it down with me, then." She followed him toward the front hallway, where Oso was stockpiling gun cases. "I should be no more than half an hour," he said to Oso. "Keep an eye on the cameras. You never know."

"You sure this trip to the office is necessary?" Oso asked.

He gave Oso a long, hard look. "This may be my last chance. I think we both know I need to be prepared to kiss my relationship with the Ramos family goodbye."

"Then go. Get out of here," Oso said. "Avery, you and I can finish up here. We'll have some men to keep fed."

Alejandro gave her a quick squeeze intended to seem casual. She didn't let him off that easily. Wrapping her arms around his waist, she clung to him, seeking some kind of confirmation that things would be okay.

But every rigid muscle in his body betrayed him. Okay was something he couldn't guarantee.

It made her ache to tell him. Just spit out those three elusive words. Instead she mouthed it silently against his chest, too afraid. Twenty-eight years old, and she'd barely ever said the words to anyone outside her own family.

Alejandro started toward the door. With his back to the two of them, he muttered something in Spanish.

She tried to break the sounds apart into words. He'd said it so fast. Deliberately, as if she wouldn't notice he wasn't speaking English. Words meant for Oso. The fact that she might comprehend any of it would never cross his mind. But she did, surprising even herself. It was only the last two words. But those two words—*sin me*—were enough.

"No!" It came out louder than she intended. "We're not leaving without you."

He stopped midstride. His grip on the back of a nearby chair left his knuckles white, but he said nothing.

She closed her eyes, hoping he would change his mind. But the eventual sound of his footsteps, followed by the click of the latch, told her otherwise.

~ ~ ~

It was like packing for an extended camping trip. "Why so much food?" she asked.

"In this country, you prepare for the worst and hope for the best. We might end up on the coast, and then again maybe in the desert. Either way, we need to stay under the radar. We've got at least three others joining us, and staying clear of shops and restaurants gives us an advantage."

The two of them boxed up fruit, cans of corn, beans, rice in commercial-sized sacks, endless cases of water, and, of course, tortillas. The walls were lined with camp stoves, water cans, sleeping bags, and half a dozen other boxes.

She checked the wall clock for the hundredth time. Without so much as a glance her way, Oso shook his head. "It's only been twenty-two minutes."

"Maybe I should help you load the car," she said.

"Safest place for you is right where you are."

Safe was one thing, but not losing her mind was important, too. "Where do you keep the alcohol?"

"You need a drink?"

"No. But I might tomorrow. Or the next day."

Oso stroked his beard. "Alejandro doesn't like his guys to drink on the job."

"And I'm not one of his guys."

"Keep it hidden where the guys can't see it." He tossed her a set of keys. "Those go to the wine cellar. It's at the end of the hall past the maid's quarters."

"How did I not know about it?"

"Maybe you had eyes for something else." With a grunt, he hefted a box of cans off the counter. "I'm making a run to the garage. I'll be right back."

She managed to conceal several bottles of wine and a corkscrew at the bottom of a box of dishtowels. Alejandro had been gone thirty-seven minutes. She paced the long hall. Oso was on what must be his third trip downstairs. Why hadn't she kept Harvey's gun in her pocket? She ran a hand across her forehead. None of this came naturally to her.

Her heart stopped at the sound of the front door. She skidded along the hallway, but as she made the turn, she could see it was only Oso.

He was breathless. Beads of sweat dotted his forehead, and he didn't look her in the eye. "I assume you know how to drive."

Her mouth felt dry, and her legs were anything but steady.

"They're already here."

"You mean Javier's guys," she said.

"Yeah. There's only two of them." He began to gather the remaining items scattered about the kitchen.

She didn't have the strength to ask more. Instead, she attempted to support herself against the kitchen counter.

He frowned at her. "Come on. We're going to pick up Alejandro. I moved the cars to the fifth floor. Morons are hanging around on the third. You'll have to follow me in the Land Rover." He nodded at the cowboy hat. "Put it on, keep your head down, and stay right behind me. There's a cell phone in the car. I'll call you. Keep it on speaker, and don't hang up on me."

~ ~ ~

She spotted the two men as they wound down past the third-floor elevators. Oso was right. Not exactly the brightest. They barely even glanced up as she passed. Oso's voice rattled through the speaker. "Good job. We'll take a right out of the parking garage. People drive like drunken fools in this city. Stay on my tail. Even if you have to run a light or two. Just lean on your horn, and try not to get hit."

He was driving a black Suburban. At least the size of it made it easy to track. "Okay." She was still shaky. "How far?"

"Less than a mile."

He was right about the crazy driving. Along the way, drivers of smaller cars tried to wedge their way between them. But she was determined. She never allowed more than a few feet between the two vehicles. It was the motorcycles that terrified her. Weaving in and out fearlessly.

"Two more blocks. He'll be on the right. Says he's standing under a tree."

It had started to rain. The red of the Suburban lights intensified, and she slowed the Range Rover to a crawl. Alejandro's dark form appeared at the passenger door as she fumbled to unlock it.

"Thank God," she said.

He was soaked. Oso's voice came over the speaker. "Nice job. I'm headed to my house. Where to and what time?"

"*Lagarto Tranquilo*. 10:00 p.m.," Alejandro said. "The rest of the guys are already on their way." He clicked off the phone and leaned over to kiss her cheek. Cold and wet, the stubble of his jaw scratched her face. Never before had she felt anything so reassuring. "We'll get out of downtown and switch. Unless you want to keep driving."

"No thanks. Oso's right, these people are crazy."

~ ~ ~

Lagarto Tranquilo turned out to be a dive bar in a desolate little town. It was easy to understand why Alejandro chose it. It was so dark that even his security team would have trouble identifying her.

The place was empty. Their party totaled seven now. The men congregated around the table as Alejandro laid out plans in Spanish. Though physically they were nothing alike, the men all shared a haunted look. Shifty-eyed and ready to strike at any moment. A side-effect of the job, she guessed.

Next to her, a man named Leo cleaned his fingernails with a switchblade. Across from him sat Spider. Aptly named, since his entire neck was one continuous tattoo of a web. No one made eye contact with her, except one. A wiry guy who leered at her whenever she glanced in his general direction. Something about him warned her to keep her gaze down.

Alejandro sent Leo and his partner, whose name was Gato, to the bar. They'd been assigned to watch the front door. Spider and the creepy guy made their way to a dark corner in the rear of the bar, leaving Oso, Alejandro and her alone at the large table.

"Since Javier's coming in from the southeast, I think we should head southwest," Alejandro said.

Oso cocked a brow. "The Ramos cartel has nothing but enemies in that direction. Are you forgetting who you are?"

"No." Alejandro's jaw hardened. "And it's exactly why no one will expect us to run that way. It buys us some time. We can lay low for a few days."

Oso's gaze caught hers. Alejandro still had no idea that Diego had issued a threat. He needed to be back at work on Monday.

"You're not thinking, man." Oso's eyes narrowed. His next words were delivered in a language she'd never heard before. Something no one in this room could understand except the two of them.

Alejandro hung his head. "You're right." He lifted his eyes to hers. "Tonight we head for Monterrey. See how far we get by daylight."

To this point, she hadn't opened her mouth. But she needed to understand some things. "Is it okay for me to talk in here?" Alejandro and Oso were already hunkered over, keeping their voices low.

"Keep in mind that no one knows Alejandro speaks English," Oso said. "Best to keep your eyes on me regardless of who you're talking to."

"But Alejandro and I are riding together. Isn't that a little weird, since supposedly we don't share a common language?"

"You've got a big price tag on your head. It's normal that the boss would want to keep an eye on you himself. Just don't give the men any reason to question it," Oso said.

"Did you get what you needed from the office?" she asked Alejandro. It was difficult to keep her eyes on Oso.

"No," Alejandro said.

"But you have enough," Oso said.

Alejandro turned away. "Later." His voice was a low growl.

"Tell me why we can't just charter a plane," she said.

Alejandro rested his head in his hands. He seemed to enjoy the fact that Oso was forced to do all the talking.

"Same reason we aren't taking a boat, or train, or anything else," Oso said. "Charter companies would have been the first thing Javier notified. We can't pay those guys enough for them to ignore Javier's reward money."

"So what does that leave?"

"We get across the tough way. We might find an independent coyote that isn't under the thumb of the cartels. But more likely, we'll do it ourselves."

"You mean cross the Rio Grande? On foot?" The two men locked gazes. "Is there any reason you two can't get me papers? Aren't there forgers out there?"

Neither seemed willing to speak. Slowly, it began to

dawn on her. "I get it. Javier's reward is so much that they'd rat me out, too."

"Yeah," Oso said softly. He patted her arm. "It's easy to bribe people. Forgers, coyotes, even cops. But it's not so easy to know where their loyalties lie."

"But you guys should have some control. Look at who you are. There has to be a way. Right?" she asked.

Alejandro's voice was flat. "We're limited. You know that."

"What he means is that we can only take it so far," Oso said.

A nice way of saying the U.S. government did not want her kidnapping to interfere with bigger things. Alejandro slid his chair back and headed for the back of the room without a word. If his tension could be converted into energy, it would be enough to light up the bar.

"He's beating himself up," Oso said.

"He shouldn't. He's risked his career for me," she said. "And his life." All the while embedded in one of Mexico's most dangerous cartels. Even though she'd known it for weeks, she hadn't been entirely appreciative of how far he'd gone to concoct a façade of safety. Since leaving the brothel, she'd never really felt threatened. Harvey's place, Alejandro's apartment, and even in Valerone, he'd managed to cocoon her. Her chest ached, and it took all she had not to look over her shoulder at him.

"It's not that. He just learned there's price on his head now, too."

She gripped the table to steady herself. It was easier to downplay the danger when it was only your own. Fear for his life surrounded her like a stifling cloud. Her mind reeled, desperately struggling for a solution. "He has to turn me in to Javier. He can claim that was his plan all along. Javier won't kill me. And Diego will protect Alejandro."

"Diego's halfway around the world right now. He can't protect him. And don't delude yourself into thinking Javier won't kill you. He's one sick guy. And if he didn't kill you, you'll wish he did."

Avery slumped in the chair. Oso was right, she couldn't imagine anything worse than going back to Javier. "What are you going to tell Alejandro about Diego's visit?"

"Nothing. The less he has to obsess about, the better."

"Do these men know who I am?"

"Yes. Most of them have worked for us for a couple of years now. You should be able to trust them."

"Will there be others joining us?" she asked.

"Depends." Oso sent a signal to someone at the back of the room. "Drink up. The bar's getting a little too crowded for comfort." He slapped the table and laughed loudly. All part of the pretense.

He started to push back in his chair before she stopped him with a hand on his wrist. "Alejandro has an American passport. Make him go back to the U.S. now. He could be on a plane tonight. You and I can find a way without him."

"Darling, you know as well as I do that he's not going to agree to that."

It was exactly what she expected to hear. But it wasn't acceptable. "Then what can I do to help? I need to do my part."

"Best thing you can do is keep your gun loaded and watch out for anything unusual." He shrugged. "The more eyes we have, the better. Beyond that—it's the will of God."

And to her surprise, he crossed himself.

~ ~ ~

"The Jeep would be better than this piece-of-fluff Range Rover," Alejandro said in disgust. His mood was foul, and his driving was just a step above reckless. "Aren't you going to say something?"

She was doing her best to ignore him, let him calm down. She'd taken Oso's advice and was trying to decide how best to carry the pistol. It was merely a distraction, but it prevented her from calling Alejandro out on his driving. She shoved the gun in the front pocket of her jeans, hoping it wouldn't blow her kneecap off.

"I want you to leave Mexico tonight," she said.

"Oso told you."

It wasn't a question, meaning she wouldn't answer. "Javier will be looking for you and me together. If you just get on a plane, it's that much safer. Oso and I will be fine. People will assume he's my father, and no one will look twice at us."

"He's a little young to be your father."

"Yeah, but you know how he loves disguises."

Alejandro managed a weak smile. "Nice try, but no. I'm not leaving you here."

"Because you're a control freak. You refuse to delegate."

"As much as I appreciate your psychological approach, nothing's going to work."

"Why not?"

There was a long period of silence. She could feel his effort to calm himself. He took her hand, massaging each knuckle individually. "I think you know why not."

She was tempted to make up something about his inability to trust others. But she let it go. He mumbled something to himself in Spanish. She frowned, trying to pick apart the words. "Say it again slowly."

"It's just a saying. A Spanish idiom."

"Please. I'm trying to figure it out."

He took his eyes off the road to look at her as he spoke each word with slow deliberation. "*Donde hay amor, hay dolor.*"

Her heart skipped a beat. Even she could translate that.

"Do you understand it?" he asked.

"Yes." She paused, uncertain whether she could say the words. "It means where there is love, there is pain." She swallowed. "It's just an idiom."

There was a long pause before he spoke. "It's not just an idiom. I didn't intend for it to be."

For a moment, there was nothing but the hushed lull of road noise between them. The absence of words was neither uncomfortable nor awkward. Just suspended uncertainty.

He started to say something but then stopped himself. "I do love you, Avery."

"But?"

His face was grim. She wasn't sure she wanted to hear what he had to say.

"The truth is, I probably shouldn't have said anything. Love isn't a luxury either of us can afford at this point in our lives. It makes us vulnerable."

She'd been right. She was sorry she'd asked.

"You see love as weakness? Like a character flaw?" she asked.

"No. I don't." He didn't sound entirely convincing. "But maybe I'm the only one who's vulnerable here." There was a smile behind his words. "You haven't said a word about your own feelings."

"Don't play coy," she said. "You probably knew how I felt from day one. You just want to hear me say it."

"Why shouldn't I want to hear it out of your mouth?"

Making a game of it this way made her feel like a teenager. Why didn't they just admit it after a couple of glasses of wine, in bed, like most people?

"All right, I do love you. Is that better?"

"Not much. It sounds like I coerced you. And didn't you tell me that you had bad taste in men?"

She pinched his arm. "No. I didn't say anything close to that. And even if I did, at least my taste has changed."

"Maybe it's just your judgment that's the problem," he said.

"Exactly what is your point?"

"My point is you just confessed your feelings to someone with a price on his head and headed for the U.S.-Mexico border with a crazy man pursuing him."

"No different than what you just did. Of course, I already know that your taste in women is what got us here in the first place. Thank you, Angelica."

"What do you expect? I was fifteen years old. Half a lifetime ago."

"And she's not over you yet." Avery placed a hand over her heart in a dramatic gesture. "Please tell me that in fifteen years I won't be abandoned and still pining for you."

He squeezed her hand. "Funny."

~ ~ ~

The sunlight peeking through the low clouds surprised her. How long had she been asleep? She glanced over at Alejandro, who was looking ragged.

"There's coffee," he said.

She arched her back. "I slept through a stop?"

"Snored through a stop was more like it." The side of his mouth curved upward.

"Where are we?"

"About three hours south of Monterrey. We'll be leaving the tollway in just a minute. It's side roads from here on out."

His phone buzzed, and Oso's voice came in over the speaker. "Rain to the north. Torrential from all reports."

"Doesn't matter. We need to keep going. All the way," Alejandro said.

"What about holing up in one of these little towns, even if it's just for a couple of hours? Reports are good. Javier's still parked in the city. We've got miles on him. A couple of these guys just got off sixteen-hour shifts. Someone's going to end up in a ditch," Oso said.

"I can drive too," Avery offered.

Alejandro swiped the hair off his forehead and sagged against the door. "No. Let's head for Agua Delgado. I know a guy who runs a hotel there. Let me call him, and I'll text you the address." He hung up and glanced at her. "Don't worry, this one's a big step up from Valerone. Clean sheets and everything."

"You really think that's what I'm worried about?"

"No." He tilted his head from side to side, stretching his neck. They'd already exited the tollway and were headed into the mountains.

"Tell me what the plan is. How I'm going to get across the border."

"It's not glamorous. But I think it will work. Just west of Zapata, there are a couple of places it's easy to get across the Rio Grande. For most of the year, the water's only waist high at the worst."

"But it's raining," she said.

"Not necessarily. It's raining a hundred miles north of here. But that's still some distance from the border. We might get outside Nuevo Laredo and not see a cloud. Anyway, there's one area in particular where I know the Border Patrol. If they see us, they'll just look the other way."

"So what's the big deal then?"

"Well, several things. The officers I know might not be on duty. Also . . ." He glanced at her. "I know them through Javier. You are a U.S. citizen. And it shouldn't be a big deal to prove, but word could get back to him first."

"But if I'm already across?" She didn't need to wait for an answer to her question. "They're corrupt enough to send me back to Mexico?"

"Something like that." He ran a hand over her thigh.

"That's a worst-case scenario. Like I said, it shouldn't be that difficult to find a place that will work."

"And once I get to the other side?"

"That's what I'm going to work on next. Calling your friend Sam."

Her head jerked. The sound of Sam's name had a strange effect on her. It wasn't that she didn't want to return home. It just seemed so foreign now. She'd been in this country for months now. She wasn't even sure she was the same person she'd been when she worked for Sam.

So preoccupied with life in the apartment, she'd given zero thought to the details of what came next. She had no home. No job. Of course, her mother would be begging her to move in. And for the sake of PR, Eric would make a big show of trying to welcome her back.

"You okay?"

"Not really. But it's nothing for you to worry about. Tell Sam not to say anything to anyone. Especially not my mom. If something happens . . . it's just best that she not expect me." Her eyes narrowed. "What kind of agreement do you have with Sam?"

He exhaled heavily. "Mind if we switch for a little while?" He had already pulled the Range Rover over to the side of the road.

"Are you evading the question?"

"No. There's not much to tell. I've never talked to the man. But I've provided him with updates on your wellbeing through other channels. I discouraged Sam from paying your ransom."

Her jaw dropped. "What?"

"It's not like it sounds. What I meant was that I didn't trust Javier to release you, even with Sam's money."

"In other words, Javier would never let me go because I would turn around and point the finger at him."

"Exactly."

She'd been so naïve to believe that Javier would never kill her. But maybe it was her naivete that kept her alive, too.

"Do you mind driving?" he asked.

"Of course not."

It felt good to step outside of the car. The air was crisp and clean, with the faintest scent of rain. She raised her arms in a stretch. Alejandro stepped behind her, encircling her waist with his arms and planting kisses along the side of her face.

"Mmmm." His hands slid up the back of her shirt. "I'd better sleep in the car, so that I can spend my hotel time wisely." He hooked a finger under her bra.

"Running for our lives from one of the most dangerous and certainly the craziest man in Mexico, and that's what's on your mind?"

He shrugged. "I'm not dead yet. I'd have to be dead to ride around in a car with you and not think about it."

~ ~ ~

He had her shirt off before the hotel room door closed. She wasn't any better, unbuttoning his jeans as they made their way to the bed. It might have been the tension of the last few hours or the uncertainty of their future—she didn't know—but they seemed to share a mutually desperate need for one another.

She kicked the rest of her clothes aside as he pushed her back against the bed. With her hands on his hips, she pulled him down on top of her. Arching her back and raising her hips to meet his, she gripped his shoulders.

There was no time for foreplay and no need for words. With gazes locked on one another, he entered her.

What followed was feral. Animalistic, urgent, and uncompromising.

Afterward, he threw himself against the pillow, breathless. Stroking the area under her breasts, he said, "Please tell me I didn't hurt you."

"I could almost ask you the same thing," she said. "I think I might have drawn blood down your back."

He touched an index finger to her lower lip. "Let's take a shower."

"I haven't even caught my breath yet."

"Hopefully you'll be feeling that way again in a few minutes."

~ ~ ~

By the time she stepped out of the steamy bathroom, Alejandro was already sprawled across the bed. She lifted the damp towel from his hand. It seemed a shame to cover him up and deprive herself of the view, but he'd freeze otherwise.

She uncorked the wine and decided it was time to set out to find something to eat. The manager directed her to the small hotel bar to wait while a cook prepared something to take to the room.

As she rounded a corner, she spotted Spider's lecherous partner. Perched on a barstool, cigarette dangling from his lips, and drinking something that probably had a lot more heft than wine. Fortunately, his back was to her, and he hadn't heard her come in. She chose a table behind a post, well out of his line of sight.

His phone rang, and since they were the only two in the bar, it was impossible to ignore him. Ninety-nine percent of what he said was in Spanish, delivered far too rapidly for her comprehension. Despite this, something in his tone was soft, as if he might be speaking with a woman.

His second call was different. She leaned forward in her chair. His speech had shifted to a tough guy slur. Periodically he glanced over his shoulder, scanning the room, but she made sure he never saw her. His voice ran deeper. Rough.

Silently, she tapped the table, wishing the cook would hurry up. It was tempting to blow off the food. She could crawl into that warm bed, snuggle up next to Alejandro, and forget about this smarmy little man.

But then he said something impossible to ignore. A demand that ended with the name Javier. A lengthy pause ensued. He set the phone on the bar, digging in his pocket for cigarettes. He'd switched it to speaker. There was no other voice and only static in the background. He lit a cigarette, propped the phone between his shoulder and ear, and toyed with his empty glass.

Maybe she was imagining things. This race to the border would do it to anyone. Limited sleep, little food. Anyway, this guy would have to be the world's biggest idiot to have a conversation with Javier in here. She rubbed her eyes. Too much time focused on Javier.

"*Bueno*," he said. Unfortunately, the phone was no longer on speaker. It would have been nice to dismiss her growing paranoia if she'd heard a voice other than Javier's on the line.

The man never said more than one or two words at a time. A lot of *si* and *no*. He was puffed up and sitting straight, as if trying to impress the person on the other end. His tone was anything but blasé. Now he was giving times. Naming places, including Agua Delgado. His dismissive pronunciation of Alejandro's name sparked rage within her. She clenched her fists, wanting to yank him from that barstool. He glanced at his watch and seemed to be estimating something. She edged forward in her seat.

The sound of footsteps interrupted her concentration. "Señorita, here is your food. No need to pay me. Your husband can pay later." The manager bowed and backed away.

The sound of the manager's voice had sent the man off his barstool and glancing about. He tucked the phone into his pocket as his eyes met hers. Shock was etched in his expression, though it didn't stop him from raising his chin in defiance.

The manager spoke to him in Spanish. Possibly asking him if he wanted another drink. It didn't matter. She snatched the food from the table and made a beeline for the stairs.

Alejandro's eyes flickered with the slam of the door, but he merely pulled the sheet over his bare shoulder. The panic in her voice got his attention. "We have to go. We have to get out of here. Call Oso."

"What?" He rubbed his eyes.

"That man, Spider's partner. He was at the bar talking on his cell. I think he was talking to Javier. He was reciting times and places. He didn't know I was there."

Alejandro's face paled, and he reached for his phone. He didn't bother with English. He tossed the phone aside and rose from the bed.

"How sure are you?"

"Not sure," she said. "I keep thinking only an idiot would call from the bar."

"Yeah, well, I'm not convinced he's one of Mexico's best and brightest. And it's always best to err on the side of caution." He stroked the side of her face with his thumb. "Don't panic. Even if Javier charters a plane or helicopter, he can't be here in more than an hour or two at best. It's why I chose this town. It has no airstrip. And between the mountains and this storm, no one could even land in a helicopter. We are truly in the middle of nowhere." He took a large bite. "You need to eat, too."

"How long has that guy worked for you? Do you trust him?"

"He hasn't been with us as long as the others. And no, I'm not sure I trust him." He reached in his bag for a clean shirt. "Oso and I are about to have a word with him. We'll find out the truth. Now, I want you to eat, and I'll be back in no time."

~ ~ ~

No time meant twenty minutes that felt like twenty hours. She knew by the look on Alejandro's face when he marched through the door that she'd been right. His fists were clenched, and there was blood on his shirt.

"There may be a job for you with the U.S. government if you're interested. I don't know how you figured it out, but thank God you did." He tossed two cell phones on the bed. "Luckily for us, it was the first time Burro had a chance to make contact with Javier. Until he got to the bar, he hadn't even been to the bathroom alone. We checked his phone, texts, emails, everything. Spider was as surprised as anyone."

"That guy's name is really Burro?"

"It's a nickname. Not that uncommon."

"Why'd he do it?"

"He claims his wife is sick and they need the money," he said. "A load of crap. My guys are well paid."

"And what now?"

"For whatever it's worth, we forced him to text Javier and tell him change of plans, we're headed west. We couldn't trust him to make the phone call since he was crying like a baby."

"Where's Burro now?"

"Locked up in the city jail. He'll find the accommodations a little unpleasant. The hotel manager is also a cop. Burro won't be released until we say so." Alejandro pulled a gun from underneath his shirt and laid it on the dresser. "And if he's lucky, that will be next March."

"But we should still get out of here." She had begun to circle the room, scooping up all personal belongings.

"Not so fast, Gabacha." He grabbed hold of her wrist and began to lead her toward the bed. "Oso is holding a meeting with the others. A little reminder of what happens when one throws in the towel on loyalty." He pressed up against her. "We still have plenty of time to ourselves."

"Oso says you haven't earned the right to call me Gabacha since you were born in the U.S., which makes you a *gabacho*."

"He's wrong about that. I was born in Mexico. Can we not mention Oso's name for the next hour or so, please?"

She wrinkled her nose. "Your shirt has blood on it."

"That's easy to fix." He whipped it off and tossed it across the room. His hands went to her hips, pulling her closer. "Plus, I've been told I'm beautiful with my shirt off." He smirked.

"Shut up," she said. He kissed her, hard. She drummed her fists against his pecs, finally managing to push away with a gasp. "I think I was drunk when I said that."

"Two sips of wine is hardly drunk." His lips moved the length of her throat. "Especially for you," he said. "Mmmm."

"What is that supposed to mean? Are you insinuating…" He covered her mouth with his and urged her toward the bed. No more game playing.

~ ~ ~

She was draped across him, bordering on sleep, when his phone drew them out of their reverie. Alejandro sat up, and she migrated to the opposite side of the bed without lifting her head. She wanted nothing more than to spend another forty-eight hours just like this. All thoughts of guns, and reward money, and Javier, forgotten.

Until that deceptively innocuous sound of his phone brought it all back.

"Yeah," he said. His fingertips traced the indentation of her spine. Her hand moved under the covers toward him, but he intercepted it before she could reach her destination. He shook his head, though the flicker in his eyes was no less wicked than her intentions.

He tossed the phone aside. "We're moving. Apparently, Javier has decided to send a couple of guys here from Monterrey just in case."

"I was afraid you'd say that. Where now?"

"To the border. Our best defense now is speed," he said.

"How long will it take?"

"Depends on where we decide to go in. Best case, four hours. But probably more like five or six. No major roads. And if this storm is north of here, we're going to be dealing with washed-out roads." He kissed the end of her nose. "You should like this part, though." His smile was sardonic. "We're headed for the desert."

Chapter 42

"See what I mean? This road would be nothing for the Jeep." Admittedly, it was a lame attempt at lightening the mood. He didn't fool her. Her body, typically the finest exhibition of feminine curves, had been fixed in rigid tension for the last thirty miles.

This part of the country could have that effect on anyone. It bore little of the beauty of the desert around Valerone. This was no man's land. Dusty, dry, and endless. Buzzards circled in the distance. The only other sign of wildlife was the occasional coyote searching for an elusive desert rat. The good part was that you could see someone stirring up dust from miles away. The downside was that they could see you, too.

"Now I see why Oso packed so much food. We haven't passed another car or even town for an hour," she said. She scanned the radio with futility, apparently desperate for a distraction. "Whoa. What's that?" she asked.

"The Oasis." A sprawling ranch with vegetation so lush one would expect to find Cancun on the other side of it. It always took him by surprise when he drove this route. "Home to one of the bigger coke distributors around. He's an American. He calls himself Freddy Chicano."

"Is he part of . . . a rival cartel?" She struggled with the words. He'd heard her do it before. The undercover bit seemed to mess with her mind.

"Not directly. He's more of a free agent. But his allegiance is not with Diego, if that's what you're asking. Freddy plays with the big boys. And he despises Javier."

"And the enemy of your enemy is your friend?" she asked.

"Probably not. We're kind of winning the lottery on enemies at the moment." He glanced in the rearview mirror. "Damn. Spider's pulled over." He whipped the Range Rover around.

It was only a flat tire, but the spare wouldn't take Spider too far. Leo squatted beside the car, loosening the lug nuts. The bigger problem was the attention they were drawing to themselves so close to The Oasis.

"We can ditch the car here. Come back for it later," Spider said.

"No," Alejandro said. "We're too close to Freddy's place. We've got ten minutes max before his guys are out here, wanting to know what we're up to. If we have to, we'll ditch it in town. It's only five miles.

"Five more miles of shitty road," Gato said. "Might as well be fifty."

"Ten minutes was an underestimate. His guys are on us already," Oso said. Heads turned toward the electronic gate of the Oasis. Two vehicles were making their exit.

"Shit," Spider said.

"At least it's only two. We still outnumber them," one of them said.

"There's probably twenty-five more back at the ranch," Spider said.

"Be cool. Just keep at it. I'll do the talking," Alejandro said. This could play out a dozen different ways. He glanced at Oso. "Make sure she stays in the car."

"What about the price on your head?"

"My guess is this will go one of two ways. Freddy's guys will either kill me or let us all go. They're too smart to do business with Javier."

He positioned himself in the center of the road at the rear of Spider's car. The oncoming pickups would have to either run him down or stop. Sports clichés filled his head. The best defense . . . the most effective offense . . . It was all crap. Freddy Chicano was only slightly less crazy than Javier. There was no offense or defense here. Only random luck.

The first of the trucks pulled up next to him. Freddy's security team. They bore the look of ex-cons. Heavily tattooed and mean. Probably Freddy's former cellmates, appreciative of the freedom that life in Mexico could offer someone with money.

"What's the problem, man?" the driver demanded.

"Flat tire. Almost done changing it." His gaze shifted to the second truck. Their windows were down, but at least they didn't seem ready to shoot.

The driver frowned. "I know you. You work for that Ramos lunatic."

The guy was an American. His Spanish wasn't quite there. Ex-con for sure. He looked as if he might have spent more years behind bars than not.

"No, I work for the lunatic's father." He announced it loud enough for the occupants of both trucks to hear.

It worked. His response brought on a ripple of laughter from all four men.

"What exactly brings you to this part of the country? As you might guess, we don't get too many visitors around here. And if we do, they're either trafficking or running. So which category do you fit into?"

"Definitely not trafficking," Alejandro said. Any insinuation that they were cutting in on Freddy's business would leave all of them dead.

"So that means running. Care to tell us what from?"

Alejandro grinned and removed his sunglasses. It was a strategy he'd honed for interrogating witnesses. It convinced them you were telling the truth, baring your soul. "I'm running from the lunatic himself."

More guffaws.

Alejandro turned his attention to the distant road as if he expected Javier to appear over the ridge at any minute. From the corner of his eye, he noticed that the driver of the second car was on his phone. Reporting back to The Oasis, most likely.

"Why didn't you just do the world a favor and take him out?" the driver asked.

"Not such a good idea when your paycheck comes from his father. You know what I mean?"

The driver tapped on his steering wheel as the man in the passenger seat talked on his cell. Awaiting orders from Freddy. The minutes seemed to drag. Alejandro took a deep breath as the driver leaned toward him. "We'd like to let you go. But our boss is curious as to why you're running."

The truth was a gamble. But he was betting that out here in the sticks, these guys weren't exactly up to date on the latest cartel news. There was a reason they called this place The Oasis. He shrugged, trying to appear nonchalant. "There are only two reasons to run: money and women. In my case, it's the latter."

The driver ran a hand over his scraggly beard. "I hear you, brother."

The man in the passenger seat nodded. Alejandro strained to hear what was being relayed to their base but picked up nothing useful. There was silence among the others. The minutes ticked by like molasses. Finally, the man tossed his phone on the dash. "Boss says he's got your back." He grinned, displaying no more than six or seven teeth. "Long as you don't mind if we kill him. Make the world a better place."

"Absolutely not. Help yourself to him. I'll owe you big if you do."

The driver put the truck in gear. "Any idea what he's driving?"

"Look for a caravan. He'll be driving the Porsche."

"Cool. Little target practice might help keep the boredom at bay."

Alejandro waited until both vehicles had circled back toward the ranch. It was only then that he allowed himself to exhale.

"We're good?" Spider asked. They were already collecting their tools and lowering the SUV.

"Yep," Alejandro said. He adjusted his sunglasses. "Let's reconvene in town. We need another weather report. Anyone had cell service for the last twenty miles?"

"Nope," Oso said. The others shook their heads.

He hopped back into the Range Rover and leaned in to kiss Avery. "I was wrong. Turns out the enemy of my enemy *is* my friend."

~ ~ ~

By the time they reached the town, no one needed a weather report. Dodging the downpour, everyone but Avery congregated inside the Suburban. Oso was on the phone with one of their security guys assigned to keep tabs on Javier.

Despite the downpour, Alejandro stepped out of the Suburban to make one last stab at an alternative plan. He dialed the number. "Arturo," he said.

Arturo didn't bother with pleasantries. "It's no good, man. They still won't let me release the documents to you. I'm sorry." There was a long stretch of silence between the two men. "Where are you?"

"Not far. If you could get us through Nuevo Laredo—"

"You know I can't do that. It would mean my job."

Alejandro couldn't find fault with Arturo's rationale. The guy had so much at stake. Two kids in college and all that came with it. Alejandro ran a hand through his wet hair. "Any ideas? Javier's on our tail."

"Honestly? Your only choice is the river." There was a long pause. "I'm so sorry, man."

"Yeah." Alejandro hung up.

"He's in Monterrey," Oso said, as Alejandro climbed back into the car.

"Damn. This is my fault," Spider said. "First that lying asshole Burro and then the flat tire."

"Not your fault," Oso said. "Could have happened to any of us."

"I didn't look at the tire," Alejandro said. "Did you find the leak?"

"I think so. It was tiny, so I'm not sure," Spider said.

"No nail or anything obvious?" Alejandro asked.

"No."

His eyes met Oso's. They were thinking the same thing: the flat was no accident.

"Oh, God." Spider looked as if he might rip the hair from his own head. "Shit. You think Burro did that, too?"

"When was he alone with the car?" Oso asked.

"About a dozen times when we were loading up. Shit, shit, shit."

"What about guns?" Alejandro said.

"You think he messed with my guns?" Spider asked. By now his eyes were huge.

"We need to go through everything in that SUV," Alejandro said. He glanced at Avery through the window. She was stony-faced. By now, the windows of the Suburban were almost completely fogged over. Oso's phone buzzed once more.

Alejandro turned to the rest of the men. "Before we head over to Spider's car, we should talk about where we're going." He wiped a circular pattern on the window. The rain was even heavier than before. "There's a low-water spot on the north side of San Ignacio. If it's raining like this, the

Patrol won't be leaving their cars. And they can't see the river from where they park."

"But it might not be a low-water spot anymore," Leo said.

"We won't know until we get there," Spider said, fixing his gaze on the clouds.

"How far from here are we talking?" Leo asked.

"Forty-five minutes," Alejandro said. "Let's go check the car."

Oso cleared his throat. "Hang on." Whatever he was about to say wasn't good. "Javier is closer than we thought. He's chartered a plane out of Monterrey. Leaves in fifteen minutes."

"In this weather?" Spider asked.

Oso nodded. "And he's got guys on the ground headed up highways two and fifty-four."

"How the hell did he pinpoint our location like that?" No one answered. They already knew. All four doors opened at once.

Alejandro nudged Oso. "Tell Avery to sit tight. Tell her we'll be heading out in less than five minutes."

Gato was already holding up the tracker by the time Oso and Alejandro made it to the car. Spider was in the back, tossing guns about. "He took my big box of ammo."

"We've got no shortage of ammo." Oso's voice cast a reassuring calm over the guys. Alejandro had seen it a dozen times in their years together. It always made things easier for him. "Check the back of the Suburban," Oso said. He turned to Alejandro. "We were too soft on Burro. We should have knocked out a few teeth."

"Yeah. Maybe we should swing back through on our way home." Alejandro hadn't meant to let it slip. He'd been careful to keep his plans to himself.

He started for the Range Rover, but Oso had picked up

on it. He yanked him back, out of hearing range from the other guys.

"What the hell are you thinking? You better be planning on escorting her home."

"Look, I'm going to contact Sam Rockforth. He'll meet us on the other side of the river. You know I can't escort her home. What do you expect? That I go meet her mother?"

Oso's face was no more than two inches from his. He spoke through gritted teeth. "This job is done. You're burned. If Diego doesn't know who you are by now, he will tomorrow. Get your head together. Whatever evidence you have now needs to be enough to bring him down. Because there will be no return for any of us."

Spider stepped in between the two. "Everything okay here?"

Oso backed away. "Yeah." He continued to glare at Alejandro. "Did you get all the ammo you need?" Spider nodded. "Then get in the Suburban. We're not taking any more chances with that car. You're riding with me now."

Alejandro made his way back to the Range Rover. He'd like to punch Oso's teeth out, too. Self-righteous bastard. There was no reason to assume Javier knew he was FBI. If there was any chance his undercover status hadn't been blown, he needed to finish the job.

"Let me guess. Javier knows where we are," she said.

"You're Spanish is getting good."

"I don't think it's a matter of spoken language. More like body language. So what now?"

"I need you to look up Sam's number. It's on the burner. Then hand me the phone."

It only took two rings before Sam picked up. "About damn time."

"No contacting Avery's mother till you've seen her face with your own eyes. Okay?" He shot her a quick glance.

"Yep," Sam said.

"Can you get a plane down to Zapata County in an hour?"

"You want to be a little more specific?"

"The best I can tell you right now is somewhere between Laredo and Zapata. I'm thinking north of San Ignacio. Hopefully, no more than an hour, but it depends on the river."

"You mean to tell me you're taking that poor girl across the river? Are you out of your goddamned mind?"

"I can think of a thousand other ways that I'd like to do this, but at the moment this is what we have."

"You will call me. Soon as you make it across."

"The very minute."

"Good. Because if you don't, I'm going to wring your neck."

Alejandro tossed the phone aside. "I think I see why you like working with him."

"Speaking of Zapata, you said you were going to explain the key. Box nine twenty-eight."

"Yeah, the key." The rain was blinding, and the car could use new wipers. None of it was helping his state of mind. "What's in that box is the heart and soul of this project. The only thing missing is what I couldn't find when I went back into the office last night." He rubbed his forehead. Last night seemed like two weeks ago. "If something happens to me, I want you to take the contents to FBI Agent Arturo Gonzales in the San Antonio office. No one else, understand?" She nodded. "And here's the important part." He reached for her hand. She wasn't going to like it. "If we somehow end up separated tonight, unless you hear otherwise from me or Agent Gonzales, I don't want you to open the box for six months."

"I don't really understand." She withdrew her hand. "I know you're trying to prepare me for the worst case. I've seen movies and read books. This border crossing isn't going to be a stroll along the shore. But why six months?"

Those beautiful green eyes. Much too perceptive. She was difficult to fool, even for a professional liar like him. "If things blow up, I could be exposed. If some impatient rookie from the Bureau makes it known that they have the goods on Diego, they'll never catch him. He'll go underground somewhere he can avoid extradition to the U.S. But if everything stays quiet, Diego will eventually creep out from whatever rock he's hiding under. He loves his life in Mexico City too much. Agent Gonzales will know when the time's right."

"And if your cover's blown? Where will you go?"

It was a loaded question. One he'd prefer to avoid. "I'm not sure. It won't be left up to me."

She was wringing her hands. He'd seen it before. It was their first night in Valerone when the tension between them had been off the charts, and he'd tried to push her away. He rubbed his temples. He couldn't do this now. The guilt would have to wait. He needed to stay with the plan.

"There's something you should know," she said.

Something told him he wasn't going to like it. From the corner of his eye, he attempted to evaluate her expression but couldn't. "What?"

"Diego paid me a visit yesterday."

"What?" He clenched his teeth and gripped the steering wheel.

"He showed up at your apartment." Alejandro could barely keep the car centered through the mud as she described Diego's manipulative and threatening visit. He was going to kill Oso for this. "The plan was to tell you once Diego had left the city, but when this thing with the mural happened, there was no need." She paused to evaluate his reaction. "I suspect you plan to leave me on the U.S. side and return to Mexico City."

He said nothing. The whole thing felt like one big betrayal.

"You know I'd do anything to convince you to stay." He still didn't respond to her. She continued, "None of us can ever understand what it's like to lose a parent in the way you lost your father. And as much as I wish you'd stop while you're ahead, I understand. I have to tell myself that at least you're working with the support of the U.S. government. You know, in all this time you never told me who you worked for. Until you said that bit about Agent Gonzales, I never knew for sure."

She was rambling, filling the silent void and trying to cover her pain. He owed it her to make the most of their time left together.

"And you couldn't guess?"

"I knew it was one of them: DEA, ATF, or the FBI. But I'm not sure it really mattered to me."

"I'm sorry. And I'm sorry I never told you about my father."

"And Harvey."

He smiled. "Yeah, that probably caught you by surprise."

"At first. But ever since I learned where your stubborn streak came from, it's been growing more obvious to me every day."

The small road he'd been searching for lay just ahead. Less than a mile to the river now. His stomach was nothing but knots. Lightning streaked across the sky. It should have made him smile. It meant no helicopters and small planes. But it didn't. He glanced in the rearview mirror. Both vehicles were close behind.

"We're almost at the river. There's a point up here, it will be on your right. Normally it's shallow, and there's a sandbar in the middle. I may need you to roll down your window and watch for it."

The open window brought a gusty flood of rain into the vehicle. She was quick to roll it up. "I don't think that's going to work."

He pulled the car off of the poor excuse for a road. "I'm going to check it out."

Before he got anywhere near the edge, he could see the impossibility of crossing. The river was way above its banks. Thunderous and raging, and full of debris. A tree limb the size of a small tree floated by. He could only stand and stare. Yards away was her refuge. And he couldn't get her there.

He'd never felt such failure in his life.

A car door slammed in the distance. He hardly noticed.

She leaned into him, wrapping her arms around his waist. He slung an arm around her shoulders and pulled her close. Neither cared that they were soaking wet. And she didn't bother to ask what came next. She was much too savvy for that.

One of the guys whistled from a waiting vehicle. Arm in arm, they made their way back and climbed into the Suburban.

"Let me guess," Oso said.

"She'd stand a better chance with the embassy," Alejandro said. He hung his head. "Any word on Javier?"

"No. But we can guess he's not far."

She shivered. Alejandro rubbed her arms, not that it did much good. She said something under her breath.

"What did you just say?" Oso asked. "The tunnel?"

Alejandro pretended he didn't understand, since Spider was parked in the front seat. Oso provided the Spanish equivalent.

"Oh, the tunnel," Alejandro said in Spanish. "She's right. Last time I checked, they were about done with the construction."

"What tunnel?" Spider asked.

"It's one of Javier's crazy schemes. Avery designed it. It's about twenty miles south. It may be our best bet."

"Then let's go," Oso said. "Lead the way."

Alejandro and Avery sprinted back to their car, and he gave Sam a quick update. "Sam's going to have a car waiting on the back side of the quarry," he said to Avery. "No headlights, just in case."

The roads parallel to the river were nothing more than trails that often came to abrupt and unexpected ends. More than once, they ended up driving through some plowed field. It didn't help that the storm had created a false sense of evening. Given his sleep-deprived state, it felt like midnight, though sunset was still several hours away.

"You think it will occur to him to look for us there?"

"We have to assume the worst," Alejandro said. The truth was, it would definitely occur to Javier. He'd love to show it off. Boast to his men about his cutting-edge tunnel. The question was: when?

"Our guys are tough and smart. And Oso's never fired at anything he didn't hit dead center. We can handle Javier's pack of traveling addicts. Plus, a couple of his guys belong to us. The best of the lot."

He glanced at her. There was an intensity to her he'd never seen before. It was the river. He felt the same. A screaming, thunderous warning of what might lay ahead had spiked his adrenaline, and he'd bet it had a similar effect on her. He stepped on the gas.

For the first time since leaving the city, he allowed himself to imagine what life would be like without her. No matter how he looked at it, the picture was the same. A bleak and lonely hell.

"The openings. How were they designed?" she asked.

"Huh? Oh. They're locked metal doors. There's a keypad at both ends."

"You've seen it finished?" He nodded, causing her to grin. "And I suppose you know the code."

His face grew warm. "I may have had some influence in the programing."

"What is it?" she asked.

"Zero four zero two."

"Do those numbers have some kind of special meaning to you?"

He smiled. She could be coy when he least expected it. "Yeah, April second. The day I met the most mesmerizing woman I've ever known."

"Is that right?"

He squeezed her hand as he pulled the Range Rover into a small grove of trees. There was just enough space for their vehicles. The quarry was a few hundred yards away, separated by the raging Rio Grande. He pointed to the tunnel entrance on this side of the river. The contractor had done excellent work, most of it based on her initial design. It was impossible to tell that several thousand cubic yards of soil and river rock had been stockpiled here only weeks ago.

"I think Javier's planning on covering the entrance with some kind of old building. Looks like he hasn't quite gotten around to it yet," Alejandro said.

Avery turned around. "We're all here now."

"And so far, no sign of anyone else." He gave her a quick kiss and handed her the burner phone. "Sam expects to hear from you on the other side. No one else."

The others were out of their cars and distributing firearms and ammo. Neither Alejandro nor Avery seemed to want to be the first to open their door.

"Bet you've never worn a bulletproof vest before," he said. "Special order. Just for you." He held it out to her. "How do you feel about another gun?"

"Oh yeah, I can't have too many guns." She made a face and turned around with her hands outstretched. "Why would I need a second gun? I'm lucky I haven't shot myself with the one I have. So, no. One is enough."

"When we get outside, make sure you keep your voice down." He handed her a flashlight. "I don't speak English.

Remember?" Adrenaline continued to surge through his system, but something about her sarcasm had lightened the mood. "Come on, I need to run through everything with the guys."

No one could stand still. Even Oso was wound tight. It had been a long time since Alejandro had seen him that way. "Everybody's got what they need, right?" He pointed toward a bend in the river. "Entrance to the tunnel is the metal door a few hundred yards ahead at eleven o'clock. There's a code on it, so I'll go first. I want Avery in the middle. Her safety is our top priority."

Leo was breathing fast. Hyperventilating. "I can guard this end." He kicked at a small pebble. "I can't do small places." He coughed nervously. "No tunnels."

"Fine. No need for all of us to go across. But we could be over there for a while. And this is Javier's tunnel. He's likely to show up."

"I'll take my chances," Leo said.

"Anything else?" No one said a word. "Then I want to say thanks. To each of you. I couldn't ask for a better team."

Chapter 43

Avery's nerves had never been so ragged. Her stomach clenched as they moved in single file just along the flank of a scrubby hill. To her left was the Rio Grande, now a menacing, raging monster. With the river at flood stage, only sporadic signs of sandy riverbank remained. Along the elevated flank, they had a fair view of their surroundings. Unless Javier's men found a way to approach from the southern side of the hill, the six of them would not be caught off guard.

Behind Alejandro was Gato. She was third, followed by Spider, Leo, and Oso. She hated that Alejandro was first in line. They should have brought Burro for that job. Marched him out front with a gun at his back.

Alejandro started down the side of the hill, angling toward the river. His pace was dictated by caution. Every move was calculated. Due to the recent construction, all vegetation around the tunnel entrance had been removed, leaving an exposed sandy patch roughly fifty yards in diameter. As they drew closer, Avery could see the vulnerability of the location. The bald spot was visible from nearly all angles.

They maintained a gradual pace. No one was out in the open yet. If it had been up to her, she'd have sprinted down the hill, pounded out that code, and run through that metal tube as fast as she could. But this wasn't her world. Hopefully, these guys knew what they were doing.

Unexpectedly, Spider placed a hand on her shoulder. She jumped and made a small sound in the back of her throat. He held a finger to his lips, then pointed to Gato, indicating it was her turn to relay the hand signals down the line.

Gato and Alejandro appeared unfazed by the warning. But she wasn't. From the back of the line, Oso had either seen or heard something. It only convinced her more that speed was the answer. This felt far too exposed.

Leo scrambled to the top of the ridge, then flattened himself. He pointed at something or someone beyond the tunnel entrance.

Before any of them had time to move, a shot rang out. Spider pushed her to the ground. She struggled to extract Harvey's gun from her pocket. Alejandro and Gato raced up the hill to join Leo.

"Don't move," Spider said. It was the first time she'd heard him speak, and his English was excellent. "You go when I go, okay?"

She nodded.

"Now." Avery followed Spider further down the flank of the hill and across a grassy stretch bordered by a few decent-sized bushes, staying close on his heels. A barrage of shots rang out.

She tried to catch her breath. "It's Javier, isn't it?"

"Probably. This is a good spot to wait. We're close to the gate."

Alejandro, Oso, and Gato caught her off guard as they slid into the cluster of bushes. Oso squeezed her arm. "You okay?"

She nodded. "Leo?" she asked.

"Watching from the ridge. Javier's here. At the moment, we outnumber him. But that won't last. Keep your eyes up on that point around the bend in the hill. They'll be coming from that direction."

Something had shifted. It took her a moment to realize the rain had stopped.

Alejandro said something in Spanish and pointed to the bend. With Gato at his back, he moved out.

"You have the code?" Oso asked her.

"Yeah, but Alejandro is—"

She was cut off by Oso. "You and Spider, go ahead."

A single shot rang out. Just short of the bend, Gato stumbled. She covered her mouth.

"There are more of them. Coming down over that ridge," Spider said. He pointed to a high spot beyond the bend in the river.

"Then we go for the bend. We'll have an eye on them from there. We'll have both directions covered." Oso put a hand on her arm. "Let's go."

An escarpment rose up from the bend in the river. No vegetation, but lots of rocky ledges along the steep slope. Gato had managed to crawl behind one of the smaller ledges. His leg was bleeding, but he was sitting up and capable of holding a gun.

Avery strained to watch Alejandro climbing the escarpment, using the ledges as cover. Reaching the top would give him the advantage of a 360 degree view. Avery started in his direction but was stopped by a firm grip. Oso pointed to an indentation halfway up. She would be well hidden and probably safe but also blind to virtually everything that was happening around her.

"Don't argue with me," Oso said firmly. "Keep that pistol out and listen to Spider, he'll tell you what to do next. I've got to watch Alejandro's back. Get yourself up there now, before any more of Javier's guys show up.

Avery reached the indentation in the cliff just as a gun went off nearby, followed by rounds of shots from what seemed like all directions. Not knowing anything was torture. She fidgeted. The gunfire was endless.

When the shooting finally stopped, she couldn't sit still. Spider had disappeared, and there was no one to tell her to stay put. Gradually, she began to inch her way out. Just above her, Oso leaned against a small ledge, positioned to fire. Behind him, she could see the top of Gato's head.

A single shot rang out, and she glanced further up to see Alejandro making a dash across the top of the escarpment. She could only hope that Javier's vantage point didn't offer the same view.

From somewhere nearby came a gurgling sound. Animal-like, but it was no animal. One of Javier's guys staggered frenziedly down the hillside. He came to halt along the river, clutching his throat. Fortunately, no one took a shot, though it might have been the humane thing to do. She turned away feeling sick.

From the opposite side of the bend, Javier's guys resumed with what seemed like minutes of unabated firing. Avery kept her eyes fixed on the top of the escarpment and Alejandro's location behind a small bush. More shots went off and Alejandro jerked, grabbing his left arm. She covered her mouth stifling a shriek, while the pistol shook in her other hand. Alejandro scrambled further back into the shrubbery.

This was hell. She was useless up here. At the sound of every shot, her body rocked with imaginary impacts. There were more cries, the sounds sending fireworks up her spine. It seemed as if it would never end.

Something prompted Alejandro to step out beyond the bush. She wanted to tell him no—he needed to retreat. His gaze shifted down to her perch. From the corner of her eye, Avery sensed movement nearby. In that splinter of a moment, Javier moved into her line of sight. He'd spotted Alejandro. That brief, heart-swelling glance had made Alejandro vulnerable.

Avery crouched. From this position, she might be able to hit Javier. It would be tough, but if she could even distract him . . . but before she could raise her gun, the firing resumed. Blasts resounded from every direction. Crazed chaos. Bullets pinged off the ledge next to her head, and she made a dive for her hiding place.

With no warning came a haunting silence. Eventually, Avery eased her way out. She could no longer see Alejandro, and Javier was gone.

Spider slid in next to her. "It's time for us to go to the tunnel."

"What are you saying?" She crawled over to the edge. There was no one in sight. The shots persisted, but the sound was growing farther away and less frequent. "Where's Alejandro?" Spider shook his head. Horror rose within her. "Where?"

She didn't wait for an answer. She moved along the rocky ledge with Spider at her back.

It was upon reaching the curve that she saw him. Thirty feet below and sprawled in the dirt. Oso was at his side. Blood pooled next to one leg, and his injured arm dangled oddly. She stuffed a fist in her mouth to stifle her cry.

That one foolish glance. This was her fault.

"We should go. There are people waiting for you on the other side."

"No. I'm going down there." She began to slide down along the embankment. Even at a distance, she could distinguish the straight line of Oso's mouth.

She slipped in next to Oso. He was holding a saturated t-shirt against Alejandro's leg. There was no point in asking Alejandro's status. Oso wouldn't tell her the truth. She tried to discern the rise and fall of Alejandro's chest but couldn't. "Did Javier do this?"

Oso nodded.

She stroked Alejandro's shoulder and he groaned though his eyes remained closed. Avery kept her voice low. "Where is Javier?"

"No," Oso said.

"I'm going to find him." She pulled the pistol from her pocket. "You might as well tell me."

"He's hurt," Oso said. "Not as bad as . . ." His voice dropped. "He's moving back up the hill. But you can't go up there."

Like hell she couldn't. She'd already wasted one opportunity. Standing around and watching Alejandro bleed to death, while Javier escaped, was not going to happen.

She stormed across grassy expanse and over the ledge. Spider was on her heels again. As long as he didn't die in the process, that was fine.

"Where are the rest of his men?"

"All gone," Spider said.

"Good. Then that's him I see in the distance."

Spider produced a sizable pistol from his ankle holster. "No safety," he said. "You should use it."

She shook her head and aimed the twenty-two at Javier's retreating form. It was a warning shot to get his attention, and it worked. She bared her teeth at his reaction, then moved toward him.

Like some eighteenth-century duel, the two of them faced one another. No attempt to hide. Spider was off to the side, indulging her wish, yet positioned to fire at a moment's notice.

Javier's tone was caustic. "I told you I don't like redheads."

The gun was heavier than she remembered, and she fought to keep it steady, but Javier wasn't exactly sprinting away. "This is for the girls at the brothel." Avery took aim and pulled the trigger.

She missed, but it was enough to show him she meant it. He hadn't even bothered to pull out his gun.

She took five broad steps closer. He was fumbling with his holster. Something wasn't quite right with his right arm. She didn't care.

"Up and to the right a little," Spider said.

As her nerves had steadied, so had her arm. "You know, Javier, I intend to kill you." She straightened, closed one eye, and fired. This time she managed to wing him. He shrieked in pain.

Javier's gun wobbled in his left hand. "Bitch. You can't even shoot straight."

Amazing. The psychological aspect of killing him was going to be so much easier than she imagined. Revenge was a powerful thing, but this was so much more than just revenge.

She extended her arm and focused on the spot in his chest where a heart should have been. "And this is for Alejandro."

It must have been a split second later that a bullet whizzed past her head. She didn't even flinch. Instead, she watched in fascination as the impact of her perfect shot blasted Javier backwards.

She wasn't sure how long it was before Spider pried the gun from her hand. "It's done," he said.

"You're sure?" she asked.

"Very sure."

She'd expected to feel something. Relief, remorse, even regret, but all she felt was the fading vibration of the shot.

Spider tugged on her arm. "Come on." He guided her down a rocky section of the river bank. From there, an eerie silence seemed to propel them both. Only the river made its presence known. Avery ran with every ounce of energy she possessed, sailing over river debris and loose rocks. Two of Javier's men lay face down at the base of the escarpment. Spider caught up next to her, putting himself between the bodies and her. "Just keep going."

Nothing had changed along the river, except that one of their men was maneuvering the Suburban over what little dry bank remained along the river's edge.

"Did you get him?" Oso asked.

Spider nodded. "Alejandro should be proud of her."

His light-hearted English was for her benefit, though no one would celebrate today.

She perched on the sandy bank next to Alejandro and threaded her fingers through his. His hand was limp but warm. The pool of blood along his leg was growing.

The dawning reality of it made her cold. He was losing so much blood. Too much. An uncontrollable shiver racked her body. He might only have minutes left. And in rural Mexico . . . she squeezed his hand and brushed the hair from his forehead.

"I'm keeping the pressure on it," Oso said. His voice was light, but his eyes held the hollows of defeat. "We'll get him covered up in the car. Can't afford to risk shock." Another statement without heart behind it.

The Suburban drew up only feet away. Gato limped around the back, gathering anything within reach to create a bed for Alejandro. Oso placed a hand on her arm. Avery's chin quivered, and she had to bite the inside of her lip to stop it. She bent, brushing her lips across Alejandro's temple. There was a twitch of his eyelids and the slightest movement to his lips.

"What?" she whispered. "What is it?"

The words were faint. Nearly indistinguishable. "Wait . . ." His voice drifted and his lips became still.

"Darling, we have to move fast and get him in the car right now," Oso said. "You and Spider need to get to that tunnel. If I know Javier, he's got more boys on the way."

"No. I want to go with you."

"Nope. Alejandro did this for you. And he would never forgive any of us if we didn't send you home safely."

Oso was speaking as if Alejandro were already dead. It made her want to scream. Leo and Oso began to lift him onto an improvised pallet. She covered her eyes.

It was Spider who pulled her to her feet.

"I need something," she said. Tears were beginning to make their way down her face, and the shaking was escalating to full-blown racking convulsions. "I have to go back to the Range Rover. It's something I can't go home without. I promise it won't take long." She clawed at his shirt sleeve. "Please."

"We go together. But first, we will let them get by."

She and Spider moved to the upper path watching the Suburban, which was forced to creep along, dodging the rising waters. The vehicle's slowness, though necessary, was agonizing to watch. When the vehicle finally reached the gravel road, Oso lowered the window and gave them a final silent nod.

It was the last thing she remembered of that day.

Chapter 44

Her assistant, Sarah, stuck her head in the door. "It's that reporter again. The same one that shows up every month."

Avery glanced up, her mind elsewhere. "Maria something. Maria Alvarez?"

"Yeah, I think so," Sarah said.

Avery raked her nails over her scalp as if the physical pain would eradicate any reminder of Mexico. "I don't care what you tell her. Just make her go away." After the first six weeks, most of them had given up on her. But not this one.

The assistant headed toward the door until Avery's voice brought her to a halt. "Sarah? Do you want to go get a drink?"

"Sure." There was no missing the surprise in Sarah's face. "I need to run home first. Let the dog out. Can we make it for six? Muskets has a great happy hour. You know it, don't you?"

Avery nodded, but it was a lie. Ever since moving to San Antonio, she'd done little more than work. She straightened her shoulders. Things were about to change.

She finished the remaining paragraphs of her report, scooped up her purse, and closed her door. Her laptop would remain at the office tonight.

"Ms. McAndrews."

The sound startled Avery. She gripped a nearby chair. Her other hand rested against her chest. This jumpiness never seemed to lessen. It was one of many scars that Javier's cruelty had left her with.

"Wow! I didn't mean to scare you. I was just really hoping to talk to you." The persistent reporter. Apparently,

Sarah hadn't been too successful in getting rid of her.

Avery moved as quickly as her unsteady legs would allow. "Why? I have nothing to say that would be of any interest to anyone." She tapped the elevator button.

"Maybe I think you have a story to tell," Maria said. She began to dig through an overstuffed tote bag.

Avery tried to ignore the woman, but it was impossible. She'd never paid her much attention before now, but there was no way Maria was older than nineteen or twenty. Hardly a full-fledged reporter. And she seemed desperate to find whatever it was.

"What about this?" Maria asked.

Look, I'm going to be late for—" Avery stopped mid-sentence. She lifted the photo from the girl's hand. She hardly recognized herself. That hideous picture taken in the brothel. But this wasn't the original. Someone had gone to great lengths to make her look even trampier and crazier than she'd been. "Where did you get this?"

Avery's interest lent the girl some bounce in her step. "I have family in Mexico."

Avery handed it back to her. "Everyone knows I was kidnapped and taken to Mexico. It's old news."

"Yeah, but you've never talked about it."

"And you see yourself as the one who breaks me? Gets me to cry?" The girl's excitement began to dissipate. "I'm sorry, Ms. Alvarez, but I really can't help you."

"Will you at least take my card? If there's something— even the tiniest story—I'd love to be the one to hear it."

"Well, you do get an A for effort." Avery held out her hand. "But don't hold your breath."

~ ~ ~

One step inside the crowded bar and she wanted to run. What was she thinking? This wasn't her thing. It never had been. Even before the scars and damage of Mexico.

Sarah was already sipping a margarita, and Avery signaled to the waiter to bring her one as well. The surprise on Sarah's face told her everything. She'd expected Avery to stand her up.

It wasn't a reflection of Sarah—it was based on Avery's own history of making excuses and backing out of anything social. But tonight, she would break the cycle, and she'd chosen her partner well. There was no one more grounded and pragmatic than Sarah. Plus, she was funny and always made Avery laugh. And the time had come to laugh again.

"Glad you decided to show up."

Avery wrinkled her nose. "Maybe next time we should find a wine bar."

The steely gray of Sarah's eyes seemed a further confirmation of her matter-of-fact way. "Sam said if you didn't start getting out of the office he was going to drag you out himself."

Avery rolled her eyes. "Can you imagine what kind of place Sam would take me to?"

"A domino hall with stuffed jackrabbits on the wall." Sarah held up her glass. "Here's to a civilized night out." She glared at a guy who'd slunk passed their table twice now. "Drink up and we'll go somewhere the clientele isn't so smarmy."

~ ~ ~

"So how did Sam convince you to move down here?" Sarah asked. They had migrated to a marginally quieter place only half a block away.

Avery sputtered, nearly choking on her drink. "You should have seen him." The alcohol was having its effect. She hadn't said this much to anyone since she'd been back. "My old boss was such a spineless ass." She laughed. "When I first got back from Mexico, Sam stayed at my mom's house with us. Guilt, I guess," Avery said with a shrug.

"Anyway, he took it upon himself to chase away reporters, law enforcement, pretty much anyone who dared to venture within twenty feet of the front yard." Her memory of Sam running out the front door, often with the first thing he could grab, was still vivid. "I think he really thrived on doing it."

"He would," Sarah said.

"The day my old boss, Eric, showed up, Sam came barreling out of the house with a shotgun."

Sarah laughed loudly enough for others nearby to gawk. She slipped down in the booth, wiping the tears from her face. "I can see it now. And let me guess, after scaring the guy off, he told you that he had a job for you."

"Pretty much," Avery said with a shrug.

There was a moment of silence between them before Sarah said, "Word in the office is that Jeremy Scurlock asked you out."

"I didn't think you were the type to pay much attention to gossip."

"I'm not," Sarah said. Her gaze was sharp. "But I'm the one everyone runs to with questions about you. You're a big mystery."

"Jeremy's a nice guy." Avery considered it for a moment. If things were going to change, she had to give a little. Sarah was tight-lipped. Avery had seen it a dozen times in their business dealings. If she asked Sarah to keep her mouth shut, she would. Avery took a large gulp of her drink. Even alluding to Mexico required courage. "But I'm not ready."

Sarah twisted her glass, watching the ring of condensation smear across the laminate table top. She said nothing.

"The guy who rescued me," Avery said, then drew in a deep breath. "He died." Her heart raced. It was the first time she'd managed to say the words aloud.

Sarah leaned forward and squeezed her hand. "I'm sorry."

Someone cleared their throat. "'Scuse me. Is one of you

Avery McAndrews?" The question came from an overgrown adolescent with ruddy cheeks and the body of an offensive lineman.

"Who needs to know?" Sarah asked, her hands curling defensively.

"Mr. Rockforth says for me to take Ms. McAndrews home whenever she's ready to go." Avery shot Sarah a questioning glance, but she looked as confused as Avery. "He says if you have questions to call him, and he'll explain."

Sarah held up an index finger before Avery could speak. She tapped the screen of her phone. "Sam, it's Sarah. What's this about, and how did you find us?"

~ ~ ~

The blue jacket was always the first thing Avery saw at the end of the day. It hung off of the closet door, it's function entirely ornamental. Though any scent of Alejandro was long gone, it always caused her heart to skip a beat. She pictured his too-tall frame in that tiny Jeep seat against the sun-streaked desert sunset. Tonight, the alcohol left her burying her face in it. Never once had she regretted dragging Spider back to the Range Rover to retrieve it.

Sometimes it made her laugh, knowing it would irritate Alejandro that she'd kept it. So dead set on wanting to give her something better. He'd expect her to wear the bracelet he'd given her to hide the tattoo. But the tattoo was a part of her now. A daily reminder of him and all that he'd risked for her. One thing that no one could ever take away.

She reached for her phone, wondering if she should sober up a little before calling Sam, then decided against it.

He picked up on the first ring. "I didn't tell Sarah the details."

"No. I didn't think you would," she said.

"We've got a yellow jacket in the outhouse."

"Meaning?"

"I've been getting some strange phone calls. They worry me. Someone claiming to be with the FBI. His name is Dylan Lynch. Does that name ring a bell?"

She'd barely cooperated with the FBI after returning from Mexico. As far as she was concerned, their negligence had resulted in Alejandro's death. In hindsight, the shootout at the river should never have happened. Some support from his fellow agents would have made all the difference. She was a kidnapping victim, after all. They knew about her. So why hadn't she been escorted across the border? Even if it was necessary that he remain undercover, Alejandro could have passed her off to someone else. Altogether, those facts made the FBI murderers. Not just murderers, but compliant in the death of one of their own.

Initially, Sam tried to argue with her. He couldn't exactly chase off the FBI with a shotgun. But the day she threatened to do it herself, he provided her with a lawyer who ensured she could do as little talking as necessary.

"No, but you know I don't talk to the FBI. What does he want?"

"He wants information about you. He's not asking what happened in Mexico. He wants to know what you're doing now. And he's called more than once," Sam said. There was a long pause. "Even if he is FBI, I'm beginning to think this guy's not harmless. I called the FBI myself. They do have an agent named Dylan Lynch, but that's all they'd give me. And I'm not even sure he's who he says he is."

"So, your solution is this bodyguard you've sent to stay with me?"

"Look, we're not getting sandpapered this time."

Whatever that meant. Avery pursed her lips. "What kind of questions, specifically?"

"Where you live. Details about your employment. That sort of thing."

"FBI shouldn't have to ask those questions." The tequila

was beginning to leave her with a headache. "Unless, like you said, this guy's not with the FBI." The thought was like a cold knife at her back. "Any accent?"

"Not that I could tell. You know what bothered me the most? He wanted to know if you'd been back to Mexico."

"What? What did you tell him?"

"To call your attorney. I gave him the number."

Without asking, she knew the attorney had never heard a word from Dylan Lynch.

"On a happy note," Sam said, "I'm emailing you that Harvey woman's address and her email. She wasn't easy to find."

"Wow! When you told me that detective could find just about anyone, I really didn't believe it. Especially someone in Mexico."

"What makes you so anxious to find her?"

She hesitated, reluctant to tell Sam the reason. He wouldn't like it. He wanted her living in the present. "I want to help get a school, or maybe more like a vocational facility, started for the girls that were in the brothel. I've been thinking about it a lot. Harvey has this big ranch, and she's all alone. She's a mess—diabetic, stubborn, but also smart. She's very interesting, you know? She speaks seven languages."

"And you think someone living out in the sticks, alone by choice, is going to agree to something like that?"

"She used to raise horses. But she can't handle the upkeep anymore since she's all alone. The girls could help out. Working with animals is therapeutic."

Sam's silence screamed skepticism.

"Look, most of the girls end up going back to prostitution. In fact, most probably already have. But if we could introduce them to other options… cooking, teaching, nursing, engineering. Javier took them from their families when they were as young as ten. Don't you think they deserve a chance?"

"Does this mean I'm going to lose my best engineer?"

"No way. I love my job. But if this works…." She bit her lip. "I was wondering if you'd let me have a month or so off to help get things started. Maybe I could do some teaching, too. If anyone's interested."

"Come hell or high water, I'm not giving you time off to go back to Mexico." She had to hold the phone away from her ear, he was so loud.

"Javier's dead. There's no reward for finding me. No one cares anymore."

"His father does."

Sam was right. How had she missed it? As long as Diego Ramos was running the cartel, she couldn't set foot in Mexico. She sighed. "But you'll still give me time off to get things organized from this end?"

"What's your time frame?"

"I don't have one yet. This idea just sort of came to me. Do you think your detective could help me find women with the J tattoos?"

"Yes, but you've put the cart in front of the donkey. Talk to this Harvey woman first, then we'll talk."

~ ~ ~

Harvey's single sentence reply came four days later. *ARE YOU OUT OF YOUR MIND?* Avery laughed. She would have questioned Harvey's health if the message had been any different. The point was—Harvey hadn't said no. It reminded her of Alejandro's insistence that Harvey take her in. Harvey hadn't outright refused that time, either. Only grumbled from the balcony about how she was retired.

Avery waited two more days before sending a second email. Followed by a third and a fourth. By the fifth email, Harvey had agreed to speak on the phone, but nothing more.

That's when she knew she'd won.

Chapter 45

Avery glanced at the time. Five-thirty, and she was starving. There hadn't been time for lunch, and Sam's bodyguard was eating her out of house and home. She gazed across the street at the line of bustling restaurants and bars. She really didn't want to request a table for one. Why hadn't she made plans with Sarah?

"Ms. McAndrews." Maria Alvarez was parked on a bench nearby. The girl scrambled to gather her belongings and catch up to Avery. "You're early today."

"Stalker," Avery said under her breath, though she glanced over her shoulder to signal the bodyguard that things were okay. "Maria, you're getting desperate. It's only been a week."

"I know, but I'm going be writing obituaries again if I don't have a story."

"Shadow a homeless person for a week or go over to Lackland and interview some vets about PTSD." Immediately Avery regretted saying it. It sounded callous, and it wasn't the message she intended. The girl was only trying to make a name for herself. Avery slowed her pace. "Maria, what really makes you think I have a story to tell?"

Maria stopped and Avery turned to face her. Maria looked older; her usual enthusiasm had been replaced with something harsh. "Ms. McAndrews." It was impossible to miss the girl's bitter undertone. She reached out, fingers curling around Avery's forearm and twisting until the *J-41* tattoo was exposed. "This is the story I want."

Avery yanked her arm away. "Don't you—"

Maria cut her off. "My mother is *J-11*."

Avery's blood went cold. She let her purse slide to the ground and made no attempt to retrieve it. "You could have said that in the first place."

Maria held the purse out to her. "I didn't know how you would react. My mom refuses to talk about it."

"Come on. "Avery practically dragged Maria across the street to the nearest restaurant. It was busy enough that it was unlikely anyone would hear them. Avery insisted on a table at the back, anyway. Her hand shook as she drained her water.

"Tell me what you do know about your mother."

"No way." Maria shook her head. "You first."

Avery's mouth was dry. Maria's pronouncement had thrown her off balance. She shook her head. "Honestly, Maria, I don't know if I'll ever be able to give you what you want." She gestured over Maria's shoulder. "You know I have a full-time bodyguard."

"Why can't you sleep at night?" Maria asked with a spiteful hiss.

Avery stared her down. "No wonder you're stuck with obits, if this is the way you deal with sources."

Maria bowed her head, apparently trying to regroup. "Sorry. Maybe I get a little defensive. I mean, your return was huge news, but my mother spent years in that hell hole and no one cared."

Avery leaned across the table. "Look, there's no one I feel for more than those girls. It would be an honor for me to meet your mother. But the reason I have a bodyguard has nothing to do with the brothel. And that's all I can say on the matter. If you want to talk about it further, then I can give you the name and number of my lawyer." She steadied herself in the chair. "Now, if you lose that attitude, I will tell you about the foundation that's been established for those girls. It may be the story that keeps you from writing obituaries."

Chapter 46

Six months to the day. The thought sent goosebumps along Avery's forearms, even though it was nearly ninety degrees outside. She was making good time. At this rate, she'd be in Zapata before noon and back at the office before four. The bodyguard wouldn't show up to escort her home until after five.

Her mind spun. She probably needed grief therapy. Her mother certainly thought so. It might have prepared her for today and how she would feel when she opened that safety deposit box. Maybe she should have emptied it out right away. It would have violated the promise to wait six months, but she could have spared herself the prolonged pain.

Instead, she'd been foolish enough to allow herself to hope.

Now, gripping the steering wheel with sweaty palms, each road sign was beginning to chisel away at her resolve as the numbers stating the distance to Zapata got smaller. Every decrease caused her gut to tighten further. She turned up the music on the car stereo even though it was already blasting. It did no good. Twenty miles, then fifteen. By five miles out she could barely drive. It was by sheer luck that she reached the bank parking lot.

Her phone was abuzz with texts. She kicked it to the floor. She didn't have the energy.

Gnawing her lower lip until it was bloody and never taking off her sunglasses, she marched through the small bank, directly toward the open door of the vault. Heads turned. It was obvious that strangers weren't a common sight in this small town. By now, there was a deep red imprint of the safety deposit box key etched across her palm.

"Need to get in a box?" The woman's name tag read Darrel Ann.

"Yes."

"Sign in over here. What box number?"

Though she could remember perfectly, Avery struggled to articulate the numbers. Darrel Ann held out an expectant hand. Something in Avery urged her to hand the woman the key and walk away. Never look back. But she couldn't.

Darrel Ann unlocked the small door and set the box on a table. "I'll be just outside."

Avery stared at the ceiling, unable to will herself near that box. He couldn't have imagined how cruel this was. Why the hell didn't he just mail the key to the guy in San Antonio?

Minutes passed.

"Everything okay in there?" It was a rhetorical question. The woman could see for herself that Avery hadn't moved.

"No," Avery said.

The woman stepped inside. It occurred to Avery that this wasn't the first time Darrel Ann had had to deal with distraught next-of-kin.

Avery leaned against a wall of boxes and closed her eyes. "Do you mind just raising the lid for me?" She could hear the woman's movement. "Is it empty?"

"No, ma'am."

The sight of his handwriting made her sway. But the fact that it was all still there sent her grabbing at a nearby table for support. She couldn't even remember the name of the agent in San Antonio.

"Ma'am, are you okay?" Darrel Ann asked.

"No."

With the assistance of her fellow employees, Darrel Ann boxed the paperwork and helped Avery to her car. "Is there someone I can call for you?" she asked.

Avery shook her head. "I think I just need to sit in my car for little while."

Darrel Ann patted her arm. "Take all the time you need."

For what seemed like hours, Avery rested her forehead against the steering wheel. She hadn't expected that this could still hurt so much. But her pain was as raw today as it had been six months ago.

~ ~ ~

She glanced around the bar, not even sure how she'd gotten there. It looked exactly as it had that night with Manuel and Bruce. She held her head in her hands. Why in the world was she here? It bore no fond memories. Just the opposite. Even from across the room, she could hear the waitress smacking her gum.

"What can I get ya?" Avery lifted her head, and the waitress did a double take. "You're the one that went missing."

"Yeah."

"Why are you back here?"

Avery shook her head. There was no answer that made sense. "Fusty Mule, please."

The waitress frowned and glanced at the clock. It wasn't even noon. "Sure you don't want something to eat, too? It's on the house. All of it."

"No, thanks." As the waitress disappeared, the reality of Avery's situation became apparent. One drink of that swill and she'd be under the table and spending another night in the Tumbleweed Inn.

Her phone buzzed. Sam. *Finally got to the bottom of this Dylan Lynch thing. Long story, but he's been trying to reach you on behalf of an Agent Gonzales. I think you're supposed to know that name. He wants you to call right away. I'll shoot you his contact info.*

Agent Gonzales. That was the guy's name. She dropped a ten-dollar bill on the table and started for the car.

After zero to drink, she felt half drunk. Her legs were rubbery, and her brain was only slightly less foggy than it had been thirty minutes earlier. She staggered forward.

She put a hand above her eyes to eliminate the glare from the sun. Across the parking lot, two men were hanging around her car.

"Hey, get your hands off my car!" Without thinking, she retrieved Harvey's pistol from her purse.

Both raised their hands, and she realized as she drew closer that neither of them were actually touching the car.

"We're FBI ma'am. It would probably be in your best interest to drop that gun."

"I have a permit," Avery said, though he was right. Even though it wasn't loaded, she really shouldn't be pointing a gun at anyone without cause. Slowly, she returned the firearm to her purse.

The man continued, "We have reason to believe you're in possession of federal property." His voice cracked as he spoke. He seemed like nothing more than a kid, all elbows and freckles and feet that were far too big for his size.

"What?"

"I believe you just retrieved some documents from a safety deposit box. I'm afraid you'll need to turn those over," the freckled agent said.

Avery threw back her head in disbelief. God, how she hated this town. It was cursed. If she'd just gotten the hell out of here, she'd be a third of the way home by now. "What I was doing at the bank is none of your concern."

"We have the word of bank employees that you accessed the contents of box number nine twenty-eight."

"So what if I did? I had legal access to that box. And its contents belong to me."

"Not according to our information, ma'am."

The second agent stepped forward, blocking Avery from her car door. Unlike his partner, he was stocky and mean-faced. "If you refuse to turn it over, we're going to take you in."

"Take me in? For what? I don't see any kind of a warrant or legal document. How do I even know your badges are for real?" Amazing. This was exactly what Alejandro had feared. She couldn't let it happen. Even if it cost her life, she'd get that box to Agent Gonzales.

The freckled one glanced at his partner. "They didn't say we should bring her in. They only said to get the box."

"Yeah, well she threatened us with a gun. That's reason enough to bring her in. She's probably linked with that cartel. Go ahead and cuff her."

"Cuff me? Are you out of your mind? Have you ever even *met* a cartel member? I bet you two have just broken three or four federal regulations yourselves." She might have worried that they had some cartel connections themselves, but these two, with their obvious lack of street sense, wouldn't last a day in that world.

"Get out of my way. If you want what's in the box, then come back with a warrant."

Mean-face rested a warning hand on his holster. "Cuff her now, Briscoe."

"No!" She twisted though her efforts were futile. The two men had her boxed in.

"If you're arresting me, you need to be reading me my rights."

The young one paused. He obviously didn't want to be the one to cuff her, much less overlook her Miranda rights. "Brian, you sure about this?"

"Damn it, Briscoe. Throw her in the back. We'll see what the committee wants to do with her. They can read her her rights."

At least there were no injections. No blindfolds. But they'd claimed her purse, her gun, her cell phone and worst of all, the box of Alejandro's documents.

They drove for miles, eventually leaving the highway for a dirt road. There was nothing around but scrubby ranch land. Mesquite, prickly pear, and yucca covered the sandy soil in sporadic clumps.

She was forced to perch on the edge of the seat because of the handcuffs. Every pothole knocked her bouncing in a different direction. These roads couldn't possibly lead to any kind of federal building.

Eventually, they came to a stop in front of a single-story ranch house. Built in the sixties or seventies, never updated, and barely maintained. Briscoe, the young one, led the way up to a sagging porch. The screen door dragged across the wooden floor.

"What kind of FBI office is out here in the middle of nowhere?" Avery asked. She was beginning to second guess her assumption that they weren't affiliated with a cartel.

The freckled agent glanced at his partner though neither offered an answer.

Until this moment, she'd felt too raw to be afraid. Her limited capacity for extreme emotions had left her only remotely concerned for what happened next. But seeing this place, and its potential for backwoods evil, that perspective was rapidly changing.

The mean-faced one, apparently named Brian, ushered her through the entryway to a long, narrow room with no windows. The sparse furnishings consisted of a couple of metal folding chairs and a mustard-colored velour couch. A pervasive odor of wet dog made her want to hold her breath.

"Sit there and don't move," Brian said, pointing to one of the folding chairs. "Briscoe, you keep an eye on her. I'm going see what they want us to do with her."

Avery's fear of who *they* were was escalating by the second. Recalling the icy indifference in Diego Ramos's eyes, she knew that if he was behind this, her time left on this earth was limited.

Young Briscoe seemed reluctant to be left behind. He alternated between fidgeting, toying with his phone, and pacing.

"You need a new partner. Or you've got to show some backbone," Avery said. "What are you planning on doing with the contents of that box?"

"I can't answer that. Brian—I mean Agent Goodson—is in charge."

"I guess that means you're not going to take these handcuffs off, either." The kid didn't answer. The weight of the day was beginning to bear down on her. She slunk down in the uncomfortable folding chair. Why hadn't she told Sarah where she was headed?

Avery attempted to flex her shoulders. There was nowhere to run. She'd seen the surroundings driving in. Nothing for miles.

A burst of all-male laughter rang out from nearby. "Where's Briscoe?" someone asked.

Someone else mumbled something unintelligible.

"Speak up. What did you say?" It was the authoritative voice of someone older.

"Watching the suspect, sir." It was mean-face, sounding considerably less sure of himself than he'd been in the parking lot.

"Suspect? We asked you to pick up a box of files from a bank. How the hell do you come back with a suspect?" another voice asked.

Someone else chimed in. "Goodson, you're a bigger idiot than we gave you credit for. Do they teach you IT guys anything?"

IT guys? Avery's heart skipped a beat. Maybe these guys really were FBI. She glanced at the freckled agent. He looked terrified.

"A gun? What the hell kind of fairytale are you concocting, Goodson?"

There was a cackle of laughter. "Some girl pulled a gun on you in the parking lot, and you brought her back here? Are you kidding me?"

Avery fought the urge to smile. There was no guarantee she was safe. And there was still the problem of getting Alejandro's documents back. But it seemed unlikely that Diego Ramos was part of the boisterous group. She glanced at the young agent. "Are you really FBI?"

He nodded nervously and kept his voice low. "But we don't normally work in the field. In fact, I never have." His voice dipped. "They brought us here to do computer work and we didn't have anything to do so they sent us to the bank to empty the box."

"Your name's Briscoe, right?"

He nodded.

"Who told you to empty the safety deposit box?"

He shrugged. No help to her. She needed to know. Maybe she could still make Alejandro's wishes known. She glanced back at the young agent. "It wasn't your idea to bring me here. It sounds like you're going to catch some hell. Let your partner take the fall." It would serve mean-face right for being so arrogant.

An older voice called out, "Maddox, go deal with this girl situation so we can move forward with this meeting."

"Excuse me, sir, but I believe DL might prefer to handle this."

Avery's heart stopped and she tried to breathe. But the sound of his familiar voice stole her breath away.

"Oso!"

She hadn't said it loudly, but the kid's head jerked up. He was wide-eyed and growing more aware that he and his partner had screwed up majorly.

"Where is DL? Someone get him and let's move on," the older voice said with impatience.

"Who is DL?" she asked.

Briscoe shrugged. His face was flushed, and he was fumbling in his pocket for something.

Avery stood. "I need to speak with Oso."

"You can't. Just sit down."

"Get these cuffs off me!" Her voice was loud enough to rock the whole house.

"I've got it." The voice—rich, deep, and heart-melting—came from the entryway.

~ ~ ~

She staggered to the wall for support. He was barely recognizable. Long hair, a full beard and a mustache. He'd lost weight, leaving his face with the cruel angles of prolonged illness. A shadow of the Alejandro she once knew.

He snapped his fingers at the kid. "Where's your key?"

"I'm trying to find it, sir. I can get one off of my partner."

"Then do it."

As he moved toward her, she saw it: the slight hitch in his gait and drag to his foot. If her hands had been free, she might have brushed the hair from his face and stood on tiptoe to whisper how much she'd missed him.

Or she might have kicked him in the shins for leaving her to believe he was dead. Six months of hell. And the last two hours possibly the worst of her life.

But neither was an option. He hung back.

"DL?" she asked.

He seemed relieved by the simple question. "DeLeon."

"And Dylan Lynch?" His face was a blank, but the confirming twitch in his fingers betrayed him. She fought hard to keep her eyes on him, wishing the kid would hurry and at the same time wanting him never to return. Her voice faltered. "Why didn't you empty the box yourself?"

"Because I had until tomorrow." He kept his gaze even. Giving nothing away. "You were early."

"No, I wasn't. You're wrong. Today was six months," she said it as a taunt, hoping to raise the faintest hint of a smile. Instigate a meaningless argument over the definition of six months and alleviate this horrible tension. But he didn't take the bait. She whispered, "You might have spared me the worst few hours of my life today."

There was a whistle followed by applause from the other side of the house. Someone called out for DL.

"What's that about?" she asked.

One corner of his mouth lifted, as if he intended to smile but something prevented him. "They're watching a live feed of Diego. He's being escorted into the U.S. by Federal Marshals."

Briscoe stepped into the room, waving a hand above his head. "Got the key, sir."

For a moment she thought Alejandro might have the kid do it, but slowly, he extended his hand. He stepped behind her, holding her wrist in one hand while manipulating the lock with the other. She held her breath. There was not a single thing in this world that could match the warmth of his touch. He slipped the key into the lock and paused.

"Is there a problem, sir?"

Tentatively, Alejandro's thumb traced the outline of her tattoo. The connection between them seemed thread-like, as if anything might sever it. Even the reckless thud of her heart might be too much. The heat of his breath played upon her hair. She leaned back a fraction, testing the weight of her body against his.

"There's no problem." He turned the key and removed the handcuffs, passing them over to the boy. "Better get to that meeting."

Against her back, she felt the indecision of his sigh. Letting him skip out of here would be the biggest mistake of her life. She twisted to face him.

"Look, I don't know—"

She didn't finish. He took her face with both hands. "Shhh."

There was nothing tentative or delicate in his kiss. She felt every bit of his six months of pain and emptiness. It left her dizzy.

"What were you going to say?" He peered down at her through lowered lids.

"I don't know." She reached up to run a hand along his beard. "But I think it's time for you to drive me home."

Epilogue

Neither Avery nor Harvey heard him enter the house. Voices rang out from the courtyard. Alejandro positioned himself at the far end, pausing to take in the sight of Avery unaware. His throat nearly swelled closed at the sight of her.

A girl looped her arms about Avery's neck. "I want you to sit by me at the picnic."

Avery stroked her head. "I promise I will. I just need to finish a few things. Everyone else is down there already, so you'll need to save me a seat."

Her pronunciation had a long way to go, but her Spanish was otherwise nearly grammatically perfect. He shook his head. And she always claimed to be terrible at foreign languages.

"That girl is going to take apart my kitchen sink if I don't keep my eyes on her," Harvey said. She and Avery turned to watch the girl dart away. "It's good to see her finally acting like a typical twelve-year-old, though." She leaned over Avery. "You don't need to miss the picnic for this. I can take care of the books."

"I'm almost done."

Harvey sank into the chair next to her. "I owe you big. I never thought I'd say it."

Avery pushed the laptop aside. "How many girls have decided to stay on?"

"Six total. Two that want to work with the horses. The other four, I'm not sure. But that reporter's mother is considering it. If I can convince her, we have a shot at getting that restaurant started, and we'll need all four of them."

"Whatever loans you need," Avery started.

Harvey shook her head. "Let's just see how it goes." She rose from the chair, and the sight of Alejandro caused her to do a double take. He held a finger to his lips, and she winked conspiratorially before turning back to Avery. "What time are you leaving?"

"This afternoon. I'm taking the bus to Mexico City." Avery raised her arms over her head in a stretch. It was too much for Alejandro. He could resist her no longer. Creeping forward, he touched her outstretched hand.

Predictably, she jumped. Hand to her chest and trying to catch her breath, she said, "What are you doing here?"

He leaned in to kiss her. It had been worth every second of the trip just to catch that flash of excitement in her eyes.

Harvey shook a finger at him. "You have five minutes. No longer. She needs to put in an appearance at that picnic. And after the past four weeks, I'm no longer convinced you deserve her."

"There was a time when you told me I didn't deserve him," Avery said as she pushed back in the chair.

Alejandro smirked, but Harvey shook her head. "Never said anything like that." She called out over her shoulder, "I mean it, don't make her late."

"How did you get here?" she asked.

"Flew into Mexico City." He stepped behind her and wrapped his arms around her waist. She leaned back against him as he nuzzled her neck.

"But why? I'd be home tonight."

"Someone's got to walk you down to the picnic through all those chickens."

"Funny." She made a half-hearted attempt at stomping on his foot. "Is this your way of saying you miss me?" She glanced at him over her shoulder.

"In about a thousand different ways."

"Name some."

"Number one, San Antonio is nothing but work without you. Number two, the apartment is too empty. Number three, I miss the way you wake me up in the middle of the night to—"

"I don't think I'm the one initiating that." She ran a hand along the line of his jaw. "Why are you really here?"

"It occurred to me that this might be a good time to pick up the Jeep. It's out front. And I was just thinking—if Sam can part with you for just a few more days . . ." He rested his chin on her head.

"What?"

"I was just thinking that my beautiful girlfriend might like to do a little camping." He leaned over her shoulder to gauge her reaction.

"Hmm, spontaneity." She grinned. "Did you bring some of Diego's wine?"

"I'm afraid it's out of my price range these days. But I've got some decent stuff and plenty of red bananas."

~ ~ ~

The reporter stuck her head through the open window of the Jeep. "So, do you have a story for me yet?"

"God, Maria, do you ever stop?" Avery started to crank up her window. "You've just spent a week with these girls. Isn't that enough for a while?"

Alejandro squeezed Avery's thigh. As he'd anticipated, Maria didn't miss it. Her eyes widened in curiosity. "It's all right, Avery," he said. "Tell you what, Maria, I've got something that—with some research—will sell a lot of papers." He gestured for her to move to his side of the Jeep.

Maria didn't hesitate.

"Ever heard of anyone named Tony Fox?" Alejandro asked. Maria shook her head. "Enrique Martinez?" Another shake of the head. "You do keep your sources confidential, right?"

"Absolutely," Maria said.

"What I'm asking of you is tough. If you manage to get to the bottom of this, you cannot give me up."

"Yeah, yeah, I get it. I would never reveal a source."

"Tony's a low-level clerk at the American Embassy. A lot of important documents pass through his hands. Why don't you see if you can find out how Tony affords an apartment in Zona Rosa on a clerk's salary? And I believe Tony just purchased a new German sports car."

"And who's Enrique?" Maria asked, scribbling furiously.

"Enrique was a fugitive given asylum by the U.S. government about two years ago. He disappeared in transit on his way to El Paso. You'll have to take it from there. Do some digging. I'm sure you'll find much more."

Waving her notebook, Maria backed away. "Thanks."

Alejandro nodded and put the Jeep in gear.

"You trust her?" Avery asked. "How do you know she won't give you up?"

He shook his head. "The only power Tony Fox has is that no one knows he's the mole in the embassy. Once she gets her facts together, he's done. I was told to let Secret Service figure it out for themselves. But so far, they haven't. Let the girl have her success."

"Do you think she has a clue who you are?"

"Sure. Dylan Lynch," he said. "Same as the name on the Jeep registration. I caught her recording the license plate number."

"Why? I mean, why are you using an alias?"

"It just makes putting together Diego's case a little less chaotic. No interference from her type," he said, and hit the gas.

"As far as I'm concerned, you'll never be anyone but Alejandro." Avery said with a smile, gathering her hair into a ponytail. "Are you going to tell me where we're going?"

"Nope. You'll just have to trust me on this one."

~ ~ ~

Alternating bands of pink and violet stretched across the western sky. Avery stretched, surprised by how long she'd been asleep. The sun was edging its way down along the horizon.

"Well?" Alejandro asked.

"Well what?" She could barely take her eyes off the shifting sky ahead. "It's incredible. No better sunset anywhere."

He waved a hand toward the scrubby desert landscape. "I think our campsite is just off to the right."

She surveyed the area, trying to find a single distinguishing landmark. There was so little vegetation it was virtually impossible, and yet with its sprawling hills, the area was still so beautiful to her. Alejandro pulled the Jeep off the road. "Does this work for you?"

She smiled. "Do we have firewood?"

"Yes. No outhouses necessary this time." He leaned over to kiss her. "It's in the back."

Alejandro opened the rear door handed her a single bottle of wine and tossed out a couple of logs "There's no camping gear back here," she said.

"No." Without elaborating, Alejandro took the wine from her and focused his efforts on removing the cork. "Hand me those two glasses, please."

She held out the glasses as he poured. "I don't understand."

Alejandro set the bottle on the rear bumper and reached for his glass. "This is a toast to the strongest woman I've ever known."

Avery frowned. "That's hardly true. Look at your mother." She shook her head. "Where are you going with this?"

"You really don't believe I'd make you sleep out here on the ground with rattlesnakes."

"When you put it that way–maybe not." Hugging herself, Avery attempted to stifle a chill.

"I wanted to come back here–to the one place on earth that there's just us. No one else. Nothing else." He touched his glass to hers. "A place where we have our own private sunset. Undisturbed. That's all I want."

Avery's throat constricted.

He set his glass aside, did the same with hers, then took her into his arms. With one hand at the small of her back and lifting her hand with the other, Alejandro began to sway.

"I don't dance," she said.

"Yeah," he whispered, "and I thought I'd never set foot out here again."

"And your point is?"

"That together we can make anything happen."

She laughed. "More like together we attract trouble."

"No, that's not true." He paused, holding her still. "Now that Diego's trial is essentially drawing to a close, and Sam is somewhat willing to be flexible with your time off, I think we should take some time for ourselves."

"What did you have in mind?"

"Maybe a little trip somewhere. Somewhere different." He resumed their slow dance, dipping her slightly. "Maybe a Tahitian island."

"Hmmm. Or maybe a trek in the Himalayas," she murmured against his chest.

"Deep in the heart of some African jungle."

She raised her eyes to his and planted her feet, refusing to take another step. "I will go anywhere with you, with one exception."

"Name it."

"Zapata, Texas."

He grinned down at her, his dimple showing. "You'll get no argument from me."

As a child Harper McDavid watched her mother ride the rollercoaster of writing books, swearing she'd never do it herself. But some things are just hardwired, and luckily for Harper, the world has moved on beyond typewriters and ten-pound manuscripts.

Harper's gritty romantic suspense incorporates her own background in science and engineering and work experience along the border. The result is a collection of brainy, hardhat-wearing heroines that occasionally appreciate the utility of the little black dress.

Harper is the mother of three daughters and lives in the foothills of Colorado with her husband, two dogs, and a fat cat. Her free time is spent traveling the world in search of that next story and perusing her local library for funny book covers.